Sunshine on the Crooked Road

NDIRANGU GITHAIGA

BON ESPRIT BOOKS

Copyright © 2025 by Ndirangu Githaiga

All rights reserved.

No part of this publication may be reproduced, distributed, or transmitted in any form or by any means, including photocopying, recording, or other electronic or mechanical methods, without the prior written permission of the publisher, except as permitted by U.S. copyright law. For permission requests, contact [include publisher/author contact info].

This book is a work of fiction. Any references to historical events, real people or real places are used fictitiously. Other names, characters, places and events are products of the author's imagination, and any resemblance to actual events, places or persons, living or dead, is entirely coincidental.

Cover design by Christine Horner

For Wanjikū, the hopeful citizen.

". . . I will lead them in paths that they have not known: I will make darkness light before them, and crooked things straight."

Isaiah 42:16 (KJV)

Preface

Following Kenya's independence from Britain in 1963, many people left their villages and flocked to Nairobi, seeking better prospects. Here, they encountered fellow citizens from other parts of the country who looked and sounded different, as well as immigrants from India and Europe. The way Nairobians switch between English, Swahili, and their vernacular in informal conversation, often midsentence, is evidence of the resultant cultural blending. In this narrative, words like atĩ/ati, mũthee/mzee and Mũthũngũ/Mzungu are examples Gĩkũyũ and Swahili words one might hear injected into ordinary English dialogue.

Commonly used untranslatable exclamations are employed for authenticity. The meaning of the sentence will be discernible from the context and the English portion.

Prologue

Hartford, Connecticut, May 1976

If Wanjikū had the power to turn the clock back to six thirty that evening, she would have gladly done so. She had known that Kabogo's announcement that they were heading back to Kenya would elicit a negative reaction from the Atkinsons but never expected it to come down to anything more than a polite tsk–tsk or frown of disapproval, mostly from Bill. Karen would take it in stride, she assumed, and come up with a sunny interpretation of what really was not good news. When the two people she counted on not to lose their composure did exactly that, it was obvious that things would not be the same with the couple that they—she, more precisely—considered best friends.

"You what?" erupted Bill, completely out of character.

Kabogo shrugged dismissively and slouched in his chair. Wanjikū shifted gingerly in hers. When her eyes met Karen's, she saw an unmistakable look of alarm.

"That's rather unexpected," Bill continued. "Has this been your plan all along? Did I miss something? And what time frame are we talking about?"

"End of next month," replied Kabogo.

A long pause followed. "Hmm . . . it's about six weeks to the middle of June. Help me out here, Kabogo. Has this just come up, or did I miss something in all our earlier conversations?"

Kabogo did not reply. There was a peculiar glint in his eye that suggested not just defiance but possibly a hint of sadistic enjoyment at Bill's reaction, and this unnerved Wanjikū. Their host's breathing had become audible, and his glasses were fogging up. A scarlet tone had suffused the usually pale skin of his face and neck.

Karen cleared her throat to catch Wanjikū's attention. Wanjikū turned and immediately understood, rising from her seat and following her friend into the kitchen.

"What's going on?" Karen asked in a frantic whisper.

"*Ngatho* [Goodness gracious]! What a disaster!" Wanjikū mumbled, her legs feeling as if they were about to give way.

"Is this for real?"

Wanjikū nodded weakly and let out a big sigh. "Yes. I know it's unexpected, but Kabogo got this crazy idea a month ago after something he saw on TV about returning to Kenya and working for the government—something about all that nation-building jazz, whatever . . . Anyway, he has a cousin who's helping him look for a job back home, and he really wants to go."

"So he doesn't have a job yet?"

"Er, not yet," replied Wanjikū awkwardly.

"I don't mean to sound rude, Wanjikū, but all that from something he saw on TV? That's a bit much, don't you think? I mean, was he already looking? How come you never mentioned this before?"

Wanjikū shook her head in dismay. "Karen, you know how Kabogo does things . . ."

"But what about the faculty position? Bill talked to all those people in the biochemical engineering department in order to make sure Kabogo had a job in hand when he graduated. Was he planning to move back to Kenya all the while? I don't really expect too much from him, but I would have thought that *you* would at least tell me there was something in the works. I didn't think we had any secrets between us."

Wanjikū cringed and fixed her eyes on the tiled kitchen floor, avoiding Karen's gaze.

"Bill isn't taking this well at all, as you can see. You know, Kabogo is the baby brother he never had, which is why he has been so invested in trying to get you guys to stay. The last three months, he's knocked on countless doors, trying to get Kabogo an adjunct faculty position. He's twisted arms and called in favors, something that doesn't come naturally to him. And now this! You know what? It's not just Bill who's struggling with this; I am too. What happened to all those plans we had for the things we'd do together—living in the same neighborhood, driving out in the fall to see the leaves changing color, summer vacations on Martha's Vineyard—or was that just me? I thought we were both looking forward to it. You said it came up about a month ago—a full month! In that time, Bill has probably talked to four or five people among the faculty and in the administration. You and I are together practically every day. I'm just wondering why you didn't let me know sooner, so we could quit planning our lives on the assumption you'd be here."

"Karen, it's not like that. It's . . . it's . . ." Wanjikū's voice faltered, and she let out a weary sigh. She had wanted to tell Karen the very day Kabogo decided he had changed his mind about the faculty position, but he'd insisted he wasn't ready to tell Bill yet and asked her to wait. If she had told Karen, it would have been unreasonable to expect her to keep it from her husband.

For an entire month, she had shuddered and gritted her teeth anxiously whenever Karen talked about all the fun and exciting things they would do together, especially since she had looked forward to them too. After those conversations, Wanjikū tried to pressure Kabogo to disclose his plans before things got out of hand, but he had been dismissive.

"Why do you spend so much time with that woman? My career plans are none of her business. I still need to finalize some things before I disclose what I intend to do."

"It's her business because her husband is spending a lot of time talking to people in the department to make sure you have a job offer before you graduate, since you told him you were interested."

"I didn't tell him to go around campaigning for the position on my behalf. He asked me if I was interested in staying on as faculty, and I said yes, but I don't remember telling him to help me find a job."

"Kabogo, you know how people here operate. When somebody asks you a question like that, it's not idle talk. If you're not interested in the job, let him know, so he doesn't waste his and other people's time."

Kabogo had stalled and dodged for the entire month, then agreed he would bring it up this evening after she'd threatened to do so herself. Now, as she talked to her friend, Wanjikū knew she wouldn't get any credit for the times she had admonished Kabogo to let Bill know sooner about the change in his plans. Couldn't Karen see that there was a reason she was unable to divulge the information sooner? She was the one person Wanjikū had told how difficult Kabogo could be.

"I just can't believe you didn't tell me sooner, Wanjikū! I thought there were no secrets between us," Karen said, turning her gaze to the floor. There was an unfamiliar edge to her voice as a tear rolled down her cheek, then another.

Wanjikū took in a deep breath, fumbling for a reply. The evening was turning out to be even more of a disaster than she'd expected.

Hartford

Chapter 1

Kenya, 1970

Wanjikũ felt her heart soar with pride whenever she watched the grainy archival footage of the Union Jack descending at midnight as the black, red, and green flag of the new nation ascended in its place. She had been thirteen years old on the night of Kenya's independence in 1963, living in her parents' home in Gĩthakainĩ, where there was no television. The village was abuzz with excitement as people clustered around the handful of transistor radios that provided a minute-by-minute update of the events of the momentous day.

"Let the *Mũthũngũ* [White man][1] go back to his village—right over there!" She remembered the wizened Mũthee Gĩchũkĩ croaking with glee, emphatically pointing his *mũtirima* [walking stick] in the direction he believed England to be. He was the oldest man in Gĩthakainĩ, well over a hundred years old, but he had a greater vigor of spirit than most people several decades younger. Throughout the Emergency[2] he had declared that he would only die once the Mũthũngũ had gone

---

1. Plural: *Athũngũ*

2. A state of emergency was declared during the bloody war of independence (1952–1959).

SUNSHINE ON THE CROOKED ROAD

back to his country. Because of his age, the Home Guards and even Wilkinson, their Mūthūngū boss, avoided engaging him in conversation as he trailed them around the village, singing tunelessly about a pack of hyenas working to persuade a herd of skeptical goats that they had come to protect them and preserve order in the grazing grounds. Wilkinson had been with the Kenyan colonial government for almost twenty years and had lived in different parts of then–British East Africa. Somewhere along the way, he had developed a fear of being bewitched. He was convinced that Mūthee Gīchūkī's hoarse, phlegm-rattling ditty was some kind of incantation and tried to maintain a healthy distance from the sprightly old fellow when he pursued them, quickening his pace as they did theirs. His Gīkūyū[3] sidekicks had not failed to notice how his bold, swaggering demeanor seemed to vanish at those times. They simply lengthened their stride to keep up with him and sought to minimize their boss's discomfiture by avoiding references to the old man in their hushed conversations.

After the *Athūngū* departed and Jomo Kenyatta became president, Mūthee Gīchūkī reneged on his pact with death and continued prancing merrily around the village, making conversation with anyone who crossed his path. Seven years after independence, Wanjikū and Kabogo had come home to say goodbye before they left for America, and they encountered him near the main entrance to the village.

"Gacikū!" he called out to her. "Are you well? I haven't seen you in many days. Who is this nice young fellow with you?"

"I am well, Mūthee Gīchūkī. This is my husband, Kabogo," she said with a friendly smile. His memory had deteriorated in recent years, and he still addressed her by the version of her name reserved for prepubescent children. He couldn't remember the names of most of the younger members of the village, and children often giggled out of

---

3. A Kenyan ethnic group, living in the highlands. Commonly spelled *Kikuyu*. Plural: *Agīkūyū*.

earshot after being asked for the umpteenth time who they were and to which family they belonged. Mūthee Gīchūkī had attended Wanjikū and Kabogo's wedding, as well as the gathering in which Kabogo's family came to pay the dowry, but apparently had no recollection of those events.

Kabogo had won a scholarship to study biochemical engineering in Storrs, Connecticut, about a half-hour drive from downtown Hartford. He and Wanjikū were students at the Nairobi campus of the University of East Africa, later known as the University of Nairobi. In January, he had come across a brochure about the University of Connecticut in the administrative office. As he'd flipped through it, he'd noted that the application process seemed straightforward, so he'd applied without much expectation. He was surprised six weeks later when the secretary sent word that there was a letter addressed to him in her office. Inside the large manila envelope, he found a letter of acceptance along with additional forms to fill out that would secure him a scholarship to cover the entire cost of his studies.

Until that point, he hadn't really thought through the implications of attending a university in America. He hadn't even felt it worthwhile to mention the application to Wanjikū, with whom a serious relationship had been developing over the previous six months.

They were sitting in the mostly empty campus cafeteria at about four o'clock that afternoon. Kabogo was a lanky six foot two, with a walnut complexion and humorless countenance. He had a meticulously trimmed Afro and sideburns and a high-pitched, nasal voice that was somewhat incongruous with his physical frame, often eliciting raised eyebrows from people who had just met him. Of the two, Wanjikū spent less time worrying about her appearance, often giving little thought to color coordination, makeup, and such. But she had a quiet, self-assured demeanor, with long eyelashes, lively brown eyes, and a graceful manner that would have turned heads even if she was dressed up in *makūnia* [gunny sacks].

SUNSHINE ON THE CROOKED ROAD

"America? For real?" she exclaimed when he broke the news.

"Yes, I'm still in shock. I hadn't really expected them to reply when I sent in the application."

"Well, that's exciting. I guess I'm happy for you." Confusion quickly replaced her initial flash of excitement.

"I'll wait to see how things go before I decide. I didn't think it was going to be that simple when I started the process. I'd assumed they would either say no or not reply at all."

"Well, you're going to have to decide soon if they're expecting you to start in August. That's only five months away."

In the silence that followed, each of them grappled with the implications of this development, which appeared to herald a fork in the road. If Kabogo traveled alone to America, it was doubtful that their relationship could withstand so great a distance, with communication restricted to aerograms or postcards. Telephone calls were possible but would be expensive and need to be coordinated with time zones in mind.

Neither Wanjikū and Kabogo, both in their first year at the university, had given much thought to the long-term objective of their relationship by this point. In the days that followed Kabogo's announcement, this consideration loomed large in Wanjikū's mind. She had expected Kabogo to hold off on sending the scholarship application until they'd had a chance to talk more about it, but was surprised the following week when he offhandedly mentioned having already mailed it.

"You already sent it in? I thought we were going to talk about it first."

"There's not much time before the application deadline. We can still talk about it while we wait for a response. Even if the scholarship is granted, I'm not obligated to go. On the other hand, if I don't get the scholarship—like if I miss the deadline—then I won't be able to go anyway."

It seemed like a reasonable argument. However, Wanjikū felt it would have been nicer if he'd said something about it to her before submitting the scholarship application. Since their initial conversation, she felt a rising need to clarify the status of their relationship with respect to this recent change in his plans. She'd dropped a hint here and there to which he seemed oblivious, so she decided to be more direct. "America sounds like an interesting place. Hopefully, you won't forget to write and keep me updated on all the new experiences."

"Well, I haven't decided if I'll go," he replied. "Right now, I'm just following through on what they asked me for, to see where it leads. But I haven't made up my mind."

Wanjikū's eyebrows arched, the skepticism impossible to disguise.

"Kabogo, you're telling me you're going through all this without any intention of following through? So if they write to you and tell you they'll cover all your expenses one hundred percent, you're going to write back and tell them, 'Actually, never mind. I wasn't really serious'?"

He smiled crookedly and shook his head. "Well, that's not what I meant. I'm just, er . . . saying . . . you know . . ."

As he fumbled for a coherent answer, it became clear to Wanjikū that despite his protestations about not yet having committed to a decision, Kabogo would certainly pursue his studies in America if he received a scholarship. She was a bit frustrated by his unwillingness to broach the topic of what would become of their relationship.

As it turned out, she was not the only one who was anxious about the unclear status of their relationship. Among the older members of the families of Mūthee Mūchoki of Kīunangū and Mūthee Waihenya of Gīthakainī, there had already been a fair amount of restlessness and hand-wringing about a relationship between their children with no stated intention of marriage. In the old days, discussions about marriage began as soon as a young man showed interest in a particular woman, who might not even be aware of a potential suitor mobilizing elders in his village to make a formal request to her parents. But times were changing. Young women were now getting the Mūthūngū's education and wanting to choose their own husbands. Some were even opting not to get married, remaining in school long after they became adults

SUNSHINE ON THE CROOKED ROAD

capable of starting families, chasing things called *ndigiri* that many young people in Nairobi were obsessed with. *Ndigiri* were black robes with matching square hats that the young people got at the university. On one appointed day every year, all those who had earned theirs would put them on and gather together, looking from afar like a large flock of crows. If a person was initiated into that gathering of crows, they could start looking for one of those Mūthūngū jobs where you could sit in a chair all day and scribble on papers.

Even from the carefully manicured grounds of the University of East Africa, worlds away from the rust-red footpaths weaving through the villages, word traveled. Whatever one did was likely to find its way through relayed whispers to one's family, for better or worse. The people of Mūthee Mūchoki's household knew of Kabogo's relationship with Wanjikū, not just from what he had mentioned, but from other sources in the village. News of the scholarship arrived in mid–April, which brought matters to a head in Kabogo's home. The issue was brought to his father's attention by Kabogo's mother, the senior wife in the home. She expressed concern that the oldest son in the family—on whom the responsibility of maintaining the family name rested—might travel to America and marry a Mūthūngū woman, some of whom even wore trousers, or so it was rumored. Mūthee Mūchoki was usually a confident man, at ease with himself and his surroundings, but the urgent whispering of his wife resulted in a night of tossing and turning in which images of Kabogo speaking through his nose like a Mūthūngū plagued him.

The next morning, he dispatched Ngotho, Kabogo's half brother, to the university to find the young man and bring him home to discuss a pressing matter. Ngotho was thrilled to travel to the city, quickly took the money he was handed for fare, and sprinted to the intersection about two miles from Kĩunangū, where *matatus* [minibus taxis] and buses headed to Nairobi picked up passengers. When Ngotho's matatu reached its final stop in Nairobi, the *taniboi*[4] pointed him in the direction of the university. He walked onto the campus, found the administrative office, and stated his case.

Kabogo was located in class about an hour later. As he approached the administrative building and saw Ngotho, a sense of dread filled him. "Ngotho, is everything all right at home?"

"I believe everyone is well, but Baba said you need to come right away. He wants to speak to you."

Kabogo's brow furrowed. "Really? What's going on?"

Ngotho said nothing, as their father had not disclosed the reason for dispatching him to Nairobi.

"OK. Let me drop off my books. I'll be back here shortly, then we can go."

By the time they made it back to Kīunangū, it was almost midday. They found their father sitting on his stool in the shade of a *mūkūyū* [sycamore fig] tree outside his hut. "You're well, Kabogo?" he called out without any inflection, sounding as if he were stating a fact rather than asking a question.

"I am well, Baba."

Mūthee Mūchoki gave Ngotho a look, which the latter correctly interpreted as his instructions to find a stool for Kabogo to sit on and then make himself scarce, something he did with alacrity. As Kabogo lowered himself onto the stool, his mother came around from behind her hut and called out a greeting, which he returned with a smile. She then entered her hut and proceeded to warm up some porridge for her son and husband.

"How is school?"

"Everything is fine."

---

4. Matatu driver's assistant, responsible for loading passengers and collecting fare. From English word *turnboy*. By the 1980s, this term had largely been replaced by the word *manamba*.

"The Athūngū in America are still making arrangements for you to go there?"

"Yes, Baba."

Mūthee Mūchoki paused a few moments before continuing. "What became of the lady friend you once brought here to visit?"

Kabogo's breath caught in surprise. He had brought Wanjikū once for a brief visit and couldn't remember if his father had even been present at the homestead on that day. His mother had, quite naturally, begun a sly interrogation of Wanjikū, who squirmed anxiously as she gave an account of her family. Her cowife, Nyina wa Mūmbi, joined the fray as Kabogo looked on helplessly from a distance, pretending to repair an area on the thatched roof that appeared to be coming apart.

"You said your people are from Nyeri?" Nyina wa Mūmbi asked a second time, almost as if she didn't quite believe what Wanjikū had told her a few moments before. "Where in Nyeri?"

"Gīthakainī."

"Gīthakainī? I've never heard of a place like that."

"It's near Gatarakwa."

"Oh, I think I've heard of Gatarakwa. I have a cousin who married into a home in Gatarakwa. Hmm . . . All the way from Nyeri . . ." That last comment seemed to imply that a hundred miles of distance, even within the borders of Gīkūyūland, brought with it the potential for suspicion.

Kabogo shifted his weight on the small three-legged stool and addressed his father. "We are still friends."

"Are you going to leave her behind when you go?"

He tilted his head weakly from side to side. "Um . . . I don't really know, Baba."

Their eyes met, and Kabogo's gaze quickly shifted to the ground between them. His father wasn't one to beat about the bush. "If you're planning on making her your wife, you should do it before you leave. You need to tell me soon, so we can begin making visits to her home and get it done before you leave. If this is not your intention, you need to release her so she can find another man and get on with her life."

If Mūthee Mūchoki's words sounded like an ultimatum, that's because they were. A young man spending time with a young woman with no clear plans for marriage was not an acceptable state of affairs. He was not interested in his family getting caught up in a scandal involving somebody else's daughter, and even less eager for his son to leave for America as a single man.

Kabogo nodded hesitantly. His father's answering silence indicated the conversation was over. He rose and excused himself politely, then went to his mother's hut and talked briefly with her, as well as the siblings and half-siblings who happened to be in the compound. Before walking back to the matatu stop with Ngotho at his side, he promised Mūthee Mūchoki he would return over the weekend with a definite answer.

Two days later, he returned at midmorning and announced his presence in his mother's hut. "Where is Baba?" he asked. Almost as if in response to his question, there was a loud eruption of sneezing from the direction of Mūthee Mūchoki's hut that indicated he had started his morning ritual of sniffing *mbakī* [tobacco].

"Take this stool and go under the mūkūyū tree. I'll tell him you have arrived," his mother said, picking up a stool and handing it to him. All the younger members of the household were either out grazing the goats or working in the fields.

Kabogo went and sat on his stool. The tension he had felt when he'd sat there two days earlier was gone. In its place, he had a clear picture of the next steps, having talked things over with Wanjikū. His father emerged from his hut accompanied by his mother and lowered himself onto a stool she placed there for him. She stood by unabashedly within earshot, even though she would not have been expected to be present. Mūthee Mūchoki didn't seem to mind.

"You have thought about the thing we discussed?"

SUNSHINE ON THE CROOKED ROAD

"Yes, Baba."

"And?"

"I think we should go ahead and visit her home," Kabogo said without hesitation, noticing a look of relief spreading across his mother's face.

***

Two weeks later, Mūthee Mūchoki rounded up some respected men and women from the village to travel to Gīthakainī to pay a visit to Wanjikū's home. A friend from the nearby Kahunguro village had graciously provided one of his matatus to ferry the contingent to their destination. Most of them had never been to Nyeri, and a few had never been in a matatu, so there was cause for excitement. Kabogo and his two childhood friends, Mbūrū and Mūriūki, whom he had asked to accompany him on the trip, were the only young people in the vehicle. On big occasions such as this, the role of a young person was to be seen and not heard, silence in the presence of elders being seen as the most persuasive display of wisdom. If a question happened to be directed to the prospective groom, his reply was expected to be courteous and brief.

Two goats, their legs bound with sisal twine, lay on the floor between the back rows of the minivan. These were gifts for the prospective bride's family, intended to generate goodwill as the bride price was discussed. So were the makūnia containing maize, beans, and millet, as well as two five-pound bags of sugar.

As the vehicle trundled down the dirt road to where it joined the tarmac highway that would take them to Nyeri, Mūthee Maina, one of the elders Kabogo's father had asked along on the visit, turned around and said to no one in particular. "I heard Nyeri people don't have *mūratina* [traditional Gīkūyū beer] at their weddings."

"*Ehe*, that may be so," replied Mūthee Mūchoki. He had sent an emissary a few days prior to Gīthakainī village, and somewhere in the conversation, the issue of mūratina came up. The representative of Wanjikū's family had stated clearly that they did not wish this beverage to be included either in the meetings or the subsequent wedding. They were followers of Jesū—a famous chief of the Athūngū from long ago—and they didn't follow all the old Gīkūyū practices. For example, they were only allowed to marry one wife, and they skipped the *ngurario* [traditional wedding ceremony] and instead had their wedding in a Mūthūngū church.

Mūthee Mūchoki had heard that the people of Jesū were reputedly lenient during negotiations involving bride price because they didn't want to create the impression they were trying to sell their daughters. So whatever relaxation was given up by the absence of mūratina was sometimes made up for by less of the contentious haggling that sometimes characterized these meetings. Still, the part about the mūratina didn't really make sense, because the Athūngū had a story about how Jesū once attended a wedding, and the *ndibei*—the type of mūratina they had in his village—ran out. He told the servants of the house to put water into the empty ndibei pots. When it was taken out to the visitors, it had turned into ndibei, which probably made him the kind of person everyone wanted at their party.

"How is it possible to have a wedding without mūratina?" Mūthee Maina continued to muse aloud, shaking his head. "What do they drink?"

Mūthee Karimi was the most traveled among them, having made several trips to Nairobi, Mūranga, Nyahururu, Nyeri, and even the other side of the mountain, where people spoke something similar to Gīkūyū, except that they always sounded as if they were singing. "Some of them drink *ūcūrū* [porridge] or chai after the wedding feast," he said, "and they get back to their homesteads even before the cows and goats are back from grazing. I've even heard of people who went to their *shamba* [farm] after a wedding and continued digging because if you get home in the daylight and you're still sober, you might as well make use of what's left of the day."

"*Haiya!*" cackled Mũthee Maina. "Even those of us who were too old to go to the Mũthũngũ's school will learn something new today."

Chapter 2

Five months between receiving an acceptance letter to a university halfway across the world and sitting in an airport terminal waiting to leave feels like barely enough time to blink, particularly if three elaborate traditional ceremonies and a wedding have been shoehorned into that time frame. As soon as Kabogo communicated his willingness to comply with his parents' wishes, things took on a life of their own, culminating in a large wedding ceremony at Kahunguro Presbyterian Church in early August, attended by more than five hundred people from Kabogo's and Wanjikū's villages combined. Anyone who remotely knew the bride or groom showed up, and somehow the food never ran out, something the women of Kabogo's village noted with pride. They were responsible for the catering, and all the neighbors pitched in without being asked. By the time the day was over, there was no doubt in the minds of the visitors from Gĩthakainĩ that their daughter would be well taken care of in her new village.

Two weeks later, Kabogo and Wanjikū sat at the departure gate at Embakasi Airport waiting to board a BOAC flight to London, with a connection from there to New York and then on to Connecticut. They reflected on the clamor and excitement of the past few months with nostalgia and a rising awareness that some of the wonderful things they had always taken for granted would soon be out of reach.

The singing and dancing of the women at the wedding had left a profound impression on the young couple as they watched them, young and old, move in rhythm, their colorful dresses swishing left and right in unison as their feet followed well-choreographed movements they had learned through many weddings over the years. Children twirled around merrily in the grass and sang along, clapping their hands in time to the music. By the time the girls were young women, they knew the songs and dances by heart and could seamlessly join in without needing to be told what to do. When acne, scratchy voices, and thin tufts of chin hair appeared, the boys would retreat to the sidelines where the men sat, quietly humming the words they knew so well and watching with a tinge of envy as the women danced.

Wanjikū and Kabogo hadn't known what to do with the presents they received, which would be impossible to take with them to America. The dairy cow, nanny and billy goats, two-acre plot of land, bags of maize, beans, arrowroots, and the like would have been great for starting a life in the village had they remained there. It would have been offensive to try to sell them—though the cash would certainly have come in handy—so they left them in Mūthee Mūchoki's compound to be absorbed into his herds and granaries. Kabogo would be able to claim replacements when the time came. As a matter of fact, the dairy cow was from Mūthee Mūchoki's herd, so it would continue to graze on the same grounds and sleep in the same shelter it always had until Kabogo came to take it away. If it died in the meantime, he would receive another one.

The bed Wanjikū received from her family symbolized the fact that she no longer belonged to her parents' home but was now a member of Kabogo's family. She'd been surprised by the emotion this gesture stirred in her when her father's eldest sister, Nyina wa Nduta, triumphantly presented the gift at the reception. "Wanjikū," she said aloud, waiting until there was a hush in the crowd. She was a school-teacher who was used to taking command of crowds with her firm voice and theatrical flair. As her eyes bore on Wanjikū, everyone's attention focused on the four young men who shuffled forward, carrying a bed. They set it down right in front of Nyina wa Nduta.

"You know what this is, Wanjikū?"

She nodded nervously.

"Say it out loud, my dear, so everyone can hear."

"It's a bed."

"Whose bed?"

"My bed."

Nyina wa Nduta frowned and cupped her right ear. "*Atī*[1] what? Say it again so I can make sure I heard you properly, and so that those people over there"—she pointed—"can also hear you."

There was a ripple of laughter through the crowd.

"It's my bed."

"Did you all hear that?" she asked the crowd.

"We have heard!" they roared, amid much laughter.

"*Ehe* . . . Wanjikū, how did your bed come all the way from Gīthakainī to Kīunangū? Did it end up on the matatu by mistake?"

Wanjikū shook her head.

"It was not a mistake, *sindiyo* [right]? Your bed is here because it now belongs *where*?"

"Here."

"Your bed now belongs in Kīunangū. These are your people now. You are always welcome to visit us in Gīthakainī, and when you come, we will sit and drink *ūcūrū* and tell each other all kinds of stories. But

---

1. Gīkūyū word most commonly translated to "What?". Often used alongside the equivalent English word for emphasis. The Swahili "*Ati*", similar in meaning, does not have the tilde over the letter "*i*" also appears later in the book. Occasionally the word, both in English and Swahili, may be used to mean "You heard what I said," when used as a reply rather than a question.

when it gets dark and everybody starts looking for their bed, you'll remember your bed is where?"

"Kĩunangũ!" the crowd replied in unison.

"Not where?"

"Gĩthakainĩ!"

Nyina wa Nduta stopped, beaming with delight as she scanned the rapt crowd. Then she turned to Wanjikũ with a twinkle in her eye and added, "But you must visit and bring us *tũcũcũ* [grandchildren], yes?"

There was more laughter, and Wanjikũ and Kabogo smiled self-consciously.

All afternoon, Wanjikũ cast quick glances to where her mother and father were seated. Her father wore a slightly crumpled gray suit, the only one he owned, reserved for special church occasions. On most other days, he wore a sweater or wool vest over his long-sleeved shirt and tie. She rarely saw him leave home without a tie. He was a deacon at Gatarakwa Presbyterian Church, a soft-spoken man who thought carefully before venturing a comment on any issue or question, and whose level-headed opinion was often sought. As a girl, Wanjikũ had wished he was more demonstrative and jovial but had come to accept him for the stoic person he was. She never doubted that he loved her—his only daughter and youngest child—even though he never said it aloud. Every time he asked her to bring him a cup of tea and invited her to sit with him as he talked about mundane matters at the church or asked her to take a walk with him in the shamba, she knew he valued her presence. Her three older brothers would comment that the *mũthee* [old man] had been much sterner in their youth and had never taken the time to sit and talk in a leisurely manner with them. They reckoned he had become sentimental with age, or maybe was softer on her because she was a girl.

Wanjikũ's mother had a practical disposition, constantly shuttling from one task to another around the home. Time spent with her always involved doing something, and in the bustle leading up to the wedding, she was in her element. She had a hard time sitting still, and the only thing that helped her stay focused during the two hours of speeches during the ceremony was the abandon with which she had danced and sang herself hoarse at the start of the reception.

Both parents had been at peace with their daughter's marriage, which was a great comfort to Wanjikū, but her heart melted when her father put his hand awkwardly on her shoulder as she and her bridesmaids busied themselves before leaving the house for the church. She turned to face him. His lips began to move, but his voice failed him, and his eyes welled up with tears.

She swallowed hard, and her own eyes began to mist up. "Baba," she whispered, then impulsively threw her arms around him and began to cry.

"It will be OK," he said, his arms hanging limply at his sides. Hugging was not something a Gīkūyū elder did. In fact, freely expressing one's emotions—except perhaps in the case of extreme, justifiable anger—was considered undignified.

Now, at the airport, she had time to reflect on the incidents and interactions of the past few weeks as they replayed in her head and to feel a sense of loss at the prospect of saying goodbye to her family, homeland, and former self. It was 10:30 at night, and their flight would be boarding in about half an hour. Most of the people at the gate were Athūngū, with a few Africans and *Ahīndī* [people of Indian descent].[2] Now, she would experience what it felt like to be the odd one out, identified first and foremost by her ancestral origin. It was an unnerving prospect. Most of the Athūngū she had encountered seemed nice enough, though they did have their peculiarities, such as the way they worshiped the clock and got red in the face if the person they were meeting didn't show up at the exact time specified. Wanjikū knew that in the Mūthūngū's homeland, she might meet some who were not as friendly—the kind who had

---

2. Singular: *Mūhīndī.*

taken people's farms, packed them onto reservations, and responded with surprise and brutality when the locals decided they'd had enough of the outsiders. Now she would be the outsider.

Kabogo scanned the information on their boarding passes for the umpteenth time. Like Wanjikū's mother, he was most comfortable when he was busy, and mulling over the contingencies of their journey helped him calm his nerves as they awaited boarding. "The lady from the university said they might have a Ugandan student pick us up at the airport. I hope he's a good person."

"Yes. At least he shouldn't have too much trouble identifying us."

"She said there was no guarantee the Ugandan student would be available, but that whoever came to the airport would have a signboard with my name on it, and that we should make sure they have a campus ID badge before going with them," he rambled on. "If for whatever reason there isn't anybody to meet us, I still have the telephone number of the university as well as instructions on how to take a bus or taxi to the college."

Wanjikū gave a big yawn. The fatigue from the rush of preparation for their departure was beginning to catch up with her. "I was talking to Mueni at the wedding—remember her from college? She told me her older brother and his wife live somewhere in Massachusetts. I don't know if that's anywhere close to Hartford, but—"

She was interrupted by a female voice over the loudspeaker: "Good evening, ladies and gentlemen. Welcome to boarding gate D with BOAC Flight BA 026, service to London's Heathrow Airport. We will begin boarding in ten minutes." The travelers near them began to gather their belongings. Exchanging glances, Wanjikū and Kabogo did a quick survey to make sure they had all their carry-on bags, then waited nervously as the minute hand on the wall clock counted down to boarding time. It was the first time either of them had ever been on an airplane.

***

Despite all their excitement and anxiety about the flight, neither Wanjikū nor Kabogo could keep their eyes open for more than half an hour after takeoff. They were surprised when the lights came back on what seemed like moments later, and the cabin crew came down the aisles calling out meal options in cheery voices as they handed out breakfast trays. Before long, the captain announced their descent to London. In contrast, the flights from London to New York and then on to Connecticut seemed to drag on forever, and their stiff legs, puffy ankles and rancid breath erased any traces of the fascination their first flight had held for them.

On the transatlantic leg, Kabogo kept half an eye on the movie on the tiny screen at the front of the cabin, gazing out the window every few minutes at the billowy white ocean of clouds beneath them, while Wanjikū leafed through the in-flight magazine, wishing she'd brought a book. Eventually, having lost track of time, she stared dully ahead, feeling exhausted, though not exhausted enough to sleep.

The landing in New York, transfer to yet another plane, and yet another takeoff were all a blur to her, but when the pilot's voice announced they were beginning their descent into Bradley International Airport, a surge of excitement shot through her followed immediately by intense anxiety. Once they got off the plane, they would be on their own, and all the details that needed to fall into place—their ride from the airport, the apartment the university had arranged for them, where they would shop for groceries on a tight budget—suddenly loomed large. Next to her, Kabogo had fallen asleep and was snoring, his mouth half-open. He was normally the one who did the worrying on their behalf, and she was a bit dismayed, even irritated, to see him so peacefully oblivious. She resisted the urge to wake him solely for the purpose of making him share her discomfort.

When the plane dipped beneath the clouds, an expanse of greenery and buildings appeared through the window, marking the place that would be their home for the next few years. "We've arrived!" she whispered excitedly, tapping Kabogo on the shoulder, unable to contain herself any longer.

He opened his eyes and stared blankly for a moment or two, then craned his neck and squinted to see through the window. "That was a long journey," he mumbled.

Now that he was awake, she could relax, knowing she wasn't going through the experience alone. She realized that some of her nervousness might have sprung from listening to his anxious musings before boarding their flight from Nairobi, but now he seemed calm, as if his nap had managed to exorcise all of his lingering worries. The plane landed with a jarring bump, which startled them, though none of the other passengers seemed perturbed. It took them half an hour to reach the concourse, where they looked for someone who might be a Ugandan holding a sign.

"I don't see anyone," said Wanjikū, feeling her heart begin to sink.

"We'll give them about ten minutes. If they don't show up, we can go to those phone booths there and call the—"

"Mr. Kabogo?" came a voice from behind them, and they turned around. Standing there was a *Mūhīndī* man with large ears that stuck out from his head like an elephant.

"Er, yes, hello," replied Kabogo and shook the outstretched hand.

The man had a small board with Kabogo's name on it. He had a cheeky smile and friendly eyes, and they both took an instant liking to him. "My name is Ravi Mehta. I'm pleased to meet you, and you as well, madam. You may be wondering what happened to the Ugandan fellow who was supposed to meet you."

"Well . . . I . . ." stammered Kabogo, trailing off when he noticed a huge grin spreading across Ravi's face.

"Aha! Beware of assumptions. What does a Ugandan look like? This one was born and raised in Kampala and went to Makerere University before coming here for further studies."

Kabogo returned Ravi's grin sheepishly.

As they exited the air-conditioned airport terminal, Wanjikū was unprepared for the stifling heat, dressed as she was in layers for the cool Nairobi evenings. Her discomfort must have showed. "So, Wanjikū, I bet you didn't think it would be so hot in America." Ravi said.

"No. The only thing they warned us about was the winter!"

They walked across into the parking lot and stopped next to an ancient, battered, lime-green Ford Thunderbird. "It's borrowed, and it's old, but it will get us where we need to go as long as the transmission doesn't fall out," Ravi declared as he opened the trunk and began to load their suitcases. In response to the worried look on Wanjikū's face, he quickly added, "It's been reliable the few times I've driven it, and we have only a forty-five-minute drive, so I think we'll be fine."

The car moved forward with a series of lurches as he left the parking lot onto the airport exit road, a cloud of gray fumes rising up behind them. Ravi didn't have much use for the brakes, and Wanjikū, sitting in the back seat, found herself unconsciously stepping on an imaginary brake pedal and holding her breath as he tailgated whatever car happened to be in front of them, her fingers tightly gripping the door handle. If Kabogo had any reservations about Ravi's driving as they chatted amiably in the front seat, he wasn't showing it.

Ravi was studying for his doctorate in mechanical engineering and had been in Hartford for five years, having initially come for his master's degree. He was thinking about moving to Boston after he completed his studies if an opportunity there became available. "I want to get as much learning and experience as I can, Then I'll try to go back to Makerere so I can strut confidently down the hallways the way I always imagined I would: *Professor Mehta, PhD, back from the USA with answers to questions you didn't even know you had . . . Step aside and learn from the man himself!*"

He delivered this pronouncement with such comical pomposity that both Kabogo and Wanjikũ erupted in laughter, dropping the veneer of careful politeness that they had maintained to that point. Ravi clearly enjoyed the success of his joke.

"All right, my friends, this is Greenwood Park, our housing complex," he announced as he turned onto a tree-lined street with low-rise buildings on either side. "We'll be coming back here shortly to pick up your keys at the apartment manager's office, but first, let's go over and see the program coordinator to let her know you're here."

Chapter 3

Hartford, 1970

Greenwood Park was a quiet neighborhood, and once Kabogo started his program, Wanjikū was often home alone, sometimes going the entire day without seeing or speaking with another human being. She was homesick and frequently found herself gazing forlornly through the window at nothing in particular, wiping tears from her face. Minutes seemed like hours on days like this, and thinking fondly of her family and friends back home only worsened the ache.

She kept on the small black-and-white television that came with the apartment—either part of the standard furnishings or left behind by a previous tenant—for background noise while she did her chores. There was also an ancient-looking radio they'd found in the apartment, which she turned on sometimes for the midday news. Rarely was there coverage of events in Africa, and when it came, it typically featured famine, wars, epidemics, and military coups—things that seemed quite removed from life back home as she remembered it. With no mention of Kenya in general or Nairobi in particular, she concluded that no news was probably good news.

Sometimes, instead of listening to what the presenters were saying, she would focus on how they said it and slowly repeat phrases or words with pronunciations she thought peculiar, such as the way they made their *t*'s disappear or sound like *d*'s. "The *presen'er* from *Atlan'a* said the ship was detained in *in'ernational wa-ders*," she repeated cheerily to herself one morning as she vacuumed the house.

Occasionally, a familiar entertainer like the Jackson Five, who were a sensation in Nairobi by the time they'd left, came on TV. The effect of watching this magical quintet had been to convince most young people who had not yet adopted a bouncy Afro hairstyle that sitting on the sidelines was no longer an option. Wanjikū's hair didn't grow as fast as that of some of her friends, so her earnest attempts at an Afro were easy to overlook. The upshot was that she never experienced the stern looks from elders in the village that some of her friends did. Her experimentation with hoop earrings ended early when, on a visit home from university, she ran into her aunt, Nyina wa Nduta, just as she was approaching the village.

"Haiya! Is that you, Wanjikū? Have you started wearing *hang'i* [traditional earrings] like the *cūcūs* [grannies] of long ago?"

The older woman seemed genuinely surprised, and Wanjikū felt mortified.

Noticing her niece's discomfort, she quickly added, "Sorry, my dear. I didn't mean to embarrass you. I was just surprised because I haven't seen anybody wearing hang'i since I was a child."

Wanjikū finished politely exchanging banalities with her aunt, then pulled off the earrings before continuing to her parents' home. She never wore them again.

★★★

It was a conversation they had a week after arriving in America that made Wanjikū realize marriage wasn't going to be smooth sailing. Up until then, it seemed to her that they were on track to have a marriage like the one her parents had, where each person was sanded down so completely into the other's likeness by routine and familiarity that they effortlessly completed each other's sentences. She had never seen her parents argue. Looking back now, as an adult, she realized they'd probably had their differences, though by the time she came along—the lastborn child with a seven-year gap between her and the brother she followed—they'd probably worked through the kinks in their relationship and decided which fights were worth having and which weren't.

She and Kabogo had previously had minor disagreements over the course of their relationship, but nothing close to what happened that day. They were sitting in their apartment one afternoon, catching some respite from all the busyness of settling into the new country, each caught up in their own thoughts.

"Marriage is one of those things that should never be rushed into, no matter the circumstances," Kabogo said out of the blue. For a moment, she couldn't tell if he was talking to himself, but given the nature of the statement, she looked up from her book. Rather than elaborate, he repeated it in a matter-of-fact tone.

"Are you speaking about a particular situation?"

"Well, yes and no. Not that I have anything against marriage per se, but looking back over the last few months, I've realized I shouldn't have let my mūthee push me into having a wedding at such short notice, given everything else that was going on."

Wanjikū's brow furrowed.

"I wasn't aware your father had pressured you into anything. Why didn't you tell me?"

"Er, there were so many things happening at the same time. It's not that big of a deal—"

"Kabogo, what do you mean it's not a big deal? This is our marriage we're talking about. Are you saying you didn't want to get married? I'm confused."

SUNSHINE ON THE CROOKED ROAD

"No, no, that's not what I'm saying. All I'm saying is that if my father—"

"You're a grown man. If you didn't feel ready to have a wedding, why didn't you just tell him no?" she cut in, her voice trembling with anger.

He let out a heavy sigh and fidgeted in his chair.

"Now, look—you're getting angry, and all I was trying to do was have an honest conversation."

"What am I supposed to say when you tell me the reason we got married was because your father pressured you into it? And why are you telling me this now? What do you want me to do since we're already married? If you'd told me this before, I wouldn't have agreed to get married in circumstances like that."

He let out another frustrated sigh and was about to say something, then checked himself.

"Kabogo, I don't understand how your father could force you—*a grown man*—to get married if you didn't feel ready. Why was it so important to him that you get married before leaving the country? It could have waited till later."

"Agh! You know how particular those old people are."

"No, I don't know. I've never heard of a man being pressured to get married quickly unless there was a baby on the way, which wasn't the case. And what about me? Didn't you think it was important to tell me what was going on, particularly if you weren't really interested in getting married?"

"Now, look what you're saying! I didn't say I wasn't interested in getting married—I just said things were rushed. Why are you bringing *kiherehere* [drama]?"

"I'm not bringing kiherehere. You just told me something very troubling about what is probably the biggest event in my adult life so far, and somehow I'm the one bringing kiherehere?"

"Ngatho! Never try to win an argument with a Nyeri woman!" he remarked softly with a strained laugh.

Wanjikũ rolled her eyes and decided she'd had enough. Getting up from her seat, she went to the bedroom and flopped onto the bed, trying to make sense of what had just happened. She was irritated by Kabogo's attempts to minimize the situation. And rather than see what the problem was when she expressed her concerns, he was accusing her of overreacting and even resorting to making stereotypical jokes.

★★★

In the days that followed, Kabogo became angry at Wanjikũ's reaction. As far as he was concerned, he had simply been sharing his thoughts about what might have been done better in planning the marriage, not questioning the decision to get married. But she had come back forcefully, cutting him off and bringing so much kiherehere into the conversation that he decided it was best to stop talking before things degenerated into a shouting match. Why did she have to raise her voice? When they were courting, he was keenly aware that words came much quicker to her than him. She routinely finished his sentences, assuming she knew what he was going to say, almost as if she were impatient to move on to the next thing. It was something that occasionally bothered him, but he had come to terms with it and had not seen it as a problem in their relationship.

This recent episode was different because she had mostly talked—yelled—at him, and even when she asked questions, she didn't wait for an answer. When she implied that his behavior fell short of what was expected of a grown man, he was deeply offended. That was disrespectful. He had never seen either his mother or Nyina wa Mũmbi speak to his father in such a manner, and he felt the stirrings of resentment within him. The whole incident appeared to confirm his premise that rushing into marriage had been the wrong thing to do.

***

It was mid-September, only a few weeks after they had arrived, but the temperature had already dropped significantly. Wanjikū needed a light jacket except in the middle of the day when the sun was out. She had gone for an afternoon walk and come across two women chatting near the playground as they watched a pair of four-year-olds playing on the slides. She was about to walk past when one of them called out to her. "Hello there! Are you one of the new students or student spouses?"

Wanjikū nodded.

"Welcome to Greenwood Park. I think I saw you and your husband moving in a couple of weeks ago. You're in Block B, right?"

"Yes, that's correct."

"Nice to meet you—my name is Ugochi, and this is Lihua. I'm from Nigeria, and she's from China. and those are our boys, Emeka and Wei, on the playground."

Wanjikū introduced herself and told them where she was from.

"Welcome to the international club," said Ugochi with a self-deprecating smile. "We have people from India, Ghana, Brazil, Egypt, Mexico, and a few other places. Our husbands are students here, and since we're dependents on their visas and can't work or enroll in study programs, we keep each other entertained and look around for interesting things to do that don't cost any money, like going to the public library, outdoor concerts, art exhibitions . . . There's quite a bit going on."

"A library—that's nice! I'd been hoping there was one nearby. I looked through the telephone directory and saw a few listed, but I couldn't tell how far away they were."

"The Dickinson Library is less than half a mile down that road there, though it feels much farther in the middle of February when you're walking through two feet of snow."

"Is it open to everyone? I mean, do I . . . ?"

"It's open to everyone. When I first came, I was afraid to go there, even though one of the women in my building told me it was free of charge. I assumed it was only for Americans and wasn't about to go in and embarrass myself by getting turned away. So I kept putting it off until my friend literally grabbed me by the arm and marched me there after I complained to her once again that I was bored to death. The only thing the librarians care about is that you don't dog-ear the pages. Do that, and you'll try their patience very quickly."

Wanjikū smiled as she recalled a couple of heated conversations she'd had with Kabogo regarding this annoying habit of his. Then she remembered something else she had been hoping to ask when she found someone knew the area. "Is there a post office nearby?"

This time, Lihua answered. "If you keep going on Poplar Street past the library, the post office is about two blocks down the road."

"Perfect," said Wanjikū. "I wasn't going anywhere in particular on my walk, but now I think I'll go and see the library and pick up some postcards and aerograms from the post office. I've been meaning to write our families to let them know we arrived safely, but there was so much else going on that I completely lost track of time."

They spoke for a few minutes longer until Emeka fell off the jungle gym with a soft thud followed by a loud whimper. Ugochi rolled her eyes, then started in his direction. Lihua excused herself and followed to where her son stood next to Emeka, trying to comfort him.

"Thank you for the information. I think I'll go now!" Wanjikū called after them. "Hopefully, I'll see you around soon." She made a beeline for Poplar Street.

***

SUNSHINE ON THE CROOKED ROAD

Wanjikũ's older cousin, Nduta, worked at the post office in Nyeri, so she'd had a post office box even before she had any expectation of receiving mail. As Wanjikũ and Kabogo's departure became imminent, this minor fact took on immense significance as it was decided that she would be the default point of contact between the couple abroad and their families.

Dear Nduta, she wrote on a postcard. *Please tell everyone that we arrived safely. America is nice. Autumn is already here, but it's not too cold yet. Much love from me and Kabogo.* Sitting at their dining room table, she studied the postcard intently for a few moments, then put it down and rose to her feet, taking in a deep breath. She couldn't keep her eyes from brimming, recollecting those eventful final weeks in Nairobi. She had so much she wanted to say but was reluctant to put it on the open face of a postcard, so she resolved to write a letter as well.

She picked up an aerogram and began to think of what to say to her parents. Kabogo would have to take the lead in writing to his own family. Even though they were her new family in the eyes of Gĩkũyũ tradition, it would have been improper for her as a new bride to address her parents-in-law directly. Nduta had graciously agreed to forward Kabogo's family's mail through Mũthee Mwĩhoko, who owned a fleet of matatus on the route from Nyeri to Nairobi. The driver would drop it off at one of the shops at Kĩunangũ, and a marketplace urchin would be dispatched to deliver it to Mũthee Mũchoki's homestead. The letter would be read aloud to them by a younger relative since neither Mũthee Mũchoki nor his wives could read. Wanjikũ's parents, on the other hand, were literate.

She set about scribbling furiously and decided that she would also ask Nduta whether she knew of anyone near Gĩthakainĩ who had a telephone. Maybe she could set up a date and time when her parents could wait to receive a call. The prospect of talking to them over the phone sent a thrill of excitement through her. An international call might be expensive, but it would be well worth the cost. Ugochi was probably a good person to ask how to go about it since she was from Nigeria and might have made similar calls in the past. She would ask her tomorrow.

***

Ugochi was only five feet two, but she had a towering personality, though not in a loud or obnoxious way, Wanjikū would learn. She expressed herself with such crystalline confidence that most people couldn't help but agree with her. When she smiled, her perfect teeth appeared from behind full lips, a striking but delicate contrast with her unblemished ebony skin. And when she laughed, which was often, it was with such explosive abandon, slapping her palms together, that her good humor was contagious.

She and Lihua were constantly at each other's side, having initially been drawn together by their sons, who spent every minute of their playtime together. Even when the boys went to prekindergarten on weekday mornings, the two women remained inseparable. Ugochi was the talker. Lihua mostly listened and could have been mistaken for severe if not for the mischievous twinkle in her eyes and the witty under-her-breath comments she interjected into the conversation, which often provoked Ugochi's dramatic paroxysms of mirth.

Wanjikū decided she would walk around the neighborhood the next morning, hoping to run into them, as she didn't yet know where either of them lived. The idea of making a phone call to Kenya had escalated into a nagging obsession, and she was keen to get additional information from Ugochi about this. At present, she didn't have a number in Kenya to call, but she had mentioned it both in the letter to her parents and in the margin of her postcard to Nduta, and she wanted to be prepared when the pieces fell into place.

When she mentioned the idea of calling home to Kabogo, he was not enthusiastic. "We're already sending them letters, and now we want to ask my mūthee to walk to the *ndūnyū* [marketplace] with his two wives to borrow a phone from the shopkeeper just so we can talk to them?"

Wanjikū felt the blood rushing to her head and stopped herself from responding with a sharp retort. She drew in a deep breath. "Are you going to write your letter?" she asked once she'd regained her composure.

"I already said I would. I'm in the middle of something that I have to finish for tomorrow."

She got up and retreated to the kitchen. Ever since the argument they'd had a week after they arrived—the one where he'd called her an argumentative Nyeri woman—it didn't take much for conversations between them to go off the rails. The day after that exchange, her anger had subsided, and she was willing to get to work ironing out the new kinks in their relationship. He also seemed willing to remedy the situation, though she noticed he became rather prickly whenever there was any semblance of criticism or questioning of his decisions. He referred to her using the argumentative Nyeri woman trope one other time, disguising his comment in a jocular tone. It was only after this that the thought occurred to her that as the oldest son of the senior wife in his family, he was probably not used to being verbally challenged, except by his seniors. After he became a man—the bearer of the family name—even his mother and her cowife would likely have exercised tact when expressing disagreement. The few times she saw him interacting with his siblings and half-siblings, they all seemed very deferential toward him.

Maybe, she thought, the way she had confronted him was the reason things had changed. But how was she supposed to have responded to his saying in essence that their marriage had been a mistake? Just smile and agree that it wasn't really a big deal? Whatever the reason for the change in his demeanor, it was noticeable. Now, when Kabogo came home at night, he always seemed to have work to do and rarely had any time or patience for her.

Kabogo did write a letter to his parents, and the next morning, Wanjikū walked to the post office and mailed the letters and postcard. On her way back, she walked toward the grassy area behind Block C, where the playground was located. She found Ugochi and Lihua chortling together about something. They heard her coming and turned.

"Well, hello, new friend! You came back."

Wanjikū grinned. "Yes, I'm back. Is your son OK?"

"My son?" Ugochi asked, looking puzzled.

"Yes, he fell off the monkey bars yesterday."

The two mothers exchanged glances, then burst out laughing, leaving Wanjikū perplexed.

"Oh, that's nothing! They fall all the time. We already forgot about that," said Lihua.

"Yes, Emeka is fine. The kids go to prekindergarten in the morning, but they'll be back here in the afternoon, climbing and swinging as if nothing happened. We're so used to coming to the playground that we often end up here without them."

Wanjikū cleared her throat. "I wanted to find out how to make an international phone call. I'd like to call my family."

"It costs quite a bit of money," said Ugochi, a grave expression on her face.

Wanjikū's heart sank. "Oh."

There was a long pause, then Lihua snorted in amusement and punched Ugochi playfully on the arm. "Stop it, Ugochi! See how upset she is? Tell her the truth!"

Ugochi's eyes shone with mischief as she tried to keep a straight face. "Sorry, I was just being cheeky. It costs about twenty dollars for three minutes."

"Ugochi!"

SUNSHINE ON THE CROOKED ROAD

"Heh heh, I don't know why I'm getting my numbers mixed up today," she said as Lihua shook her head in exasperation and held up five fingers. "OK, let me get serious. Lihua's right. Five dollars should be enough to call your family and have a decent conversation. The best time is on the weekend. You just need to call the international operator, and they'll connect you. I assume you have a phone in your apartment?"

"No . . . not yet."

"Come to my place when you're ready. You can pay me when they send the bill."

"Oh, thank you!"

"Of course. The first minute of the call is the most expensive, so you have to make sure to arrange with your family to be wherever you plan to make the call at the right time. Unless, of course, they have their own phone . . ."

"No. Nothing like that, but thanks again. I'll let you know when I'm ready to call."

★★★

She heard back from Nduta on a Tuesday two weeks later:

Dear Wanjikū and Kabogo,

Very nice to hear from you! Call Gatarakwa Presbyterian Church at four p.m. any Sunday at the telephone number below—your baba and maitū are usually there in the afternoons for activities like fellowship, Women's Guild, etc. They'll be waiting for your call.

Nduta.

For Wanjikũ, Sunday couldn't come soon enough. She let Ugochi know that she hoped to make the phone call on Sunday at nine a.m., which would be four p.m. in Kenya.

"Sure, no problem. Emeka never sleeps beyond six, even on weekends when we wish he would, so Nnamdi and I gave up all hope of sleeping in a long time ago."

She let Kabogo know in case he wanted to come over and say hello, but his noncommittal response made it clear that he would not be coming. On Sunday, she got up early and headed over to Ugochi's apartment. At nine a.m., Ugochi called the international operator, gave her the number from Nduta's card, and hung up. Wanjikũ's looked crestfallen.

"She'll call back when she connects with the other number," Ugochi explained. A short while later, the phone rang. She picked up the receiver, listened, then handed it to Wanjikũ.

"Hello . . . hello?" For a few moments there was only a soft crackling on the line. "Hello? Baba? Can you hear me?"

"Yes, Wanjikũ. And can you hear me?"

"Yes."

"I'm here with your mother. How is America?"

"Everything is OK. We are settling in well, and Kabogo is very busy with his studies."

"Oh, that's good to hear! Is he there so I can greet him?"

"He isn't here because I had to go to a friend's place to borrow a phone—we don't have one in the house yet—but I'll give him your greetings."

"Oh, that's OK. Yes, please give him our greetings. Let me give your mother the phone so she can say something before it cuts."

SUNSHINE ON THE CROOKED ROAD

After some fumbling on the other end, Wanjikū's mother came on the line.

"Wanjikū? Hello . . . hello? Can you hear me?"

"Yes, Maitū. I can hear you. You are well?"

"We are very well and thanking God for it. How is America?"

"Everything is going well, and we're settling in," Wanjikū repeated. "Kabogo is busy with his studies."

"It is good for him to be busy since that's what he went there to do."

"Yes."

"Everyone here is well. I have spoken with all your brothers this week, and they told me to pass on their greetings. Nyina wa Nduta also said to give you her greetings."

"Tell them I said hello."

"Yes, I'll do that. And greet Kabogo for us."

"OK."

"All right, then. Call us again when you get another chance. And thank you for the letter—we enjoyed reading it."

"All right. Goodbye."

"Goodbye."

The phone clicked at the other end of the line, and she reluctantly replaced the receiver. Ugochi, who had gone into another room to give her some privacy, returned with a surprised look on her face. "Finished already? That was quick!"

Wanjikū nodded. Though the call had been nothing more than an exchange of banalities, she was pleased to hear her parents' voices and know that everything was well at home.

"Anytime you need to call again, just let me know."

"Thanks, Ugochi. I really appreciate it. It was nice to talk to my parents."

After she left Ugochi's apartment, she felt a heaviness in her heart as she realized how much she missed home. The novelty of moving to America was wearing off fast, and she would have given anything to get her old life back—the people she knew, familiar food, the sunshine and matatus . . . She missed her life as an unmarried woman when she didn't have to be around someone who seemed interested only in the things that mattered to him.

Chapter 4

Wanjikū had somehow managed to make it through a series of monumental decisions—dropping out of university, getting married, and relocating thousands of miles—without the slightest of doubt as to whether they had been the right ones. But as the gray overcast days of autumn continued, she began to feel an uncertainty about her new circumstances. It might have been triggered by a chance conversation she had with Lihua in which she learned that her friend already had an undergraduate degree—though she hardly looked old enough to be out of high school—and had applied to get into a master's program in the biochemical engineering department the following year. Lihua's did not disguise her surprise at learning that Wanjikū had left university prematurely to follow Kabogo.

"So are you going to go back to school?" she asked with an uncharacteristically solemn expression on her face.

"I . . . I haven't really thought about it. I'd probably have to get my own scholarship and probably my own visa, and um . . ."

"And?"

"Oh, I don't know. It sounds like it would be very complicated."

"How will you know unless you try?"

Wanjikũ shrugged, unsure of what to say and, at Lihua's insistence, promised unconvincingly to think about it. It had initially felt like a rash decision to abandon her studies, but everything else seemed to have worked out so well that she assumed it was meant to be. There had not been a single naysayer among her friends and family. In fact, many of them acted as if she had won the lottery by getting married and moving to America.

That evening Kabogo came home and went through his usual routine of scarfing down his dinner without making any effort to talk to her before relocating to the living room to study.

"Kabogo?"

"Huh?" He glanced up with a frown, sounding mildly irritated at having been interrupted.

"How is your coursework going?"

"It's going OK; there's just a lot to do," he replied, his tone softening. "I feel like nothing I learned in Kenya carries over into what I'm studying." Their eyes met briefly, then he resumed reading.

"I'm thinking of applying to a bachelor's program here, for next year."

He looked up with incomprehension. "Why?"

"Why? Because I want a degree as well."

"But who will take care of . . . ?" He raised his arm and gestured around the room. "Who will take care of everything around here? Also, it's not that simple . . . I mean . . . getting accepted into an undergraduate program, then getting a scholarship, then getting your own student visa . . ."

"It didn't seem that difficult when you did it," she said dryly.

He let out a snort, and his eyes betrayed a brief flash of anger before he reined himself in. "OK. You go ahead and figure it out. Don't let me be the one to stop you."

She returned to the kitchen and began to wash the handful of dishes in the sink. While he had not objected to her plan, it was a hollow victory because she wasn't really sure she wanted to resume her studies with so many other things she was still trying to adjust to. In fact, she wondered if bringing it up with Kabogo had been a subconscious act of self-sabotage, hoping he would push back aggressively and give her a valid excuse for inaction.

When she told Kabogo two weeks later that she planned to phone her parents again and asked if he wanted to come along to say hello, he demurred with the sardonic comment that a second scholarship, if she got one, could be put toward paying the phone bill. As usual, she hid her irritation. Her mother and father would ask about him, and she would once again offer an excuse on his behalf. It wouldn't take long for them to begin to wonder if something was amiss. Once she and Kabogo had a telephone in their apartment, maybe he would feel more inclined to take part.

Ravi stopped by one Saturday around this time. It was the first Wanjikū had seen of him since the day they'd arrived, but he and Kabogo had crossed paths a few times in the engineering department. "Hello, my neighbors both here and in East Africa! I decided to pop in and make sure you're settling in well."

"It's nice to see you, Ravi," said Wanjikū, her eyes shining with excitement. Even Kabogo gave his usual brooding demeanor a break, and the three of them had a lively conversation for the two or so hours Ravi was there. His colorful descriptions and self-deprecating humor had them in stitches. *I wish Ravi came here every day so Kabogo and I could have a nice time together*, Wanjikū thought as they prattled merrily about the peculiar first impressions and misconceptions associated with arriving in a new country.

"So, Wanjikū, have you found ways to stay occupied during the day when Kabogo is away?"

"Yes, I've met some of the other international student spouses: Ugochi, Lihua, Elsie, Lakshmi, and a few others."

"Have you met Nnamdi, Kabogo? That's Ugochi's husband. He's in the electrical engineering program—very nice guy, but silent as a mouse. His wife, on the other hand, has enough personality for both of them. Probably one of the most fun people I've ever met! Many of the students get together for Thanksgiving dinner since we don't have families here to spend the holiday with. It's always a lot of fun, with plenty of food from all over the world."

"That's sounds great!" exclaimed Wanjikū. "When is it?"

"Sometime in late November. I think this will be Nnamdi and Ugochi's last Thanksgiving with us, because he's graduating next spring and moving to California for his PhD."

"Oh yes, Ugochi mentioned they would be leaving next summer. I'm going to miss her," said Wanjikū dejectedly.

"That, unfortunately, is one of the downsides of an international student community. You meet people from all over the world, but everyone is on their own journey. You travel together for a while, and then you have to say goodbye."

"I'm not looking forward to it."

"Enjoy them while they're here. Lihua is probably going to struggle the most when Ugochi leaves, and their boys as well." They shared a somber pause before Ravi continued, "Well, I came to bring joyful conversation to this house but managed to bungle it. While we're on the subject, I might as well add that if all goes well with my doctorate program, I may also be gone in a year or two."

"Yes, you said something about moving to Boston after graduation, so we can't accuse you of not having warned us," replied Kabogo.

"All right, I need to be on my way now," Ravi declared as he rose to leave. "I'm glad to see that you're both settling into life at Greenwood Park."

Chapter 5

970–1971

1 Wanjikũ met a lot of new people at the international students' Thanksgiving dinner and the Christmas party that Kabogo's department hosted. She got to spend some time at the party with Elsie and Lakshmi, whom she had met previously but only interacted with superficially. Elsie was soft-spoken with a warm smile. She was from Ghana, as was her husband, Bob, who studying for a doctorate in political science. Lakshmi was from India. Her husband, Amit, was Ravi's classmate and close friend.

They'd installed a telephone in their apartment in late October, so it became easier to call her family, and Kabogo had even participated in some of the calls, which she found reassuring. He had still not expressed any interest in telephoning his own family, but they had exchanged correspondence with Wairimũ, his stepsister, who had taken on the responsibility of reading his letters to the family and writing the replies. She was married to a man from Gachororo village—about a half-hour walk from Kĩunangũ—where she taught at a primary school. It had proved much easier to mail Kabogo's letters to her there instead of sending them through Nduta in Nyeri.

Wanjikū wore trousers for the first time that November. While some of the other female students at the university in Nairobi had routinely worn trendy bell-bottoms, she'd had neither the courage nor the desire to experiment with something that was considered unthinkable for women in Gĩthakainĩ village. As the frigid temperatures of winter came around, practical considerations superseded tradition, and she bought two pairs of woolen pants she found at a local thrift store. Much to her relief, Kabogo seemed untroubled by this innovation.

Lihua found out in January that she had been accepted into the master's program in biochemical engineering and was elated. With Ugochi's looming departure, the demands of the program would help fill the imminent void. Wanjikū, however, would effectively lose the two people she'd spent most of her days with. She had met some of the other women in the neighborhood and hoped that those nascent relationships would grow into something more meaningful. Occasionally, she remembered her promise to Lihua to consider applying to a degree program, but she'd become adept at coming up with excuses for putting it off. She admired Lihua's conviction in pursuing her own educational ambitions, especially with a kid.

Not having met Lihua, Kabogo was surprised when an unfamiliar woman approached him in the department with a huge smile and outstretched hand, asking if he was Wanjikū's husband. Since there were only two Black students studying biochemical engineering, her assumption had not been much of a gamble.

"Yes," replied Kabogo hesitantly, "and you are?"

"I'm your neighbor from Greenwood Park. Wanjikū is my friend. I'm looking around the department because I'll be starting my master's program here in the fall."

"Master's, or did you mean bachelor's?"

"Master's. I already got my bachelor's in my home country before moving here."

"You look very young."

"Thank you," she replied, smiling self-consciously. "Well, I just wanted to say hello. I'm sure I'll see you around. It was nice to meet you."

Wanjikū, who had spoken with Lihua that afternoon after the encounter, was eager to bring it up as soon as he walked into the house. "My friend said she met you in the department today."

He grunted and dropped his books and folders onto the coffee table, then proceeded into the kitchen. Wanjikū's eagerness melted away as she watched him wordlessly serve his dinner onto a plate.

"Is everything all right?"

"Everything's fine. I'm just very busy," he mumbled.

Of course, she thought. *Very busy as usual.* Lihua had been excited about meeting Kabogo, and Wanjikū had hoped for some answering spark from Kabogo. Instead, he seemed even surlier than usual. After a while, she gave up trying to talk to him and retreated to the bedroom. She couldn't help wondering if his sullenness was related to the discovery that Lihua—one of the neighborhood housewives—was his academic superior. She wouldn't even have considered it were it not for his reaction when she said she was thinking going back to school, and his comment that she ought instead to "take care of things" around the apartment.

There was no further conversation between them that night or the next, but the night after, he went on at some length about his schoolwork and how he was now considering doing a master's and even a PhD. Wanjikū listened with forced enthusiasm, trying to restrain her mind from wandering. She noticed how eager he was to talk about his plans, but noticeably less so when she tried to get him to engage in a discussion about issues in their relationship that were troubling her. It was almost as if he had decided to steer clear of anything that might lead to an argument, instead preferring anodyne topics that were better suited to casual conversation between strangers, which is what, in effect, they were becoming to each other.

She was mopping the kitchen floor on a Monday evening at the end of January when she overheard an announcement on the TV that there had been a military coup in Uganda. Setting the mop against the wall, she rushed to the living room in time to see images of heavily armed soldiers standing around their tanks among throngs of ecstatic Ugandans as a burly, fresh-faced General Idi Amin shook hands with supporters and waved at the crowds. She wondered how this would affect Ravi and whether he had spoken to his family. The jubilant atmosphere reminded her of her village on that night in 1963 when Kenya had finally thrown off British rule. But in this case, she was surprised because she had not been aware that the deposed president, Dr. Milton Obote, was unpopular with his people.

Once the newscaster moved on, she waited a few minutes to see if there would be a follow-up about Uganda or some other African nation, but there was nothing more, so she returned to the kitchen and resumed mopping.

When Kabogo came home about forty-five minutes later, she met him at the door. "Hey, Kabogo, they just announced on the news that there's been a coup in Uganda. I don't know if you'd heard or talked to Ravi."

"Oh, really? I wasn't aware, and I haven't seen him today," Kabogo said. "But he's probably home by now. Let's go check on him, so he can tell us what he knows."

Wanjikū grabbed her coat and put on a pair of boots as Kabogo dropped his books onto the kitchen counter. They'd never been to Ravi's apartment, but he had told them where he lived. After ringing the doorbell a couple of times, they heard hurried footsteps approaching. Ravi opened the door.

"Hey guys, come in," he said in a subdued tone, visibly distracted. He didn't offer to take their coats, and they made their way through a labyrinth of boxes and furniture piled with papers and clothes to get to the love seat. "Sorry about the mess. I wish I could tell you there are times my apartment looks better, but I'd be lying. Some tea?"

Wanjikū was about to decline the offer, but Kabogo nodded. Ravi put some water in the kettle and set it to boil. "You heard the news?" he asked.

"We did. We're not sure what it means, so we wanted to hear your thoughts," said Kabogo.

"And to make sure your family is OK," Wanjikū quickly added.

Ravi let out a deep sigh and shook his head. His large ears turned very red. "I've tried calling several times, but the operator says the lines are busy. Maybe that's from a higher call volume than usual, or maybe the military government has temporarily shut down the telecommunications system. I don't know."

"Oh no!" exclaimed Wanjikū softly.

"I spoke with them just this Saturday, and everything seemed OK. They must have been unaware of whatever was brewing."

"On TV, it looked like people were celebrating. I didn't think Obote was that unpopular."

"I don't think the Baganda ever forgave him for destroying their kingdom and sending their *kabaka* [traditional monarch] into exile, and every leader has enemies. But you're right. If there was a strong anti-Obote sentiment, my family and I missed it. Or maybe the people were rejoicing on TV because what else are you going to do when a group of armed men say they've come to liberate you? It's not like you can tell them, 'No, thanks, go back to your barracks. I think we'll stick with the devil we know!'"

"What do you think is going to happen?" asked Kabogo.

"I have no idea. The uncertainty is what makes this so difficult." The kettle started to whistle, and he set about making them tea. "I never imagined this would happen in my country. You hear about these things happening in other places, but you always assume it will never happen to you."

"Man, I'm sorry," said Kabogo. "Let's hope things work out, and Uganda comes out better off."

"No harm hoping at this point," replied Ravi without a trace of conviction. "There's not much else we can do."

★★★

Ravi stopped by Wanjikū and Kabogo's apartment three nights later with an update. He was finally able to reach his family. He was relieved to learn that they were OK, and that everything seemed calm where they lived.

"But how did they sound?" Kabogo probed. "Did they sound like they usually do, or was it the way people talk when they think someone might be eavesdropping?"

"See, that's the thing. They sounded very formal and careful, like someone was listening."

Wanjikū's eyes widened. "You mean like someone in the room . . . ?"

"No, no, not in the room. I mean the way the government can tap people's phones—at least in Uganda, they can. I'm sure it's the same in Kenya."

She nodded. "So do you think your family will try to leave?"

"And go where? Uganda has been our home for four generations. My great-grandfather was among the people brought by the British in the 1890s to build the railway. It's the only place we know."

It was hard to know what to say, so they sat in silence for a minute until Ravi got up from the sofa armrest where he had perched and walked to the door. "I just wanted to keep you updated, since you're the only people I know who seem remotely aware of what has happened or how it might affect me. Everyone else is going on with their merry lives, and the media has already moved on to the next disaster."

As he stepped out into the darkness, a cold blast of air from the open door hit Wanjikū, who shivered and crossed her arms over her chest. "It's hard to get any real news from home here," she said to Kabogo. "You can hope that no news is good news, but as Ravi's situation shows, that isn't always the case."

Chapter 6

Unless the kids were playing in the snow, it was too cold that winter to meet in the courtyard or playground, so Wanjikū and her friends usually congregated in the common room in Block B. It was spacious and furnished with plush couches, a color television, and a kitchenette with a kettle, coffee machine, and fridge. There was also a Ping-Pong table at the far end of the room. Since they usually went there on weekdays when the kids were in day care, they typically had the place to themselves. They would get some tea, coffee, or soda, then sit around the table playing cards or board games—"bored-people games," Ugochi called them. Most of the games were new to Wanjikū, and she wasn't a skilled player, but she thoroughly enjoyed the nonstop chatter and camaraderie.

In addition to Lihua and Ugochi, Elsie and Lakshmi often joined in. She saw much more of them now that it was winter. Even for Elsie, who rarely participated in their activities, having company was preferable to sitting alone on a dreary winter day. They had gotten used to her coming in and greeting them enthusiastically before politely excusing herself and curling up on a couch to lose herself in Tolstoy, Achebe, Jane Austen, or whichever author had her attention that week. Lakshmi, on the other hand, was as boisterous as Ugochi and spoke twice as fast, so a competitive game of Monopoly with the two of them was something that Lihua and Wanjikū found tremendously entertaining. As rambunctious as they were, the atmosphere never grew hostile or uncomfortably tense.

"Has anyone talked to Ravi lately?" asked Lakshmi amid the clatter of rolling dice and *tap-tap-tap* of pieces being advanced on the Monopoly board. "I ran into him yesterday and tried to start a conversation, but he seemed rather edgy and in a hurry to get away, which is unusual for him."

"Lakshmi, didn't I already tell you what that man needs is a wife? You need to get together with those Indian friends of yours and introduce him to a nice woman. That chap is dying of loneliness!"

"No, seriously, Ugochi, there was something wrong. I've never seen him looking like that before."

Wanjikū, who was usually more comfortable taking it all in, cleared her throat and spoke up. "Kabogo and I spoke with him recently. His family is in Uganda, and he's worried for them because of the coup."

There was complete silence, and all eyes turned to her. Elsie's curious face appeared from behind the cover of *The Brothers Karamazov*.

"Is he really from Uganda?" asked Ugochi. "I thought he was joking when he told me that. It's always hard to tell if he's joking or being serious."

"His whole family lives there. He's been able to talk to them on the phone, but he couldn't tell what was really going on because—"

"Wait, let me guess: The government people were eavesdropping, just like they do in Nigeria and I'm sure in most other places."

"Yes."

"I didn't know there had been a coup in Uganda. I must have missed it on the news," said Lakshmi.

"When it comes to news stories from Africa, all you have to do is step away from the TV for two minutes, and you'll miss it completely. Isn't that right, Elsie?"

"Huh?"

"Dear Lord, this poor Ghanaian bookworm!" Ugochi moaned.

"Sorry, I was in the middle of a very interesting passage. What was the question again?"

"I was just telling them I thought Tolstoy was a better writer than Dostoevsky. I wanted to hear what you thought."

Elsie shrugged. "It's actually a very good book, Ugochi. You should try reading it sometime."

"Maybe I'll have time to read it when Emeka leaves for college." she said as she rolled the dice and moved her piece, slowing down as she realized where it would land.

"Aha! Go to jail—again!" exclaimed Lihua excitedly.

Ugochi made a face as she moved her piece directly to jail, without passing go or collecting $200. "Well, at least I won't have to pay rent for the next round."

Elsie, who hadn't yet resumed reading her novel, spoke up. "Did you know that Monopoly was invented by a woman?"

"Yeah, I think I heard that somewhere," replied Lakshmi. "It had a different name originally."

"Right."

"Ordinarily, I would be excited to hear that," said Ugochi, "but that woman is currently on my blacklist."

Lakshmi suddenly snapped her fingers. "You know what Ravi needs? A shortwave radio. Then he can get news from home through the BBC or one of those international broadcast stations. I have an uncle in India who swears by his shortwave. My dad makes fun of him, saying that even if he saw a group of Pakistani soldiers setting up camp in his backyard, he wouldn't believe it unless it was on the BBC."

"That might work," agreed Ugochi. "A shortwave radio *and* a wife—then Mr. Mehta would be a happy man. You have the keys to his happiness, Lakshmi."

"Amit and I will go over to his place this evening. He's good friends with Amit, but they haven't spoken in a couple of weeks, so we weren't aware of what had happened in Uganda."

"What was the coup about, anyway?" asked Ugochi. "We don't hear much about coups in East Africa, unlike all our coups in West Africa. We've already had two in Nigeria plus the war in Biafra. How many in Ghana, Elsie?"

"One, so far."

"I heard that one of the complaints was that there hadn't been any elections since independence," said Wanjikū.

"Well, let's hope they will follow through with organizing an election. The problem is that elections only seem to be a priority to the people out of power. Once they're in power, they start coming up with excuses for why the timing isn't right. Even the great Nkrumah fell into that trap and made himself president for life. Isn't that right, Elsie? You're the one from Ghana." Elsie raised an eyebrow but said nothing. "Sometimes coups just lead to more coups until that becomes the normal way to respond to whatever you don't like in a government."

"It's eleven fifteen. Time to go pick up the kids!" announced Lihua as she put the game pieces back in the box. "Same time tomorrow?"

"Same time tomorrow," they replied in unison.

★★★

Wanjikū never really had any interest in sewing, so she had no idea why she felt the compulsion to buy the shiny black Singer sewing machine at the thrift store that day. She had gone in with no specific intention other than to pass the time, but when her eyes fell on it, she was inexplicably drawn to it. It looked to be in excellent condition, and for five dollars, she could hardly go wrong.

"That's quite a bargain!" exclaimed the shopkeeper, a plump bespectacled woman with a sanguine complexion and a ready smile.

"Thank you."

"I've always wanted to learn to use one of those, just never got 'round to it."

"I don't know how to, either, but I want to learn."

"Good for you! Well, we've all got to start somewhere. Say, if you look in the corner over there where the books are, you'll find one called *It's Not Sew Difficult! Sew* spelled S-E-W. You might want to get that as well."

Wanjikū found the book and paid for her purchases. The machine was a little heavy, but the bus stop right next to the thrift store dropped her off just outside Greenwood Park. Once home, she opened the book and started reading, stepping into a world that hadn't existed for her even a couple of hours earlier.

When Kabogo got home that evening, he eyed the machine with detached curiosity. "A sewing machine? What for?"

"They were selling it at a throwaway price, so I figured I'd give it a try."

He shrugged and continued to the kitchen, his fleeting interest having been satisfied. "I met your friend Lihua's husband in the department today," he said over his shoulder. "Chen. He's doing mechanical engineering. Seems like a nice guy."

"She's mentioned him, but I've never met him."

"He told me she's a talented painter. Apparently, she considered doing it professionally, but it's hard to make a living."

"Yes, she showed me some of her paintings, and they're beautiful—flowers, mostly. She said it makes her feel like she has her own private garden in their apartment." Wanjikū enjoyed evenings like this, all too rare, when Kabogo seemed at least moderately friendly. Usually, he came home in a foul mood or simply not interested in engaging with her. She never knew which Kabogo would come through the door.

"I saw Ravi today, but I didn't talk to him."

Wanjikū was silent. She had spoken with her father last weekend, and he had relayed worrisome news regarding the neighboring country. "Many people are crossing the border from Uganda, and they're describing horrible things: people being killed and abducted by soldiers, unexplained disappearances," he'd said. "It's all over the radio and newspapers here."

She'd told Kabogo about it after the call, and they'd decided that nothing would be gained from forwarding secondhand reports to Ravi. He had purchased a shortwave radio at Lakshmi's prompting, and between that and speaking with his relatives, he would find out what he needed to know. Unfortunately, being so far away, he was powerless to help.

Chapter 7

Wanjikū had never cared for eggs. Kabogo, on the other hand, loved them, especially boiled. It was one of those differences a new couple notices early in their marriage and, if wise, dismisses as inconsequential. On many a morning, she would boil him two eggs for breakfast without thinking anything of it. One such day in early spring, she sipped tea at the kitchen table as Kabogo sat down to a hurried breakfast. Everything seemed normal until Kabogo struck the shell of an egg with his butter knife, deftly peeled it, showered it generously with salt, and took a big bite. As the smell hit her nostrils, a wave of nausea made Wanjikū jump to her feet and dash to the bathroom, where she leaned panting over the toilet bowl. She'd felt mildly nauseous off and on for the past few days, but nothing like this.

"Hey, are you OK?" asked Kabogo, who had followed her, perplexed.

"I should be fine. I just need a minute."

"Are you sure?"

"Yes." She didn't want to turn toward him because she was sure the smell of eggs on his breath would push her over the edge.

"OK. I have to go now. If it doesn't get better, you should go to the student health center."

She nodded and took several slow deep breaths as she listened to the sound of his retreating footsteps followed by the door slamming shut.

After a few minutes, the nausea subsided. She slowly straightened and returned to the kitchen. "One, two, three!" she whispered before taking in a gulp of air, making a grab for Kabogo's plate, emptying the pile of eggshells on it into the trash, tossing the plate into the sink, and turning on the faucet. She backed away from the sink, threw open the kitchen window, and hungrily inhaled the cool springtime air. After a few minutes, she felt confident enough to walk back to the sink and turn off the faucet without having to hold her breath, though by midmorning, not having been able to eat or drink anything besides water, she still felt nauseated enough that she decided to go to Student Health.

"Hello!" chirped the bright-eyed receptionist when she walked through the door. "What good timing! Dr. Jones just walked in, and there's nobody else in the waiting room. This must be your lucky day!"

Wanjikū smiled feebly, filled out the required form, and took her seat. The nausea had subsided somewhat, and she was beginning to doubt whether she needed to be there when an inside door opened, and a middle-aged nurse in a starched white dress with matching shoes and cap appeared. Scrutinizing her clipboard, she opened her mouth, then closed it again. "I'm sorry, I'm not sure how to pronounce your name. How do you say it?"

Wanjikū pronounced it slowly for her as she rose from her seat.

"*Wan-jee-coe*," she repeated. "That's not so hard. I'm Paula. Please come this way." As she took Wanjikū's blood pressure, temperature, and pulse, she asked, "Was there a particular concern that made you come in today?"

"I've been having some nausea off and on for the past week, and it's really bad around eggs. I don't know if I'm developing an allergy to eggs or what. But I also haven't had my period in three months, so . . ."

"Understood," replied Paula with a knowing smile. "You're in the right place either way. Let's get you in see Dr. Jones. Come with me."

Dr. Jones was a little man with a bald dome rising above a half ring of jet-black hair. The thick lenses on his black plastic glasses made his eyes seem larger than they really were, and his bulbous nose must not have functioned well, since he did most of his breathing through his open mouth.

"What seems to be the problem today, er, Mrs. *Wan-jee-coe?*" She was surprised at how well he pronounced her name until she glanced at the clipboard Paula had placed on the table when she'd brought her in and saw a phonetic spelling of her name there in big block letters.

"I've been nauseous for the past week or so . . ." she began. "My last period was in February. Certain smells, like boiled eggs, really make it worse. I don't know why I didn't put it together before, but maybe I'm pregnant."

Dr. Jones smiled. "Yes, that would be my guess. We'll do a pregnancy test, and if that gives us our answer, we can stop checking. Any fevers or chills? Any problems with dizziness or lightheadedness?"

"No."

"OK, then. If you get up on the examining table, we'll take a look, then do a pregnancy test. We should have the results in a couple of hours, so that you and your husband don't have to sit up all night wondering what to expect."

Wanjikū felt more anxious than nauseated as she climbed onto the examining table. She and Kabogo hadn't had any conversations about having a child. She wondered how he would take the news if she were pregnant.

***

Kabogo's reaction was muted. At first, she wasn't sure that he had heard or understood her, because he simply nodded and said, "Oh, really?" and then proceeded to put the kettle on for tea.

"You have nothing else to say?"

"I'm just trying to understand what this means," he said, still without much affect. "It's a big development."

Big development, she thought, a bewildered expression on her face.

"When would the baby be born?"

"November."

"Do we know if it's a boy or a girl?

"Not yet."

"Well, I hope it's a boy so my father can be named." Naming children in the Agĩkũyũ tradition was very structured, with children named after paternal grandparents, then maternal grandparents, followed by siblings from alternating families in descending order of age.

"What if it's a girl?" Wanjikũ pushed back.

"I don't think it will be." Kabogo was not one to recognize when he'd put his foot in his mouth and recalibrate. He felt he had said all he needed to say and moved on to his coursework, leaving Wanjikũ to stew in a toxic mixture of confusion and irritation. She was baffled by his reaction and his bizarre choice of words. It didn't seem to register to him that her body was going to go through major changes, some of which would come with big health risks, and that after the baby came—boy or girl—their lives would never be the same. From his comments, it seemed that the entire pregnancy was her business, with his involvement being only when the time came to name the baby, if it happened to be a boy.

In the weeks that followed, he saw just about everything, including Wanjikũ's symptoms of morning sickness—her aversion to eggs, her fatigue—as signs that the baby would be a boy, to the point where Wanjikũ thought she might lose her mind, though she couldn't decide whether it was more from annoyance or worry. Every time he spouted one of his irrational pronouncements, she would think frantically, *What if it's a girl?*

Wanjikũ didn't feel she had anyone she could talk to about her predicament because it was the kind of thing one could discuss only with a very close friend or a sister. While her friends in the neighborhood were great companions, she felt she didn't know them well enough for this type of discussion. Nor did she have anyone in Kenya she could talk to this early in the pregnancy, even if she could magically dispel the complexities of getting in touch. Back home, people never mentioned they were expecting a baby until it was obvious from one's appearance, probably in part from superstition that it would bring misfortune. Fortunately, there hadn't been any visible change in her appearance that might prompt awkward questions.

She found relief from her state of isolation in the long hours she spent trying to unravel the complex mysteries of the sewing machine. The previous owner had taped the manual to the underside of the machine's housing in a clear plastic bag, along with some leftover supplies such as spools of thread, bobbins, and an unopened pack of pins. She read the manual and *It's Not Sew Difficult!* a couple of times, then cut a pair of old bedsheets into four-inch squares so she could practice basic stitching techniques. It took time and concentration to figure out how to thread the bobbin and then the needle. She overlapped two of her fabric squares and felt a thrill of excitement as she gingerly stepped on the foot pedal and heard the machine suddenly come to life with a high-pitched hum and a vigorous *thump-thump-thump*. The needle shuttled up and down through the fabric, and a crooked line of black stitches appeared as the cloth emerged on the far side of the needle. Once she had fed the cloth all the way through, she cut the thread and carefully pulled it out to admire the joined pieces with a sense of triumph, then readied the fabric to make another pass.

It wasn't long before she had completely used up her sheet scraps and needed to find more fabric. Fortunately, Ugochi was cleaning out her family's apartment in preparation for their relocation to California and was more than happy to part with threadbare sheets, dish towels, and other fabric. Once all her friends knew what she was up to, they provided her with a steady stream of discarded cloth so that she could continue to practice her stitches. None of the other women considered sewing an activity of recreational value, so they were fascinated by this development.

"Are you going to start making real clothes soon?" Ugochi asked.

"I haven't gotten that far. Right now, I'm just working on improving my technique." Even as she said that, she was smiling on the inside as she thought of the tiny outfits she hoped to start putting together soon for the baby that was growing inside her.

"I don't think I've ever met anyone who just woke up one day and decided to buy a sewing machine and teach themselves to sew."

"If I hadn't come across the machine in the thrift store, it would never have occurred to me, either." She was grateful it had, as it helped to clear her mind and make her worries about Kabogo and her pregnancy seem less important than they'd been before.

Kabogo looked baffled whenever he saw her communing with the machine, hunched over and feeding scraps of cloth in one side and out the other. She would see him from the corner of her eye but pretend not to, feeling a perverse sense of pleasure at having a place she could retreat to in plain view where he could not follow. There was also the satisfaction of acquiring a skill he didn't possess, since it sometimes seemed that the only things he still liked to talk to her about were his accomplishments in his field. She struggled not to resent having quit the university so that she could marry him. She hadn't entirely abandoned the idea of enrolling in a degree program, but that didn't seem compatible with caring for an infant. For the moment, mastering the sewing machine felt like accomplishment enough.

Chapter 8

In early June, some of the Greenwood Park students and families arranged a farewell gathering for Ugochi. There was a good turnout of more than fifty people. Besides the international families Wanjikū had met at the Thanksgiving dinner, many of the couple's American friends and Emeka's friends from day care were in attendance, as well as Nigerian friends and relatives who had driven in from elsewhere in Connecticut, Massachusetts, New York, and New Jersey. The celebratory atmosphere and brightly colored springtime outfits complimented the blossoming flowers and bushes in the bright sunshine of the courtyard.

Nnamdi was a soft-spoken, deliberate man who measured his words carefully. He tended to ask questions rather than offer observations and listened closely to whatever was being said, before responding with, "I see," or asking another question. At six foot three, he towered over his diminutive wife, even with her platform sandals and Afro. But with her quick wit and magnetic personality, she was the one most people knew. Nnamdi's colleagues from the electrical engineering department had come to say goodbye to him, but even more of those in attendance had been dragged there by their wives who had bonded with Ugochi. If Nnamdi was the sage of the family, Ugochi was the diplomat. Together, they moved in perfect synchrony, communicating by raised eyebrows and cocks of the head amid the clamor of the festivities as Emeka, Wei, and their friends ran amok in the courtyard.

When Ugochi and Lihua had told their sons about the move, they'd been crestfallen for all of thirty seconds before Wei thought up a new game to play, and off they ran.

"That's it?" Lihua had asked incredulously.

When they returned sometime later, Emeka asked his mother if Wei could come to California for a sleepover.

"California is far away. If Wei's family happens to be in the area, we can definitely have them over for a visit."

"Yay!" erupted the four-year-olds in unison. And that was that. Though the boys made references to the move many times after that, the prospect of a sleepover erased any trace of sadness.

Kabogo came to the farewell party but only briefly. He ate, greeted a few people, including Nnamdi and Ugochi, then made an excuse and left. He and Nnamdi had never really connected. "That guy is a bore—he's too quiet!" Kabogo had said after they'd met at the Thanksgiving dinner. Of course, when he'd met Ugochi several weeks earlier, he'd complained that she was too talkative, though she'd eventually won him over. She had even managed to get him to laugh at his own expense.

The party, which had started around two o'clock, was still going strong when Wanjikū left at eight. It was pleasantly warm. The late sunsets in spring and summer still boggled her mind, as these were nonexistent back home. When she spoke to her parents by phone, her reports of daylight until eight or nine at night were a source of wonderment.

Kabogo lay on the couch watching TV when she got home. He grunted in acknowledgement as she walked in, then turned his attention back to the police drama he was watching. She was tired and headed straight to the bedroom. This was one of those times when the near absence of casual conversation in their house was a relief. As she changed into her nightclothes and burrowed under the sheets, she noted with satisfaction that despite all the food and drink smells at the party, she had managed to make it through the day without any significant nausea. Before long, she was fast asleep, the gentle sound of her snoring filling the dark room with its hypnotic rhythm.

She awoke from a peculiar dream in which she was at a party stuffing one hard-boiled egg after another into her mouth until her stomach hurt. When she awoke, Kabogo lying insensible next to her, she was drenched in sweat and nauseous, her abdomen cramping. She clambered out of bed and hurried to the bathroom, determined not to throw up until she got there. As she closed the bathroom door and flicked on the light, she lifted her foot reflexively, having stepped in something moist and sticky. When she looked down to see what it was, her whole body went numb. Dark red liquid trickled down her legs, forming a growing circle on the floor.

She swung open the bathroom door, and the light flooded the bedroom. "Kabogo! I'm bleeding!" she whispered urgently.

He mumbled in his sleep and turned over.

"Wake up, Kabogo!" she shouted. "I need to go to the hospital!"

He lay silent and immobile for a few seconds, then sat up bolt upright in bed. "*Ati* what? What's going on?"

When she told him, he jumped out of bed and ran to the living room to dial 911, the emergency number that the campus authorities drilled into the heads of the international students at the beginning of the school year. At the time, Kabogo's reaction was, "*Kwani*[1] , how many times will they keep repeating that number? If we're unable to remember something so simple, we shouldn't be here."

Now, it was a lifeline. Curled up against the bathroom wall in a glassy-eyed stupor, grimacing each time a spasm gripped her belly, Wanjikū could hear him explaining the emergency to the dispatcher.

---

1. Swahili word which, when added to the beginning of a sentence, turns it into a question.

The ambulance crew arrived within about five minutes, and everything was a blur after that. She remembered a stocky man with a blond buzz cut and pale blue eyes loudly asking her name and birthday as her limp body was lifted onto the gurney. She heard him say something about her heart rate and blood pressure followed by the quick sharp pain of needles going into both forearms before she lost consciousness.

When she awoke, she was in a hospital bed surrounded by a curtain and could hear two calm female voices in conversation a short distance away. Looking around nervously, she wondered what had happened to her and what lay beyond the curtain. Soon, some rapid footsteps approached, and the curtain opened. A nurse in her fifties with a pair of tortoiseshell spectacles hanging on a chain over her bosom seemed surprised to see Wanjikū but gave her a friendly smile. "Oh, hello! I didn't expect you to be awake yet. How are you feeling?"

When Wanjikū mumbled a noncommittal reply, the nurse said, "I'm going to let Dr. Anderson know you're awake. I'm sure you must have some questions." She stepped out, closing the curtain behind her. Wanjikū waited in a kind of suspended animation.

When the curtain opened again, she wondered if she'd dozed. Another woman appeared, younger than the first. "I'm Dr. Anderson," she said. Wanjikū's mouth fell open as she searched for words. She had never seen a woman doctor before. Dr. Anderson pulled up a nearby stool and sat down beside Wanjikū so she was at eye level. "I'm afraid I have some bad news," she began, looking grave.

Chapter 9

Losing the baby might have been more bearable if not for Kabogo. The two times he'd showed up at the hospital, he seemed ill at ease when he was alone with her but magically transformed into a charming, dutiful husband whenever a nurse or doctor appeared, asking concerned questions and repeating their instructions back to them to confirm his understanding. The pretense vanished as soon as they left the room, replaced by a disinterested silence. In her emotionally vulnerable state, it was harder for her to cut him as much slack as she usually did for his callousness.

The day they got home from the hospital, Ugochi stopped by to say goodbye. Kabogo stood partially blocking the doorway, making an excuse for why Wanjikū couldn't see her. When she heard that Wanjikū was unwell, she pushed right by him and made her way to the master bedroom, which was in the same place as in her own apartment, saying, "Oh, then I must see her, as we are leaving town today." She opened the bedroom door. "Hello, Wanjikū? Can I come in? I just came to say goodbye."

Wanjikū, lying in bed, replied wanly but was moved by Ugochi's concern. When Ugochi sat on the bed next to her, the story of her miscarriage came out in a flood. As she finished, the words caught in

SUNSHINE ON THE CROOKED ROAD

her throat, and tears began to stream down her cheeks. It was the first time she had allowed herself to cry since it had happened.

Ugochi took her in her arms, the floral scent of her perfume enveloping them. "Don't worry, my sister. God will give you another one. I had the same thing happen to me two years before Emeka was born, and I thought it was the end of the world. Be strong. It will be OK." She rose to her feet. "Nnamdi is waiting for me, so I have to go. Goodbye, and take care of yourself. Once we settle down in Palo Alto, I'll give you call to see how you're doing. Maybe one day you can come and visit if you happen to be in California. You will always be welcome there."

Wanjikū listened to the confident *klop-klop-klop* of her platform shoes as she walked to the front door. "Goodbye, my friend," she said to Kabogo as she walked past him in the living room, where he stood, completely nonplussed.

Maybe because he was smarting from his inability to intimidate or control the little hurricane named Ugochi, he promptly came to the bedroom door and commented that the miscarriage might not have happened had Wanjikū taken better care of herself rather than spending so much time with her friends, especially the six hours on her feet at Ugochi's farewell party. He dressed up his remarks as an expression of concern, saying that the next time around, she really needed to rest more, but she understood that he was telling her the miscarriage was her fault. She said nothing and rolled over in the bed to face the wall just inches away. He waited silently for a minute, then returned to the living room and resumed his schoolwork.

Lihua checked in on her a few hours later. Clearly, Ugochi had filled her in. Wisely, Kabogo did not attempt to stop her. She presented Wanjikū with an exquisite painting of a pink orchid.

"Thank you. It's beautiful," Wanjikū said.

"Every time you look at it, I hope it reminds you that there is beauty around us even when life seems difficult." She and her family were taking a road trip to Michigan to visit Chen's uncle, in part to provide a distraction to Wei as he came to terms with the finality of his friend's departure. When she got back, she'd be busy gearing up for her master's program.

***

Whenever Wanjikū looked back at the summer of 1971 in her later years, she recalled a tedious succession of sunny but empty days through which she dragged herself, one at a time. She had sustained a series of significant personal losses in June: the baby, the friends she'd spent most of her time with, the illusion of a functional marriage . . . She and Kabogo still engaged in the rudiments of conversation, but after the way he'd behaved during the miscarriage and its aftermath, she avoided him, hoping to forestall any more of his tactless comments that might completely unravel their already tenuous relationship. As to friends, she didn't feel the same connection to Elsie and Lakshmi as to Ugochi and Lihua, and she was too emotionally exhausted to make much of an effort. Even the solace she'd found in her sewing machine right up to the day before her miscarriage was gone.

She began going daily to the Dickinson Library to read books, encyclopedias, and magazines, mostly as a way to stay away from the emptiness of the apartment in the daytime, where her season of hope brought on by the pregnancy had ended in such heartbreak. It was only after she'd lost the baby that she realized how much time she had spent planning for it, especially imagining the baby clothes she would sew. After the miscarriage, she could not bring herself to sit at the sewing machine without dissolving into a puddle of tears. Sometimes she would find herself staring at an open book, her mind having wandered off into morose ruminations about how her life might be different if she had not quit the university in order to get married.

On one exceptionally slow day at the library when she stopped at the counter to check out some books, the librarian on duty said, "Isn't your husband a student in the biochemical engineering department? I think I met you once at one of the social events there. I recognized the name *Kabogo* on your library card."

Wanjikū looked up to see a cheerful woman in her midthirties with chestnut brown hair and green eyes. She had never seen anyone with green eyes before and was transfixed. They reminded her of dew-soaked Kikuyu[1] grass at sunrise, glistening like gems. After a minute, she realized that she had been staring rudely and snapped out of it. "Oh . . . yes," she said. "That's my husband."

"Great! That's what I thought. My husband, Bill, is on the faculty. I'm Karen."

"Wanjikū. Nice to meet you."

"Bill tells me your husband is an exceptional student." As Karen stamped her books, she peppered Wanjikū with questions about Kenya and told her about the small town in Kentucky where she and Bill were from. She had a kind, relaxed demeanor, and Wanjikū automatically felt comfortable with her, as if she had known her for a long time. "We worried the winters might be a problem when we first moved here, but that turned out not to be an issue. We love it!"

"Our first winter was a bit tough for me. Maybe my second one will be easier."

"It does take some getting used to. I've seen you here quite a few times; you must enjoy reading."

"I do, and it's better than sitting around the house watching TV. I don't have many friends. Two of the women I used to spend time with in the neighborhood have moved on."

---

1. Species of grass native to areas of Kenya inhabited by the Gĩkũyũ people. *Kikuyu* is a widely used variant of the word *Gĩkũyũ*.

"No place like the library to make new friends—real or imaginary!" Karen said, then looked behind Wanjikū with concern. "Well, I'd better get back to work. Maybe we can get together for a cup of coffee sometime."

"That would be nice," Wanjikū replied, hoping that Karen meant it.

Chapter 10

As it turned out, she did. Wanjikū and Karen got together many times in the weeks that followed, both in and out of the library, and it wasn't long before they became close confidantes. Karen was easygoing and had a good sense of humor. She continued to ask endless questions about life in Kenya, and Wanjikū sometimes struggled to explain things that had always seemed obvious to her but made no sense to an outsider—like why her married name was Kabogo's first name and not his surname.

"Mūchoki is not my husband—he's my father-in-law. Why would I take my last name from him?"

"Then why does Kabogo use Mūchoki as his last name?"

"Because that's his father . . . but not mine."

"So does that mean there's no such thing as a family name?"

"What's that?"

"See, like, if Bill and I had been able to have kids, our family would have been referred to as the Atkinsons. And if we had sons, their children would also be referred to as the Atkinsons, but if we had daughters, they would typically take their husband's family name. In your case, though, your husband's wife and children are referred to by his given name, not his father's name. Or am I getting it wrong?"

"No, that's correct."

"Wow, interesting."

The cultural perplexity worked both ways. Wanjikū was surprised by how matter-of-fact Karen was about information that would have been a source of shame in Kenya, such as her and Bill's inability to have children. Back in Gīthakainī, a woman who couldn't have children would never be referred to by the honorific *Nyina wa* like her peers. Even among the followers of Jesū, who no longer practiced polygamy, the commitment of a husband to a childless marriage was probably too much to hope for. To Karen, this might have been a source of consternation, like acne or arthritis, or even sadness, but not shame. Because of Karen's approach to life, Wanjikū felt she had finally found someone she could talk to about her miscarriage and the emotional turmoil it had left in its wake.

She listened without interruption, and when Wanjikū's voice trailed off and the tears started flowing, she just put an arm around her and said nothing. When Wanjikū was done crying, she inhaled deeply and turned to Karen with bloodshot eyes. "Back home, we don't talk about such things, and we certainly don't cry in public."

"You're not in public. You're pouring your heart out to a friend. There's nothing wrong with that."

Wanjikū choked out a laugh that was more of a sob. "I guess so. Thank you."

"Of course."

★★★

Karen and Bill invited Wanjikū and Kabogo to their house for dinner one Saturday in October. Initially, Wanjikū had been concerned that Kabogo might decline the invitation, given his previous reluctance to socialize and the sorry state of their marriage. However, it turned out that Kabogo had received the invitation from Bill, the head of his department, the same day she'd been invited by Karen, so saying no was not an option. For all his disregard of her at home, Wanjikū gathered that his persona at school was very congenial. He might have been two entirely different people. He also had an impressive work ethic, which had not escaped the notice of Bill and other people on the faculty.

Wanjikū stopped by Lihua's apartment for advice a couple of days before the appointed evening. Between Lihua's preparation for her program and Wanjikū's budding friendship with Karen, they hadn't seen much of each other over the summer, but Wanjikū still considered Lihua her friend. She cut right to the chase. "The head of Kabogo's department and his wife invited us to their house for dinner. Is there anything I need to be aware of? I'm still not that comfortable with American customs."

"I'm not, either," Lihua said with a chuckle, "especially when you're visiting a workplace superior. Let me ask Chen."

She called out in Mandarin, and Chen appeared, shuffling casually down the hallway from the bedroom. "Hello, Wanjikū," he said with a welcoming smile. Lihua explained her predicament.

"A social visit with a workplace superior . . . That's a bit tricky. Are other people invited, or just you?"

"Just us . . . I think."

"OK . . . Let me see . . . Well, the easiest thing might be to take a bottle of wine. It's hard to go wrong with that. Not unless they happen to be wine snobs."

Wanjikū looked skeptical. "But what if they don't drink wine?"

"It doesn't matter. They'll just give it to someone else. It's the gesture that counts. Or if you don't want to take wine, you could take a dessert, but that gets more complicated, and you'd probably have to coordinate with your hostess."

Wanjikū sighed and shook her head. "I don't know much about desserts, so I guess I'll stick with wine. How will I know what to buy?"

"Red wines are a safe bet, I think," said Chen uncertainly.

"OK, thank you."

"Which professor is this, by the way?"

"Bill Atkinson."

"I've heard he's a nice guy, though I've never met him. How did you end up getting invited to his place?"

"His wife works at the library, and we became friends over the summer."

"Oh, his wife is your friend!" exclaimed Lihua. "Then why don't you just ask her what to bring?"

"Really? Wouldn't that be rude?"

"No, no! People here are very direct. It's really weird. You don't need to try to guess what someone wants, especially if they're your friend. You just ask them."

Wanjikū realized as soon as Lihua said this that she was right, especially where Karen was concerned. She headed for home feeling much more relaxed about the coming dinner.

★★★

Karen and Bill lived only a couple of miles away, right off the bus line, which was fortunate since nighttime temperatures were getting chilly. Despite the vagaries of the bus system, they still got there well ahead of time, only to find Bill pacing behind the storm door with the main door ajar. He immediately opened the storm door and called out, "Here you are! Come on in!" Then, over his shoulder, "Karen, they're here!"

As they entered, Karen appeared from the kitchen, wiping her hands on her apron. "Welcome, we're so glad you could come!" Wanjikū handed over the bottle of wine that Karen had agreed would be welcome as Bill took their coats and ushered them into the living room.

It was a fun evening over a delicious meal. Karen and Wanjikū spent most of it talking between themselves while Bill and Kabogo ranged over topics concerning the department and their field of study. Given her own experience with Kabogo, Wanjikū was concerned that he might be taciturn and aloof, but from the snippets of conversation she could catch, Kabogo was asking Bill about the master's and doctorate programs and showering him with knowledgeable questions about his area of expertise. She knew she had nothing to worry about. It seemed to her that Bill almost levitated above his chair in the glow of Kabogo's informed interest and attention. *That sly devil*, she thought. *Not at all the boorish Kabogo I know.* Despite her resentment that he never showed her this side of himself, she was glad to see him so skillfully ingratiating himself with someone who could make such a difference to his career.

It also avoided a lot of potential awkwardness between her and Karen. The two of them were having a wonderful time together. The twinkle in her friend's emerald eyes, the warmth of her hug, and the excitement with which she took her on a tour of the house seemed to lift their friendship to a whole new level. It wasn't a very big house, but it was wonderfully furnished, with nothing out of place. "Your house is so neat!" exclaimed Wanjikū.

"I'm a librarian with no kids," Karen noted wryly. "Putting things in their right place is what I do for a living. But if you really must know, I had Bill haul a bunch of stuff that was lying around to the basement. Knowing him, it's probably right at the bottom of the stairs. Let's go see if I'm right!"

She opened the basement door and turned on the light. At the bottom of the stairs was a pile of shoes, journals, books, and clothes. She turned to Wanjikū with a triumphant grin that her friend shared.

"You know what would really be nice? Having you and Kabogo come and spend Christmas with us in Lawrenceburg."

Wanjikū's eyebrows shot up. She wasn't sure how to respond.

"I know what you're thinking. You're wondering how welcoming a little town in Kentucky would be to someone from Kenya. I can't speak for everyone you might meet, but I can tell you that my parents would absolutely fall in love with you. I'm sure of it! I can even see myself fighting with my mother about who gets to spend more time with you."

Wanjikū looked tentative. "How about Bill's family?"

Karen paused to consider. "Bill's family is . . . well, less demonstrative. They're nice, sincere people but harder to read. It took me years to get over thinking they disliked me because of their silence when I visited. Bill is an only child, and he's used to how . . . reserved . . . they are, so he didn't think anything of it until I finally broke down and asked him why his parents hated me. He just looked at me like I had three eyes."

By the time they rejoined the men, Bill was giving Kabogo a detailed description of how he'd prepared the mouthwatering honey garlic salmon they'd had for dinner and offering to take him fishing in next summer. Kabogo looked enthralled, egging Bill on, but Wanjikū knew better than to assume that he was genuinely interested. Seeing the surprise and consternation on his face when he'd complimented Karen on the salmon only to learn that it was Bill who deserved the credit was a moment worth savoring. She wasn't holding her breath that he would ever help her in the kitchen, but she hoped that some of Bill's views might rub off on him with time.

The TV was on in the background at low volume, and Bill's attention was captured by an announcement about the opening of Disney World in Florida. "Hear that, Karen? That's what I was telling you about. It's supposed to be bigger than the one in California."

"But there's nothing in Florida. Why would they open an amusement park there?"

"That's precisely it! They could buy a lot more land in Florida than they ever could in California."

"Have you ever been to an amusement park?" Karen asked Wanjikū.

"I don't even know what that is."

"Well, maybe we can visit one together someday. Maybe even in Florida!"

Chapter 11

In 1972, world events that would not ordinarily have caught Wanjikū's notice turned out to be highly significant to a couple of her Greenwood Park friends. President Nixon's trip to mainland China in February would have been yet another dry and esoteric news story to her had she not run into a red-faced, fulminating Lihua. Her simple "How is everything?" had triggered a diatribe against unreliable friends who deserted you as soon it was convenient for them.

Wanjikū became alarmed. "I don't know what you're talking about, Lihua. Is it something I did?"

"Wanjikū, where have you been? Don't you follow the news?"

"When I can. Why? What happened?"

Lihua sighed deeply. "Chen and I are from Taiwan."

"Yes. That's somewhere in China, right?"

"No, it's *not* in China, at least not the China that Nixon went to visit."

"Oh! There's more than one China?"

It turned out that both Chen and Lihua's families had left mainland China for Taiwan in the late 1940s as the nationalist forces were defeated by Mao Zedong's Red Army. Chen's father and uncle had both served in the air force, fighting against Mao's troops until it became clear that defeat was inevitable.

According to Lihua, Chen, usually so soft-spoken and cerebral, had started to become agitated the previous summer, when Nixon had announced his plans to visit China, right about when the family had gone to visit his uncle in Michigan. There, they tried to hash out what the announcement might mean for their kin back home. They had little doubt that the visit would take place, but they hoped it would amount to little more than a photo-op with no major ramifications for Taiwan.

When the Shanghai Communiqué was released at the end of Nixon's visit, proclaiming that "all Chinese on either side of the Taiwan Strait maintain that there is but one China," their worst fears were realized. Lihua, Chen, and their relatives were gripped with existential dread. They felt that they had been betrayed by the United States and left at the mercy of their Communist foes.

"Do you think they will invade?" Wanjikū asked.

"I don't know. That's what we're worried about."

"I'm sorry," said Wanjikū. "I had no idea." They walked on together for a while in silence. "How's Ugochi, by the way?"

"I spoke with her last weekend, and it sounds like they're having a great time in California. We're going to try and visit them before the end of the year. I'm sure Wei will be excited to see Emeka again."

After talking to Lihua, she found herself paying more attention when China or Taiwan were mentioned in the news. She wondered whether knowing someone from Vietnam might have prompted her to pay more attention to the daily barrage of horrific news from that country, which she often tuned out for the simple reason that it did not directly affect her.

In August, another bombshell hit, this time for Ravi, with Idi Amin's expulsion of South Asians from Uganda. Wanjikū and Kabogo had seen him around campus and knew he planned to graduate the following spring. He had become noticeably more subdued since the coup. Once it became clear that the mere mention of his home country produced waves of anxiety and gloom in him, they tried to steer clear of that topic in conversation.

One day a week after the news broke, Wanjikū and Kabogo happened to be in the kitchen when she turned to him and asked, "Did you hear that Amin expelled the Ahīndī from Uganda?"

"Yes, I saw it on the TV in the break room at the department. Every time I see Ravi, he looks so gloomy, not at all his usually jovial self. We had a little chance to talk yesterday afternoon."

"How is he doing?"

"He's worried, though he says that it will primarily affect those Ahīndī who still have British passports. Since he and his family took Ugandan citizenship at independence, he hopes it won't affect them."

"Oh, good!"

"But everyone is nervous, because there have been stories of people being beaten up by soldiers for no reason, or disappearing."

"My baba mentioned that in our last phone conversation. He said the stories coming into Kenya from the people who have managed to leave are disturbing. So maybe the Ahīndī with the UK passports are the lucky ones after all. At least they can relocate to England."

"They would be, except that even with a British passport, they can't travel to the UK without a travel voucher, and the British government has cut back the number of vouchers they are issuing."

"Ati? Even with a British passport, they can't travel to the UK? What's the purpose of having a passport issued by a country you can't even visit?"

Kabogo shook his head. "I'm sure when the colonialists were gathering Ravi's forefathers from their villages in India to go build the railway, there was no problem getting them travel papers," he said dryly.

They stood together in silence until Kabogo glanced at his watch and decided it was time to move on. Wanjikū made no attempt to detain him. This was about as good a conversation with him as she could hope for these days, and it was best concluded before one of them ruined the evening by saying something that they shouldn't, or got their back up about some innocent remark. She returned to her sewing machine and resumed working on the cotton pajamas she was making for herself on the theory that something she wore to bed would not expose her inexpert tailoring skills. She was sewing again, thanks in large part to a rambling story Karen had told her during one of their regular get-togethers at Morning Buzz, a popular coffee shop and favorite hangout for students with avant-garde mismatched decor, packing crates for tables, and heavenly coffee.

Apparently, Karen's aunt had been a seamstress who had made most of the clothes that she and her siblings wore growing up. They'd been embarrassed to wear the handmade clothes and envious of their schoolmates, whose parents could afford to provide them with store-bought outfits. When two popular girls from the grade above had asked in their usual haughty tones where she got her dresses, Karen had run off crying, assuming they were making fun of her. Only later, when one of the girls' sisters told her that they referred to her as "that weird girl with the amazing outfits" did she begin to recognize how stylish and well made her clothes were.

In response, Wanjikū casually mentioned her brief flirtation with the sewing machine. Karen became excited. "Why did you stop? You should pick it up again. What's the point of having a sewing machine if you're not going to use it?"

She realized that it was time to get back to sewing again. After the miscarriage, she'd avoided the machine, spending more time at the library instead. It took a few sessions following Karen's remarks for the heaviness of those memories to dissipate. Soon, her original fascination with the machine and what it could allow her to do returned. She became restless to improve her skills, and before long, the lively whirring of the electric motor became the soundtrack for many an afternoon and evening. Kabogo complained about the noise at first, but Wanjikū ignored him, and his grumbling eventually stopped.

***

As the cool gray days of autumn rolled around, Wanjikū avoided walking to the library. Her initial experience of cold weather had included an element of fascination, but now, all she could think of was the discomfort of the biting chill and the early nightfall. She became virtually housebound, talking herself out of all but the most necessary reasons for walking past the front door. She had plenty of time to sew, and Karen often telephoned or stopped by to visit. By mid-November, she'd begun to feel more tired than she would have expected from the seasonal blues. Her monthly cycle was again overdue, and when she noticed swelling in her hands and feet and an unusual snugness in the waistband of her trousers, it supported her suspicion that she might be pregnant again. She ruefully remembered her last visit to Student Health and her ridiculous deduction that she'd developed an egg allergy. At least she wasn't experiencing any nausea.

As modest and private as she was, she did not relish going to the health center again. She had read in a magazine at the library that in Canada, tests were available to check at home if you were pregnant. An American doctor quoted in the article had called it "ridiculous and lamentable" that the same tests were not yet available south of the border, and Wanjikū couldn't help but agree.

Nevertheless, the next morning she made her way to Student Health where, just like the first time, the waiting room was empty. Everything seemed much less intimidating this time around. It helped that Paula was there when she was called back. "Hello, *Wan-jee-coe*. I remember you from the last time you were here." They walked to the nurse's station, where Paula checked her vitals and made small talk about the weather and local goings-on.

"How did you make out the last time?" she asked, her piercing blue eyes looking straight at her over her half-moon spectacles.

Wanjikū averted her gaze. "I had a miscarriage."

"Oh, I'm sorry to hear that," she said, stopping what she was doing. She sounded truly deflated by the news. "Well, I'll let Dr. Jones know you're here."

Chapter 12

Wanjikū decided she wouldn't tell Kabogo about the pregnancy until it started to show. For one, she didn't want to raise his hopes, given how things ended the last time. For another, she wasn't at all sure that his hopes would be raised. Kabogo was unpredictable, and mostly not in a good way. She also didn't want to deal with any more irrational nonsense about the baby being a boy. It wasn't like he took much notice of her frame of mind or physical appearance, anyway, so she should be able to maintain the subterfuge for some time.

If the baby was a girl, she would name her after Kabogo's mother, Nyagūthiī. Agīkūyū adults were rarely addressed by their given names but rather as *mother of—* or *father of—*. Those without children went by *son of—*, *daughter of—* or *wife of—*. Wanjikū hadn't found out her mother-in-law's given name until Kabogo had mentioned in passing during her first pregnancy that the baby would certainly be a Mūchoki and not a Nyagūthiī. The ironic juxtaposition of her father-in-law's and mother-in-law's names did not escape her. It wasn't every day that you met two people living together whose names were Mūchoki—"the one who comes back"—and Nyagūthiī—"the one who goes away."

Karen was the first to find out about this second pregnancy, though not by any conscious intention of Wanjikū's. She had been planning

SUNSHINE ON THE CROOKED ROAD

to delay her disclosure as long as possible—even to Karen—abetted by layers of winter clothing. On one of Karen's visits, she told Wanjikū that her favorite indie rock band, The Sunburnt Woodpeckers, would be performing in New Haven in the spring and entreated Wanjikū to come with her to the concert. Much as she wanted to please her best friend, nothing about The Sunburnt Woodpeckers or the prospect of a crowded, smelly, and probably expensive rock concert sounded even remotely appealing to her. Without thinking, she blurted, "I can't go, because I'm due in April."

"Due?" Karen asked, looking puzzled.

Wanjikū hoped she could finesse the situation, but Karen's eyes opened wide with surprise and recognition. "You're kidding!"

"Oops," Wanjikū said, cringing. "That wasn't supposed to come out."

"Why the secret?" asked Karen, looking miffed.

"What if I lose it again? Even Kabogo doesn't know."

The awkwardness of the unexpected revelation quickly passed, and a look of excitement came in Karen's eyes as she got up from her seat and threw her arms about Wanjikū. "I'm sure it will be fine. I'm so happy for you!" The reassuring hug from her best friend—whose wavy hair tickled the side of her face, her fruity perfume filling her nostrils—brought tears to Wanjikū's eyes. "What are you hoping to have?"

"I don't care. I'm just hoping for a healthy baby. Kabogo will insist that it's going to be a boy, which is another reason I don't feel like telling him about it right now."

Karen knew something of Wanjikū's complicated relationship with Kabogo, the Kabogo who was nothing like the seemingly thoughtful husband she and Bill knew when the couples were together. Of the four, Bill was the only one who had no clue that there was more than one Kabogo. The long sessions of confiding in each other that Wanjikū and Karen had shared meant that each knew things about the other that even their husbands did not, such as Karen's tortured relationship with her mother-in-law, and the related fact that though she'd hated their early years in Hartford, she never mentioned it for fear that Bill would apply for a position at the university in Lexington—his original choice and way too close to her in-laws.

"Karen, I was serious when I said that even Kabogo doesn't know about—"

"About what? I didn't hear anything."

"Thank you."

"So how does it feel? Are you excited? Nervous? I'm just trying to imagine what it's like."

"I'm not allowing myself to feel anything yet. When things have moved further along and I've talked to Kabogo, I'll have a better idea of where things stand."

***

Opening her heart to Karen did her good. It also reminded her that she needed to make an appointment with an obstetrician. The last time around, she never ended up seeing the doctor because she had the miscarriage. Karen said that one of the librarians who was expecting had an obstetrician she liked and gave her his name two days later: Dr. Pickmore, less than half a mile beyond the library. The following morning, she set out under a clear blue sky and dazzling sunshine for Dr. Pickmore's office. This was an important enough step that she wanted to make it in person, rather than over the phone. She was layered in clothing and snow gear, as it was freezing cold, and her boots crunched over the brittle crust of compacted snow on the sidewalk.

By the time Wanjikū got to the office, her nose was burning with cold. When she entered, a dour-faced woman looked up from the reception desk in the nearly empty office. "May I help you?"

"Yes, I'd like to make an appointment to see Dr. Pickmore."

The woman looked at her calendar with distaste before saying, "Dr. Pickmore doesn't have any openings for new patients at this time."

"How about one of the other doctors?"

The receptionist made a show of looking through her appointment book. "Not at the moment, no," she said, without looking up. "Anything else I can help you with?"

Wanjikū's brow furrowed. "No, thank you," she said, then turned around and left the office. She stopped in to see Karen at the library on her way home. She was busy at the checkout counter, so Wanjikū signaled that she'd be in the periodicals section and flipped through a magazine.

Karen slid into the chair next to her a few minutes later. "Hey, how did it go?" she whispered. When Wanjikū related her experience, Karen exclaimed, "That doesn't make sense!" then lowered her voice. "How can an entire obstetric practice not have openings for new patients? They have plenty of turnover, and Leslie just started going there a couple of months ago."

"I'm just telling you what she told me. So I'm heading home to figure out my next step. Maybe I'll go back to Student Health and ask them for referrals. They must know which practices are taking on new patients."

"OK. I'll give you a call when I get off work," Karen said, hurrying back to the checkout counter to take care of another patron.

Wanjikū returned home and busied herself with the endless chores that nibbled away at the short winter days, which were much harder to get used to than the long days of summer. When the phone rang that afternoon, she hurried to pick it up. "Hello?"

Karen didn't even bother with a greeting. "So when Leslie came in, I told her what you told me. She was surprised because her cousin just got an appointment with Dr. Pickmore last week, so I called the office and asked if they had new patient appointments. Rebecca, the receptionist, said they had openings not just with Dr. Pickmore but with all the other doctors as well."

"Well, she was quite emphatic when she talked to me, and she wasn't very friendly."

"What are you thinking?"

"Oh, I don't know, Karen, but that whole interaction left a bad taste in my mouth. That's definitely not the doctor's office I want to be going to."

"Totally understandable. Let's talk some more tomorrow. I'll come over to your place."

"OK, see you then."

As she hung up the phone and went to the kitchen to start preparing dinner, she was certain she knew what the experience from that morning had been about. Of course. She had suspected it at the time, but there were other plausible explanations, such as the lady having a bad morning and the possibility that there were truly no appointments available. But after hearing that Karen had called back later and gotten a totally different answer, she understood what the problem was.

That night, Wanjikũ lay awake, listening to Kabogo's snoring. She envied his ability to lay his head on the pillow and effortlessly disengage from the world. She wondered if she ever featured in his dreams. If so, did she have a different role than in real life, or was she still the disregarded wife who cooks and cleans and take care of the house, with no acknowledged goals or opinions of her own? Mostly, though, she replayed the scene from Dr. Pickmore's office over and over again in her head, wishing for once that Kabogo's shortcomings were her only concern. Sometime after three-thirty in the morning, she fell asleep and was awakened only by the sound of Kabogo hustling to get out of the house. She felt exhausted.

Karen arrived at her door unannounced shortly after nine o'clock.

"Hey, girl, just checking to make sure we're both thinking the same thing. What do you think was going on with that receptionist at Dr. Pickmore's office?"

"Karen, I didn't want to jump to conclusions, but I think that lady is a racist."

"Hmm, that's kind of what I suspected. Do you think we should ask to speak to the manager and call her out? The rest of the people in the office may not be like her."

"No, I'm not going back there after what happened. No thanks."

"You still need an obstetrician, though."

"I think I'm gonna go down to Student Health and ask them if they have a list of doctors they recommend. That's where I got the pregnancy test."

Chapter 13

1973

"I don't know. April might be a problem, because I'll be presenting a poster at a conference in Florida," was Kabogo's response when she finally got around to telling him about the pregnancy in January. She was dumbfounded. A scheduling conflict was not among the unhelpful responses she had anticipated hearing from him when she shared the news.

"So I guess that means you're leaving me on my own when the baby is due to attend a conference?"

"That's not what I said," he replied. She waited for more, but he declined to elaborate. After a long, uncomfortable pause, he said, "I'm sure we'll figure something out by the time April arrives," then walked back to his untidy array of books and folders on the dining table.

Wanjikū bit her lip. Despite having braced herself for the most boneheaded of responses, he had still managed to take her by surprise. Clearly, it did not occur to him that skipping the conference might be easier than expecting the baby to accommodate his schedule. She had not expected him to join her on all of her remaining prenatal visits to Dr. Patel—the obstetrician—but coming to one or two would have been nice. If Dr. Patel was surprised by his absence, he didn't show it. He was

SUNSHINE ON THE CROOKED ROAD

a soft-spoken man with kind eyes and a tousled shock of white hair, and she found his calm, fatherly demeanor reassuring, even if, given his Indian accent, he called her, *Vanjikū*.

If Kabogo seemed indifferent, Karen nearly made up for it with her boundless enthusiasm and resourcefulness. She took Wanjikū shopping for maternity dresses and baby clothes to supplement the ones she was sewing, and was always optimistic and upbeat, never seeming to tire of ferrying her around in her car. Kabogo had bought an ancient Ford Cortina with about a hundred thousand miles on it a few months earlier. Wanjikū hadn't been keen to learn to drive it because she was sure it was destined to break down at any time, leaving her stranded by the roadside.

Probably because of Kabogo's conspicuous absence, Dr. Patel had stressed, "Babies often come at night. If your husband is not home and you go into labor, make sure you call an ambulance. No delay or hesitation. Call 911, OK?"

She'd appreciated his concern and knew that she could call on Karen to take her to the hospital at any time of day or night. When she remembered how much blood she'd lost during the miscarriage, how she'd blacked out on the bathroom floor and woken up a day later in the hospital, she worried that if something went wrong with her pregnancy while Kabogo was away, it could be a disaster.

Kabogo left for Florida on a Friday in April without any show of concern, though he did joke that she should try to hold on to the baby until he returned at the end of the following week. The anger she felt for most of that day gave way to anxiety as the sun went down. Fortunately, Karen came over soon after to cheer her up and even brought a chicken casserole she'd prepared that afternoon. Wanjikū picked at it out of politeness, though she had no appetite. Bill would be heading on Sunday to the same conference. Karen had offered to come and stay with Wanjikū, but Wanjikū didn't want to impose, saying they already had a plan to get to the hospital and that she could telephone at any time. The two women had long since decided not to advertise Kabogo's unseemly behavior at home to Bill, since undercutting his career advancement would only hurt Wanjikū in the end.

After dinner, they reviewed their plan of action in case she went into labor during Kabogo's absence. Wanjikū had her bag packed for the hospital by the front door, and Karen reminded her to call her right away, no matter the hour. Karen would call first thing every morning and, if Wanjikū didn't pick up, would call the hospital to see if she was there before panicking and rushing over. Friday night passed uneventfully. Wanjikū was surprised by how well she slept, not opening her eyes from the time she turned off the bedside lamp at ten o'clock to when Karen telephoned at seven the next morning to see how she'd fared.

On Saturday night, she felt unusually restless and couldn't seem to get comfortable when she lay down to sleep. She did eventually manage to drift off, but woke up again around one. After about an hour of staring wide-eyed at the luminous dial of the alarm clock on the nightstand, she turned the light back on and decided to read. She'd left the musty-smelling copy of *Wuthering Heights* from the library in the kitchen, so she put on her robe and, once she was in the kitchen, decided to make herself some chamomile tea, which Lihua promoted as a sleep aid. It didn't have that effect on Wanjikū, but she liked the taste of it, and the routine of making and drinking the tea did seem to help her relax.

As she searched in the cupboard for the box of tea bags, a mild cramping in her abdomen lasted a few seconds and then went away. She froze midstep, regarded her protuberant belly with a look of alarm, and waited for more cramping. When none came after a minute or so, she grabbed a tea bag and made her tea, then took it and her novel to the living room. Just then, she felt another cramp, this one painful. It built in intensity until she bent over and let out an involuntary gasp. When it passed, she walked cautiously to the armchair and sat down. Her heart was racing, and she glanced instinctively at the overnight bag by the door. She lifted the hot cup of tea, shutting her eyes as the steam rose to her face.

Should she call Karen? But what if it wasn't labor? What if it was just a worse version of the indigestion she'd been experiencing lately? She didn't want to inconvenience her friend for nothing, especially since she had to get up early the next morning to take Bill to the airport. She remembered Dr. Patel's exhortation: "Call an ambulance. No delay or hesitation. Call 911, OK?" Almost immediately, she was gripped by another spasm that felt like a giant talon grabbing her insides. She let out a shriek as she realized that it had no intention of letting go. When it finally relented, she realized, *This is it. No delay or hesitation . . .* and immediately dialed 911. She was glad she did because moments later her water broke, and her contractions worsened. By the time the paramedics arrived, she had pulled a terry cloth robe over her now-moist nightdress and was waiting anxiously by the door.

They were polite but businesslike, communicating with each other mostly in jargon. One of them spoke in clipped sentences into a walkie-talkie, describing the situation.

The other one—a burly, gray-haired man with a thick mustache who helped her onto the gurney—said, "Don't you worry, ma'am. You're in safe hands."

"My bag . . ." she started, pointing to the overnight bag she had packed.

"Got it! Is there anyone else here with you?"

"No, my husband is at a conference."

"His loss." They quizzed her about potential fire hazards, grabbed her keys, and locked up after themselves, putting the keys in her bag.

Once they'd hoisted her into the ambulance, the engine roared to life, the siren came on, and off they flew. Two paramedics sat with her in the back, chatting with her to help her relax, and within a few minutes, they were at the hospital.

Dr. Patel was not on call that night, but Dr. Sorensen, a tall, thin, balding man who could look austere when he wasn't flashing his ready smile, took charge. "It looks like you're already making good progress," he said after examining her. "The baby is fine and seems to be in quite a hurry to come into the world." He offered her a relatively new procedure called an epidural that lessened the pain of labor and involved sticking a needle in her spine. The combination of relatively new and sticking a needle in her spine decided her against it.

"Are you sure?" asked Dr. Sorensen, as if this were a big mistake.

"Yes," she said firmly.

As it happened, turning down the epidural was a huge miscalculation and one she regretted as the waves of pain intensified, the minutes slowing down to a crawl as her contractions grew stronger and came closer and closer together. Soon, everything around her was swallowed by the torturous pain that mercilessly squeezed her belly and refused to let go. She screamed and gasped, the tears flowing down her face, as Dr. Sorensen and his nurse alternately shouted for her to push and told her how well she was doing, for which she wanted to punch them in the nose. Then, suddenly, they were no longer shouting but exchanging quick businesslike phrases hardly above a whisper. She thought they sounded happy, even excited. As a tiny, shrill scream pierced the air, Wanjikū's pain and distress vanished, replaced by intense joy and complete exhaustion as her head fell back against the pillow.

"Congratulations, Mrs. Kabogo!" announced Dr. Sorensen, his face lit up by one of his smiles. "You have given birth to a beautiful baby girl."

Chapter 14

Nyagūthiĩ was indeed beautiful. Wanjikū had always thought it silly when people described a newborn as beautiful, because in her opinion, they all looked like moles, squinting in the sun's glare. But now, as she held the precious creature that had come out of her own body, she was overwhelmed by feelings of love far stronger than any she had ever felt.

She also felt completely drained. Around five thirty in the morning, she reluctantly let the nurse take Nyagūthiĩ and had no trouble falling into a deep sleep. When she awoke, the room was flooded with sunlight, and her baby was asleep in a bassinet next to her bed, wrapped up like a tiny gift. A new nurse walked in moments later. "Someone named Karen is here to see you. Should I send her in?"

Wanjikū nodded, and a moment later, Karen entered the room, clutching a bunch of flowers. She tiptoed to the bassinet and looked down. "Wow, she's adorable!" she whispered.

"Thank you."

She came around to Wanjikū and gave her an awkward, flower-tangled hug. "Hold on. Let me see if they have a vase for these." She returned a few minutes later with the flowers in a plastic vase and sat by Wanjikū's bed. "I called your house this morning, and when you didn't pick up, I immediately called the hospital to make sure you were here. I'd just dropped Bill off at the airport. He wanted to cancel his trip when I told him, but I said we'd be fine. He'll give Kabogo the news. And guess what he reminded me to bring that we'd completely forgotten to pack?"

"What?"

She reached into her bag and triumphantly brought out a Polaroid camera. "First-day baby pictures! He said I could bring his other camera, too, but it has too many buttons and dials."

She walked over to the bassinet and took a picture of the sleeping baby. "Your first picture on Planet Earth! Here, let me take another one that shows this card with all her particulars on it, so she doesn't end up fighting with her siblings years from now about whether it's her or one of them."

Wanjikū listened with mild amusement. She didn't have any baby pictures. Most Kenyans her age had their first pictures taken at a wedding, a funeral, or when the family dressed up and went to a studio in town for a family photo. No one had cameras around the house when she was growing up. Mingled with her amusement was sadness that Bill, who was hardly more than an acquaintance, had offered to cancel his trip when her own husband had not.

"Is it OK if I pick her up? I'll try not to wake her."

Wanjikū nodded. Karen put down the camera and gingerly picked up the sleeping infant. "Not as heavy as I'd expected. Hey, there, little princess!"

The nurse came back into the room. "Would you like me to take a picture of you with the baby?" she asked Karen when she saw the camera.

"Thank you. That'd be great!"

There followed a whole series of pictures of the three of them on the bed once Wanjikū had taken back Nyagūthiī.

"So when do you get out of here?" asked Karen when the nurse left.

"I don't know. The doctor hasn't come in yet. I'm ready to go home tomorrow if they let me."

"I took today and tomorrow off, so I can bring you home from the hospital. And if you give me your house keys, I'll go in there and get things ready for you and the baby."

"Oh, Karen, you've already done so much!"

"Ssh! Don't mention it. I'm glad to help."

***

Wanjikū and Nyagūthiī were home by noon. Karen had cleaned the house and placed right next to the bed the crib they'd purchased at a thrift store the month before. Wanjikū glanced to where she had been standing when her water broke and saw that no trace of that event remained. As it was a warm spring day, Karen had opened the windows. The chirping of birds outside made the house feel more alive than it had in months.

"I'm not the best cook in the world, but I made us some rice, chicken, and broccoli for lunch. I was planning to go over to the grocery store this afternoon to get some milk and bread and whatever else you need."

"Thank you," said Wanjikū, overwhelmed by Karen's kindness. "I'm so lucky to have you as a friend."

"*I'm* the lucky one!" Karen countered. "And happy to be of some use."

The telephone rang about noon, and they exchanged looks before Wanjikū went over to answer it. "Hello?"

"Hello, it's Kabogo." Wanjikū felt her whole body tense. "I tried calling yesterday morning, but nobody picked up."

"I was in the hospital," she said.

"Bill told me. So how's the baby?"

"She's fine."

"Oh . . . She?"

"Yes, it's a girl." When he didn't say anything, she continued, "I'm here with Karen."

"OK. I'll be home on Friday."

"OK. Bye."

When she hung up the phone, her hands were shaking. "I regret the day I met that man!" she said angrily. Karen's eyebrows arched in surprise. "The only reason he called was to find out if the baby was a boy. He didn't even ask how I got to the hospital and back or how I'm managing with a new baby in the house. He didn't even offer to come home early. Marrying him was the biggest mistake I ever made! I feel nothing but regret!" Her words boiled over into sobs, as Karen sat frozen on the sofa, the baby asleep on her lap. She'd been well aware of Kabogo's caddish behavior from former conversations, but she had never seen Wanjikū break down like this, though it was no surprise under the circumstances.

Once her sobs subsided, Wanjikū sat on the sofa next to Karen, an embarrassed look on her face. "Shouldn't it be the baby who's crying? Instead, she's sleeping quietly while I do the crying. I'm sorry to put you through that."

"Don't be ridiculous. Better to cry than to keep it bottled up inside. I guess I hadn't realized quite how bad things were."

"You know, divorce doesn't happen very often where I'm from, which makes an unhappy marriage very difficult. And even if I could divorce him, where would I go? Right now, I'm here as a dependent on his visa, so I'd probably have to leave the country. If I went back to Kenya, who would hire me—a divorced single mother who dropped out of college? And the shame that would come to my family . . . I couldn't put my parents through that."

"Sounds like you've been thinking about this."

"Every now and then, he does something so upsetting that I can't help thinking about it. I just don't know anyone who's ever done it, and I'd hate to be the one everyone in my village points to as the first."

"But what if he did something extreme, like . . . I don't know . . . Has he ever hit you?"

"Fortunately, he hasn't. The women where I'm from have a reputation for violence. Every now and then, there'll be a story in the news about a woman from Nyeri chasing her husband with a *panga*—like a machete—after a domestic dispute. I used to laugh about it with my college friends, but maybe it's a good thing. Kabogo has mentioned it more than once, and I do nothing to disabuse him of the idea."

"You wouldn't hurt a fly."

"True, but if he ever hit me, that would be the absolute end of our marriage, and there's no way I wouldn't hit him back."

"Aha! So you're a panga-wielding princess after all!" Karen teased.

"I hope it never comes to that. In the meantime, let's spend Nyagũthiĩ's first day at home talking about something less depressing than divorce and chasing spouses with pangas. How about I get us some tea and warm up some lunch?"

"I'll do that. You take this baby. She's starting to get a fidgety."

Chapter 15

Ravi's surprise graduation party at the end of May was even bigger than Ugochi and Nnamdi's going away party—a testament to how well thought of he was—and included lots of people she had never seen before. He'd had a difficult year, and the fact that he had managed to complete his doctorate despite his personal challenges was something to celebrate.

Even though General Amin's formal declaration for Asians to leave Uganda was directed at non-Ugandan citizens, his overzealous enforcers couldn't be troubled to make the distinction. It soon became clear that even Ugandan citizens of Asian extraction would be required to relinquish their businesses and take up farming in the arid northeastern region of Karamoja. Ravi's family had somehow managed to make their way into Kenya—Wanjikū didn't know the details—and was trying to get asylum in the commonwealth countries of Canada or Australia. The UK was already overwhelmed by the Asians who still held British passports. Ravi, too, was now stateless and had applied for asylum in the United States.

Unlike the happy-go-lucky character who had picked them up from the airport when they arrived, he had a somber air these days. He spent most of his free time glued to his shortwave radio, listening for snippets of news about Uganda. Wanjikū didn't see much of him anymore and had learned most of this from Lakshmi, whose husband, Amit, was his close friend. He hadn't thought much of it when Amit asked him to keep his Saturday afternoon open so they could try a new Indian restaurant downtown. Now, surprised, and possibly aghast, by the throng of well-wishers, he seemed to be struggling to adopt his former bonhomie.

The party was Wanjikū's first trip out of the house for anything other than short walks in the commons with the baby, and many of her friends and neighbors from Greenwood Park greeted her with surprise and excitement upon seeing the newborn. Since her miscarriage and Ugochi's departure two years earlier, she had dropped off the Greenwood Park social radar, only occasionally rubbing elbows with Lakshmi and Lihua. She didn't even know if the common room gatherings she had formerly attended were still taking place. She and Kabogo arrived together and immediately went their separate ways, which was par for the course. The only thing they shared that bore any resemblance to intimacy was currently off-limits. Dr. Sorensen had recommended six weeks of abstinence, but when she told Kabogo, she had tacked on an additional six weeks for good measure.

To her surprise, what she mostly felt toward him now was not anger but detachment. She had expected to explode with rage when he'd returned from the conference, but she felt no inclination to do so. She calmly went through her new routine as if he wasn't there, addressing him when she had to, as though he were a distant relative, and enjoying his discomfort when she whipped out her breast to feed Nyagūthiī. Perhaps venting her emotions to Karen had given her some perspective on the situation. She was stuck in an unhappy marriage and financially dependent on Kabogo—and now, there was a baby to take care of whose needs took precedence over hers. She needed to be strong for Nyagūthiī. After his first night home, during which the baby woke up every two hours, Kabogo decided to sleep on the sofa. That weekend, he bought a single bed, which he set up in the spare bedroom. She was surprised that she felt nothing but relief, with a hint of triumph.

Wanjikū had invited Karen to Ravi's gathering, and as soon as she arrived, she scooped up Nyagūthiĩ and became completely oblivious to everything else. In the wake of Wanjikū's burst of candor about Kabogo, Karen had opened up to her about how difficult it had been when she and Bill learned they could not have children. Given the cavalier way Karen had first broached it, Wanjikū had assumed it was no big deal, but that wasn't the case. Karen told her that as an only child, she had envied her numerous and boisterous cousins and dreamed of having a lively household with at least three children. After several months of trying unsuccessfully to conceive when they'd first moved to Hartford, they'd consulted the leading fertility specialist in the area, who told them after a series of tests that Bill couldn't produce live sperm. The specialist held out hope for something called in vitro fertilization that was currently under development, but when Karen had learned that the sperm would be provided by an anonymous donor, she rejected the idea. She only wanted the child of the man she loved, and so they had remained childless.

On that beautiful spring day of Ravi's graduation party, as Wanjikū watched Karen lovingly coo over her baby, she rejoiced that she could share the joys of this perfect creature with her best friend.

Chapter 16

May 1976

As Wanjikū followed Kabogo meekly up the Atkinsons' front path, she felt a vague sense of foreboding about what lay ahead. In the three years since Nyagūthiī was born, Wanjikū's life had settled into a routine that revolved around caring for her adorable but strong-willed toddler, often in the company of Karen. with whom she spent lots of time, usually out on errands, at the playground, or having long chats at Morning Buzz. She still sewed, and many of Nyagūthiī's clothes as well as hers were her handiwork. With interesting activities most of the time and people whose company she truly enjoyed, the loneliness of the early years had faded, and she had come to feel at home in Hartford.

She was irritated by Kabogo's insistence on not telling their friends about their intentions until today, six weeks before their planned departure. She hoped they would understand, but she certainly anticipated some awkward moments. She'd considered dropping some hints to Karen about what was coming, but she knew it would have been unreasonable to expect her to keep it from Bill. Kabogo seemed untroubled. He had made up his mind, and what anyone else thought mattered little to him. After six years in Hartford, everything seemed to be falling into place for their life after graduation. Thanks to Bill's tireless behind-the-scenes efforts on his behalf, as Kabogo wound up his master's program, he already had an adjunct faculty position lined up. If anyone had been more excited about this than Kabogo and Wanjikū, it was Bill and Karen. Karen and Wanjikū were inseparable, effortlessly completing each other's sentences and sometimes telegraphing thoughts to each other with nothing more than a smile or an exchange of glances.

Bill and Kabogo's relationship was more formal. Neither was much of a talker, and the fact that Kabogo was a student and Bill the head of the department continued to set the tone for their interactions. Bill disparaged the pecking order and tried to get Kabogo to loosen up off campus, but Kabogo would only go so far as to call him *Bill* and with the same deference he called him *Professor Atkinson* on campus. At the university in Nairobi, even that would have been considered nothing short of sacrilege. Invitations to go fishing or hiking with Bill were still a bridge too far for Kabogo, and he studiously came up with ingenious excuses to demur. Even so, Bill persisted, taking Kabogo's excuses in stride with a cheery, "Well, maybe some other time!"

When Kabogo embarked on the final year of his master's program, it was Bill who took the initiative to find out about his postgraduation plans. His offhand comment that he'd like to get some work experience before beginning his doctorate had been all it took for Bill to launch a whispering campaign to find him a position in the department. Kabogo had a reputation for being articulate and driven and for producing stellar work, so most of the faculty did not need much persuading, but a handful seemed put off by Kabogo's foreign-sounding name. Oddly enough, they hadn't expressed similar reservations when West German Gottfried Schattschneider had been hired the previous year.

Karen appeared at the door the moment Kabogo pressed the doorbell and excitedly ushered them in. "Where's Gogie?" she asked, crestfallen. *Gogie* was how Nyagūthiī's had first pronounced her own name as a toddler, and it had stuck.

"We left her with Adele, who begged me to let her come over and play with Lexie." Adele was a neighbor whose daughter was the same age as Nyagũthiĩ. The two toddlers had become fast friends.

"I was so looking forward to seeing her!"

"I'm sorry," replied Wanjikũ, reminded of one more thing in Karen's world that was about to come crashing down. "Auntie Kawen," as Nyagũthiĩ called her, was more like a second mother to her. Both she and Karen positively lit up when they saw each other, which was almost daily.

They stepped into the house, and Bill emerged from the kitchen where he had just finished preparing the steaks they would be having.

Kabogo dropped the bombshell after dinner. When Wanjikũ thought about it afterward, this had probably been better than blurting it out as soon as they'd arrived. At least they'd been able to enjoy one last dinner together.

Karen had told Wanjikũ that Bill had been chattier than usual in recent weeks. With Kabogo's job finally in the bag, he felt that they were on the cusp of the "happily ever after" he had always dreamed of, living near cherished friends and working at jobs they enjoyed. "Maybe when Kabogo graduates, you can move to our neighborhood, so we can walk to each other's houses, drop in for dinner, all that fun stuff. That'll give me a shot at becoming Gogie's favorite aunt. I'm so excited for what's ahead!" At times like that, Wanjikũ's subterfuge was almost more than she could bear.

Was it really a newsclip that had changed the course of their lives so drastically, or was returning to Kenya something Kabogo had been planning all along? While eating dinner a couple of months before, there had been a typically brief news segment on television about Kenya's progress since independence. An eloquent government minister had urged all Kenyans studying abroad to return home and help build the motherland. Wanjikũ didn't see it as anything more than the usual empty political rhetoric, so she was surprised when, a few weeks later, Kabogo announced his intention to return home. He didn't have a job in hand since it would have been next to impossible to know what was on offer or to apply in a timely fashion, but he had spoken by phone with his cousin Mūgo, who assured him that there were jobs aplenty. All he needed to do was show up. Mūgo agreed do some groundwork and scope out some possibilities before they arrived.

Wanjikū was unimpressed by Kabogo's sudden change of plans, and the seemingly poorly thought-out nature of it. Her life was just beginning to get comfortable, and here he was, upending her plans without any warning. For the past few years, their relationship had been sustained mostly by avoidance of difficult conversations. When there was little at stake and she had her own world to retreat to, with Karen and Nyagūthiĩ, it hadn't mattered too much, but this was different. She'd confronted him on the issue, and he'd tried to mollify her, saying that going back home was the original plan and indeed the right thing to do, adding that he thought it was important that Nyagūthiĩ get to know her grandparents, cousins, aunts, and uncles.

"But if it was the right thing to do, why did you lead us on and put Bill up to everything he's had to do? You should've told him the minute he asked. And wouldn't it make more sense for you to start this job and then start looking in Kenya with a plan to transition in a couple of years?"

But talking to Kabogo when he'd made up his mind was like arguing with a rock. He nodded, dithered, and prevaricated. Ultimately, she realized that if he didn't take the job, she had no basis to remain in America since she was a dependent on his visa. And she was looking forward to reunite with all the family and introduce Nyagūthiĩ to them since they hadn't had an opportunity to visit home from the day they'd arrived.

After Wanjikū came to terms with the prospect of going home, the next source of friction with Kabogo was when he would tell the Atkinsons. If he'd had his way, he would have telephoned them from

Bradley International Airport, and thus avoid having to deal with the emotional fallout. After three heated arguments in which he wouldn't commit to a date when he would tell them, she gave him an ultimatum. They had been invited to the Atkinsons' for dinner in a week's time.

"If you haven't told them by the time dinner is over, then I will make the announcement for you. You might not think much of Bill's friendship, but I'm not going to let you ruin my relationship with Karen. Bill has done so much to help you—I feel bad seeing the way you take him for granted."

Kabogo didn't reply when she told him what she'd do. From the way she spoke, slowly and deliberately, she made it clear she wasn't bluffing. His unwillingness or inability to reciprocate Bill's kind gestures had often bothered her. Now, she wondered whether his efforts to get Kabogo a job had produced the opposite of their intended effect. His desire to help, however well intentioned, could sometimes seem a bit suffocating, and Kabogo certainly had a contrary streak.

The after-dinner announcement couldn't have had a more immediate and devastating effect on her relationship with Karen, whose tears at the impending loss had quickly shifted to expressions of anger and betrayal. "I can't believe you didn't tell me sooner, Wanjikū! I thought there were no secrets between us."

"I'm sorry, Karen. I . . ."

"Oh, well, I guess it doesn't matter anymore," Karen said with a shrug, staring at the floor, a hard expression on her face. "Best of luck in your plans," she added dismissively. "It was nice of you to come and say goodbye."

"Karen, don't say that. Please!" Wanjikū implored.

Tears had started dropping from Karen's face onto the tiled kitchen floor, but she wouldn't look to face Wanjikū, and she didn't say a word.

"Karen?"

No response.

Wanjikū took in a deep breath and waited a few moments, but it became clear that Karen did not want to talk. It was time to leave. "Goodbye, Karen. I'm so sorry." She walked back to the dining room to where Kabogo and Bill sat like sullen statues, and Kabogo rose from his seat. "Goodbye, Bill," she mumbled as she hurried to the door to catch up with Kabogo.

As they drove home, she was furious. This was all Kabogo's fault. If he'd had thoughts about returning to Kenya, he should have voiced them before Bill went out and squandered his social capital for his benefit. Or if the newsclip had indeed changed his mind—which still seemed implausible to her—he should have let Bill know at the earliest opportunity, before, rather than after, he had secured a faculty position for him. The fact that he had nothing yet lined up in Kenya seemed equally absurd. Taking the faculty job and planning a visit to Kenya to evaluate eventual job prospects there would have been much more prudent. Instead, by one impulsive act, he'd burned all his bridges, and hers as well. That he had made a decision without any consideration for how she might feel did not surprise her, but he had also destroyed the image he had so carefully cultivated within the department—and with Bill, who had even spun his inconsiderate decision to attend a conference when his wife was ready to give birth as an admirable, if misguided, dedication to work.

"Why was that *Mzungu*[1] [White person] being so dramatic?" Kabogo growled unrepentantly as they drove home. "Kwani, I need his permission to go back to my country?"

"Kabogo, are you serious? You're the cause of all this mess, and that's all you can come up with? And why are you calling him *that Mzungu*? His name is Bill, and he's supposed to be your friend. He has shown you nothing but kindness from the day you met him, but like the proverbial

---

1. Swahili equivalent of "Mūthūngū"

SUNSHINE ON THE CROOKED ROAD

donkey, all you've given him is a kick in return![2] And you might have cost me a very close friendship. Karen doesn't even want to talk to me now. And for what? For what, mister? You don't even have a job lined up in Kenya! Agh!"

Wanjikũ clenched her teeth in rage and said no more. She looked out the window at shadows of trees and buildings bathed in the pale-yellow glow of streetlights and the crescent moon. Kabogo remained silent.

Wanjikũ desperately wanted to talk to Karen, but every time she thought of picking up the phone, she remembered her friend's rebuff, and her resolve vanished. Not being able to talk to Karen was undoubtedly the most difficult thing she endured in the two weeks that followed. She could count on a single hand the number of times in the past three years that she had gone more than a couple of days without speaking to her friend, either in person or by phone. She spent the days in a languid stupor, absentmindedly packing up boxes in preparation for the move whenever she could distract Nyagũthiĩ long enough or put her down for a nap.

"Gogie help Mommie," her three-year-old would say, pulling out items from the boxes nearly as quickly as Wanjikũ could put them in. "Where Auntie Kawen?" she asked repeatedly, innocently rubbing salt into Wanjikũ's wound.

Kabogo had found a shipping company that would pick up their household possessions at the beginning of June and deliver them to a warehouse in Nairobi in late August. The finality of the move sank in when he informed her of the pickup date. While the prospect of moving back to Kenya and seeing friends and family had unquestionable appeal, there were so many things about Hartford she would miss—the vibrant springtime and late summer sunsets, the endless selection of books and magazines in the library, becoming proficient in sewing, going to

---

2. Swahili proverb: *Asante ya punda ni mateke* [The only way a donkey knows to express gratitude is with a kick].

the playground with Nyagūthiī, the amazing items she purchased for ridiculously low prices at the thrift store . . . and most of all, Karen.

She had hoped that Karen would telephone in the days that followed the disastrous evening, but one, two, three days went by, then a week, and then two. With each passing day, her anxiety mounted until she finally couldn't take it anymore. Four weeks before the departure date, as she waited for Nyagūthiī to settle down for her afternoon nap, she picked up the phone, then dithered for at least fifteen minutes before dialing Karen's number.

Karen picked up on the first ring. "Hello?"

"Hello, Karen. It's Wanjikū. I just wanted to say how sorry—"

"No, Wanjikū, I'm the one who should be apologizing," interrupted Karen. "Bill and I should have taken more time to listen, rather than assuming that our wanting you to stay was the only thing that mattered. I sit by the phone every day, trying to work up the nerve to call you, then chicken out at the last minute. I thought you wouldn't want to talk to me after how we reacted."

"And I was afraid to call because I thought you'd angry with *me*, as you have every reason to be. I wanted to tell you about Kabogo's plan since the moment he came up with it out of the blue, but he wanted to be the one to make the announcement. Since Bill is his boss, I went along. However, after he dragged his feet, I finally threatened that if he didn't say anything when we came to your place for dinner, I would make the announcement myself."

"Oh, that's an awkward situation to be in. I can only imagine. Are you home now? I'm not working today."

"Yes, I'm packing up boxes for the move."

"Can I come over and help?"

"Oh, I'd love that!"

★★★

SUNSHINE ON THE CROOKED ROAD 115

Karen and Wanjikū's final month together was even more precious to them now that they had so little time left. Packing proved to be much easier with Karen around, as she was very practical and efficient, and the conversations they had while working made time pass quickly. And Karen was more than happy to distract Gogie when she got in the way. It was hard for Karen to come to terms with the realization that she was not going to be able watch her grow up as she'd assumed. Updates by mail and the occasional photograph would be a poor substitute, but she did not waste the opportunity to shower her with love while she could.

After the moving company stripped the apartment bare, Karen brought blankets, sleeping bags, basic kitchenware, and other sundries to tide them through their last few days in Hartford. She even suggested they stay at her house, but Wanjikū didn't want to impose and knew Kabogo wouldn't go along with it, anyway. Bill had patched things up with Kabogo, mostly by apologizing for his own behavior, which, in typical fashion, Kabogo took as an exoneration for his own accountability in the debacle.

★★★

The two families sat waiting for boarding to begin on the Pan Am flight to Kenya. Bill talked in low tones to Kabogo about ways his newly acquired training could be used for the public good in Kenya. Kabogo, responding to Bill's encouragement, was chatty and courteous, and even grinned when Bill generously quipped, "Hey, if you ever change your mind and want to come back, just let me know. You'll be an asset wherever you go."

Karen played with Gogie, trying to hide the note of sadness in her voice as she taught her a new song while Wanjikū looked on. They were clapping together, Karen's antics eliciting delighted squeals from Gogie, when the flight attendant announced that boarding would begin soon.

Wanjikū felt her heart flutter. Karen picked up Gogie. Her face fell. The two friends had been anticipating their goodbyes with growing dread as the weeks fizzled to days and then to hours. "I guess this is it," Karen said, her voice cracking with emotion. Bill and Kabogo were already making their way toward the line forming at the boarding gate, still caught up in their discussion. "Make sure you write as soon as you settle in," Karen added.

"I will," Wanjikū said, the tears starting to trickle down her face. Karen handed Gogie to Wanjikū, who balanced her on her right hip as she gripped the collapsed stroller in her left hand, a handbag slung over her shoulder.

"Bye, Gogie!"

"Bye, Auntie Kawen!" said Gogie cheerily, bringing her pudgy hand to her mouth before throwing it out toward Karen.

"I love you!"

"I love you!"

Karen stepped away from the boarding line and joined Bill, who had already bid Kabogo farewell with a firm handshake. Her eyes met Wanjikū's, and she put her hand over her heart, both their faces damp.

"I'll miss you, Karen. Goodbye, Bill," said Wanjikū in a faltering voice. Then, sucking in a deep breath, she turned and shuffled to catch up with Kabogo, who was already handing over their boarding passes.

Nairobi

Chapter 17

1976–1977

Nairobi had grown a lot in the six years they'd been away. It had a fizzy, mildly chaotic air that contrasted with the mellow, unhurried atmosphere of Hartford. People scurried everywhere in an unrehearsed choreography that reminded Wanjikū of safari ants stampeding to and fro across a village path. The cacophonous *pii-pii* of automobile horns—especially matatus—would take some getting used to. Wanjikū could hardly recall hearing a car horn in the entire six years they'd lived in Hartford, and they certainly hadn't sounded like these.

They moved into a three-bedroom flat in Kariokor, a working-class neighborhood just northeast of downtown, and Kabogo immediately set out to look for a job. With a master's degree in biochemical engineering, he received an offer in no time from the Ministry of Agriculture, in the newly created Department of Agrochemical Research, which was run in conjunction with the University of Nairobi. As the assistant director, he would be responsible for creating the technical protocols and working with the university interns, some of whom, it was hoped, would join the staff after the completion of their studies.

He bought a gently used maroon Datsun 120Y, and on their first trip to his parents' home in Kīunangū, pranced around the car, twirling the keys in his hand. The *oohs* and *aahs* from his family members, including the usually taciturn Mūthee Mūchoki, were clearly music to his ears. He regaled them with stories about America that were a lot more colorful and upbeat than his demeanor had been at the time. In these tales, he was beloved by all and had made the difficult decision to return home for the sake of his family, despite his Athūngū colleagues clamoring for him to remain, immensely valuable as he was. Wanjikū had to acknowledge that the story was at least partly true. He had earned respect and accolades in his department, though unlike with Nnamdi and Ugochi, or with Ravi, no one had arranged a farewell gathering in his honor. Given their social isolation within Greenwood Park, she didn't see this as a snub in any way, but it didn't exactly support Kabogo's narrative.

Wanjikū hadn't had time to establish a relationship with her mother-in-law before they'd left for America, and her attempts to do so during that first visit since their return were not promising. That Wanjikū was from Nyeri and had attended university, if only partially, put her on the back foot to begin with. Nyagūthiĩ's screaming refusal to let herself be held by the grandmother for whom she was named and her insistent demands of "Where Auntie Kawen?" didn't help. Fortunately, only Wanjikū and Kabogo could understand Gogie's heavily Mūthūngū-accented English.

Three sons had already been born to Kabogo's siblings and half-siblings, all of them named after Mūthee Mūchoki, as was customary. The unspoken question on everyone's mind was when Kabogo and Wanjikū would bring home a little Mūchoki of their own. Not even the shiny Datsun 120Y could blunt the force of that expectation.

The weekend after their visit to Kĩunangū, they traveled to Gĩthakainĩ to visit Wanjikū's family. She was excited to see her parents again as well as her older brothers, who had come for the occasion with their families, and she only half listened as Kabogo played the triumphant son-in-law, extemporizing about their time in America. She quietly savored the green hilly landscape, the crisp mountain air, and the mooing of the Friesian cows in the fenced paddock a short distance from the veranda where they had gathered. Nyagūthiī had only seen cows in pictures, so when Wanjikū took her to the barbed wire fence to observe the unhurried munching and heavy breathing of the serene beasts, she squirmed with a mixture of terror and fascination.

So far, Kabogo had been easy enough to put up with. He tended to do well in scripted public settings, and it helped that she had more people in Kenya to talk to, along with the distractions of a city she was familiar with. She took driving lessons, knowing that in a year or so, she would need to enroll Nyagūthiī in preschool, which would likely not be in the immediate environs of Kariokor. Surprisingly, Kabogo seemed eager for her to get her driver's license as soon as possible, probably so he wouldn't have to keep taking her to the supermarket for groceries.

Shortly after their arrival, she purchased a batch of aerograms and wrote to Karen and Bill as promised, to let them know of their doings. In August, their boxes and furnishings arrived from Connecticut and were soon stowed around their flat. Overall, the move had gone smoothly, and Wanjikū began to feel that returning to Kenya might not have been such a bad idea after all.

***

Wanjikū enjoyed reacquainting herself with downtown Nairobi. It was close enough to walk from Kariokor, but with Nyagūthiī in tow, it was much easier to fold up the stroller and get on the bus. Once downtown, she would wander around for hours looking through the windows of the trendy clothing shops on Government Road or haggling over fabric prices with the *dukawallas* [ethnic Indian shopkeepers] on Bazaar Street. There was an astonishing variety of fabrics, and the prices were reasonable. Besides Bazaar Street, she knew of shops in Ngara, closer to where they lived, which often had an even greater variety and better prices. Her sewing machine had arrived undamaged, and she planned to resume her hobby soon.

Nyagŭthĩ usually fell asleep the moment the stroller started trundling along the sidewalk, and Wanjikŭ sometimes found herself walking longer than she'd intended just so she wouldn't have to wake the toddler to get back on the bus. She was familiar with the streets from her university days, though many new shops had opened in the time she had been away. One of her favorite stops was an ice cream shop on Koinange Street, right across from the university. She and Kabogo had been regulars there before they'd left for America. Revisiting it six years later with Nyagŭthĩ was oddly nostalgic. She half expected to meet her old self there, brimming with carefree optimism.

She got her driver's license without any trouble and started driving the car to the grocery store on weekends, especially Sundays, when the roads were not busy. Kabogo drove the car to work on weekdays. When she'd asked him to accompany her to the supermarket on her first trip as a licensed driver, he replied dismissively, "*Si* you passed the test? They wouldn't have given you a license if they felt you were incapable of driving. *Wĩringie nĩ rwa nyarĩrĩ!* [It's shallow enough here—you can cross on your own!]" Her initial irritation with him for being unsupportive gave way to the realization that driving with him in the passenger seat—yelling instructions and second-guessing her—would have been far worse than going alone.

A slow and nervous driver at first, she lived in constant fear of seeing a matatu or double-decker bus appearing in her rearview mirror, bullying her to move faster by getting too close. Since the Datsun had a manual transmission, she also dreaded stopping on hills at traffic lights and feeling the car begin to roll backward as she tried to engage the gears when the light turned green. After a few weekend trips, she became more confident and no longer had to psych herself up before getting in the car. This was just as well, since it was only a matter of months before she would be driving Nyagũthiĩ to preschool every day.

The post office was close to where Kabogo worked, so he usually picked up the mail on his way home. About three weeks after they'd arrived back in Kenya, he presented her with a letter from Karen. She opened it carefully, her hands trembling with excitement, and began to read:

Dearest Wanjikũ and Gogie (and Kabogo),

Bill and I were thrilled to receive your letter the other day! We're glad to hear you're settling in back home. Hartford is not the same without you! I miss the fun times we spent together, talking about anything and everything. I felt I could share my deepest hopes and fears with you without being afraid you'd misunderstand me. I always knew we had a special friendship, but I've come to appreciate it so much more since you left.

I hope Kabogo's job search went well, and that he found what he was looking for. Bill often comments what an excellent addition he would have been to the faculty and misses him a lot. I can see it in his eyes whenever his name comes up. I think he saw in Kabogo the younger brother he always wished he'd had. (Maybe that's part of how we ended up getting carried away with all those plans about living next to each other and doing everything together, etc.)

SUNSHINE ON THE CROOKED ROAD

How is Nairobi? I try to imagine what it's like and what a normal day looks like for you. Nowadays, anytime Africa is mentioned on TV or in a magazine I find myself paying close attention, almost as though I'm expecting to hear or read something about you. I hope one day we'll get a chance to come and visit. That would be amazing!

I miss Gogie, my sweet little princess! I can't think of her without my eyes misting up. Please give her a big hug and kiss for me. Tell her Auntie Karen misses her very much.

Please stay in touch. We look forward to hearing from you soon.

Love and kisses,

Karen (and Bill)

Wanjikū smiled as she folded the letter. "Bill and Karen say hello," she called out to Kabogo, who was in the living room "They said they'd like to visit someday." He grunted in reply. Nyagūthiī sat on the floor, playing with blocks. "Nyagūthiī, do you remember Auntie Karen?" she asked.

Her daughter looked up expectantly, but the name seemed not to ring a bell. She held up one of the colored blocks she was playing with. "Mommy, gween!"

"Yes, Nyagūthiĩ, that is green," she replied, suppressing a twinge of disappointment.

★★★

Kabogo hadn't intended to remain in touch with the Atkinsons after they left America. In the final months before returning to Kenya, he had grown weary of hearing Wanjikū going on and on about Bill-this and Karen-that to the point he began to feel smothered. When he overheard Karen and Wanjikū daydreaming about living in the same neighborhood, a sense of disquiet overtook him. Bill was a nice guy, but much too nice—like that perfectly good cup of tea ruined by an extra spoonful of sugar. Also, Kabogo couldn't stand the way he and Karen were always touching, holding hands and kissing in public—something so at odds with his own undemonstrative upbringing that he often found himself averting his eyes in anticipation. He couldn't imagine living close to them and witnessing more of this, or having Wanjikū start to expect the same from him. For all he knew, she might expect him to help out in the kitchen as well.

When he saw the newsclip about opportunities in Kenya, he spied a ready escape from a future he was starting to dread. He'd assumed the relationship would be significantly diminished by the distance, but now, the Atkinsons were talking about coming to Kenya to visit. Having seen how they followed through with decisions, he knew this wasn't idle banter, and it worried him. The years in Connecticut had served their purpose, but they were back in Nairobi now, and he was ready to move on and leave that all behind.

Chapter 18

During World War I, the British conscripted hundreds of thousands of Africans to carry heavy loads to the front lines of their battles with the Germans in East Africa and to provide other menial labor. These laborers—known as the Carrier Corps—worked in hellish conditions for little pay. When they died, as so many of them did, they were buried in unmarked mass graves, unlike the Athūngū soldiers they served, whose graves still dot the landscape of countries that were never theirs. While the individual names of the porters, cooks, and other laborers went unacknowledged by the colonial government, they live on in their descendants. In an ironic reversal, it is the Athūngū soldiers left behind by a receding empire and with no kin to honor them who have faded from public remembrance. When the name *Carrier Corps* rolled off the African tongue, it was transformed to *Kariokor*, still the name of the neighborhood where the Carrier Corps was based. The legacy of the Carrier Corps is passed on to another generation every time a child in Nairobi wonders from which of the forty-two native Kenyan languages the strange-sounding word comes.

Kariokor was a working-class neighborhood of boxy, unpretentious, four-story buildings covered in flaking paint, with a kaleidoscope of colorful laundry flapping on the clotheslines stretched between them.

In the daytime, the unrelenting rumble of slow-moving traffic mixed with the loud cries of matatu *manambas*[1] calling for passengers and the carefree hollering of neighborhood children playing soccer or *blada*.[2] It wasn't until ten at night that the noise usually began to die down, and nothing resembling quiet could be expected until well after midnight. By five in the morning, the streets were astir once again with townspeople hurriedly going about the business of the new day.

Wanjikū had a nodding acquaintance with most of the fellow occupants of their building. A few of them had children Nyagūthiï's age, and she took more of an interest in these, always on the lookout for potential playmates for her daughter. However, she never let Nyagūthiï go alone to the yard to join the children who played there, because the open and unmonitored gate to the busy Ring Road made it accessible to anyone.

A few weeks after moving to the neighborhood, she had discovered a *duka* [shop] a five-minute walk away. Before that, she had driven to Uchumi, the big supermarket in town. Bhatia, the shop owner, was a short, stout man with a squint in his right eye and thinning gray hair. His impassive expression was often mistaken for hostility, but on further acquaintance, it became obvious that he was a kind and attentive man. He spoke often in an ungrammatical Nairobian dialect of Kiswahili that was the bane of language purists. The first time Wanjikū went to his shop, she had run out of bread and didn't want to drive to the supermarket. Once she established that he was out of her preferred brand, she made her way toward the door.

"*Mama, we 'pana taka jaribu hiyo ingine? Mkate ni mkate, sindiyo?*" ["Ma'am, don't you want to try this other brand? Bread is bread, right?"]

---

1. Matatu driver's assistant, responsible for loading passengers and collecting fare. This term superseded *taniboi*, mentioned earlier.

2. A girls' game where the players jump into and out of a narrow space between two stretched out lengths of inner tube that are raised higher and brought closer together with each attempt. Whoever completes the highest jump without getting snagged wins.

SUNSHINE ON THE CROOKED ROAD

"*Ai, hii mkate ni tofauti. Sijawai ona aina hii . . .* [*Ai*, this bread is different. I've never seen this brand before . . .]" she replied lamely.

"*Haya, fanya namna hii: We chukua hiyo—kama hapana penda, rudi kesho halafu chukua ile ingine free of charge.*" ["OK, let's do this: You take this one—if you don't like it, come back and take a loaf of your usual brand free of charge."]

Wanjikũ reluctantly agreed and found that the bread was just as good. When she stopped in the next day to let him know, he flashed a rare smile. After that, she found herself going to Bhatia's for most of her routine groceries, with occasional trips to Uchumi for the things his duka didn't carry.

A first-time visitor to Bhatia's shop could not fail to notice the giant of a man who sat wordlessly in a plastic chair under an acacia tree next to the shop. He had a dour expression, staring at the ground without so much as a flicker of movement. This was Otondi. Passersby gave him a wide berth, intimidated by his towering size.

Otondi was a *bubu* [mute] and had some strange mannerisms. He never looked anyone in the eye, and he always picked up his plastic chair and shook it upside down before sitting in it, even though there was nothing on it. If his routine was disrupted, he got very agitated. At night, he slept in the veranda of Bhatia's shop, a shapeless mass obstructing the doorway, and was particular about lying down for bed in the exact same spot at precisely nine o'clock. Since the door normally opened outward, once Otondi lay down to sleep, there was no way in or out of the duka until the next morning. While Bhatia was not one to turn away a customer easily, he had no time for browsers and hagglers in the fifteen minutes before closing, needing to have everyone gone, including himself, before Otondi claimed his space for the night.

When Bhatia arrived at six each morning to open the shop, he brought a lunch box packed by Mrs. Bhatia with delicacies such as chicken curry, chapati, yogurt, mango slices, and samosas for Otondi. "*Otondi, we lala mzuri* [Did you sleep well, Otondi]*?*" he would ask, at which Otondi would tilt his head slightly before reaching for the lunch box.

Wanjikũ was curious about Otondi and picked up his story in bits and pieces from Bhatia and other shoppers. Many years prior, Otondi and his mother had started coming to the shop at the end of the day to see if he had perishable food that he'd be throwing out. At that time, Otondi was about twelve, shyly following his mother—who was very protective of her son—like a shadow. From what Bhatia could tell, they lived on the street, probably among the families that camped near the Globe Cinema Roundabout. However, unlike those others, they wore presentable clothes and had respectable manners. Otondi did not seem at all like the raggedy *chokoras* [street children] who often came by, smelling of the glue they sniffed from bottles or *mkebes* [tin cans].

Bhatia's youngest son was slightly older than Otondi, so he would bring in clothes from time to time that his son had outgrown and give them to Otondi. One morning, he was surprised to come to the shop and find Otondi, barely eighteen then, curled up on the veranda in front of the doorway. He was alone. "*Otondi, wapi mama* [Otondi, where's your mother]?" he asked. Otondi had looked at him blankly. Bhatia went into the duka, brought out a white plastic chair, put it under the acacia tree, then gave the boy two scones and a soda. All that day, he frequently came to the shop door to check on Otondi, hoping to see his mother as well, but there was no sign of her. The young man just sat there, motionless, staring at the ground. When Gĩkonyo—a *mkokoteni* [pushcart] driver who sometimes ran errands for him—stopped by, Bhatia asked if he had heard anything about Otondi's mother. He had not and was as troubled by this development as Bhatia.

"Let me walk over to Grogon and ask my friends there if they've heard anything," said Gĩkonyo. As a mkokoteni man, he knew people everywhere, and the people on Kĩrĩnyaga Road—which most people still referred to as Grogon, a bastardization of *Grogan*, its colonial-era name—were usually good sources of information. It was a winding,

SUNSHINE ON THE CROOKED ROAD

potholed road with dense traffic, and was lined with auto-parts stores frequented by grease-stained mechanics hunting for parts that were either not available or exorbitantly priced at dealerships. One had to be careful, though, because it wasn't unheard of for someone to go into a shop to purchase a missing side mirror for their car only to find the other side mirror missing on their return.

Bhatia, who overpaid Gĩkonyo for some of his wares, indicated his concern for the welfare of Otondi's mother and his appreciation for Gĩkonyo's attention to the matter. Gĩkonyo came back about four hours later, looking grave. He lingered outside the shop while Bhatia took care of two customers, then hurried in, looking over his shoulder to make sure nobody had followed him. In hushed tones, he recounted what he had learned.

The previous night, a couple from the camp where Otondi and his mother lived had gotten into a fight. It started with shouting, then escalated to blows. Finally, in a fit of rage, the man grabbed a metal pipe and started hitting the woman with it. Otondi's mother rushed over and grabbed the man's arm to prevent him from hitting the woman again. Blind with rage, he turned on her and brought the pipe down twice on her head. As she crumpled to the ground and lay motionless, he dropped the pipe and bolted as neighbors rushed to the aid of the fallen woman. They carried her to the nearest taxi stand on Grogon and persuaded a driver they knew to ferry her and two of the men from the camp to Kenyatta National Hospital. By the time they got there, however, it was clear to them that it was too late, a fact confirmed by the doctor on duty who directed the body be taken to the morgue. By the time the men returned, looking dazed and forlorn, Otondi had disappeared. Nobody remembered seeing him after the initial commotion, but the body of the man who had killed his mother was found the next morning on the bank of the Nairobi River, about half a kilometer away, his head so bashed in that he could be identified only by his clothes. The next morning is also when Bhatia found Otondi sleeping on the veranda of his shop.

Since then, Otondi had made the shop his home. He sometimes visited his people at the Globe Cinema Roundabout during the day but always returned to Bhatia's in the evening. Some patrons assumed he was the security guard, though it would be odd to have a guard whose nine o'clock bedtime forced Bhatia to hurry shoppers out before closing time and who was greeted with kind words and steaming dishes of food every morning. But in a very real sense, he was the duka's security guard.

According to Baba Opiyo, one of the neighborhood drunks, thieves tried to break in one night, unaware that Otondi was asleep on the dimly lit veranda. One of them accidentally stepped on his hand, and the ground came alive with a wild roar. A hulking figure seemed to sprout from the cement, at which point any sensible person would have beat a hasty retreat, but the three startled crooks unaccountably chose to stand their ground. One of them swung a tire iron at Otondi, who bellowed like a charging bear as he lunged at the man and lifted him over his head before hurling him onto the tarmac several yards away. The man screamed, writhing in agony as his terrified comrades carried him to safety. At the hospital, where he was found to have several fractured bones, they reported the incident as a hit-and-run. Loosely speaking, this was true.

Otondi had gone straight back to sleep. When Bhatia arrived in the morning, he didn't know what to make of the tire iron lying in the grass until he heard from Baba Opiyo about the incident. There was never another burglary attempt on Bhatia's duka.

Chapter 19

Kabogo's first few days at his new job were exciting. The department staff, who numbered somewhere between fifteen and twenty people, welcomed him with enthusiasm, evidently impressed by his credentials, and his office was right next to that of the director. His secretary, a diminutive woman in her midfifties with a Miriam Makeba hairstyle, was named Riziki. When she first addressed him as *sir*, he half turned to see if there was someone important standing behind him. When he realized she was speaking to him, it was as if an inch had been tacked onto the soles of his platform shoes.

Riziki was quick to perform the tasks he assigned her, and he could hear her clacking away furiously on her typewriter through the door that separated their offices. She was also punctual and made sure that Amina—the tea lady—delivered tea and *mandazi* [fried dough snacks] to his office promptly at ten a.m. and three p.m. Sometimes, though, if his office door was partly ajar, he could hear her talking softly on the phone in a way that was clearly not work-related. This irritated him at first, but her sunny yet respectful disposition and attention to detail quickly won him over. That she made sure her boss's tea and mandazi always arrived on time also spoke in her favor.

The Department of Agrochemical Research was new, and although his office was right next to the director's, the director himself had yet to be hired. He'd met Monica, the future director's secretary, when he happened to walk over there, exploring his new surroundings. He felt some envy that the director's office was about twice the size of his own and much more elaborately furnished. Monica had been working intently on a stack of documents, though he couldn't imagine for whom, when he'd stopped by. In the absence of a director, Kabogo was for all intents and purposes in charge.

During his hiring interview, he had met a couple of senior ministry officials whom he assumed would stop by once he'd started work in case he had questions or concerns regarding the twelve-page document he'd received that outlined his mandate and responsibilities. They did not. In fact, the two people who helped him most to understand how things worked—or didn't—were Riziki and a man named Wairagū, who had been transferred from the main offices of the Ministry of Agriculture on the sixth floor to take charge of accounts for the fledgling department. Wairagū was in his late fifties and spoke in a slow, croaky monotone. The odor of Sportsman cigarettes permeated the air around him and lingered long after he left the room, so that Kabogo could always tell where he'd been. When he stopped by Riziki's desk to chat, Wairagū's Sportsman funk clashed with her vivid citrusy scents to create an olfactory Armageddon. At least Wairagū seemed to have a thorough understanding of how the ministry worked and its vision for the new department.

Kabogo had been eager to visit the much-vaunted agrochemical research lab he'd been told about in his interview, but it quickly became apparent that there was no such lab on the premises. After his morning tea break on his third day, he walked over to Wairagū's office to see if he could get more information.

"Yes, of course. They've been talking about the lab, and I think the plan is to put it on the university campus in Kabete, but it hasn't been

SUNSHINE ON THE CROOKED ROAD

built yet. In all probability, part of the reason they were excited to hire you was so they could get your technical input right from the outset. You see what I mean?"

Kabogo had already noted that his compulsive use of that last phrase, along with equally useless phrases such as, *I think that's the case* (or not the case), *in all probability*, and *These things take time*.

"It hasn't been built? I understood that the infrastructure was in place, and they were just waiting to staff it."

"No, no, that's not the case—not at all. I'm not even sure they've identified where on the campus it will be located. These things take time, you know."

Kabogo couldn't help wondering if there had been some miscommunication during the interview. "So how long has this department been up and running?"

"Er . . . Let me see . . . About eleven months. Yes . . . yes, I think that's the case."

"And there hasn't been a director or an assistant director in all that time? Who decides . . . ? I mean, what does . . . ?"

"You're wondering what we do all day?"

"Yes . . . Can you give me an overview of daily operations?"

"That's a fair question, but starting a new department takes time; it really does. It may look like we don't have much to show for it yet, but it's like when you put a *mboco* [bean] seed into the ground. You have to be patient for it to sprout. Someone who comes after you will see nothing but soil, and they might think you haven't done anything. But if they come back a week later, it will be a different story. That how it works in situations like this."

Kabogo winced. "OK, I appreciate the information."

"My pleasure. Let me know if you have any other questions."

He returned to his desk and looked at the stack of folders in his "out" tray with documents he had worked up, outlining and refining protocols for the research lab he had just discovered didn't exist. If this department had been up and running for the past eleven months—without a director or assistant director—what was the busy staff doing? What had Riziki been working on before he arrived? What was Monica, the director's secretary, working on in the absence of a boss? He sidled up to Riziki's desk, hoping for some answers. She was murmuring in low tones to someone on the phone but quickly said goodbye and hung up.

"Yes, sir," she said cheerily. "What can I do for you?"

"Riziki, I was wondering . . . For the past year or so since the department opened, who has been in charge of things? Who tells people what to do? For example, where does Monica get her assignments, if there's no director? And before I came, whose paperwork did you handle?"

She hesitated, a look of mischief flitting across her face, then mostly succeeded in adopting a serious expression. "There's still plenty of work from our old jobs to do."

"Oh, I see. Did they not hire people for your former positions?"

"Not all of them, exactly," she replied evasively. Just then, the phone rang, and she snatched it up. "Department of Agrochemical Research, assistant director's office, may I help you?" As she listened intently to the person at the other end of the line, Kabogo glanced at his watch and decided to head across the street for lunch. As he moved away, Riziki looked up, and he indicated that he was going out for lunch. She nodded, and her expression relaxed as though she were relieved that their conversation had come to an end. Kabogo's simmering frustration with his workplace became harder to conceal as the months went by. One after another, his ideas dead-ended in bureaucratic cul-de-sacs. Even his most straightforward queries about workflow and accountability were met with shifty silence or long-winded explanations that made little sense. Riziki seemed to have perfected the art of making the phone ring the moment he approached her desk.

It didn't take him long to realize that the research lab would never be built, and his initial feelings of anger and betrayal about this gradually gave way to resignation. He tried to set up a meeting with Messrs. Koech and Mūkundi—the ministry officials who'd interviewed him and sold him on their glorious vision for the department—but their secretaries claimed that their calendars were full, and he should check back later. The energy and enthusiasm with which he'd started the job began to falter, and he watched in puzzlement as people continued to scurry industriously around the office day after day. He had no idea what they were doing, much less to whom they reported.

The two meetings he'd convened as acting head of the department had been well attended. The staff had nodded agreeably at his proposals and even laughed politely at his jokes. When he asked them for input, they gave impressively nebulous-sounding suggestions, such as, "creating an atmosphere that fosters scientific creativity" or "maximizing agricultural productivity by closing current gaps in efficiency." Listening to them, he suspected that they had mastered the art of regurgitating platitudes they'd heard their superiors spout to create an illusion of progress toward a nonexistent goal. It was the same high-sounding bombast he had naively swallowed during his interview with Koech and Mūkundi, who had also played to his vanity, repeatedly referring to him as *highly skilled* and *exceptionally well suited to this position.*

His regular paycheck provided much appreciated proof that he was officially on the payroll. However, it depressed him to realize that his salary would come even if he sat at this desk all morning reading the newspaper. His increasing despondency did not escape Riziki, who lingered one day in his office after delivering a document he'd asked her to type. Clearing her throat, she began, "Mr. Kabogo, I hope you can see that most of us in this department are hard workers."

"Sorry, what?" he asked, emerging from the stupor of his ten o'clock tea break.

"We're hard workers," she repeated, her usually cheery expression now somber. "When they decided to start this department, we were taken from our former jobs and told to come here. They didn't give us a choice. This department was a pet project of one of the senior ministry officials, but he was reassigned to the Ministry of Foreign Affairs shortly after it was set up. The person who succeeded him didn't consider it a priority, but because the budget had already been approved, he couldn't close it down. So we've been left on our own like orphans. None of us enjoys being idle, so we've been getting work from our former bosses or whoever needs help at our old jobs to stay busy."

"So the higher-ups stuck you in a department with no work to do?"

She shrugged apologetically.

"Why are you telling me this?"

"Because, sir, you came in with a lot of energy and good ideas, and I can see that you've started to become frustrated that nothing seems to get done. I wanted to let you know that even for a government office, this is not the way things normally work. Eventually, the ministry will wind down this department and have to find new jobs for us, since they already hired replacements for our old jobs. All of us want to have work to show for the time we've been here, so our old bosses can vouch that we've been productive. Your case is different, since you were hired from outside. You might have to go to a different ministry."

"Well," said Kabogo thoughtfully. "Thank you for letting me know."

"Yes, sir." She turned to go, then stopped and turned around. "By the way, I heard a rumor today that they've hired a director."

"Even though the department will likely be shut down?"

"Probably because of it," she answered, lowering her voice and glancing furtively at the open door. "From what I hear, he has a bachelor's degree in literature, which might not sound like a suitable qualification for the head of the Department of Agrochemical Research. But he is the nephew of the new ministry official who has no interest this department."

"That doesn't make any sense! Why would he hire a relative to join a department that's going to be liquidated in a few months?"

Riziki's looked surprised by his simplicity. "It will give him an entry into a government job. Even if the department closes down, it will be the ministry's responsibility to find him a job at a similar level. Nobody gets fired or laid off from government jobs—we just get reassigned."

Kabogo snorted and shook his head.

"Yes, sir. Some people are very cunning. But please remember that many of us are honest people trying to do a good job."

"I know you're a good worker, Riziki. And thank you for being so honest with me."

★★★

Kabogo applied for a job as a research director with Koenig Pharma, one of the top two pharmaceutical companies in the country, and within three days was invited for an interview the following Wednesday. When he told Riziki he would be stepping out for a couple of hours—the first time he had ever left the office in the middle of the day—she nodded knowingly. Since their recent conversation, they'd become something akin to coconspirators, and she sensed that he was unlikely to remain with the ministry much longer.

He toured Koenig's sprawling complex in Ruaraka, about half an hour from downtown Nairobi—including two well-furnished research labs that would be under his purview if he got the job—and interviewed with five or six executives of the company. At the end of the visit, he was elated. This was precisely what he'd had in mind when he'd decided to leave Connecticut and return to Kenya. Everyone he met seemed knowledgeable and passionate about what they were doing, and they seemed as enthusiastic about him as he was about them.

The salary they offered was about three times what he was earning at the ministry, and the benefits package was generous. When they offered him the job, he accepted without hesitation, submitted his letter of resignation to the ministry, and informed Riziki that he would be leaving at the end of the month. Only when he told Wanjikū about the new job did he fill her in on the turmoil of dissatisfaction he had felt at his government job over the past several months. Seven years before, she would have been miffed that he hadn't sought her input or even kept her informed, but her expectations in that regard had long since been starved to death, deprived of the crucial nourishment of thoughtful actions and kind words. What remained most resembled a business partnership, with each party striving to meet predefined obligations through a series of joyless transactions; in that regard, the income was obviously a big plus. They would be able to get the second car sooner, and would probably be in a position to take out a mortgage rather than continuing to make rent payments.

In the midst of this was the happy, inquisitive Nyagūthiī. While she was a source of joy to her mother, she seemed a source of discomfort to her father. When she tugged at his leg or plopped down next to him on the sofa, he responding stiffly, if at all, like a stranger who'd been forced to engage with a four-year-old through no fault of his own. From the time he'd returned to their apartment in Hartford after his conference, he'd kept his distance and almost seemed relieved by Karen's enthusiasm for the baby, which took some pressure off him. Wanjikū could not recall any occasion on which he'd voluntarily picked up or held Nyagūthiī. Was it because he was disappointed he didn't get the boy he'd hoped for? Fortunately, Nyagūthiī seemed oblivious to her parents' strained relationship and her father's remoteness toward her.

One Saturday morning, when he was reading the paper and studiously ignoring Nyagūthiī, who was playing quietly with her doll, he commented, "This one is going to need to use one of those skin-lightening creams when she gets older. Otherwise, she'll never get a husband."

Wanjikū caught her breath and stopped what she was doing. Had she heard him correctly? She shot him a venomous look and hissed, "She looks like you!" Her hands were trembling, and she looked away to hide the tears of rage that had formed in her eyes.

"Look, I was just making an observation. It's different for me because I'm a man. My appearance doesn't matter as much."

She resisted verbalizing the unkind thought that immediately popped into her head. Instead, she walked to where Nyagūthiĩ played with the Mūthūngū doll with curly blond hair he had bought her for her third birthday and took her by the hand. "Put that down now, dear," she said, gesturing to the doll, which she resolved to throw away at the earliest opportunity. "Come with Mommy and let's go for a walk." Nyagūthiĩ happily obliged. Wanjikū hastily helped her put on her shoes and sweater, and they hurried out, the one eager to escape her husband, the other excited to go out into the sunshine with her favorite person in the world.

***

When the Mūthūngū left in 1963, he did not take everything he'd brought with him back to England. One of the things he left was a strange madness that infected the minds of many Africans—a madness so powerful it was like *ūrogi* [witchcraft]. As followers of Jesū, many of the Athūngū despised ūrogi. Yet they still managed to cast spells that burrowed deep into the minds of those with whom they came in contact.

The Color Bar, which was the system the Mūthūngū introduced to his obvious benefit, separated everything into three categories: The best schools, hospitals, places to live, and so on went to the Mūthūngū. Next came the Ahĩndĩ. The African got all the shabby things that were left over. After a few generations, people began to believe that the Mūthūngū was in fact better than everyone else and deserved the best things.

Color Bar should have ended in 1963, when Jomo Kenyatta took over leadership of the country from Malcom MacDonald, the last Mūthūngū governor. Yet certain ideas lingered in people's minds even after the Mūthūngū with his guns and snarling dogs had gone, even if they were more difficult to see and could only have been the result of ūrogi. For an educated person like Kabogo—with six years of university training in biochemical engineering from America—to look at his daughter and conclude that she was not beautiful because her skin was darker than a Mūthūngū's rankled Wanjikū immensely. His comment popped up relentlessly in her mind, taunting her with such ferocity that she found herself gritting her teeth, clenching her fists, and muttering angrily in the days that followed. When she turned on the TV, it struck her for the first time that a staple of the advertising was skin-lightening creams that promised to make you more beautiful. She stabbed off the TV.

Nyagūthiĩ's doll mysteriously vanished and had probably already found a new home among the eagle-eyed chokoras who sifted through the pile of garbage at the landfill for anything of value. The few times Nyagūthiĩ asked about her doll, Wanjikū distracted her with an exciting new game or adventure until the doll faded from memory. It might have helped that Nyagūthiĩ had never named it. The next time she was downtown, Wanjikū went to a big toy store on Bazaar Street to get her daughter a doll that looked like her. The Mūhĩndĩ shopkeeper shook his head regretfully. All the dolls in stock looked just like the one she had banished from her home.

***

Within a month of starting his new job, Kabogo bought a Peugeot 504, which let Wanjikū have the Datsun to herself. She would need it once Nyagūthiĩ started preschool in the Hospital Hill area, especially since Kabogo now left home early in the morning and didn't return until nine or ten at night. It wasn't that he worked late or that the traffic on Thika Road was bad. He had started what he called *networking*, which apparently involved eating dinner out and coming home with the smell of Tusker beer on his breath. He said he needed to do this to position himself for future promotions and career growth in the company, so Wanjikũ no longer included him in her dinner plans. She rather enjoyed the quiet evenings playing with Nyagũthiĩ, her precious dark-chocolate-skinned daughter.

Chapter 20

August 1978

Two years had gone by since they'd returned, and their life in Nairobi had fallen into a somewhat predictable rhythm. Kabogo had settled into his job at Koenig Pharma, and as far as Wanjikū could tell he was energized by what he was doing there, mentioning on a few occasions that this was exactly what he'd had in mind when leaving Connecticut. Nyagūthiī had started kindergarten and was enjoying it.

After the sounds of the city died down and the television programming from Voice of Kenya—the sole broadcast station—ended for the day, Wanjikū, who was a light sleeper, usually listened to the activity in the street below, still clear enough from their third-floor flat. She could hear the sound of cars zipping by on Ring Road and the hoarse crooning of the occasional drunkard staggering home. One Monday night in August, she lay awake listening, though she didn't know why. It wasn't as if anything bothered her, such as one of Kabogo's boneheaded comments. Glancing at the dial of the alarm clock, she saw it was midnight, and when she looked again after what felt like ages, only ten minutes had passed. Kabogo was sprawled on his side of the bed, lying so still and silent that she put her hand on his back to make sure he was breathing.

SUNSHINE ON THE CROOKED ROAD

A little after one-thirty, she was jolted by the ominous *hoo-hoo* of a *ndundu* [owl] that made her blood curdle. She had always laughed off the belief in her village that whenever an owl called out at night, an old person in the village would die, but the sinister, mournful cry of the ndundu unnerved her. She took a deep breath and turned over, covering her head with her pillow. When the low-pitched call came again from the nearby trees, her whole body shivered.

It seemed almost immediately after she finally fell asleep that the alarm went off. Rolling over in bed and rubbing her eyes, she saw that Kabogo had already left for work. She hurried out of bed and got in the shower, then woke Nyagūthiī and prepared her for kindergarten. Wanjikū had grown accustomed to driving in the busy Nairobi traffic, dodging matatus and aggressively merging into a neighboring lane when needed. She marveled at her own sangfroid when she remembered how nervous she had been when she first started driving. Even in her sleep-deprived state, she could get Nyagūthiī to Saint Anne's Kindergarten in fifteen minutes and return home in even less time.

Around lunchtime, she turned on the radio and heard martial music. She twisted the dial, but martial music seemed to be the order of the day. She turned off the radio, then turned it back on. Nothing had changed, so she resumed what she had been doing—shelling maize and peeling potatoes in preparation for the *mūkimo* [a traditional Gīkūyū meal] she was making for dinner. Nyagūthiī's school let out at around three o'clock, and she wanted to have everything ready so she could start cooking when they got back home.

The music had receded to background noise, so she was startled when a voice interrupted it. The voice announced in a solemn tone that the Mzee[1] Jomo Kenyatta was dead. Her mouth went dry. She dropped what she doing and hurried over to the radio. "*Wūi, Mwathani* [Oh, dear

---

1. Swahili equivalent of *Mūthee,* a respectful way to address an old man.

Lord]*!* How can he be dead?" she asked aloud as she lowered herself into a chair.

That Kenyatta, the only president Kenya had known, could die was nearly unimaginable. Not long before, the attorney general, in response to some political shenanigans, had declared that it was a criminal offense, punishable by death, "to imagine, devise or intend the death or deposition" of the president. Besides, the old man had seemed full of health in recent public appearances, waving his famed fly whisk and rousing the crowds as he bellowed, "*Harambee!*"[2] his signature expression.

If her first reaction was dread and panic, her first act was to run out of the house and drive to Nyagūthiī's school to pick her up. Outside, the people she saw looked dazed, hurrying home from work, afraid of what was going to happen without knowing exactly what that might be. For most, the notion of a Kenya without Kenyatta was unthinkable. It wasn't so much that he was an irreplaceable leader as a fear of the instability his death could bring.

When she arrived at the school, she formed part of a clutch of nervous parents also picking up their kids and barely speaking. She was surprised to find Kabogo at home when she got back. "We closed our offices when they made the announcement. Nobody knows what's going to happen," he said.

It was a strange afternoon, with both the TV and the radio on, she and Kabogo shuffling around the flat in an agitated silence. It was reassuring when Vice President Daniel arap Moi was sworn in as president, but there were still a lot of unknowns. The image of Ravi's troubled face after he'd learned of Amin's takeover in Uganda haunted Wanjikū.

"Mommy, what's happening?" Nyagūthiī had asked several times from the minute she had picked her up. It wasn't normal for kinder-

---

2. Expression frequently used by Kenyatta, exhorting citizens to rally together to accomplish a task. In modern Kenya, a *harambee* is a fundraiser.

SUNSHINE ON THE CROOKED ROAD   145

garten to shut down early and for everyone to be sent home, and she could tell that her parents and teachers were worried.

"I'll tell you later," said Wanjikū as she fought the traffic on the way home, then bustled her daughter to the safety of their flat and thought about how best to explain the situation to her. The seventh or eighth time Nyagūthiĩ asked, Wanjikū squatted to be at eye level with her daughter. "You know the man who comes on TV and waves that white *ninii* [thingamajig] that looks like a cow's tail and shouts 'Harambee!'? You know who I'm talking about?"

Nyagūthiĩ nodded. "You mean Mzee Jomo Kenyatta?"

"Yes, that's him. I didn't realize you knew his name."

"He's the president, Mommy. We learn about him in school."

"Oh, I see. Well, they announced today that he died. That's why everyone is sad."

"Is that why they didn't put up the flag properly this morning?"

"What do you mean?"

"You know how normally they put the flag at the top of the pole? This morning on the way to school, it was in the middle instead, like they just gave up. I hope they learn how to do it correctly."

She hadn't noticed the flag on their way to Saint Anne's. It seemed odd that the flag would have been a half mast, since the president's death was not announced until early in the afternoon.[3] "Yes, Nyagūthiĩ, it looks like they have a lot of learning to do."

---

3. While flags had been flying at half mast since early that morning, mostly unnoticed, it wasn't until later in the day that the news was made public because Vice President Moi, Kenyatta's successor, was nowhere to be found. He reportedly had concerns for his safety and made himself scarce when the president's death was announced. *Untold Story: Details from the night Jomo Kenyatta died, KTN News, Kenya: https://www.youtube.com/watch?v= N_6CHAvqYN8*

Chapter 21

Though Kabogo returned to work and Nyagŭthiĩ to school the very next day, the general mood over the next several days was subdued and off-kilter. Despite the president's death being an officially acknowledged fact, people hesitated to speak about it in public for fear they might say something that landed them in trouble. On TV, a winding line of mourners queued to pay their last respects to Mzee. They even showed him lying in state.

"Mommy, are they sure he's dead?" asked Nyagŭthiĩ when she saw him. "To me, it looks like he's sleeping."

"I expect the people in charge would have been able to tell the difference."

Nyagŭthiĩ wasn't persuaded and wanted to go check for herself, but Wanjikŭ refused.

After Mzee's funeral came speeches by the youthful Moi, who promised to follow in the footsteps of his predecessor. Once things settled back into their familiar rhythms, Nyagŭthiĩ's attention returned to matters more suitable to a five-year-old such as the new girl at Saint Anne's whose family had just come from America. "She's called Milka. Didn't we used to live in America, Mommy?"

"We did."

"I thought so! I told her, but she didn't believe me. She doesn't talk like the rest of us. She talks like a Mzungu, like Mrs. Campbell, the headmistress."

"What do you mean?"

"Oh, just the way she talks." Nyagūthiĩ scrunched up her face. "She . . . talks . . . like . . . this," she said in a laborious imitation of an American accent before collapsing in giggles.

Wanjikū chuckled. "Look at you, making fun of her! Do you know you sounded exactly like that when we came back? When we went to visit Cūcū and Guka, everybody kept asking, 'Ati what is she saying?'"

"You're teasing me, Mommy."

"Haiya, it's true."

"How come I don't talk like that now?"

"Once you started playing with your cousins and the kids in school, you began to sound more and more like them. That's what will happen to Milka."

"Mrs. Campbell still sounds like a Mzungu, and she lives here," said Nyagūthiĩ skeptically.

"That's because she probably came here as a grownup. Just like me and Baba—even after six years in America, we still didn't sound like we were from there."

"Can Milka come to our house on Saturday to play?"

"I don't know. I'll have to meet her mother first."

Nyagūthiĩ nodded, then went to the living room to continue work on a Lego set. Wanjikū assumed that was the end of the discussion, so she was surprised when her daughter came home the next day with a handwritten note addressed to *Mama Nyagūthiĩ*. It was from Milka's mother, Millicent Obonyo, asking if she could pick up Nyagūthiĩ on Saturday for a playdate at their house. Wanjikū dialed the included telephone number.

"Obonyos," answered an uninflected woman's voice.

"Um . . . hello," began Wanjikū. "This is Mrs. Kabogo. I'd like to speak with Mrs. Obonyo."

The voice at the other end of the line suddenly became animated and friendly: "Mama Nyagūthiī? My name is Millie, but you can call me Mama Milka. *Tusiongee kirasmi hivyo*[Let's not be so formal]*!*" Soon, they were chatting like old friends. They arranged for Wanjikū and Nyagūthiī to drive over to the Obonyos' on Saturday, only two days away. By the time she hung up the phone, Wanjikū was even more excited about the playdate than Nyagūthiī.

The Obonyos lived in Madaraka Estate, a fifteen-minute drive from Kariokor. Wanjikū and Nyagūthiī started out around ten, before Kabogo had gotten up. When they arrived, Milka and her mother met them excitedly at the door, and the girls rushed off to play in Milka's bedroom. Mama Milka was tall and slender with high cheekbones and lively eyes full of merriment. She often threw her head back and cackled with laughter when she found something funny, and if a joke was off the charts, she would hold out her palm for a high-five as she doubled over, tears streaming down her cheeks. Mama Milka was the type of person who could walk into a dying party and bring it effortlessly back to life.

While they were chatting in the kitchen, a short, potbellied, serious-looking man entered the room. "Hi, Fred," said Mama Milka. "This is my new friend, Wanjikū. Fred—or Baba Milka—is the quiet one in the house, while I'm the *domo ya sokoni* [marketplace chatterbox]."

Baba Milka proceeded to ask Wanjikū about her family and their life in Connecticut. He had a mellow voice and unhurried manner that put her at ease. Mama Milka watched him affectionately as he spoke. "So how is Baba Nyagūthiī adjusting to working in Kenya?" he asked.

"He had a job with the agricultural ministry, which was challenging, so he went to a pharmaceutical company. He seems to be enjoying his new job."

"I'd be interested in getting his thoughts on how to navigate government employment. I'll be starting with the Ministry of Works as a civil

SUNSHINE ON THE CROOKED ROAD

engineer in a couple of weeks, and it would be helpful to hear from someone who has gone through a similar experience."

She promised to pass along the request to Kabogo, and the three of them continued to talk. The girls emerged intermittently from Milka's bedroom, giggling conspiratorially and evidently having a good time. Wanjikū was surprised when she looked at her watch. "Haiya! Where did that time go? It's already four o'clock. I have to leave!" she exclaimed, rising from her seat. They had been talking for more than five hours. The whole time, Mama Milka had shuttled back and forth across the kitchen, preparing omelets, pancakes, and cups of chai spiced with ginger for themselves and the girls, even as she remained fully engaged in the conversation.

"*Haraka ya nini, lakini* [What's the rush, seriously]? You just got here," protested Mama Milka. Etiquette required the host appear reluctant when a guest announced their intention to leave, but Mama Milka and Baba Milka seemed genuinely disappointed that she had to go, an impression supported by the fact that Baba Milka had just stopped in to stay hello and had ended up staying the entire time.

Wanjikū and Nyagūthiī happily exchanged stories about their experience with the Obonyos on the drive home. Upon entering the flat, they found Kabogo sitting in the living room, his feet on the coffee table, reading a newspaper. "I didn't realize you'd be out all day," he said, though for once he sounded more conversational than annoyed.

"We went to visit one of Nyagūthiī's school friends. They just moved here from Massachusetts."

"Oh?"

"Yes. the father, Fred, got a job with the Ministry of Works and wants to talk to you about what it's like working for the government." She handed him a folded piece of paper with Baba Milka's full name and contact information. He opened and read it. "*Sawa* [OK]," he said dismissively.

She thought something about the curl of his lip seemed even more disdainful than usual, but decided she was being paranoid. Toward the end of the week, she saw Mama Milka at Saint Anne's when they both arrived at the same time to pick up their girls, and they spent twenty minutes talking in the parking lot as the girls played hopscotch. "Baba Milka is still waiting to hear from Baba Nyagũthiĩ, if he has time to call," remarked Mama Milka as they bade each other farewell.

"I gave him the number last Saturday, but I'll definitely remind him."

She didn't see Kabogo that evening because he was once again out "networking." It seemed that he got home later and later nowadays. Even on the weekends, he usually went out around five or six p.m. and didn't get home until late. It no longer bothered her. In fact, life at home was more pleasant when he not around, particularly for Nyagũthiĩ. After multiple unsuccessful attempts to get him to talk to her, play with her, or show any interest in her and her activities, she had had given up, avoiding him when he was home by staying in her room or in the kitchen with her mother. On the rare occasions he spoke to her, her terse replies were delivered in a monotone. It made Wanjikũ sad. She'd caught the look of surprise in Nyagũthiĩ's eyes at the Obonyos' when Milka had snuggled up to Baba Milka at lunch. He had put his arm around her and gently stroked her hair. Clearly, not all fathers were as emotionally distant as hers.

It wasn't until Saturday that Wanjikũ had a chance to talk to Kabogo again. When he shuffled into the kitchen around eleven, he found Wanjikũ trying out a recipe for jam tarts, which Nyagũthiĩ had eaten at school and had been badgering her to make. He poured himself a cup of tea from the flask on the countertop and sat at the dining room table without saying anything to her. After a few minutes, she asked, "Did you get a chance to talk to Mr. Obonyo, the one whose number I gave you last Saturday?"

He looked up and cleared his throat. "No."

SUNSHINE ON THE CROOKED ROAD

"I ran into his wife on Thursday at Nyagūthiǐ's school, and she asked me to remind you, if you get the time."

"What does that *jaluo*[1] want from me?" he growled. She lifted her wooden spoon, her eyebrows arched in surprise, and she stared at him disbelievingly.

"Kabogo, what is it with you and stereotypes?" she hissed in a low voice. "Either someone is a jaluo or a Mzungu or a Nyeri woman . . . Why can't you just see people as human beings instead of putting them in categories?"

She glanced down the hallway to make sure Nyagūthiǐ was in her room and had not heard the offensive comment. It had never occurred to Wanjikū to number tribalism among Kabogo's many unsavory attributes. That someone so highly educated, who had lived abroad among people from all over the world, would take such a reductive view seemed inconceivable to her. Of course, there had been no occasion for it to come up during their years in Connecticut. When she thought back to his few friends at university, she did not recall his ever having an association with someone from western Kenya.

She fumbled with the pastries on the countertop, drew a deep breath and, ignoring his outburst, persisted with her request. "So are you going to call him or not?" She felt her voice had come from outside her body, but even she could recognize the menacing edge to it. Kabogo looked up uncomfortably, gruffly mumbled, "I'll see," rose from his chair, and went to the bedroom.

***

Wanjikū wrestled with what to tell Mama Milka once it became clear that Kabogo had no intention of calling Baba Milka. It made her mad.

---

1. Reference to someone from the Luo ethnic group, sometimes expressed in a derogatory way, such as in this instance.

Calling Baba Milka required so little of him, and his refusal to do so was endangering her budding friendship. She decided that, when it came up, she would not offer up any elaborate lies or excuses to cover for him. This was his problem, not hers. So when Mama Milka mentioned it again as they walked together to the parking lot of Saint Anne's, she blurted, "He's a tribalist, so he might not call."

Mama Milka stopped and turned to her, looking surprised and then outraged. She opened her mouth, but nothing came out. Finally, she choked out, "Ati what?"

"I didn't even know it until I forwarded Baba Milka's request. Kabogo said he didn't want to associate with jaluos."

"Ngatho! Is that for real?"

Wanjikū was surprised to hear her friend use a Gĩkūyū expression, and her surprise must have shown on her face.

"I grew up in Eastlands, with kids from everywhere," she explained, "so when we talked among ourselves, we used words and expressions from every language without even thinking about it. Some parents would try to keep their kids from playing with kids from other tribes. We called them *washalee*, slang for *washamba* [country bumpkins], because they were still trying to live like they were back in their village."

"Well, now you know about my *mshamba* husband," said Wanjiku with a rueful laugh. "Despite living six years in America, his *ushamba* [provincialism] hasn't left him. I hope you won't hold it against me."

It was Mama Milka's turn to laugh. "That would make me as bad as him. If you're not too busy this weekend, we should get together. I'm sure the girls would enjoy it, and so would I. You can come to our place again."

"Sawa," replied Wanjikū gratefully.

Chapter 22

Wanjikū's sewing proficiency had come a long way since those first misshapen pajamas she made for herself in Connecticut, which Kabogo had thought funny to mistake for curtains. She made her own outfits nowadays, proud that, as with the dresses Karen's aunt had sewn for her, people asked admiringly where she bought them. She also sewed Nyagūthiī's clothes, but Nyagūthiī seemed to care even less about what she wore than the boys in her class, and Wanjikū found herself wanting to display her skills on a bigger stage.

One day, walking along Ring Road, she noticed a sign outside Upendo Children's Village—an orphanage—appealing for donations of food, cash, clothing, or other supplies. She had walked past that sign dozens of times, but on this day, it caught her attention. Impulsively, she backtracked to the entrance and told the guard that she wanted to have a word with whoever was in charge regarding a donation. He led her to the office of Mrs. Makokha, the director, a petite woman in her fifties with lively eyes and graying hair that she wore in braids. "Come in, come in, please!" she said, rising from her seat and enthusiastically shaking Wanjikū's hand.

Wanjikū proposed to make some clothing for the children, and Mrs. Makokha couldn't have seemed more pleased. She insisted on giving her a tour of the orphanage, walking surprisingly fast, the staccato *kop-kop-kop* of her heels ringing in the hallways as Wanjikū hurried to keep up. As she showed her the facility, her hands glided through the air in rapid, flowing gestures that Wanjikū found irresistible to watch, the colorful bangles on her wrists clinking noisily with every movement.

"So you're a tailor? Oh, God is great! The children will be so excited to get smart, matching uniforms. This is such good news! They're about to gather in the lunchroom. I'll take you there and introduce you to them."

Wanjikū took in a sharp breath. Uniforms? "Well, not a tailor, exactly," she hedged.

Seeing her hesitation, Mrs. Makokha chose to interpret it as nerves about seeing the children. She put a reassuring hand on her arm. "Don't worry. They're very friendly, and quite well behaved. They'll be most excited to see you."

"So . . . how many children do you have?"

"I don't have any! This is not my orphanage."

Wanjikū looked confused.

"It belongs to God," explained Mrs. Makokha. "I'm just the custodian."

"OK, but how many . . . ?"

"Right now, we have fifteen children, fourteen from four to thirteen years old, and one older one, age sixteen."

Wanjikū let out her breath. Fifteen uniforms might be manageable, as long as she wasn't expected to make more than one per child. She decided not to ask, for fear that Mrs. Makokha would misinterpret the question as an offer.

As they walked into the lunchroom, all the heads turned, accompanied by excited chatter. The moment Mrs. Makokha raised her hand, the room fell silent. "Good afternoon, children. We have a very special visitor today whose name is Mrs. Kabogo. Mrs. Kabogo is a tailor. Luka, do know what a tailor does?"

SUNSHINE ON THE CROOKED ROAD

Luka sat up straight and declared, "Tailors make clothes."

"That's correct. Now, Mrs. Kabogo has offered to make uniforms for all of you . . ."

The room erupted with such cheering and banging on tables that even Mrs. Makokha seemed startled. She let it play out for a minute, then raised her hand again. "All right, now, boys and girls, what do we say to Mrs. Kabogo?"

"Thank you, Mrs. Kabogo!" they choroused.

Wanjikū couldn't suppress a smile and nodded self-consciously. Then she and Mrs. Makokha left the cafeteria. "Where do they attend school?" she asked as they walked back to the office.

"The younger ones go to Saint Stephen's Primary School, which belongs to the church that supports this orphanage. A van picks them up in the morning and brings them back at four. Jonah, the sixteen-year-old, goes to one of the nearby high schools, and he usually takes a matatu there and back. He was our first child and the reason we started the orphanage in the first place."

"Oh?"

"Yes. He was abandoned by his mother near Saint Stephen's. Someone from the church found him wandering in the parking lot. It was a Monday, and I happened to be there. I had lost my shawl and went to check if I had left it at church the previous day. I found this six-year-old boy in the office with the vicar, the secretary, and the caretaker. They called the police, who promised to send an officer to get the boy's details so they could trace his relatives, but they asked us if someone could look after him in the meantime."

"So you volunteered?"

"Not exactly," she said, looking a bit chagrinned. "I just happened to be the obvious candidate. The vicar already had too much on his plate. The caretaker was a young, single man, and the secretary had three children below the age of five. My two boys were teenagers at the time, so when the secretary repeated what the police had said, everybody just looked around nervously until their eyes settled on me. I ended going home with my shawl, which had been turned in to the lost and found, and a new son."

"Wow!"

"Yes. Wow! Jonah was a blessing to us, and we couldn't help thinking about all the other children who weren't lucky enough to find someone to take care of them. My husband and I mentioned it to the vicar, Reverend Njoroge, who gave a sly smile and asked us if we were volunteering to start a ministry for abandoned children. That certainly took us aback! It's easy to talk about a problem and expect someone else to fix it. It's much harder to recognize that you might be the solution." She paused, shaking her head. "Mrs. Kabogo, if you had told me then that I would end up running an orphanage, I'd have called you a *mwendawazimu* [crazy person]. But here we are. Reverend Njoroge and the church have been very supportive, including buying this house so we could accommodate more kids, and I have become a shameless and relentless beggar, going to churches, offices, homes, and community groups to raise money for our needs. And of course, there are people sent by God who just call or show up, like you did today, with pledges and donations."

"How do you find the children who come to the orphanage?"

"We don't find them. They find us. Some are orphans, but some are just abandoned. There are more of both every day. Back in the old days, in the villages, this would never happen, because every child was everybody's child. Even if your parents weren't there, you still had aunties, uncles, grandparents, friends, neighbors—everyone was involved. But here in Nairobi, everyone is trying so hard to get by that they're not able to take care of someone else. Many people come here from their village thinking life will be easy and end up struggling to survive. If you're in desperate straits, having a child following you around all day may be the last straw, both for you and the child."

"Can't they return to the village when things don't work out?"

"To do what? Even there, life has gotten harder. That's why many of them come to the city in the first place. It's not like the old days when there was plenty of food in the shamba. Even in the villages, most people can only take care of themselves and the few people in their immediate household. Those of us who live in the city have to try to make our own little villages by helping each other when we can. No single individual can fix all the problems in Nairobi—not the mayor, not even the president—but if each person helps a few people, and they in turn help a few people, we might make things better."

Wanjikū glanced at her watch and realized almost two hours had passed since she'd walked into the orphanage. She needed to get going. She arranged with Mrs. Makokha to come back the following week to get measurements for all the children so she could begin working on the uniforms. Mrs. Makokha was also able to tell her more precisely what she had in mind. The children often sang in church on Sundays, so she thought it would be nice if they had matching outfits.

Once Wanjikū understood her vision, she no longer felt any hesitation; in fact, she could hardly wait. Mrs. Makokha's sincerity and enthusiasm turned out to be contagious.

★★★

Mama Milka wholeheartedly supported Wanjikū's plan to make clothes for the children at the orphanage. Accompanied by their daughters, the two went shopping for fabric in Ngara the following weekend. The girls seemed bored to tears as they were dragged from one shop to another, haggling over prices with the Ahīndī shopkeepers. With fifteen uniforms to sew, finding suitable fabric that was also cheap was key. She'd set aside some money every month after all the household expenses because Kabogo usually gave her a discretionary two thousand shillings above whatever she needed for the month. By the time they got to the fifth shop, the routine had become tedious, even for the mothers. They bought the girls the sodas they had promised to keep them in line, then decided to look at one or two more shops before calling it quits for the day.

At the seventh shop, Mama Milka spotted some rolls of African print fabric in a corner on the top shelf. "*Na hiyo kitenge pale* [And that *kitenge* fabric over there]*?*" she asked the shop attendant, a young man in his late teens. He must have been the proprietor's son, because he looked up and, without hesitation, quoted a price that was about half that of the other fabric they had seen.

Trying not to look too surprised, she called to Wanjikū, who had been wandering through the shop, and pointed to the fabric. "What do you think?" she asked.

Wanjikū, who had not heard the price, shrugged.

"*Hebu nione, tafadhali* [Let me have a look, please]," Mama Milka said to the attendant. He instructed his assistant to climb up and bring down the two large rolls, each with a different pattern. As they examined them, Mama Milka whispered the price in Wanjikū ear, which immediately got her attention.

Nyagūthiĩ looked on, perplexed. "Mommy, you're going to make us kitenges?"

"I don't know, maybe. What do you think?"

"I think they look nice."

"And you, Milka? What do you think?"

Milka adopted an appraising look, then said, "I like them!"

Mama Milka nodded her approval to Wanjikū, who fussed over the two rolls indecisively. "I like them both. It's so hard to decide." Finally, she set one aside. "*Haya, tutachukua hii* [OK, we'll take this one]."

As the assistant reached to take back the second roll, Mama Milka put her hand on it and said, "*Hata hii tutabeba* [We'll take this as well]." Seeing the startled look on Wanjikū's face, she said, "It's my

SUNSHINE ON THE CROOKED ROAD

contribution. You can make them each two outfits . . . I like orphans, too." She smiled.

"Oh, thank you!" said Wanjikũ, returning her smile.

"*Nguo nyingi ya watoto mbili* [That's a lot of clothes for two children]," remarked the attendant as he rang up the purchases.

"*Hapana. Kuna wengine, siyo hawa tu* [No, there are others, not just these]," she replied. He looked skeptical but kept his mouth shut, not wanting to jinx a good sale.

As they picked up their purchases and made to leave, Mama Milka still had a nagging question. "*Kwa nini hii material ya kitenge ni bei kidogo kulingana na hizo zingine* [So why is the kitenge material so much cheaper than the other ones]?"

The young man shrugged and shook his head. "*Sijui. Watu hapana nunua. Wanataka style kama ile iko London.*" ["I don't know. People just don't buy these. They prefer the styles that people wear in London."]

Chapter 23

W anjikū labored over the outfits in the following weeks, but as she worked for several hours every day, she became more efficient, her hands moving more quickly and effortlessly about her tasks. She made dresses for the girls and shirts with matching trousers for the boys. The cotton kitenge fabric turned out to be an excellent choice. The first roll she worked with was midnight blue, adorned with repetitive interlocking rings of gold and lilac. The contrast between the blue, gold, and lilac was stunning and became even more striking when draped as clothing. She sewed the first trial dress for Nyagūthiĩ. Watching her daughter, usually so oblivious to fashion, laughing in delight and twirling in front of the mirror when she tried it on boosted her confidence.

"Do you like it?"

"Oh yes, Mommy. It's beautiful!"

They drove to the Obonyos' the following evening with Milka's outfit, even though it was a school night. Milka, beaming, thanked her shyly, and she and Nyagūthiĩ rushed excitedly to Milka's room to admire their matching dresses in the mirror.

"Wah! I'm impressed, *lakini*. I knew you would do a good job, but this is outstanding! You should start your own clothing business."

"Now, Mama Milka, why are you enjoying[1] me? I'm not a professional tailor."

"Haiya! I'm not enjoying you. I mean it. Those dresses are very beautiful."

Baba Milka, who had just come in after getting a fashion show in the hallway, agreed wholeheartedly. "It's true, Mama Nyagūthiĩ. Those dresses are very stylish. Top quality!"

"Thank you."

Fueled by those hearty encomiums, Wanjikū went about working on the remaining outfits with a newfound self-assurance. She completed the outfits with plenty of cloth to spare and immediately picked up the second roll. This other one had an earthy red background, which reminded her of the rich soil in the hillside farms in Gĩthakainĩ, splashed with whimsical, multicolored whorls of yellow, red, green, and turquoise that stood out like giant lollipops. If the first fabric was stately in appearance, this second one was bold and playful, like a carefree second-born child, free of the pressure of parental expectations yet commanding in its own right. The magic of kitenge was its ability to put together potentially conflicting colors in vivid geometric patterns that made them mesh. When the second round of uniforms was completed, the response from Nyagūthiĩ and the Obonyos was equally enthusiastic. She packed up everything the following day and went to Upendo Children's Village.

The unrestrained excitement of the kids at the orphanage when they tried on their uniforms, and the admiration of their caretakers, was finally enough to convince her that her handiwork was, indeed, good. The talkative Mrs. Makokha was temporarily struck dumb, tears of joy on her cheeks. "Goodness, the kids look so smart!" she said hoarsely when she could finally speak.

---

1. *Making fun of*, in Kenyan colloquial English.

One of the orphans noticed the tears in her eyes and asked, "Mom, why are you crying?"

"I'm crying because I'm happy, Daniel. I'm happy to see all of you so happy."

"But you don't laugh when you're sad."

"That's true," she said, putting her arms around him, "but sometimes people cry when they're very happy."

As Wanjikū drove home later, reveling in her achievement, she thought about Mama Milka's exclamation that she should start a business. Though she hadn't the faintest idea how to go about it, the idea intrigued her. Seeing the joy on all those faces as they relished their new clothes was an intoxicating experience. She felt an overwhelming need to do it again. The next time Mama Milka suggested she go into business, Wanjikū wasn't dismissive, though she wasn't sure where to begin and had misgivings about trying to run a business.

"*Si* you just apply for a stall at Kariokor Market?" said Mama Milka, as if it were obvious. "Once you submit the application, you can start sewing, since it will probably take months before you get a stall. Then you'll have enough clothes to sell by the time you're ready to start."

"But where would I even go to apply?"

"*Ai, nyako* [girl]! I can see you didn't grow up in Nairobi! Ati where? *Si*, you just go to *Kanjo*[2] [City Council]? I haven't done it myself, but that's what people do for those kinds of things." Put like that, it did seem pretty obvious.

"So are you going to do it, or do you need me to keep pushing you like a mkokoteni?" asked Mama Milka, pretending to push an imaginary pushcart. "I will, if that's what it takes."

"No, I'll do it! I just need some time to think it through and do some planning."

---

2. From the Gĩkũyũ corruption of the word *council*.

SUNSHINE ON THE CROOKED ROAD

163

"*Sawa*, but remember, the other word for thinking and planning is procrastination. It will take months before you can get a stall in the market, so you'd better apply now and do your planning while you wait."

***

It took about nine months for Wanjikũ to get her stall and move into it—much longer than the three to four weeks the Kanjo official had promised. In that interval, she sewed a number of outfits in various styles for display. Though her intention was to sell made-to-order garments, which would require less money upfront, she resolved to use only kitenge fabric. While her initial attraction to kitenge fabric had been its price, she had come to appreciate the versatility of this multicolored cloth, producing vivid, colorful designs that stood out from the staider Western-style apparel that Nairobians wore. And something about what the young shopkeeper said when she bought her first kitenge cloth, about people preferring styles from London, had lit a defiant flame in her. She still remembered the incident involving Nyagũthiĩ's Mũthũngũ doll and her frustration about being unable to get her daughter a doll that looked like her.

She had already started receiving orders through Mrs. Makokha from congregants at Saint Stephen's after the children made their uniformed debut there, performing a song at the front of the church. With the money Wanjikũ made from those orders, she bought more cloth in a variety of colors and designs. She returned time and again to Lalji and Sons, the shop where she had bought her first two rolls of kitenge, and soon got to know Mukesh, the proprietor's son. Kioko, the old, stooped, wordless assistant, faded so well into the rolls of cloth on the shelves that he startled her when he moved suddenly to retrieve an item that she'd requested. Mukesh called her *Mama Kitenge*, a nickname she wore with pride. Recognizing a good customer when he saw one, he began to stock more kitenge, so that she always had a number of options to choose from. Before long, Lalji and Sons became the go-to place in Ngara for kitenge fabric.

Kabogo had seen a number of outfits hanging in the closet and her work area in the spare bedroom. The sewing machine sat surrounded by rolls of cloth and aluminum boxes containing pins, measuring tape, thread, scissors, and other sewing accessories. Her workspace was a scaled-up version of the sewing she had been doing all along, and he didn't seem particularly interested in learning the reason behind this. Their conversations were mostly superficial nowadays, discussing events in Nyagūthiĩ's life, their respective families, or the news. She could tell from the way he talked about his job when it came up that he was enjoying what he did. One thing she appreciated about him was that, despite his many flaws, he never quibbled about household expenses, making sure she had whatever she needed for bills, shopping, or Nyagūthiĩ's school. There was usually money left over at the end of the month with which to buy cloth and other sewing essentials.

When she finally took possession of her stall at the market, numbered D64, she was ecstatic but also nervous. It was located deep in the bowels of the market, far from the main entrance, and was only about six feet deep and ten feet wide, with just enough room for a counter in front and shelves on the back wall. It had large, green accordion-style wooden doors that she could open outward like enveloping arms at the beginning of the market day and shut securely with a padlock at its close. The doors already had nails in them from which she could hang her display outfits, though she had to remove several nails that threatened to tear her fabric. Despite her unpromising location, she saw a steady stream of foot traffic and soon had a trickle of orders coming in.

Sellers in her corridor offered in a variety of items. Njaū sold sachets of laundry soap, cooking fat, spices, soda, exercise books, and sundry household goods similar to what one might find in a grocery store but

SUNSHINE ON THE CROOKED ROAD

repackaged in smaller amounts for buyers on a tight budget. Nyaga sold a variety of grains and flours: beans, lentils, *njahĩ*,[3] maize flour, sorghum, millet, and many others. He measured out his merchandise with an aluminum scoop, pouring it into brown paper bags placed on his scale, sometimes topping up, sometimes taking a little out in order to get the desired weight.

Next to him was Gaturu's repair shop, with radios, TVs, and other household appliances in various stages of disassembly and reassembly, the counter littered with electronic detritus. He was a small, restless man who spoke in short, quick sentences, often eliciting a bewildered "Ati?" from customers on the other side of the counter. When Wanjikũ moved in, she caught very little of what he said, but after a few weeks, she understood his every overheard word and would wait with concealed amusement for the expected "Ati?" in reply.

Then there was Njogu—a heavily built, cantankerous man whose prominent ears reminded her of Ravi—who sold fruit of all kinds: mango, pineapple, custard apples, blood fruit, loquat, sugarcane . . . He had terrible allergies and blew his nose loudly at frequent intervals. Wanjikũ usually walked across to his stall at least once a day for sugarcane. She normally preferred to chew on sugarcane in one footlong stick, sucking out the delectable juice and spitting out the desiccated fibers as she made her way from one end to the other. Here in the market, though, she had Njogu cut it into small pieces so she wouldn't look undignified if a customer happened by while she savored her treat.

Joyce Mubiru occupied the stall right next to hers. Like Njaũ, she sold household merchandise. Because she was from Uganda, everyone called her *Mganda* [the Ugandan]. She was a stocky woman in her late thirties who spoke in a voice barely above a whisper and had a gaze so intense that even those with a good conscience could hold it for only a few seconds. Her left arm hung limply at her side. Most

---

3. A species of black bean of great cultural significance to the Agĩkũyũ.

of the traders spoke Kiswahili or Gĩkũyũ, but Joyce—though she had no trouble understanding those around her—mostly communicated in English.

All the stall owners had been gracious and welcoming to Wanjikũ when she arrived, but she connected best with Joyce. She often took her stool to sit and chat outside Joyce's stall as she waited for customers to come by. It didn't take long for them to become friends. For some inexplicable reason, even though Wanjikũ was fluent in English, she usually spoke to Joyce in Kiswahili with Joyce replying in English. One day, at closing time, Wanjikũ asked her about her arm.

"I was shot," Joyce said matter-of-factly.

"Shot? You mean with a gun?"

"Is there another way? Yes, with a gun! And I'm grateful to be alive, because that's not what the man who shot me intended."

Wanjikũ drew in a breath, unsure of what to say.

"In Kampala, I had a comfortable life, with a husband and daughter, just like you. My daughter, Janet, was about five, and my husband was a professor of economics at Makerere. One day, Amin's men came to our home in one of those unmarked Peugeot 504s people used to talk about and took my husband at gunpoint from the house. It was common knowledge that if you were taken away, you were never seen again. Sometimes there would be reports of a leg or a head being found in the Nile—whatever the crocodiles hadn't bothered with, since they had a lot to choose from."

She seemed unnaturally calm as she spoke, and because she spoke softly, Wanjikũ found herself instinctively moving closer.

"Since the coup, I had been telling my husband, Edwin, that we should leave the country. I had a bad feeling about that man Amin, but Edwin was dismissive, saying we had nothing to fear. He thought that no one in their right mind would harm intellectuals, as that would be destroying one of the country's most important resources for development. He was an educated man but very simple in some ways. Anyway,

SUNSHINE ON THE CROOKED ROAD 167

my daughter and I were in the backyard, so we hadn't seen the men come in. When we went back inside, we could see through the open front door two men pushing my husband into a car. Janet screamed and ran out the door, shouting for her father, and I followed her. One of the men ran back and grabbed Janet, carrying her to the car. She was kicking and screaming, and the man slapped her hard. Then one of the other men saw me coming, and the next thing I knew, I felt something slam into my shoulder, followed by intense pain. I collapsed, and when I opened my eyes, I was lying on the driveway in a pool of blood. The couple who lived next door helped me up and into the house while I told them over and over that I needed to find my daughter. Then I lost consciousness again."

Wanjikū felt too stunned to speak.

"My neighbors were afraid of keeping me in their house lest they get in trouble with Amin's people, and they felt it too risky to take me to the hospital, since someone coming there with bullet wounds was likely to attract the wrong kind of attention. Instead, they did something very daring. They patched up my shoulder as best they could, put me in the boot of their car, and took me to one of the wife's relatives in a village near the town of Busia, which straddles the Kenya-Uganda border. I was in and out of consciousness through all this, so I don't remember much.

"The night I arrived at the house, I was awakened by a hand tapping me on the arm. It was completely dark in the room, so I got very scared. Then a man's voice whispered to me, 'Don't worry, Joyce, you'll be fine.' I asked him where I was, and he said he was taking me to Kenya. 'Who are you?' I asked. I thought maybe it was the owner of the house, and I was afraid of what he might be planning to do to me in the dark. Instead of telling me his name, he said, 'Edwin and Janet are fine. Don't worry about them.' At that, I became confused and began to cry. He touched me again on my arm and said, 'Don't be afraid.'

"When morning came, my neighbor's sister, the woman who owned the house, came in to check on me. I asked her about the man. She looked at me as though maybe I was delirious and said she lived alone. She told me she was taking me into Busia, to the house of someone who helped people cross the border. It was about two hours away on foot, and we would need to stay away from the roads so as not to get caught by the police or soldiers."

"But if you thought your family was OK . . ."

"No. I knew they were dead. I wondered if the experience from the night before had been a dream. It seemed so real. Maybe it was an angel. Who knows? The strange thing is that after I talked to him, I didn't feel sad about them anymore. It's like God was telling me that they were safe from Amin and his people, that I would see them again someday."

"I can see why . . . but how could you cross the border? Did you have a passport?"

"I had nothing: no money, no documents . . . nothing, except some money the neighbor had given her sister to pay for the border crossing. She gave me her blouse and sweater because mine were caked with dried blood. In fact, she cut up my old blouse and used it to rebandage my shoulder. Everything else I had on was what I had been wearing when the soldiers came to our house. I was very weak from losing blood, so the walk to Busia was very challenging. I would get dizzy and have to stop after a short while to rest. The lady was very patient and encouraged me to keep going. I knew that walking to Busia was my only hope of staying alive, and hers as well, because being found with me would have put her at grave risk. The journey, which she had said would take an hour and a half, ended up taking almost four hours.

"She took me to the house of a man in Busia where about ten other people were hidden—all men—and gave him the money from her sister. Then we waited for it to get dark. The plan was to walk to a place about forty-five minutes north of the border post and cross into Kenya, then find our way through the forest on the other side. I was so exhausted

SUNSHINE ON THE CROOKED ROAD

from walking earlier in the day that I couldn't see how I would be able to make another journey without resting for the night, but the man was nervous and in a hurry to get rid of us. He told us someone in the town preparing for a similar mission had been found with people in his house, and Amin's soldiers shot him in the head, right there and then—in front of those people. The man could see I was weak, but he said the best thing was to try to cross into Kenya. If I got too exhausted, I could rest in the forest once I was on the Kenyan side. Even as he said that, I tried not to think of all the wild animals that might be in the forest. Since he had already received payment for my crossing and I had nowhere else to go, I decided I would make the trip. I remembered the strange man in the dream telling me he was taking me to Kenya, and I felt that God would protect me."

"So you went with the men?"

Joyce paused for a moment, then shook her head and laughed. "The night we crossed the border was pitch-black—you couldn't see your hands in front of your face! On top of that, it started raining. It rained so hard that I was afraid we might drown in the river we had to cross to get to Kenya. It was chest deep and flowing fast, but we managed to cross together, holding hands. On the other side, everybody took off as fast as they could into the dark. I couldn't keep up, and before long, I was all alone. So there I was, wandering aimlessly, tripping over roots and bumping into trees. I was so turned around that I was afraid I might end up right back at the river or, worse, at the border post.

"After what seemed like forever, I saw a light in the distance that turned out to belong to a house. I decided the best thing to do was to climb over the fence and hide in the backyard until morning, but as soon as I got near the fence, a dog started barking and ran toward me. Before I could turn to run away, a light hit me, and a man shouted. '*Weh!*' ['You!'] He was pointing a gun right at me. I thought, *Now I'm finished. I came all this way to Kenya to die.* He took me into the house and made me sit on the floor. I was shaking so hard from cold and fear that his wife went and got me a blanket. The man asked, 'What's your name?' When I said nothing, he started to get angry, but the woman told him to calm down. She said, 'You will say your name now or at the police station.' So I told them. They looked at each other in amazement, and then the woman started crying."

"She started crying?"

"Yes. I was very confused. After a few minutes, she said, 'Let me get you some dry clothes. You can stay with us if you want.' Since I had nowhere to go, I was glad to accept, though I still didn't know what was going on. The next day, the woman, whose name was Wangũi, told me that the previous year, they had been expecting their first baby and had decided to name her Joyce if she was a girl. She was, but she died because the umbilical cord was wrapped around her neck. I arrived on the first anniversary of that event. The night before, Wangũi had dreamed about the baby they had lost, only she was grown up, and the name Joyce kept repeating in her head. When I told them my name was Joyce, I think they saw it as an omen of some kind."

"I can see why. That's amazing."

"It is. For me it was more than amazing. It was a miracle, and it saved me from being shot or turned over to the police. As it turned out, Wangũi's husband, Kĩgotho, was a policeman, which is why he owned a gun. So there I was, a fugitive hiding in the house of a policeman. They looked after me for three days. Kĩgotho told me that the men I had crossed with had all been arrested by the border guards. In the heavy rain and darkness, they had entered the town very close to the border post and were spotted immediately."

"Oh no! What happened to them?"

"I never found out."

"So how did you get to Nairobi without a passport or a Kenyan ID?"

"Well, I got an ID later, but that's another story. Everything happened so strangely, though. Kĩgotho and Wangũi—mostly Wangũi—saw it as their mission to find a way to get me safely to

SUNSHINE ON THE CROOKED ROAD

Nairobi. Do you remember hearing about the *magendo* [illicit trade] in Chepkube Market?"

Wanjikū shook her head.

"When things became difficult in Uganda, coffee farmers started smuggling their produce into Kenya so they could get better prices from buyers who relabeled it as Kenyan coffee and exported it abroad. After the US imposed a trade embargo on Uganda, coffee smuggling became an even bigger business. Many powerful people were involved and made millions of shillings. Kīgotho's brother was involved, sending lorries twice a week to pick up coffee in Chepkube and take it to Nairobi, while Kīgotho and his colleagues made sure the lorries weren't impounded—for a fee, of course. So I ended up one morning in one of those lorries, being driven straight to Nairobi. I sat right in the front seat next to the driver, watching policemen wave us through. Kīgotho's brother, whose name is Mwangi, owns many properties in Nairobi, and he put me up in one of his bedsitters. He even had one of his people take me to a private doctor where they dressed my wound and put me on antibiotics. The doctor said the nerve in my arm was damaged, which is why this hand is shriveled, but that if the bullet had hit the artery, I would have died from the loss of blood. He thought the best thing to do with the bullet was to leave it where it was rather than try to take it out, since it wasn't going to do any more damage. Now, I manage this stall for Mwangi, whom I've never met. He pays me enough to cover my rent and living expenses."

"You said you managed to get an ID?"

"Yes. One of Mwangi's men took me to get an ID a few days after I arrived. He just took me to some government office where I had my picture and fingerprints taken. No way that was legal, but it's a real ID, though it says I'm from Busia—on the Kenyan side, of course—and the name on the ID is Joyce *Muriru*, not Mubiru. I thought it was a mistake at first, but when I tried to point it out, Mwangi's man told me to keep my mouth shut. Turns out it's a Kikuyu name, not that I look like a Kikuyu, but there's nothing to say I can't have a Kikuyu husband."

"Wow!"

"I'm very grateful. If I wasn't a fat woman with a withered arm, I'm sure people would think I traded something with Mwangi for his kindness. I try to repay him by doing a good job with this stall, but it doesn't seem like enough. One day, I went to one of his offices to report a problem with a leaking pipe in my flat. The secretary—you know, one of these young, beautiful ones with red lipstick and shiny hair—gave me such a mean look. I could see she was wondering how a shabby market woman had dared to enter that air-conditioned office and leave a message for her boss. I started to wonder myself if it had been a good idea, but by the time I got home from work, one of his handymen had already come and fixed the problem. And I don't know who he knows in Kanjo, but when the Kanjo people come around looking for bribes, they never ask me. In this corridor of ours, the only two people who don't pay bribes to the Kanjo people are myself and Njogu."

"Njogu? How come?"

"I don't know, but you see how that man is—big as an elephant and with a rotten temper. And the way he strips the peel off sugarcane with that gigantic knife? If I was them, I wouldn't want to mess with him, either."

"But he's always so kind!"

"To us, sure. But we're not those Kanjo parasites, Ngatia and Ngarĩ, who come around trying to reap where they haven't sown."

Wanjikũ felt a knot in her stomach. She knew it was only a matter of time before they came calling at her stall. "What should I do when they come?"

She shrugged. "You'll have to decide. It's not an easy decision. If you pay them, they'll keep coming back. If you don't, they won't take it kindly. They could even shut down your stall."

Wanjikū thought about that for a bit, then tried to put it out of her mind and asked, "Do you think you'll ever go back to Uganda?"

"I don't think so, but who knows what the future holds? You know, I've never told the story of how I left Uganda to anyone before, but it feels good, like there's less pressing me down."

"It's quite a story. Thank you for confiding in me."

"Thank you for listening. You probably didn't expect a question about my arm would result in a long, convoluted story. Maybe one day my story will give you hope if you're going through a hard time."

"Maybe," said Wanjikū, hoping she would never have to go through anything that difficult.

Chapter 24

Kaka Josiah was unlike those modern preachers who had titles like *bishop* and *apostle,* drove around in big, shiny SUVs with quiet engines, and wore expensive clothes and jewelry that they proclaimed were evidence of God's favor in their lives. The glorious rays of Providence bore down with singular intensity on these highly esteemed servants of heaven, often without any visible spillover to their faithful congregants, who in fact provided their pastors' bounty. These disciples of the prosperity gospel preached that a Range Rover was within reach of anyone who ventured to ask without doubting—so long as they provided proof of their sincerity by how much they were willing to give. The bigger the request, the bigger the seed that needed to be sown. Unfortunately, whatever return the worshipers got for their generosity seemed disproportionately small.

How Wanjikũ found herself joining Hallelujah Bible Fellowship certainly had something to do with Mama Milka. But the fact that she had taken to getting out of bed early on Sunday morning, driving across town with a somnolent Nyagũthiĩ, and spending three hours under a tent with no sides through which the bone-chilling wind tunneled mercilessly in July and on which the sun beat down with equal ferocity in January was still impressive. Prior to joining the church—if showing

SUNSHINE ON THE CROOKED ROAD 175

up regularly was indeed the same thing as joining—the only times in her adult life that she had been to church had been her wedding day and Nyagūthiī's christening in Connecticut. As a child, she had regularly attended Gīthakainī Presbyterian Church, where her father was a deacon and her mother a stalwart of the women's guild, but she'd fallen out of the habit in college. That lapse was reinforced by marrying Kabogo, for whom Sundays served as a buffer between the indiscretions of Saturday night and the hard-edged impositions of Monday morning.

The first time she and Nyagūthiī visited Hallelujah Bible Fellowship was when Milka had a lead role in the Christmas play. Nyagūthiī wanted to see her friend's performance. She was already familiar with Milka's character—Mama Teddy—and had herself played various minor roles in the course of helping Milka practice her scenes: a talking sheep, the village drunkard, the argumentative Mama Tony . . . By the time they saw the show, Nyagūthiī gleefully anticipated the responses to Mama Teddy's lines and burst into giggles before the punchlines came. She probably had as much fun as Milka, if not more.

After the play, which was greeted with rousing applause, Kaka Josiah stood up to speak. Because everyone referred to him as *Kaka Josiah*—Brother Josiah—Wanjikū assumed he was one of the congregants sharing a personal story of God's goodness in his life. The story was about a Kisii man from Donholm who had recently gone across town to Eastleigh to visit a friend. On the way, he was mugged and left unconscious in a ditch with only his trousers, having been relieved of everything else. It was early evening, and people were still out and about. First, a Gīkūyū man came by and decided the injured man was a decoy for a trap, so he crossed the street to avoid becoming the real version of what lay before him. Then came a well-dressed Luo man who thought the bloodied person on the ground might need help but didn't want to soil his immaculate three-piece suit. After that came a Kisii man—a fellow member of the man's tribe. He concluded that the unfortunate man had picked a fight when he didn't have the strength to take down his opponent and so deserved what he got.

Then a Somali man came by—Kaka Josiah referred to him with the ethnic slur *wariah*. Wanjikũ could hear a pin drop as everyone waited to hear what ridicule would be heaped on the Somali. They were still viewed as immigrants and outsiders despite having lived in Kenya for generations and were often targets of prejudice.

To their surprise and disappointment, the Somali called a taxi, took the man to Kenyatta Hospital, and came back the next day to check on him. When Kaka Josiah asked the congregation who they considered to be the man's friend, their answer, *Msomali Mwema* [the Good Somali], was an obvious stand-in for *Msamaria Mwema* [the Good Samaritan]. This brought the parable to life, since none of them had ever seen a Samaritan or known anyone who had, but they had all seen a Somali. Kaka Josiah had gently induced them to reflect on the destructiveness of the seemingly harmless game of ethnic stereotyping, especially to the smaller tribes that were frequently marginalized.

Wanjikũ was hooked and began to regularly attend the Hallelujah Bible Fellowship to hear Kaka Josiah's contemporary riffs on parables that had previously seemed like irrelevant tales from long ago and far away. Even when he mentioned Jesus in his stories, he depicted a hip, *Sheng*[1] -speaking guy from Eastlands who told witty jokes and often resolved a companion's conundrum by launching into his signature phrase, "*Lakini cheki hivi nanii . . .* [But look at it this way, guy . . .]" followed by a fresh take on the gospels.

Kaka Josiah was a natural storyteller, but he was also notable for owning very little, unlike the preachers who mistook wealth for godliness. In fact, he didn't even own a car. Every Sunday morning, he either took a matatu or caught a lift from a congregant from his home in Donholm

---

1. Nairobian slang combining Swahili, English, and local Kenyan languages in proportions that vary widely depending on what part of the city you're in.

to the Hallelujah Bible Fellowship tent in the big *kiwanja* [field] near Nairobi West. Most of the matatu drivers knew him and refused to charge him. If he or his wife, Mama Hilda, had any reservations about riding to church in matatus, even as many of their congregants arrived in sleek, air-conditioned cars, they kept these to themselves. The proceeds from the church's overflowing collection plates instead supported orphanages, congregants' hospital bills, supplies for health clinics in slums, books for primary schools, and other worthy causes.

It was surprising that buying a tent with canvas sides that came all the way down never became a priority, given the inadequacy of the current structure for keeping out the vagaries of weather. Kaka Josiah felt there were too many other pressing needs in the community to waste resources on another tent. People who came late to Kaka Josiah's church were soon disabused of the notion that either rain or sunshine fell straight down. Those at the periphery of the throng usually ended up soaked, either from rain or sweat. As a result, even congregants who were perennial latecomers in other aspects of their lives showed up early—an impressive feat for Sunday mornings in a part of the world where scheduled meeting times were often taken as no more than vague suggestions. It was just as well, since Kaka Josiah started his services promptly at nine.

The Obonyo family had been members of the congregation for a couple of years, and Mama Milka seemed to know everyone, lingering for an hour or more after service. She introduced Wanjikū to so many people—dozens of Mama So-and-sos or Baba So-and-sos—that she couldn't keep track of them all, but their genuine smiles and warm handshakes gave Wanjikū a sense of belonging. Nyagūthiī also made friends in the children's ministry and began to look forward to going to church on Sunday.

Even as she expertly navigated the social scene, Mama Milka fed Wanjikū words of caution: "Mama Nyagūthiī, most people here are very nice and easy to relate to. But you have to *chunga siri* [guard your secrets]. Make sure you never tell anyone here anything you want to keep private, because people talk. Sometimes people go up on stage and say very personal things. Think twice before you go up there and ask people to pray for you because Baba Nyagūthiĩ did this or that, unless you want all Nairobi to know. Am I making sense?"

Wanjikū nodded, though she wondered why Mama Milka felt the need to tell her this. It wasn't like she had any urge to bare all.

***

As Wanjikū spent time with Mama Milka, she was fascinated by her friend's ability to adapt to different situations. Already accustomed to her being one of the very active members of Hallelujah Bible Fellowship—singing in the worship team, leading loud prayers of intercession, and rallying congregants to this activity or the other—she was surprised one Saturday to see a different side of her. They had gone shopping downtown. As they walked near Kenya Cinema, they crossed eastbound lanes of traffic on Moi Avenue and waited on the traffic island for westbound traffic to stop. Suddenly, Wanjikū saw her friend make an abrupt motion, almost too quick to notice, then heard a muffled thump like a sack of grain hitting the sidewalk.

"What—" she started.

The light had just turned green when Mama Milka grabbed her elbow and hustled her across the street. "Let's go," she said without turning around.

Wanjikū turned her head and saw a couple of people helping to his feet a man who had fallen. The two men walking behind them were laughing under their breath. "*Hajakufa—ni kuzimia tu* [He's not dead—he just passed out]," one said.

"*Ai, huyo mama ni mkali! Umeona vila amemgonga* [Wow, that woman is vicious! Did you see how she hit him]*?*" asked the other.

Mama Milka hurried them on, only slowing down when they got to Aga Khan Walk. "Never stop if you get into something like that," she said, breathless but exhilarated. "Get away as fast as possible. Those people don't usually work alone."

"Which people?" asked Wanjikū in bewilderment. "What happened?"

"That guy back there was trying to steal my bag," she said, holding up her handbag. The strap had been sliced cleanly through. "They usually cut the strap, then just pull it away and run. They like those traffic islands because everyone is looking in one direction, waiting to cross. They take your bag or wallet and run back the other way, dodging through the cars."

Wanjikū was startled and impressed by her friend's street smarts. "So what did you do? I just saw a slight movement and heard something fall."

Mama Milka jabbed her elbow out and to the side. "Don't play with me! When we were kids, we used to watch Bruce Lee movies and have fighting competitions. The rules were: No weapons, no hitting in the face, no going home to tell your parents you got beaten up . . . things like that. We didn't want parents finding out and spoiling our fun, so if you got bruises, you had to say you fell down while playing: otherwise, you'd get kicked out of the club. We called ourselves *Kaloleni Martial Arts*. Many of the kids I fought with—and most of them were boys—were afraid of me because I had long legs. I kicked very hard, so my nickname was *Millie Mateke* [Millie Kicks]."

"Wow, I don't know what I would have done if it was me. I probably would have started screaming."

"I guess growing up in Kaloleni had its benefits, though at the time, I just assumed all kids played those kinds of games. Because of all that fighting, I just reacted without thinking back there."

Chapter 25

Wanjikū had heard that rather than walk up and down the corridors of the market, shaking down the traders for their hard-earned shillings, the Kanjo men—Ngatia and Ngarī—usually held court during the first week of the month at Wanjohi's Bar, near the market entrance. Whoever's annual lease was due for renewal within ninety days, based on the month their stall permit had been issued, would be summoned to sit and chat with them over a complimentary soda. In the course of the brief conversation, an envelope full of money would change hands under the table, after which their next victim would be called.

Because the two Kanjo men kept close tabs on whose payments were due when, it was considered unwise to try to evade them. Gaturu advised Wanjikū that when her turn came, she would receive word, though he didn't say how. When she pressed him on this point, he said only that they knew where she was and how to reach her.

She thought it would happen at the one-year anniversary of her permit, but it didn't. When she had gone nearly two years without being summoned, she began to hope that proximity to Njogu and Joyce had somehow rubbed off on her or that her stall had magically failed to make it onto their list. Then the message finally came. Nyaga, whose permit was also due for renewal at the same time as hers, came to her stall and told her that Ngatia and Ngarĩ wanted to see her at Wanjohi's for a chat. They wanted ten thousand shillings, which was more than her entire household budget, including rent for the flat, and monthly lease payments for the stall. At this point, she was making about five thousand shillings from the stall on a good month. Her heart sank.

"How will I know who they are?"

"Don't worry, you'll know. If there's any confusion, just ask at the counter."

She popped over to Joyce's stall and, when Joyce was done with her customer, whispered shakily, "They're asking for me."

"Who?"

"The Kanjo people."

"Oh," she said grimly.

"What should I do?"

"Go hear what they have to say."

"Nyaga said they want ten thousand shillings."

"Those crooks!" she hissed. "Shame on them."

"Watch my stall while I'm away?"

"Of course."

Wanjikũ made her way toward Wanjohi's, her palms sweating and her mind spinning as she considered what to say. They were seated at a table on the veranda of the *makuti* [palm frond]-thatched establishment and rose to greet her as she entered. Ngatia was about six feet tall with a broad chest and a huge Afro, apparently indifferent to the fact that they had gone out of style. Ngarĩ was lean and shifty-looking, with a gravelly voice, probably from the Rooster cigarettes he puffed on constantly. His face was scarred from acne, his eyes bloodshot. He had a dank, unwholesome quality that made her want to keep her distance.

"*Karibu* [Welcome], please," said Ngatia graciously, gesturing for her to sit. "Let me call the waiter to get you a drink." The waiter appeared without having to be called.

"Njoroge, please find out what this lady will have, and put it on my bill."

Wanjikũ's heart pounded as she scanned the menu. The Kanjo men were drinking orange Tarino drinks, the kind Nyagũthiĩ and her friends liked, which struck her as oddly incongruous, almost comical.

"Er, give me a Tangawizi," she said told the waiter hoarsely.

"Oh, you like the bitter ones," remarked Ngarĩ.

She couldn't tell if that was good or bad.

Ngatia made cordial small talk about local politics, the delayed rainy season causing farmers like his mother a lot of heartburn, the relative merits of sweet versus bitter drinks . . . Were it not for the looming shakedown, he would have seemed just the person to pass the time with for a couple of hours on a lazy afternoon.

Ngarĩ, on the other hand, seemed impatient, restlessly waiting to make his move, which he did when Ngatia finally paused in his chatter to take a sip of his drink. "You know why you're here?" he said unceremoniously.

"No," said Wanjikũ, wanting to hear it from his lips.

"The permit department at City Hall has become very strict about code violations. We don't agree with what they are doing. Because we have longstanding friendships with many vendors in this market, we try to help by expediting the renewal process so that you don't have to close your shop and spend weeks waiting in line. That way you can do what you do best. We can be your representatives in the permitting process. But we also have mouths to feed, and we're putting ourselves and our families at risk by helping you."

If the situation hadn't been the opposite of funny, Wanjikũ might have snorted at such a preposterous lie.

"All we want is for your business to do well," Ngarĩ continued. "By letting us take care of the permits, you can take care of your business, so we both win. We might even come and buy something from your shop! In short, everything works well when we work together."

SUNSHINE ON THE CROOKED ROAD

"How much do—"

"Ten sticks is normally what we ask," he interrupted. "But because you're a relatively new business, we'll take seven."

"My business has been slow to pick up. I don't know—"

"You've been in business two years already," he interrupted again, an edge creeping into his voice. "I'm sure you can manage it. We're willing to work with you if you can't pay it all at once."

"OK, let me go and see what I can put together, then come back in a week or two."

Ngatia cleared his throat. In a conciliatory tone that seemed anything but, he said, "Let's respect each other, mama. We'll be waiting for you here on Friday at noon. Don't delay." Today was Wednesday.

"OK," she muttered, then rose to leave.

"Please, mama, why don't you stay and finish your drink?"

"Thanks, but I need to get back to my shop."

She walked out of Wanjohi's Bar and returned to her stall. Joyce looked up eagerly as she approached. When she got close enough, and out of earshot from the other vendors, she said, "They're asking for seven thousand. I told them I don't have the money right now, and they gave me until Friday."

"What are you going to do?"

"I don't know." She spent the rest of the afternoon dithering. Normally, she closed her stall at four thirty, but it was a slow day, so she locked up an hour early and went home. The market was close to home, so she walked, as usual when she didn't have much to carry, pondering the situation on the way. She made about five thousand shillings a month from selling her kitenges at the market, which wasn't much, out of which she had to pay a twenty-five hundred monthly lease payment for the stall. In addition, she frequently got orders through Nyagũthiĩ's school, Saint Stephen's, and word of mouth that amounted to another ten thousand shillings or so per month. It was always helpful to be able to direct those customers to her stall to look at samples and have their measurements taken.

Seven thousand shillings took a big bite out of a business her size. More than that, she knew it wasn't the right thing to do. Gaturu said that greasing the cogs of the Kanjo machine was the cost of doing business, that it was just the way things worked. She knew that for nearly everyone in the market, that was true, but it still didn't feel right. One of Kaka Josiah's sermons had been pivotal in Wanjikū's decision not to pay a bribe to the Kanjo men. In it, he had excoriated Christians who looked down on their neighbors who smoked or enjoyed their Tusker while at the same time giving "something small" to a policeman when they got pulled over for speeding or offering a loaded handshake to a government clerk to expedite processing a document. That was probably the most uncomfortable service she attended. There was no laughter or nodding of heads, just nervous coughing and shifting in seats as congregants wished he would turn the spotlight back on the "sinners" outside the tent—but he was relentless. She hadn't realized how much impact he'd had on her until now.

By the next day, she still hadn't come up with a plan, and she felt keenly that she was running out of time. Images of Ngarī and Ngatia kept popping into her head. She wasn't sure which of the two was more ominous: Ngarī with his pockmarked face and bloodshot eyes and snarling, "I'm sure you can manage it." Or Ngatia with his gracious manners and faintly ridiculous Afro telling her in a cordial tone, "We'll be waiting for you on Friday. Don't delay."

Joyce observed her quietly for most of Thursday, then said, "If you want to move your things to my stall, we need to do it without attracting too much attention." Wanjikū looked puzzled. When Joyce added, "That way, if you decide not to pay and they come to close your stall, there will be nothing inside."

Wanjikū understood and recognized it for the generous offer it was. That was all she needed to make up her mind. She knew that retribution

SUNSHINE ON THE CROOKED ROAD 185

from the Kanjo men would eventually come, but there was nothing she could do to prevent it, short of paying the bribe, and that was the one thing she had decided she would not do. Waiting for a lull when most of the other vendors were occupied with customers or rearranging their merchandise, they spirited most of the clothing, equipment, and ledgers from Wanjikū's stall to Joyce's. When they were done, the only thing left were four or five display outfits on hangers—easily movable at short notice.

"I'd better keep these on display. I'll move them to your shop to-morrow at midday, around the time those Kanjo people realize I'm not going to pay."

Friday at noon, she didn't even bother to go to Wanjohi's but remained in her stall, conducting business as usual, albeit while constantly glancing up and down the corridor. She ended up having one of her better afternoons, racking up six new orders, but she knew she was living on borrowed time. Sooner or later, they would come after her, probably timed to include an element of surprise. She only hoped they didn't come with their *askaris* [enforcers] in the middle of the day, embarrassing her in full view of customers and fellow vendors.

The end finally came the following Friday morning. When she arrived at her stall, she found the wooden doors barred with thick red tape in a giant X. More tape sealed the doors where the two halves met, running from top to bottom like the teeth of a zipper.

"*Wamekufungia* [Did they close you down]?" asked Nyaga. "*Hao watu siyo mchezo* [Those people are no joke]." He sounded less sympathetic than self-congratulatory. After all, he had done what was required to avoid her fate and had conveyed to her exactly what she needed to do.

Joyce didn't say much. She waved her to a chair at the back of her stall, and when the tears started flowing gently rubbed her back. Then she disappeared, only to return with a steaming cup of tea from Mama Oloo's that she set on a stool in front of her. "Don't worry about it," she said, then returned to the front of her stall.

Wanjikū sat sipping her tea for about an hour, listening to Joyce make conversation with her customers in her soft, soothing voice. One or two asked about the red tape on the neighboring stall. "It's going to be a Red Cross dispensary," said Joyce, as much for her own entertainment as for Wanjikū's.

Eventually, Wanjikū got up, feeling more composed. "I'm going to leave now."

"OK. If anyone comes to your shop, I can give them your contact information. You can leave your samples here for them to look at if you want."

"Thank you."

Gaturu was craning his neck, trying to glimpse his disgraced former neighbor. "Don't bother about him," said Joyce. "You would think I have a bag of money hidden back here the way he keeps trying to get a look. This is none of his business."

Gaturu seemed to drink in her ignominy as she emerged from Joyce's stall, but she ignored him and walked briskly through the market to the back exit.

***

A week after her stall was closed, Wanjikū received a certified letter from the City Council with a list of seven bullet points of alleged violations at her stall that had required it to be shut down. They seemed to have been randomly selected from the Kanjo manual, including a couple from the restaurant section, such as the requirement that she have two clearly marked bathrooms with running water and adequate drainage. Her hands shook with rage as she scanned the document in disbelief. The letter stated that if these shortcomings were not satisfactorily addressed, not only was she at risk of permanently becoming ineligible for a permit, she also faced potential legal liability as well.

SUNSHINE ON THE CROOKED ROAD

"Those people are devils from hell!" exclaimed Mama Milka the next day when Wanjikū showed her the letter. "I knew they were bad, but not this bad. Maybe you should hire a lawyer."

"With what money?" retorted Wanjikū sourly. "It would have been cheaper to pay the bribe than to hire a lawyer. And who knows if a lawyer would be of any use in such a crooked system?"

"*Lakini*, seriously, these people just wrote down things without thinking. It would be very interesting seeing them trying to explain in court why they want you to fit two toilets into a tiny market stall when there isn't even any running water."

"If the judge was in their pocket, taking the case to court might just make things worse."

Mama Milka clicked her tongue in frustration. "Seriously, where are we going as a country? It's like a tick that sucks so much blood that it becomes bigger than the cow and won't stop sucking until the cow shrivels up and dies. Only then does it realize that without the cow, it will also die."

Wanjikū couldn't see a way out of the situation, but she decided to go to City Hall the next day, nursing the slim hope that a sympathetic official might assist her or point her in the right direction. She went to the main counter and picked a number. There were about ten people in line ahead of her, with a range of facial expressions from ill-masked anxiety to complete insouciance.

The line moved fairly quickly.

"Yes, how may I help you?" abruptly asked the woman behind the desk without so much as a greeting.

"Er . . . My stall at Kariokor Market was closed for a code violation, and I wanted—"

"Where's the letter?"

She slipped the document under the glass pane and watched as the clerk skimmed through it, her lips moving wordlessly.

"Are you here to pay the fine?"

"Um . . . I wanted to find out what my options—"

"You have only two options: You can pay the fine, or you can dispute it."

Her eyes brightened when she heard of the second option. "So how do I go about disputing the fine?"

There was a flicker of surprise in the clerk's otherwise impassive face. "You go to Counter Seventeen and fill out the form. Then you'll get a case number. When you case comes up, you explain your situation to the magistrate. If they rule in your favor, the case is dropped, and you don't have to pay the fine. They will then give you authorization to resume business operations. You'll still have to pay the monthly dues and remain current on your lease until the date of the court case."

"Er . . . How long does it usually take for that process to be completed?"

"Two years."

Two years! Wanjikū's head almost exploded. She knew that worst thing she could do was lose her composure before a government official because dramatic displays of emotion were usually perceived as a challenge to their authority. Anyone who did this would suddenly encounter an inexplicable number of roadblocks, with files going missing and inordinate delays between steps.

"Oh, I didn't realize it would take that long," she said calmly. "That's a bit longer than I'm able to wait. Would you mind telling me about the other alternative?"

Her demeanor must have earned her a few merit points because the clerk's gaze softened a little. "The other option is you pay the fine and any other outstanding monthly dues. Then we schedule a follow-up inspection. If everything is satisfactory, they'll give you a date when you can resume your business."

Wanjikū pressed her for more, in an almost ingratiatory tone that had the effect of pacifying the clerk who was already fidgeting in her seat, ready to move her along and call up the next person. "In terms of

SUNSHINE ON THE CROOKED ROAD 189

inspectors, how do they decide who will do the follow-up inspection? You know . . . scheduling and all that."

"That's normally done by the zone inspectors, the ones assigned to your location. In most instances, they would have been the ones who identified the code violations in the first place, so they're best suited to ensure that the recommended remedial action has been taken to satisfaction."

"Well, I guess that makes sense. Is there ever a situation where they would allow a different inspector from the ones who did the original inspection?"

"Only in the case of a dispute, for which you would need—"

"Counter Seventeen?" said Wanjikū with a smile.

A trace of a smile appeared on the clerk's face, and she dropped her voice. "How long do you have left on your lease?"

"Three months."

Glancing furtively to her left and right, she said, "If I were in your situation, I'd just let it expire when the time comes. You'll still owe the fine and late payment penalties if they ever catch up with you—that is, if you ever try to open another business here—but these people are pathetic at collecting anything that's not going into their own pockets! I'm not supposed to tell you this, but that's what I've seen many people do in situations like yours."

"OK. Thanks for the advice. How much is the fine, by the way?"

"What are the first letter and number on the top right-hand corner of the document I just returned to you?"

"C5."

Her brow furrowed. She pulled up a slender manual and leafed through the pages, then looked up. "Hmm . . . *C*'s are expensive, but better than *D*'s. The fine for a C5 is eighteen thousand shillings."

Wanjikū nodded politely, hiding her dismay. She thanked her for her time.

"I wish I could do more to help," added the clerk, looking genuinely apologetic, as Wanjikū turned to leave.

***

Between the church, the school, and her customers at the stall, word of mouth about her kitenges continued to spread, and she received many calls at home. Once or twice a week, she met with Joyce at the back entrance, and they chatted about what was going on in each other's lives. When the conversation invariably came back to the closed stall, Joyce, in her soft, unperturbable voice, would say, "It will be OK," with such certainty that Wanjikū sometimes wondered if she knew something she wasn't telling. Had she enlisted her benefactor's help—the one who made sure she never had trouble with the Kanjo people? If so, why wasn't she saying anything about it? Wanjikū thought of asking her on one or two occasions but decided she didn't want to put her on the spot if it turned out not to be the case.

At the end of that month, her bill for the monthly lease payment for her stall came as it always did. She considered walking away from what was left of her lease, as the Kanjo clerk had suggested, but decided she would finish out the three months in the hopes that it would be easier to restart her business if things ever got sorted out. From what the clerk had said, there could still be a fine even if she let the lease expire. She felt that disputing an unjust fine might be easier if she'd made the monthly lease payments to the end of the term.

The orders coming in kept her from stewing at home all day while Nyagūthiĩ was at school and Mama Milka at work. Given the probability that she would never get her stall back and would face the same problems with the Kanjo people even if she did, she considered applying for a "real" job. She had applied for several at the same time Mama Milka had, but with no university degree and no special skills besides sewing,

SUNSHINE ON THE CROOKED ROAD

that had come to nothing. There was no reason to think she would do any better now.

In the three months since her stall had been closed, her anger and anxiety over the situation had gradually begun to fade. Then she received another certified letter. Her mind was racing as she ripped open the envelope with trembling hands. The letter was terse and opaque.

Dear Kabogo, Wanjikũ (Mrs.),

With reference to Permit No. 339876 pertaining to Plot No. D64, Kariokor Market, you are hereby requested to appear in person at Nairobi City Council, Department of Permits and Licenses, City Hall, no later than November 15, 1981. Failure to comply may result in permanent revocation of the aforementioned permit.

Yours Faithfully,

Francis Msakwa

Director, Department of Permits and Licenses

She read it over twice, and then again. The instructions were clear enough, but what did it mean? There was no way to tell. When she showed the letter to Mama Milka the following day, she squinting at it at length before irritably smacking the paper with the back of her hand.

"So many big words, just to say nothing! If this Msakwa fellow is trying to ask you for a bribe, he should just say so."

Wanjikū managed a weak smile. "Should I go?"

"Well, it sounds like if you don't, they will cancel your permit, even though the lease has already expired. So I don't think you have much of a choice in case you ever need another business permit in the future."

"They will probably cancel it, anyway. I hope it's not one of those things where I show up and the person calls Kanjo askaris to escort me to Lang'ata Women's Prison until I've paid the fines."

"I doubt it. That would be too extreme, even for them. When are you thinking of going?"

"I don't know. Monday or Tuesday, maybe."

"Let me see if I can talk my boss into giving me a couple of hours off, so I can go with you. That way, if they try to take you to jail, I can show them how we used to settle matters at Kaloleni Martial Arts!"

Wanjikū laughed.

"You know what? I have an even better idea!" Mama Milka exclaimed, snapping her fingers.

"What?"

"You'll see . . . If I can work it out. So what day and what time?"

"Let's say two o'clock, Tuesday, in front of City Hall."

"Sawa, let's do that."

★★★

At the appointed time, Wanjikū saw Mama Milka crossing the street in animated conversation with a big man wearing a bowler hat, a tight black T-shirt, and baggy trousers. His bulging biceps rippled as he gesticulated. When they got to where Wanjikū waited, Mama Milka flashed a big smile and said, "I brought an insurance policy." Seeing Wanjikū's questioning look, she continued. "This is Okoth, an old friend. He's a bouncer and works security for many VIPs in town. Remember when I told you we used to have fighting matches in Kaloleni? Okoth knew the wrath of Millie Mateke. He was a lot smaller then, as you might imagine, but I think he's still afraid of me."

Okoth cracked a smile, then let out a deep rumbling laugh. "*Eh, ni kweli. Alikuwa ananitandika sana tukiwa wadogo.*" ["Yes, it's true. She used to clobber me when we were kids."] His large meaty hand engulfed Wanjikũ's as they shook. While he understood English, he was clearly much more comfortable expressing himself in Kiswahili.

"We'll stay in the waiting area. If things start going sideways, make some noise, and we'll come and rescue you."

Wanjikũ was dubious. "*Ai*, Mama Milka, are you sure? This doesn't seem like a good idea."

"Don't worry, we won't try anything heroic. But if they try to arrest you on made-up charges because you refused to pay a bribe, maybe just having us there will make a difference."

Wanjikũ still looked skeptical.

"It's just a precautionary measure. Kanjo askaris don't carry guns. Not only is Okoth big, he also knows a lot of important people. If he expresses concern about where they're taking you, they might think twice about doing anything foolish."

"*Usijali, mama, hatutaleta shida* [Don't worry, ma'am, we won't cause any trouble]," Okoth echoed with a mischievous grin that didn't exactly reassure her.

They walked into the crowded lobby of City Hall and stopped at the reception desk, where they were directed down a long, dimly lit hallway to Mr. Msakwa's office. She knocked softly on the door with his name on it followed by *Director, Department of Permits and Licenses*, then cautiously opened it. Mama Milka and Okoth remained in the hall. Inside, a gray-haired woman with horn-rimmed spectacles sat typing. "May I help you?" she asked.

"I'm here to see Mr. Msakwa. I received a letter from him telling me to come here. It's about my stall at Kariokor Market."

"Do you have the letter, so I can pull up your file?"

Wanjikū removed the letter from her handbag and handed it over.

"Please wait here," she said, rising from her seat and disappearing through a door behind her desk. She returned shortly with a manila folder, then knocked lightly on the door to Mr. Msakwa's inner sanctum before entering. Wanjikū waited nervously for about five minutes until she came out again and ushered her in.

Mr. Msakwa was an obese middle-aged man with a round face and jowls that quivered when he spoke. He had a lazy half smile that never left his face, and he spoke in a slow, droning voice. "Yes, madam, you have come about your stall in Kariokor Market," he said once she was seated.

She couldn't tell if this was a question or a statement, so she nodded.

"What circumstances led to the stall's closure? I have a report here, but I want to hear it from you, because sometimes there are discrepancies."

She realized that this could well be a trap. Wouldn't accusing representatives of his department of bribing her just get her into trouble? After all, she had no proof. Maybe this was another attempt, albeit dressed up in politeness and officialdom, to extract money from her. Remembering Ngatia's cordiality prior to closing her stall reminded her that even pleasant-seeming people could ask for bribes and become vengeful when they didn't get them.

On the other hand, she hadn't paid the bribe and no intention of doing so now. She had done nothing wrong, and by speaking the truth, she had nothing to lose—or so she hoped. If this man summoned the Kanjo askaris to arrest her anyway, she would have to rely on Mama Milka and Okoth to liberate her, however unlikely that seemed. The askaris would certainly have to enter through the hallway and take her out again that way, so her friend would see them at least.

SUNSHINE ON THE CROOKED ROAD

"Madam," prompted Mr. Msakwa, clearing his throat. "Would you like to tell me what happened?"

She took a deep breath. "My permit was approaching its renewal date, and two City Council officers told me that I had to pay them if I wanted it renewed. I refused. About a week later, I came to the market and found they had closed my stall and sealed it with red tape. Later, I got a letter saying I had several code violations that needed to be corrected before the shop could be reopened."

"What sort of business do you run?"

"I'm a tailor."

"Anything else besides tailoring?"

"No."

He frowned, then looked down and studied the contents of the open manila folder in front of him.

"You don't sell food or own a restaurant?"

"No."

"How long have you been running this business?"

"Two years."

"Did you have any other business in the market before that?"

"No."

"Do you own any other stalls in the market?"

"No."

He sighed and shook his head as he took a final look at the file in front of him before closing it. He scribbled a few short sentences on a yellow legal pad, tore off the sheet, and placed it on top of the folder. Summoning his secretary on the intercom, he handed her the folder with the paper on it and, as she left, turned back to Wanjikū. "Give us a few days to sort this out. You should be able to reopen your stall by Friday at the latest. And you don't owe any fines."

Her heart skipped a beat. With difficulty, she swallowed down the hundred objections she had at the ready and managed to murmur, "Thank you" instead.

"Anything else I can do for you?"

"No. Thank you very much."

"OK. Good luck."

As she rose and walked toward the door, he asked, "So you know Bwana Osotsi?"

"No," she said uncertainly, searching her mind. "No. I'm sure I don't know him."

"Just wondering." When she didn't move, he made shooing gestures with the back of his hand. "Have a good day."

She said goodbye to the secretary and went out into the hall, where Mama Milka paced restlessly while Okoth stood alert, looking ready for anything.

"*Ehe* [Yes]*?*" asked Mama Milka eagerly as they walked down the hall to the lobby.

"Good news! He said I can reopen by Friday. He just asked me some questions, then told me they'd sort it out."

"What? Just like that?"

"Just like that."

"And you believe him?"

"Well, we'll see. But I don't see any reason not to. When I was leaving the office, he asked me if I knew someone called *Omusotsi*, or something like that. It wasn't anyone I know."

★★★

There was a lot of excitement in the corridor on Block D when Wanjikũ showed up on Friday to reopen her stall. The red tape had been removed the previous day by some Kanjo workers, generating heated discussion about what this meant. Had Wanjikũ met the requisite conditions for reopening her stall? Had it been leased to someone else? When she appeared on Friday afternoon carrying large Uchumi bags full of

SUNSHINE ON THE CROOKED ROAD

cleaning supplies, some of the other vendors came out to welcome her back. Wanjikũ even noticed some money changing hands, as if from bets.

"*Umerudi* [You're back]?" asked Nyaga as he emerged from his stall and shook her hand, a huge smile on his face.

"*Eh, nimerudi* [Yes, I'm back]."

"*Haki hao watu wamekutesa bure* [Honestly, those people harassed you for no good reason]," he added sympathetically. He had certainly changed his tune from when he'd admonished her for not giving Ngarĩ and Ngatia what they'd asked for. She knew he hadn't simply come out to greet her—he wanted to know how things had played out with Kanjo.

"*Walikulipisha ngapi* [How much did they make you pay]?" he asked eagerly, clearly prepared to gloat.

"*Sikulipa chochote* [I didn't pay anything]," she said, unable to hide a note of triumph.

"*Kweli* [Really]?"

"*Kabisa* [Absolutely]."

He looked baffled, even dismayed, but nodded graciously and welcomed her again before returning to his stall.

Gaturu called out a loud "Karibu sana!" from behind a disemboweled television he was working on. Joyce, hearing the commotion, emerged from behind her counter, beaming, and gave her a tight squeeze with her good arm.

"Let me finish with this gentleman," she said, turning to the irritated-looking customer waiting at her counter. "Then I'll come over so you can tell me how everything went."

As she opened and cleaned her stall, she realized how glad she was to be back. Not so much that she had a place of business again—she had continued tailoring through her ever-growing network of friends and friends of friends—but because of the genuine sense of belonging she felt here. It didn't hurt when Njogu ambled over from his fruit stand and set a plate piled with sugarcane pieces on her counter.

"*Nimefurahi sana kukuona* [I'm very happy to see you]," he said gruffly, his eyes moist.

"*Asante sana* [Thank you very much]."

Joyce wasn't able to come over for another hour due to a steady stream of customers, but when she did, her eyes shone with excitement. "So, tell me, what happened?" she asked.

Wanjikū had already told her during their weekly rendezvous about the first letter from Kanjo. Now, she told her about the second one and her visit to Mr. Msakwa's office.

"Just like that?"

"Just like that."

"I wonder what happened?"

She studied Joyce's face to make sure she wasn't being facetious. "But Joyce, wasn't it your person who called Kanjo to sort out my issue?"

"My person? What are you talking about?"

"The one who protects you from Kanjo people?"

"Who, Mwangi?"

"I guess that's his name. The brother of the policeman whose house you stayed at."

"Why would Mwangi call Kanjo?"

"I thought maybe you had asked him to."

Joyce looked somewhat deflated, even guilty. "I'm sorry, Wanjikū. I wish I'd felt that I could ask him. Maybe if I were a better friend and a stronger person, I would have, but in all the years I've been here, I've never even spoken to the man. I did pray every day for God to open a way for you."

"Don't be sorry, Joyce. I'm grateful for everything you've done for me. The only reason I thought you might have something to do with it is because I couldn't think of any other explanation for why Kanjo made such an about-face. I still can't."

She was more baffled than ever. Why had Mr. Msakwa contacted her out of the blue and given her such a favorable hearing? That couldn't have happened without someone powerful pulling the strings. If Mwangi hadn't been behind it, who had? "I was so afraid of what they might do to me, I even went there with a bouncer!"

That got a laugh out of Joyce. "You must be joking."

"No, I'm serious."

"What did you think they would do?"

"I thought they might arrest me for unpaid fines and march me off to jail."

Joyce laughed again. "Only if you're lucky. The usual punishment for a first offense of not paying your market stall bribe is the firing squad!"

Now, it was Wanjikū's turn to laugh. "I'm just glad to be back."

Chapter 26

August 1 1982

Wanjikũ tossed and turned as she listened to the scattered *twa! twa! twa!* in the distance, wondering what it was. Had it been November, she would have chalked it up to the fireworks the Ahĩndĩ in Ngara and Parklands set off during Diwali, but this was late in the night on July 31. On other nights, she'd heard similar-sounding bursts that she'd learned to associate with a robbery or police chase, but these were more continuous and widespread, suggesting strings of firecrackers. Was there some victory or holiday being celebrated that she wasn't aware of? That seemed possible, especially since it was a Saturday.

Kabogo often came home late, around three or four in the morning. His long-winded explanations usually involved some last-minute crisis at work that only he had the expertise to handle. She internally rolled her eyes at each successive tale of his quick wit and dedication and the company mandarins' gratitude. Though she felt more relaxed when he wasn't there, on a night like this, she would rather he'd been home early, if only for a second opinion as to what was going on.

When she awoke in the morning from her restless sleep and realized it was six thirty, she was unnerved to see his side of the bed empty. Where was he? She knew he went to the office sometimes on weekends, so she decided to call to see if he was there. The phone rang unanswered, and she replaced the receiver. Sometimes he went out with friends and people from work, but she didn't really know them besides hearing their names mentioned, and certainly didn't have their phone numbers. She decided she would try to call the office again a little later.

Nyagũthiĩ was still asleep. Opening the fridge, Wanjikũ realized the half packet of milk would be insufficient for breakfast. Slipping on a dress and sweater, she headed over to Bhatia's shop. It was typically open by seven on weekends, but when she got there about ten after, the doors were still shut. Otondi was up, though, slouched in his chair and staring at the ground. She decided to try one of the kiosks on Ring Road. As she walked through the gate onto the main road, it was immediately apparent that something wasn't right. There were plenty of people out and about, but all of them were carrying consumer goods—televisions, stereos, piles of clothes—none of which were in boxes or shopping bags. Some people walked in pairs carrying bigger items between them such as furniture and appliances, and a few pushed *mikokoteni* on which several large items had been stacked.

"*Nini inaendelea* [What's going on]?" she asked one man who passed by, a large Sanyo television perched on his shoulder.

"*Serikali imepinduliwa* [The government has been overthrown]," he replied without any hint of emotion.

"*Ati nini* [What]?"

"*Kweli kabisa, mama. Hata town kumejaa maiti* [Very true, ma'am. In fact, the streets in town are littered with corpses]."

She gasped and felt her body go numb as she realized now what the popping sounds she'd heard all night had been. Watching the steady procession of people carrying looted merchandise, the calmness of the scene, even with the intermittent sound of gunshots in the distance, added to the sense of unreality.

"*Kuna mali ya bure huko nyuma* [There's free stuff back there]," someone else said to her as he passed. When someone carrying a shop mannequin passed by, she wondered if she were caught up in a surrealist dream. She decided to return to the flat and turn on the radio to see if there was news about what was going on.

Back at the flat, she found Nyagūthiĩ awake and wondering where she'd been. She would have preferred not to tune in the radio to potential mayhem around her nine-year-old daughter, but she was desperate. At first, all she could find was martial music playing on a loop, but after a few minutes, a broadcaster said that the announcement a few hours earlier about the government having been overthrown was nothing more than *porojo* [idle chatter], and that President Moi's government was firmly in control.

"What's going on, Mommy?" Nyagūthiĩ asked.

"I don't know. I think I'm going to call Mama Milka to see what she knows."

"Mommy, are we safe? Where's Daddy?"

"I don't know. I don't know where Daddy is."

"But Mommy—"

"Shh! I need to concentrate," she said impatiently as she dialed Mama Milka's number.

She answered on the first ring.

"Hi, Mama Milka. Are you and your family all right?"

"We are safe here. We are going to wait until things settle down before going out of the house. Please be safe as well." Her tone was cautious and unnatural.

"Do you know what's going on?"

"Apparently, there was an attempted coup, but fortunately, the government forces have prevailed," she said stiffly.

This was very unlike Mama Milka. Wanjikū wanted to ask her what was really happening with her, but she knew her odd response was probably because government security agents routinely eavesdropped on the phone lines. "OK, Mama Milka. You know you can call me if you need anything."

"Yes. Thank you. Goodbye."

Wanjikū slowly hung up the phone, a pensive expression on her face.

"Mommy, what's going on? Tell me!"

"Well, some people tried to take over the government by force, but they were defeated. That's all I know. We need to wait for more updates on the news."

"Are we going to be OK?"

"I think so."

"And Daddy?"

"I'll try calling his office again to see if his there. Maybe I'll check with Uncle Ngotho as well. Or hopefully he'll call and let us know where he is." She got up quickly to fill the kettle so her daughter wouldn't see the irritation mixed with fear in her eyes. Where was Kabogo? Even if it wasn't safe for him to come home, he could at least call to let her know he was OK. She felt her blood curdle remembering the man on Ring Road's comment that the streets in town were strewn with corpses. *Please, God, let him be alive*, she thought. *I'm not ready to be a widow!* She could feel that she was starting to hyperventilate and tried to slow her breathing.

"Turn off the kettle when the water boils, Nyagūthiĩ. I'm going to the bathroom." Nyagūthiĩ, seeing that her mother was upset, looked alarmed. "It's OK. I'm not leaving the house."

Nyagūthiĩ nodded warily.

Deep breaths. It's going to be OK, she told herself when she closed the door behind her. But was it? If Kabogo was dead, she would have to figure out what to do for income. The clothes she sold at the market didn't bring in enough money to cover household expenses. Yes, Kabogo was thoughtless and insensitive. She remembered that he had never seen the need to replace her rickety and capricious Datsun that sometimes stalled in traffic—a danger both to her and his own daughter—while at the same time buying a brand-new Peugeot for himself. But she had to admit that, for all his annoying habits, he at least worked hard and provided for their needs without too much grumbling. She wasn't prepared to start over as a single mother without any money.

"Mommy, are you going to come out?" called Nyagūthiī from outside the bathroom door.

"I'll be right there," she said, roused from her musings. In the mirror, she saw a frightened woman who had no plan for what to do if her worst fears were realized. She practiced a reassuring smile for Nyagūthiī, but it looked more like a grimace. Not falling apart would have to be enough. "No fear and no tears," she whispered to herself as she opened the bathroom door.

When she answered the phone a short while later, she was annoyed at herself for being almost crushingly disappointed that it wasn't Kabogo. Her mother and father had heard about the trouble in Nairobi and wanted to make sure that they were OK. They had installed a phone in their Gīthakainī house two years earlier, so now Wanjikū spoke to them often.

"Are you people well, with everything that we're hearing?"

"Things are tense but OK so far," she replied. "We're still waiting for more news about what's going on." Over time, her parents had stopped asking about Kabogo after picking up on the awkward pauses in her replies and the unconvincing explanations she offered for his unavailability whenever they asked to say hello to him. She was especially glad that they were out of the habit of asking about him today, because telling them that he wasn't home and hadn't been in touch would have made them nearly as frantic as she was. Besides, if she expressed her fears, she might break down, which she didn't want to do in front of Nyagūthiī.

After the phone call, she tried Kabogo's office again and got no response. She also called Ngotho, who hadn't heard from Kabogo, either, and grew rather concerned. "I hope he's safe," he said. "There's chaos everywhere. I'll let you know if I hear anything."

It was a long morning. First, she hovered over the radio, waiting for updates as she sipped a mug of acrid-tasting *turungi* [black tea], having

SUNSHINE ON THE CROOKED ROAD 205

run out of milk. Later, she decided to cook some rice and lentils to give herself something to do while she waited for updates. Television broadcasts on VOK wouldn't start until midday. Through it all, she waited for the phone to ring, even double- and triple-checking to make sure she had replaced the receiver properly after speaking with her parents. Her one triumph was that Nyagūthiĩ seemed reassured by her veneer of calm, looking through books at the kitchen table and humming quietly to herself as she always did.

When the phone rang again around eleven o'clock, they were both startled. Wanjikū turned down the flame on the stove and ran to pick it up. Nyagūthiĩ got there first but waited for her mother to answer. It was Kabogo.

"Kabogo, where are you? We've been worried about you!" she said irritably.

"Wah, it's been a crazy night! I'm at my cousin Mūkuria's place in Rūirū, which is where I went when the chaos started. We heard from people leaving town and coming this way that there was fighting in Eastleigh, around the air force base, so I decided it wasn't safe to try coming that way."

"You should have called and let us know where you were!"

"I wanted to call earlier, but Mūkuria doesn't have a phone in his house, and we couldn't risk walking around at night with everything that was going on."

"When are you coming home?"

"We're getting ready to walk over to where the matatus from town drop off passengers so we can hear what the manambas are saying about the situation downtown. If things have settled down, I'll come. Either way, I'll let you know. I don't want to try coming when the situation isn't safe."

"OK, but let us know as soon as you can."

Wanjikū hung up and heaved a sigh of relief. Nyagūthiĩ looked at her expectantly, though she had already pieced most of it together from her mother's side of the conversation. "I didn't know I had an Uncle Mūkuria," said Nyagūthiĩ when her mother relayed the part she hadn't heard.

"Your father has many relatives. I don't know most of them, either, but it doesn't matter. At least he had somewhere to go rather than risk driving here last night."

Based on newscasts later in the day—both on the radio and the TV—the coup attempt had indeed been quashed. A massive security crackdown ensued, with arrests of many people suspected of having been involved. The universities—perennial hotbeds of political activism—were shut down and students directed to report on a weekly basis to the local chiefs in their home districts. A dusk-to-dawn curfew was imposed, and citizens were required to have their identification cards ready for inspection at the numerous police checkpoints that appeared throughout the country.

Kabogo called back an hour later and reported that, based on what they'd heard from the people in the trickle of matatus that had managed to leave downtown, it wasn't safe yet. He did make it home the next day around noon and seemed none the worse for wear. In fact, he held forth on the events of the previous forty-eight hours with relish, though most were secondhand accounts. In fact, Wanjikū wasn't sure that he had even been in earshot of the gunfire. Since he said that things had looked peaceful in their immediate environs on his way in, she decided to go down to Bhatia's to get a few groceries, desperate not to have to endure another cup of turungi.

Otondi was sitting in his plastic chair, staring vacantly at the ground as usual. She wished she could peek into his brain to see what he had made of the commotion yesterday and the sound of gunfire the night before.

Inside the shop, everything seemed normal except that the shelves of staples were mostly empty. The two customers inside had piled much of what was left into their baskets. She grabbed the two loaves of brown

SUNSHINE ON THE CROOKED ROAD

bread that remained on the bread shelf and hurried to the milk section, only to find it empty.

"*Maziwa imeisha* [Is the milk finished]?" she called out to Bhatia, who was ringing up another customer.

"*Pole, mama. Kwisha kabisa. Imekuja kidogo sana leo* [Sorry, ma'am. It's completely finished. I only got a small supply today]."

She groaned in disappointment.

"*Kesho mimi naweka yako mbili* [I'm gonna save two packets for you tomorrow]."

"*Asante, nimeshukuru* [Thanks, I appreciate it]."

She walked up and down the aisles, looking for other items that might run out soon—soap, toilet paper, rice—then walked up to the counter with her odd assortment of groceries. Bhatia smiled at her, then started adding up the purchases. He glanced over her shoulder as the previous customer exited the store, then said, "*Jeshi pana mzuri kuongoza nchi; najua bunduki tu* [The military is not suited to run a country; they only know how to use guns]."

"*Kweli kabisa* [Very true]," she replied in a low voice, turning to make sure they were alone.

"*Nimeona hii wakati ya Amin. Mi naishi Kampala mbeleni lakini Amin nafukuza Mhindi yote, ndiyo nakuja hapa* [I witnessed this in Amin's time. I used to live in Kampala, but Amin drove out Asians, so I came here]."

Wanjikū was surprised to hear this. "*Haiya, sikuwa najua wewe ni Mganda* [Oh, I didn't realize you were Ugandan]."

"*Pana Mganda sasa—Amin nasema hiyo. Nazaliwa huko lakini mimi Mkenya sasa* [I'm not Ugandan anymore—Amin told us that. I was born there, but I'm Kenyan now]."

"*Kweli. We ni mmoja wetu sasa* [True. You're one of us now]."

She remembered Ravi and his experience around the time of that episode, recounting this to Bhatia. The details were hazy in her recollection, but his eyes lit up nonetheless.

"*Kweli? We nasikia hiyo habari America* [Really? You heard the news in America]*?*"

"*Kabisa* [Absolutely]."

He wanted to know more about Ravi, and she wasn't sure why. So many years had passed since she'd last spoken to Ravi that she didn't remember his last name, which seemed to frustrate Bhatia as he offered a couple of last names that didn't ring a bell. Then he put his fingers behind his years, fanning them outward and asked, "*Masikio kubwa kama chapati* [Big ears like chapati]*?*"

She burst out laughing at the vivid description but still had doubts they were talking about the same person.

"He is engineering professor in Boston, no?" Bhatia pressed on, making a rare switch to English.

"I think so! Ravi moved to Boston before we left. But how would you know Ravi?"

Bhatia chuckled with glee, shaking his head in disbelief. "*Ravi ni kama mtoto yangu. Yeye na kijana yangu, Anuj—best friends, kabisa! Kila siku pamoja. Wakati sisi nafukuzwa, familia yake yote naenda Canada, sisi nakuja Kenya. Anuj sasa iko America—wako pamoja kila wakati.*" ["Ravi is like my child. He and my son, Anuj, were best friends, joined at the hip. When we were forced to leave, his family went to Canada, and we came here. Anuj now lives in America—they're together all the time."]

Wanjikū was amazed by this coincidence, and the joy of the discovery took away the sting of returning home without milk. As she turned to leave and another customer walked in, Bhatia called out after her, "*Pana sahau kesho, mi naweka hiyo vile tumeongea* [Don't forget tomorrow. I'll set it aside like we discussed]."

"*Sawa, asante* [Great, thanks]," she replied as she emerged from the store and out into the bright sunlight.

Chapter 27

One day in early 1983, Kabogo came home and announced that he had received a promotion and would be heading the newly established Mombasa division of Koenig Pharma, due to open in a few weeks. Wanjikū hadn't kept close track of his career, but a promotion sounded like a positive development. *Maybe we'll finally get a house of our own somewhere nice, like Racecourse, instead of continuing to pay rent here,* she thought. They had been in Kariokor for almost seven years, which was far longer than she had imagined they would stay.

The way he explained it, he would fly to Mombasa on Sunday evenings and return to Nairobi after work on Thursdays, working at the Ruaraka office on Fridays. The company would provide an apartment for him in Mombasa.

"Yay! Then we can come to the beach during school holidays!" Nyagūthiī exclaimed. She had been sitting at the dining table doing her homework, and Kabogo hadn't realized she could hear him.

"Now, look at this one," he said with a rare grin, pointing in her direction. "You're supposed to be doing your homework, and instead you're eavesdropping on other people's conversations."

"I wasn't eavesdropping. I just heard it. If you were discussing something private, you should have told me to cover my ears."

"OK, cover your ears."

She rolled her eyes. "So can we come to Mombasa when school is closed?"

"Let's wait and see. I don't even know what kind of place they'll give me."

Given the number of evenings he came home late, and the times he was so surly and unpredictable she wished he hadn't come home at all, there didn't seem to be a downside to this new arrangement. She had readily gotten on board with the plan, but when she mentioned it to Mama Milka that weekend, her friend's reaction was a lot more nuanced.

It was Saturday morning, and they were sitting at a café in Nairobi West, near the Obonyos' house. Baba Milka was watching the girls while the two women stepped out, ostensibly to get groceries but mostly to talk privately about the new development with Kabogo's job. It was impossible to have a conversation during the week, with Wanjikũ at the market and Mama Milka at her job. Even when they were together on the weekend, they usually had the girls with them.

"Wouldn't it make more sense for all of you to move there? Even if Kabogo has to be at the Nairobi office once a week, he can fly back to Nairobi on Thursday evening and return to Mombasa after work on Friday."

Wanjikũ visceral reaction to this suggestion made her realize how much she was looking forward to having Kabogo out of the house from Sunday through Thursday. At the same time, she recognized Mama Milka had a valid point. "Well, for one thing, I don't want Nyagũthiĩ to change schools. Most schools in other parts of the country are not as good as what we have here. And I'd hate for her to be separated from Milka and her other friends."

"OK," said Mama Milka, rocking her head from side to side. "I can see how that might be a problem . . . and obviously, I don't want you

SUNSHINE ON THE CROOKED ROAD

to go. *Lakini* . . . this business of having a part-time husband . . . How does that even work?"

Wanjikū's lips curled into a sardonic smile. "Nyako, you know that zero divided by two is still zero? Right now, I don't even see him, so why should I worry about him commuting to Mombasa? It would even be worse for Nyagūthiĩ and me if we moved with him, because we would be far away from all our friends and family."

Mama Milka still looked skeptical. "I don't know about those long-distance relationships. It's certainly not going to help your marriage."

Wanjikū sighed, trying to hide her irritation. "You know, you're fortunate to have a husband like Baba Milka, who actually thinks of someone other than himself. My situation is different from yours. I dropped out of college to follow Kabogo to America, and now . . ."

"Yes, I know. But if you're interested in working on your marriage, this is not the way to do it."

"*Ai,* nyako, seriously! These things only work if both people are interested," snapped Wanjikū.

Mama Milka decided it was time to back off. "Sorry," she said quickly. "I'm not helping. Let me shut up now." She glanced at her watch. "Forgive me for being *kimbelembele* [presumptuous]. You know, even a fool can be mistaken for a clever person if he keeps his mouth shut. I should have thought of that before I opened mine."

Wanjikū felt abashed as she realized that Mama Milka wasn't whom she was mad at. "Sawa, I'm sorry I snapped at you."

The waiter brought the bill for the tea and mandazi, which Wanjikū insisted on paying. Then they picked up a few items at one of the grocery shops and started the short drive back.

What Mama Milka had said made perfect sense, and pointed up the obvious issue Wanjikū had been unwilling to consider. However, given her familiarity with all the messy details of life in the dysfunctional

Kabogo household, Wanjikū had expected a more understanding response.

Chapter 28

That August, Wanjikū and Nyagūthiĩ visited Kabogo in Mombasa during Nyagūthiĩ's school holidays. Nyagūthiĩ was ten years old and full of excitement, having heard stories from her schoolmates about their family vacations at the coast. Only well-off families could afford to take these trips, and even among these, there was a hierarchy based on the specific location one visited and whether they traveled by road, rail, or airplane.

"On an airplane! For real? Yay!" Nyagūthiĩ exclaimed when Wanjikū informed her of this detail in the plan that had just fallen into place earlier in the day. The trip wouldn't have materialized if it were not for Nyagūthiĩ relentlessly hounding Kabogo about it. He warned them that he would be mostly working and unavailable during their visit, but it was clear from their faces that neither of them expected this to have any meaningful impact on their plans.

When they landed at Moi International Airport, they were met by a stout smiling man with graying hair who held up a sign that read, "Kabogo Family." He was a driver at Koenig, and Kabogo had sent him. After a polite exchange of greetings, he took their suitcases and led them to a sleek, burgundy Volvo, opening the doors for them. Wanjikū caught the look of astonishment on Nyagūthiĩ's face and winked at her, trying not to let her own excitement show. However, it was her turn to be awestruck twenty-five minutes later when they drove into a gated complex with white two-story houses with red-tiled roofs in Nyali, an upscale part of town.

"Karibuni," he said as came to a stop outside one of the homes and opened the car doors. He then proceeded to retrieve the suitcases from the trunk. They stood hesitantly next to the car until the front door of the house opened, and a wiry, energetic man in his thirties emerged. He introduced himself as Rashid, the domestic help. Ushering them in, he took their suitcases from the driver and followed them into the elegantly furnished living room. They surveyed their surroundings in awkward silence.

"Karibuni sana," he said. Upon seeing the bewildered looks on their faces, he added, "Oh, you don't speak Kiswahili? Welcome to Mombasa."

Wanjikū told him she did indeed speak Kiswahili. It wasn't until minutes later when they were alone in the Nyagūthiī's bedroom that they could talk.

"Mom, are we in the right place?"

"It's a very nice house, Nyagūthiī. ! I think we're in the right place. Unless it was a case of mistaken identity, which would be a very strange coincidence . . . but no, the driver did say he worked for Dad's company—"

Just then, the phone rang in the living room, followed a few moments later by a soft knock at the door. It was Rashid. "Mrs. Kabogo, your husband is on the phone." He turned around, and Wanjikū and Nyagūthiī followed him into the living room.

"Hello?"

"Hi. I was checking to make sure you got here OK."

"Yes, we did. We're getting settled in."

Kabogo sounded cordial. He said he was busy at work and got right down to business, suggesting activities they might find interesting, such

SUNSHINE ON THE CROOKED ROAD

as the beach, the swimming pool, and the ice cream shop. "If you need anything, ask Rashid. He can show you what there is to see because he worked for many years at one of those tourist hotels. I don't get around much, so you may end up learning more about Mombasa than I do by the time you head back to Nairobi."

Rashid was a great cook and had made a pasta dish for lunch. After they had eaten, he showed them the swimming pool in the compound, then took them about a hundred yards down a shaded path onto a quiet spot on the beach. There was no one else there. Nyagūthiĩ, already in her swimsuit, squealed with excitement when she caught sight of the ocean and took off running across the smooth white sand. A satisfied grin came over Rashid's face. "You can rest here for a while," he said, spreading out *kikois* [multipurpose woven Swahili cloths] onto the sand for her and Nyagūthiĩ to sit or lie on. "When you want to come back to the house, just go through that black gate there, and come to the third house on the left."

Wanjikū thanked him and sat on a kikoi, watching Nyagūthiĩ splashing blissfully in the water. A mild breeze kept it from getting too hot, and the booming of the waves lulled her into a serene torpor that was interrupted when Nyagūthiĩ came running, dripping wet, and lay down on her kikoi. "This is going to be so much fun, Mom! We're living like rich people."

Wanjikū frowned. "It's a very beautiful place, dear, but we're not rich."

"But Mom, Dad must be making a lot of money. Otherwise, he wouldn't be living here."

"It's not his house. It belongs to the company."

"But still, they wouldn't give him a house like this if they weren't paying him a lot of money."

Nyagūthiĩ was savvy for her age in matters like this. Even the fact that they flew to Mombasa rather than take the train or a bus had not escaped her attention. Wanjikū remained silent. She was thinking about the times she had told Kabogo that they needed to find a house of their own, rather than continuing to pay rent in the Kariokor flat. He always had an excuse, and she had assumed he was unduly cautious. Now, it was hard to see how he could continue to live here for part of the week and spend the weekends in Kariokor—two worlds that were wholly unlike each other.

They spent about two hours at the beach and then returned to the house. Rashid was preparing four o'clock tea, which they felt a bit excessive, as they were still full from lunch. But he was very gracious, and they didn't want to offend him.

Kabogo didn't come home until after dinner, around nine o'clock. After a perfunctory exchange of greetings and an inquiry into how they'd spent their afternoon, he sat down to the warmed-up dinner Rashid placed on the table for him and started flipping through a folder from work. Wanjikū and Nyagūthiï lingered in the living room until Rashid announced he was headed home for the day. After he departed, both Wanjikū and Nyagūthiï headed to the bedrooms, leaving Kabogo deep in thought at the dining table.

★★★

The week went by fast, and it was soon time for them to return to Nairobi. Rashid had done an exceptional job ensuring their stay was pleasant, and they'd both enjoyed kicking back and savoring his delightful cooking. For Nyagūthiï, the beach was top on every day's agenda. They sometimes spent hours there in the morning, then returned after lunch. She learned that Rashid had a daughter her age and had been excited at the prospect of a playmate. However, Rashid, in a firm but courteous tone, said it would be inappropriate for him, the domestic help, to bring his daughter to socialize with his boss's child. Nyagūthiï thought this absurd and was about to press the issue but caught the sharp look in her mother's eye, warning her that doing so would put Rashid in an awkward, uncomfortable situation.

They saw little of Kabogo all week save for his late-evening appearances, where he was usually preoccupied with work-related matters. Even though he had warned them ahead of time, his absence still seemed excessive—almost as if he was going out of his way to minimize the time he spent with them. By the end of their visit, Nyagũthiĩ appeared resentful about this, and it seemed to drain the joy from the happy experiences they'd had on the trip.

Chapter 29

Wanjikū noticed that whenever Nyagūthiī spoke about the Mombasa trip afterward, she mentioned only the two of them and Rashid, as if Kabogo hadn't been there. When he came to Kariokor on the weekends, she interacted with him in a manner that was cold and aloof.

In Mombasa, Wanjikū had again brought up the issue of buying a new house and moving out of the rented flat in Kariokor. While admitting it was something worth considering, Kabogo remained non-committal. She mentioned it once more when they were back in Nairobi, but he gave a meandering answer that was light on specifics. Undeterred, she planned to revisit the issue in a few weeks, not wanting it to fall off the radar as before, but something happened about ten days later that caused a significant change in their relationship.

She woke up one Tuesday morning with cramping in the lower part of her belly. Initially, she thought it was a urinary infection, something she'd experienced before. However, when she developed an itchy discharge, she was overcome by dread and confusion. Then anger set in as she reflected on the fact that Kabogo was the only person she had been intimate with. Even before he'd started work in Mombasa, they'd had a few heated conversations about his coming home late. He had stated

SUNSHINE ON THE CROOKED ROAD 219

that his work was demanding, and that he needed to put in lots of extra hours to meet the expectations of his superiors, but that explanation seemed unconvincing.

Having weighed her options prior to the most recent conversation, she had acknowledged the grim reality that she and Nyagũthiĩ were still dependent on him financially. When she'd started the kitenge business, she had hoped to remedy the imbalance, but her business hadn't taken off as well as she'd hoped. Even now, in the 1980s, divorce was not common, and what terrified her most about divorce cases was that the odds were often stacked against the woman, based on how the laws were worded or interpreted. It was conceivable in a situation like hers that a judge would assign Kabogo primary custody of Nyagũthiĩ on the grounds of his demonstrable ability to provide financially for her. And this was assuming a judge approached the case with a neutral mind as opposed to having auctioned off a favorable verdict prior to the hearing. The fear of having Nyagũthiĩ taken away from her eclipsed all other fears, including the fear of dying.

On this day, as she looked back at how things had turned out, she wasn't angry at herself for not having walked away from the marriage—she was angry at those occasional nights when he had sidled up close to her at bedtime, and she gone along without making a fuss, including on the recent trip to Mombasa. If staying in a difficult marriage for the sake of her daughter's welfare had been strategic, perhaps even honorable, those lapses in discretion, with his pattern of staying out late, had been utter foolishness.

She rarely called him at the office unless she had to, and this was one of those situations. The receptionist asked if it was urgent, and she replied that it was important, which led to an awkward pause as the other party attempted to decipher whether there was a meaningful distinction between those terms. Ultimately, she decided there wasn't and patched her through to Kabogo, who had been called out of a meeting.

"Hey, what's going on? Is everything OK?" he asked.

"Kabogo, I have a discharge."

"A what?"

"A discharge, like an STD."

"I'm not sure I'm following—"

"You know what an STD is! How did I end up with an STD? You're the only one I've been with," she said, feeling the blood rush to her head. Her hand holding the telephone receiver was shaking.

"I have no idea, Wanjikũ. How would I know? I don't have an STD, so I don't know where you got it. Are you even sure it's an STD?"

"You think I don't know my own body?"

"That's not what I said. I was just asking if you were sure it was an STD or something else. I don't know how you got it because—"

Wanjikũ abruptly hung up and sat at the kitchen table, her face buried in her hands. Tears started to flow. The phone rang. It was probably Kabogo. She had no desire to talk to him anymore and let it ring unanswered. Not only was she certain he was lying, but she was upset by his insinuation that she might have gotten the infection from someone else. Her immediate priority, however, was to see a doctor. She picked up the phone book and was about to call their family doctor's office, then had second thoughts. Dr. Mueke took care of all three of them, and was on cordial terms with Kabogo, which would make this situation extremely awkward. She flipped through the yellow pages and stopped on a familiar clinic she recognized from TV commercials. As she prepared to make the phone call, she glanced up toward the door of the spare bedroom. When she returned from the doctor's office, she would work on new sleeping arrangements.

★★★

She decided to proactively let Nyagũthii know of the bedroom changes that evening, worried that her daughter might come looking for her in

SUNSHINE ON THE CROOKED ROAD

the night and be alarmed to find the master bedroom empty. Usually, Nyagũthiĩ slept through the night, but she didn't want to take any chances. Nyagũthiĩ already knew she spent a lot of time during the day in the spare room because that was where she did her sewing. It wasn't very spacious, and with the sewing machine and kitenge material, it felt even more crowded. To reduce the clutter and make room for her clothes, she stored most of the kitenge fabric and some of the completed outfits in her now-empty closet in the master bedroom.

A grave look fell across Nyagũthiĩ's face when she told her the news. "Why, Mom? Are you and Dad getting a divorce?"

"Not exactly. But we haven't been getting along lately, and I need my space."

"But why can't he sleep in the spare bedroom and not you?"

Wanjikũ held her breath for a few moments. "Well, I . . . er, I spend a lot of time in that room, anyway, because that's where I do my work. I don't mind sleeping there."

"He's never home. I still think you should get the bigger room."

Wanjikũ didn't reply. She studied her daughter. There was an indignant look on the ten-year-old's face. "Are you OK, Nyagũthiĩ?"

"Dad is mean. We should move out of this house and live on our own."

"I'm sorry you have to go through this. But divorce isn't that simple, either," she said softly.

All day, she had been mulling over the financial implications of leaving Kabogo. Even though she had put aside as much as she could from the sale of kitenges, it was an erratic business, making it impossible to plan. It was not unheard of to go a week, sometimes two, without a single order. Her returns from the market stall were even less consistent than those from the orders she got at home. Reflecting on this earlier in the day, she had concluded that her monthly lease payment at the market would be better applied to a rent payment or savings for a rainy day. She planned to go to Kanjo the following day to inquire about canceling the remainder of her lease. Since this wasn't a situation like the previous time, when she had been fined and her stall shut down, she hoped the process of cancellation might be simpler. If it wasn't, she would simply do what the clerk advised her the last time—walk away from the lease, and hope she would never need to apply for another permit in future. Without an official business location, she would either have to have customers come to her house for measurements or meet them at theirs. This had worked for many of the word-of-mouth referrals but would certainly limit the size of her customer base. It wasn't an ideal situation but would have to do for the time being.

Nyagūthiī's observation about her getting the master bedroom made sense, and she had initially considered this. However, moving into the room where she already did her sewing was the most straightforward option and the one least likely to require any interaction with Kabogo.

She considered returning to her parents' home in Gīthakainī but ruled it out as a viable option. While her parents would not refuse to take her in if she asked, Gīthakainī was an hour and a half away, and there were no schools there of the same caliber as the one Nyagūthiī attended. She also remembered Nyina wa Nduta's lesson on her wedding day, with the young men carrying a bed to the reception hall to indicate to her that Gīthakainī was no longer considered her home.

On Thursday, which was when Kabogo normally returned to Nairobi, he didn't come home. In fact, he didn't show up all weekend. This reinforced her suspicions about his having been the source of the STD, identified as gonorrhea at the clinic. He showed up the following weekend but did not make any mention of the STD issue or the new sleeping arrangements. In fact, he was courteous and even asked if there were any additional household expenses that needed attention. Nyagūthiī avoided him the entire weekend, staying in her bedroom and coming out only when she was sure he had left the house.

Life settled into this peculiar equilibrium in the weeks and months that followed. Kabogo still came home on most weekends, which

SUNSHINE ON THE CROOKED ROAD

Wanjikũ found baffling since neither she nor Nyagũthiĩ showed much interest in interacting with him. Nyagũthiĩ, now a preteen, had no use for subtlety when expressing anger or hostility, and hiding in her room when Kabogo was home was typically the most charitable treatment she accorded him. Wanjikũ still talked to him about household administrative matters like rent, bills, and occasional updates regarding family members from either side. That he still took responsibility for all the expenses around the home was helpful, though hardly deserving of her gratitude.

As Nyagũthiĩ entered upper primary school, Wanjikũ felt a growing apprehension knowing that in a few years, her daughter would be done with primary school and ready to move on to secondary school. The most desirable schools for her next step in her education were boarding schools. Having spent a lot of one-on-one time with her daughter, she wasn't looking forward to not having her around. Besides this, she wasn't particularly excited at the thought of being alone in the house with Kabogo when he came home on weekends.

Chapter 30

June 1985

Wanjikū and Nyagūthiĩ usually referred to the Datsun as *KMT*, based on the first three letters of its license plate. For an old car, it was surprisingly resilient, bouncing back from one mechanical problem after another under the care of Owino, the local mechanic whose shop was a short distance from Bhatia's duka. Owino was a big man with a twinkle in his eyes and a booming laugh, which announced where he was in the garage when Wanjikū brought in KMT with a new problem or walked there from her house when it refused to start.

Even after Kabogo began spending most of the week in Mombasa, she never felt comfortable driving his Peugeot 504. In part, this was because she was upset that it had never occurred to him that she might need a newer car, and her rejection of the car was a stand-in for how she felt about him and his thoughtlessness. There had been a few occasions when KMT wouldn't start that she had taken the Peugeot, but she always referred to it with slight distaste as "my husband's car."

KMT felt more like a person than a car to her—quirky and unpredictable, but an important part of her life. It had featured in many memorable events: their first drive around Nairobi with Kabogo at the wheel and Nyagūthiĩ in her lap; the stir it had caused with their parents when

SUNSHINE ON THE CROOKED ROAD

they'd visited their respective homes to show it off; those first terrifying solo outings after she'd learned to drive; the nerve-racking occasions when it stalled out in an unfamiliar part of town; even the reassurance she felt when Owino popped open the hood and started tinkering as he sang softly to himself in Dholuo. None of those memories, however, was as vivid as what happened one Saturday night in June.

She had dropped off Nyagūthiĩ at Mama Milka's around midday for a sleepover. After spending the early afternoon alone in the house, she'd decided on a whim to visit her Aunt Nyagura, her mother's older sister, who lived near Dagoretti Corner. Aunt Nyagura lived alone and was delighted by the unexpected visit. She had insisted on preparing an entire meal from scratch, starting with diced onions and tomatoes, *dhania* [coriander], and Kimbo cooking fat. Though it was fun to work together in the small kitchen, chatting while they prepared dinner, Aunt Nyagura was much the better cook. She worked so fast and effortlessly that Wanjikũ sometimes felt she was getting in the way. Within two hours, they were sitting at her dining table enjoying a delectable dinner of rice, chicken stew, *sukuma wiki* [collard greens], and chapati.

She liked that Aunt Nyagura treated her like a friend, even though she was a couple of years older than Wanjikũ's mother. They exchanged updates about relatives they had spoken to recently, and she was gratifyingly incredulous when Wanjikũ told her all about Nyagūthiĩ. "But how is that even possible? *Si* I was just holding her the other day! Just a *ka*-little baby when you people came back from America! Ati now she's almost a teenager? Ngatho! Kwani, what are you feeding her?"

The hours went by quickly and pleasurably, and it was only when Wanjikũ looked at the clock and realized that it was almost nine that she decided she needed to get going. The traffic on Ngong Road was starting to thin, so she made good time to the Haile Selassie Roundabout, where her trouble began. Stopped at the traffic light with several cars ahead of her, she heard a tapping on the front passenger window and looked up, expecting to see one of the chokoras who asked for money at traffic lights, though not usually at night. Instead, she saw a gun pointed at her through the glass. Her whole body went numb. She opened her mouth to scream, but no sound came out. The man behind the gun pointed at the lock. Trembling, she reached out and pulled it up to unlock the door, her eyes fixed on the gun.

"*Kanyaga mafuta, twende* [Step on it, let's go]!" said a bearded man who wore a hat and had a booming voice as he slid into the passenger seat, keeping the gun pointed at her. The light had turned green, and the other cars began to move. She let out a frightened whimper.

"*Ala! Unangoja nini? Twende* [What! What are you waiting for? Let's go]!"

As she released the clutch and stepped on the gas pedal, the car moved forward with none of its usual jerkiness. Her heart pounded in her chest, and her peripheral vision became hazy. As they continued down Haile Selassie Avenue, she wondered if any of the other drivers had seen what had happened. Even if they had, there was little they could do. The police rarely responded to carjackings in progress, and when they did, it was usually with a hail of gunfire that made no distinction between carjacker and victim.

She slowed down as they approached the roundabout at Railway Station, even though the light was green. "*Weh! Nani amesema usimame? Twende!* [You! Who told you to stop? Let's go]!" the man barked. She shuddered and picked up some speed.

The pale, lemon-yellow light of streetlamps shone into the car, and she could tell that the man was tall from the way his knees stuck up against the glove compartment. She was scared to turn and look at his face. From the corner of her eye, she could see the gun glimmering in the light, pointed at her head. Heading up Ring Road, she felt a sudden desperation as they passed the Kariokor flats where she lived. So close to home, yet so far. She fought back tears as it occurred to her that this might be the last time she would drive up Ring Road.

SUNSHINE ON THE CROOKED ROAD

Approaching a roundabout somewhere near Pangani, she began to worry that he was taking her to Karura Forest, a haven for robbers and killers that the police dared not enter. The light at the roundabout turned red, and she came to a stop. She could see the man moving from side to side and looking behind them, though she couldn't tell why. Suddenly, KMT began to shudder violently, and its engine died. The light turned green.

"Wũi, Mwathani!" she exclaimed as she tried to restart it, her hand trembling so hard, she could barely turn the key in the ignition.

"*Nini* [What]*!*" he growled as he put the pistol to her head, the cold metal pressing against her temple.

"*Siyo makosa yangu! Gari ni mzee* [It's not my fault! It's an old car]*!*" she shrieked.

"*Anzisha, ama nitakufyatua risasi* [You better start it; otherwise, you'll get a bullet]."

Cho-ngio-ngio-ngio, groaned the motor wearily as she turned the key a second and third time. The man's breathing was getting heavy with frustration.

Lord, don't let me die like this, she thought. *Please don't let me die!* A shiny Range Rover pulled up in the next lane, and the driver honked his horn and waved. The man turned, and she felt the pressure of the gun ease from the side of her head. The driver of the Range Rover rolled down his window and beckoned, and her assailant chuckled softly as he recognized who it was. He jumped out, ran to the other car, and got in, after which it sped off. She presumed it was her tormentor's accomplice, possibly in another carjacked vehicle.

She sighed with relief as the other car disappeared, but her joy was short-lived. She was on a lonely, dimly lit road, late at night in a broken-down car. She turned the key in the ignition again, but she got the same lethargic *cho-ngio-ngio-ngio* as before.

"KMT, *'ebu wacha mchezo* [KMT, please stop playing games]*!*" she pleaded.

She got out of the car and desperately tried to flag down passing vehicles, hoping a kind soul would see her plight and offer help. Instead, other drivers kept their windows rolled up and accelerated as they passed, assuming it was the familiar setup where a seemingly helpless woman stopped on the side of the road lured an unsuspecting Samaritan into the clutches of thugs lurking nearby. Even when the light was red, cars slowed down just enough to make sure the roundabout was clear before gunning their engines to run the light.

She considered walking to the nearest petrol station, but there were none in sight, and walking alone in the dark to Pangani, the nearest populated area, was even riskier than staying where she was because of pedestrian muggings. As time passed, she felt more and more like a sitting duck. So while it was a relief to no longer have a gun pointed at her head, it had not dramatically improved her prospects.

About twenty minutes passed as she sat helplessly in her car, praying and trying to figure out what to do. She wished she had a way to call for help. *If only someone would invent a telephone you could use from your car.* She had once mentioned to Kabogo how useful this would be for letting someone you were meeting for lunch know you were stuck in traffic. He had laughed at her and suggested that such fanciful imaginings were typical for a housewife with less than a year of university education and no scientific background. "The sound has to be converted to electricity and then sent through wires," he scoffed. "What are you going to do, send electricity through the air?" Not knowing enough to argue with him, she had said no more.

From the corner of her eye, she caught a flicker of movement in the shadows among the trees. Terror gripped her as she saw the silhouette of a man running toward her with what looked like a *rungu* [club] in one hand. She let out a gasp and instinctively turned the key in the ignition once again, knowing full well how hopeless it was. *Cho-ngio-ngio-ngio* . . . The running man had almost reached her when she realized she hadn't checked that all the doors were locked after her encounter with the carjacker.

The man grabbed the handle of the front passenger door and opened it just as KMT's engine sputtered to life. She put the car into gear and jammed her foot on the gas. It lurched forward, just as the interloper scrambled to get inside. The sudden movement destabilized him, but he held fast to the door frame with his free hand.

"'ebu simama, auntie! Unaenda wapi [Stop, auntie! Where are you going]?" he shouted as the odor of stale sweat, cigarettes, and alcohol filled the car. She gripped the steering wheel and pushed her foot down on the gas pedal. As the car picked up speed, he continued running alongside, holding on to the door frame. He swung his rungu against the window and covered her in a shower of glass. As she entered the roundabout, she saw his hand reach in and grab the steering wheel. He managed to jerk it just enough to force the car partially onto the curb with a loud thump, but KMT kept moving forward, with the driver's side on the road and the passenger side on the curb. The man had gotten hold of the steering wheel and was still hanging on despite the jolt of impact. Had it not been for the road sign that appeared ahead of them, he might have managed to get into the car, or yanked on the gearshift lever to slow her down. As it was, he smashed into the sign and let go with an agonized howl before disappearing from view.

Suddenly, KMT was back on the road, swerving precariously from one lane to another. Fortunately, she was the only car on this stretch of road. She kept going, slowing down but not stopping for red lights, until she finally pulled into a parking space at Kariokor Estate, her chest heaving, her hands locked in an iron grip on the steering wheel. She had survived.

When she took KMT to Owino's the following Monday and told him what had happened, he listened impassively, then grinned and said, *"Unajua gari mzee ni kama mtu. Inajua mwenyewe. Ikiona mtu mwingine analeta shida, inakataa kwenda."* ["You know, these old cars are like people. They know their owners. If they see someone trying to cause trouble they refuse to move."] He speculated that the timing of the stalling and restarting might indicate an issue with the fuel pump, and he had friends who could replace the broken window with one from a scrapyard.

She gave her faithful jalopy a fond look as she turned to leave the garage, reflecting on what Owino had said about old cars knowing their owners. While KMT's stalling issue was clearly a problem she wanted fixed, by stalling last night, it had probably saved her life. Had she been driving Kabogo's car instead, she might be lying dead in Karura Forest by now.

Chapter 31

Nyagūthiĩ completed primary school at the end of 1986 and started boarding school early the following year. She and Milka were accepted to Precious Blood Secondary School in Rirūta. It was a bittersweet moment for Wanjikū, who had grown used to her companionship—her cheeky humor, loudly voiced opinions, and the way she often came where Wanjikū was and sat quietly with her homework, each person comfortable in the other's presence with no need for words. All this notwithstanding, Wanjikū was excited to see her daughter moving on to the next stage in her educational journey.

Things were quiet around the house after she left. Wanjikū was still able to keep busy with her sewing business. Since she worked from home, it wasn't unusual for her to go a whole day without speaking to anyone. This was probably the only time she experienced regret about walking away from the lease of her market stall after the Kanjo people presented her with a byzantine array of steps for winding down the shop, warning her that failure to comply would render her ineligible for a permit in future. Smiling politely and thanking the clerk who had directed her to the first counter for that process, she turned around and exited the building, hoping she'd never need to return. She missed the daily conversations with her fellow stall owners, especially Joyce. Every few weeks, she went there to chat with Joyce and to savor Njogu's sugarcane, but usually couldn't stay long because they had to attend to their businesses.

She stopped by every now and then at Upendo Children's Village, either to take measurements for new outfits or simply to catch up with Mrs. Makokha, with whom she had become close and now referred to as Mama Jonah. Many of the orders she received for outfits were traceable to either Mrs. Makokha or one of the congregants from Saint Stephen's, though with time, the connection of the new customers with her original clients had become more distant.

Mama Milka was her closest confidante, and they spoke at least two or three days a week. Now that their daughters were in boarding school together, many of the conversations centered around the school and updates about their daughters. They frequently got together on weekends to chat over tea and mandazi and saw each other on most Sundays at Hallelujah Bible Fellowship.

On days when she needed someone to talk to and none of her friends was available, she would walk over to Bhatia's duka in the middle of the day. Things were usually slow, and she could use the purchase of a packet of milk or other household item as the occasion to launch into conversation. Bhatia loved a good chat and could make an hour seem like fifteen minutes, especially when he began recounting his childhood experiences in Kampala.

★★★

There were several Mrs. Kabogos in Nairobi, and maybe even one or two with the first name *Wanjikū*. Enough, at any rate, that she had received several calls for the wrong Mrs. Kabogo over the previous years. Just a few months earlier, a doctor's office had called, seeking to confirm an appointment for fibroid surgery that she knew she hadn't scheduled. So when Wanjikū picked up the telephone that Thursday afternoon in November 1989, and someone identifying himself as Dr. Kigen from Kenyatta National Hospital asked if she was Mrs. Kabogo, she assumed it was another wrong number, especially after the caller said that a patient he believed to be her husband had been admitted to his ward. "It can't be my husband. I think you have the wrong number," she replied brusquely and hung up, knowing that Kabogo had left on Sunday afternoon for Mombasa.

After going back to her sewing for a while, however, she began to have doubts. Even if the Kabogo they had admitted wasn't conscious enough to tell them whom to call, wouldn't his identification documents have given them enough information to lead them to the right Mrs. Kabogo? Eventually, she decided that she'd better make sure. She could call the hospital back, but navigating that bureaucracy could take hours, so she decided to call Kabogo's office. When she reached the receptionist at the Mombasa office, he informed her that Kabogo was at the Nairobi office, which was surprising information since he usually came home on Fridays.

She called the Nairobi office, and the receptionist assured her that once she tracked down Kabogo, she could patch her through. "Please hold," she said, treating her to exuberant orchestral music as she waited. Wanjikū began to wave her right hand through the air like a conductor and was almost disappointed when the receptionist came back on the line just as the music approached its climax. "I'm sorry, madam, but apparently he's not in the office currently. May I take a message?" Her tone was formal now, almost guarded.

"Yes, please ask him to call home as soon as he gets a chance."

The receptionist hesitated longer than seemed natural, before replying, "Certainly, madam. Thank you for calling."

The phone call from the hospital had come at about half past one, and she had called the office before two. In the hours that followed, she didn't leave the house in case Kabogo called. When it got past four, she began to get irritated. Not calling back was a typically inconsiderate thing for Kabogo to do. By five thirty, irritation had given way to worry. What if he really was in the hospital? She decided her best course of action would be to go and find out. After all, she had the doctor's name. By six thirty, she was telling the man at the reception desk about her call from Dr. Kigen and asking where she could find him. After checking her identity card, he gave her complicated directions for getting to Ward 27. After asking several more people along the way, each of whom pointed her in a different direction, she eventually arrived at the nurses' station for Ward 27, presented her ID card, then explained the situation and asked to speak to Dr. Kigen.

"Yes. We've been hoping you'd come in. Let me see if the doctor's available. Please take a seat."

It was ten minutes before Dr. Kigen appeared. He was a tall man in his late thirties or early forties with a dark-chocolate complexion, a large bald spot, and calm, kind eyes. He ushered her into a room labeled, "Family Meeting Room," and the charge nurse came to join them.

"So, Mrs. Kabogo," Dr. Kigen began when they were all seated with the door shut, "would you mind telling me your husband's full name, date of birth, and which town or village he is from? I need to verify that I'm speaking to the right person."

Wanjikū took in a deep breath, trying to calm the rising anxiety within her. "Kabogo Mūchoki, April 25, 1948, and he's from Kīunangū in Kīambu."

The doctor looked down at an identification document in the folder in front of him, then looked up again. "Thank you. The person admitted to our ward is definitely your husband."

"So what's going on?"

Dr. Kigen leaned forward in his chair.

"He was brought into the emergency department yesterday morning by a Good Samaritan after he was seen acting strangely in town—talking to himself and grabbing at passersby. He fell to the ground in a seizure.

SUNSHINE ON THE CROOKED ROAD

The only thing in his possession when he got to us was the ID card in his back pocket. No wallet, no keys . . . nothing else, but he fits the photo and description on the ID."

Wanjikū's mind raced with questions, but she started with the most obvious one. "Is he OK?"

"He's confused, and . . . er . . . quite sick."

"With what?"

Dr. Kigen cleared his throat and shifted uncomfortably in his seat. She braced herself. "He has a type of meningitis called cryptococcal meningitis. Have you heard of it?"

She shook her head.

"It's a rare disease, but we're seeing it more and more among people who have been affected with the new virus that compromises the immune system . . ."

After that, she could see his lips move, but the only thing she could hear was her own heavy breathing. Her hands trembled uncontrollably. The nurse had put an arm around her and was whispering something in her ear, but she couldn't decipher what she said, and her thoughts were jumbled. She heard somebody ask, "Mrs. Kabogo, are you OK?" and tried to answer but could not form any words. Then the room was spinning, and she could hear urgent voices that sounded magnified yet unintelligible, like words underwater. The room was getting dark, and she was falling, falling, falling . . .

When she awoke, she was lying on a couch in another room, and Dr. Kigen was standing close by in the company of a different nurse. "Mrs. Kabogo, can you hear me?"

"What happened?" she asked groggily.

"We were having a conversation about your husband, and you fainted. About forty minutes ago. I'm sorry. I shouldn't have overwhelmed you with the news. That was a lot to take in all at once."

Wanjikū looked away, embarrassed by having fainted.

"Did you understand what I was telling you before you fainted?"

She felt a lump in her throat, but cleared it and said, "Yes, you were saying something about a new type of meningitis caused by the virus."

"Yes . . . We'll talk about that issue later. Maybe I should take you to see him first, then we can talk. Is that OK?"

She nodded.

"Mrs. Kabogo," said the nurse, "do you have someone we can call to come and be with you? I don't think it's safe for us to let you drive home alone."

"I'll be fine. Just give me a minute." She tried to sit up, but that wasn't a good idea.

"No, I think you need someone here with you," said the nurse in a polite but firm tone. "Is there a friend or family member I can call?"

She gave her Mama Milka's number, cringing at the prospect of interrupting her friend's evening. The nurse stepped out and returned a few minutes later to say that Mama Milka was on her way.

Wanjikū closed her eyes. When she opened them again, she was alone in the room, and someone was knocking on the door. When it opened, the nurse ushered in Mama Milka, who sat down next to Wanjikū and took her hand. "Are you OK?" she asked.

Wanjikū nodded unconvincingly, tears in her eyes.

The nurse looked uncomfortable. "I'll leave you two here, then," she said brightly. "When Mrs. Kabogo is ready to visit her husband, you can come out to the nurses' station, and we'll see if Dr. Kigen can take you back."

***

Wanjikū had never known Mama Milka to be timid or squeamish, but the sound of groans in the open ward and the smell of stale sweat mixed with carbolic soap must have spooked her; she was surprised to see her pulling back as they followed Dr. Kigen to the rooms at the far end

SUNSHINE ON THE CROOKED ROAD

of the hallway. She turned to her and motioned with upturned palms, asking if there was something wrong, and Mama Milka shook her head.

"Even if he's awake, he may not recognize you, so please don't be disappointed," warned Dr. Kigen as they approached the door. "That's just the nature of the illness." On the bed, Kabogo lay asleep on his back, breathing noisily through his open mouth, his arms and legs tied to the bedframe. He didn't look very different from when she last saw him a couple weeks ago. The two women entered the room but remained near the door, unwilling to go farther.

"Why are his hands and legs tied?"

"He was very restless earlier, screaming and trying to get out of bed, so we tied him down and gave him something to calm him."

Wanjikū and Mama Milka exchanged horrified glances.

"You said you're giving him medicine for the meningitis. Will it make him better?"

Dr. Kigen glanced hesitantly at Mama Milka, clearly unsure of how much he could say.

"Oh, it's OK, *Daktari* [Doctor]. This is my closest friend. You can speak freely in front of her."

The doctor nodded and proceeded. "Unfortunately, the big problem in this situation is that even if we treat the meningitis and get a good response, the immune system will still be suppressed because of the virus. Even when I've seen people getting better with treatment of conditions like meningitis, they still end up with one infection after another. That is the major problem with HIV. Right now, there's no cure for it. There is a drug called AZT that they've started using experimentally in America, but the results are far from perfect. Even if it proves effective, it may be a while before it's available in Nairobi."

He went on to explain how the virus was transmitted—sexual contact, blood transfusions, and contaminated needles—of which she was already aware from all the information flooding the media. What caught her attention, however, was when he said it could remain in the body for up to ten years before someone developed symptoms. He also mentioned that people with a history of STDs were at an increased risk of getting this disease. She felt her body go numb.

He suggested that, as Kabogo's wife, she get tested, but everything inside her pushed back forcefully against this. What was the point of finding out when there was no treatment for the disease? He had already explained that the virus could not be transmitted by shaking hands or hugging, which were the only things that might have concerned her regarding passing on the infection to someone else. Nyagūthiĩ was in boarding school now, and she would make sure she used separate utensils for herself when her daughter came home from the holidays.

"Why does his skin look darker than usual?" Wanjikū remarked.

"Is it?"

"Yes."

"We've seen it in some patients with this new disease."

Wanjikū's mind immediately went to a day several years earlier when Kabogo had dismissively said that Nyagūthiĩ would never get a husband unless she used skin-lightening creams. The bleak irony was hard to overlook.

"When was he last well?" Dr. Kigen asked Wanjikū.

Wanjikū swallowed awkwardly and tried to remember the last time she saw Kabogo. Because they slept in different bedrooms nowadays, it wasn't unusual for them to go a whole weekend without seeing each other. She would hear him moving around in his bedroom when he was around, often leaving the house early and coming home late. So when she thought about it now, it had been a couple of weeks since she'd last seen him.

"Um, he spends a lot of time in Mombasa for his job. And even when he's in Nairobi, he often has company assignments, so sometimes I can go a week or more without seeing him. I'd say it has been about two weeks."

SUNSHINE ON THE CROOKED ROAD

Dr. Kigen didn't seem to notice her discomfort or hid his reaction well if he did. He shook his head and remarked, "It's unfortunate. We're living in tough times with this new disease."

Soon thereafter, he signaled his intention to leave by asking if they had questions. He had spent almost two hours with them without seeming rushed, and they recognized that he had delayed either going home or attending to other patients.

"No. Thank you very much, Daktari," Wanjikū replied.

"OK, feel free to stay as long as you—"

"I think we'll also leave now. It's getting late," she interrupted, seeing no point in spending time with Kabogo in his current condition.

Not a word was spoken between her and Mama Milka as they left Ward 27 and took the elevator to ground level. As they approached the parking lot, she felt she had recovered enough from her fainting episode to drive home, but Mama Milka was reluctant to let her go on her own.

"You've just received a lot of bad news, and you'll be all alone at home. Why don't you come and spend the night at our place? It's no big deal."

"No, nyako. You have to go to work tomorrow. I don't want to interfere with your morning routine."

"Are you sure?"

"I'll be fine. We can talk tomorrow."

"OK. I'll give you a call in the morning when I get to work. If you need someone to come be with you, I can work it out. Otherwise, I'll come over after work, and we can come back to the hospital."

"Sawa, thanks," said Wanjikū as the two parted ways.

***

Mama Milka called the next morning, and they decided she would pick up Wanjikū at home after work so they could go to the hospital together. Wanjikũ had initially considered going by herself in the morning, then returning later with Mama Milka, but the image of Kabogo from the previous night was so disquieting that she was afraid to go alone. She had an order of several outfits to work on, so the day went by quickly. She found that focusing on the sewing allowed her to take her mind off the stress of Kabogo's hospitalization and its implications.

At six o'clock, Mama Milka arrived, and they went to Kenyatta Hospital. As they pulled into the parking lot, Wanjikũ felt her heart fluttering and her palms becoming sweaty. Mama Milka must also have been apprehensive because they had been talking in serious tones about the events of the previous night but her voice trailed off as she turned into the main gate of the hospital. They made their way through the swirling throngs of people in the hallways of the hospital complex and took the elevator to the seventh floor. As they walked toward Ward 27, they saw a preoccupied Dr. Kigen walking briskly in their direction.

"Hello, Daktari!" Mama Milka called out.

He looked startled. Then, recognizing them, he said, "Oh, hello! *Poleni* [Sorry], I almost walked right past you. My mind was elsewhere. I'm so sorry about everything that has happened. How are you coping?" He was looking directly at Wanjikũ.

"I'm OK. How is Kabogo?"

He looked even more startled than before. "Did no one get hold of you this morning?"

"No."

Dr. Kigen grimaced, then turned back to the ward. "Come with me. We need to talk."

Wanjikũ felt her legs getting wobbly. She was afraid she might faint again. It helped when Mama Milka took her by the hand. Once again, they entered the family meeting room and sat.

"Mrs. Kabogo, I'm very sorry to be the one to tell you this, but your husband rested early this morning."

SUNSHINE ON THE CROOKED ROAD

Wanjikū stared blankly at him and felt Mama Milka put her arm around her shoulder. "He died?"

"Yes, I'm afraid so."

"What . . . what happened?" she asked in disbelief.

"His condition deteriorated overnight, and despite all our efforts to turn things around . . ." He shook his head.

She couldn't think of anything to say. When she'd seen him the night before, she knew that death would come with the HIV diagnosis, but she hadn't expected it to happen so fast.

"They took his body to the morgue. You will need to make arrangements with a funeral home, and they can take it from there."

She felt oddly detached about Kabogo's death, though she suspected it would catch up with her later. Instead, her mind reeled at all the tasks that spun off from it: finding a funeral home and arranging the funeral, going to Nyagūthiī's school to tell her the news and bring her home for the service, calling everyone on Kabogo's side of the family as well as her own, writing an obituary for the newspapers, as well as for the radio so that Kabogo's illiterate relatives upcountry would hear the news. What would she even put in the obituary? She knew so little of Kabogo's life anymore. It seemed ridiculous, but she couldn't help once again feeling mad at him for being so inconsiderate. Then there were the funeral costs. How much would it be, and where would she get the money? It was overwhelming. And how could she be a widow? What would she do? The image of the sad, elderly Nyaruai who lived near her parents flashed through her mind. She was too young to be like that.

Dr. Kigen cleared his throat. "I'm sorry to run off, but I was on my way to the other side of the hospital when I saw you. You're welcome to stay here for a while, since I know you'll need some time to process the news."

Wanjikū nodded. "Thank you, Daktari, for everything."

"Um, Daktari," said Mama Milka as he rose to leave. "Can I talk to you for a moment?"

"Sure," he replied, looking surprised.

"I'm be right back," she told Wanjikū, patting her on the shoulder.

When Mama Milka returned a minute or so later, Wanjikū asked her. "What's going on?"

"Turns out, it was nothing. Right now, we need to go figure out this funeral home business."

Chapter 32

Nairobians are talkers, and anything newsworthy spreads rapidly across town. So the job of the newspapers is often to validate what people have already heard. On occasions when the papers failed to communicate what was really happening—either from collusion with or fear of the authorities—the grapevine often proved surprisingly accurate and reliable.

Kabogo had died on Friday. That Sunday, Wanjikū, feeling overwhelmed and despondent, resolved to go to Hallelujah Bible Fellowship, hoping to hear some words of encouragement from Kaka Josiah. Unlike Mama Milka, who knew and spoke to everyone in the congregation, Wanjikū often left immediately after church. Since the funeral announcement wouldn't come out until Tuesday, she felt safe from having to face awkward questions. She was therefore dismayed when she saw Peris Waithegeni making a beeline toward her as she hurried to the parking lot after the service.

"Hello, Mrs. Kabogo. I just wanted to make sure you were OK because I heard some unfortunate news, and I wasn't sure you were the person involved. I thought I'd check, so I can come alongside your family in prayer if indeed it is true."

Wanjikū stiffened.

244 NDIRANGU GITHAIGA

"What news?"

"About . . . er . . . a certain Mr. Kabogo from Koenig, the drug company."

"That was my husband."

"I'm very sorry to hear that."

"Asante."

"What happened? Was he sick, or was it an accident? Such a tragedy to lose a spouse unexpectedly."

"Yes. It's tragic," murmured Wanjikū, stunned by Peris's forwardness.

Peris was an inveterate gossip. In fact, Mama Milka secretly called her Mrs. *Mūcene* [Gossip] and had specifically pointed her out when she'd first warned her about wagging tongues in the congregation. Peris usually offered to pray for fellow congregants, telling them their prayers needed to be as precise as possible because if the desired outcome was too nebulous, it would be impossible to tell if the prayers had been answered. While she did indeed pray on other people's behalf, it was clear that she relished hearing the juicy details of her fellow congregants' misfortunes—romantic misadventures, cheating spouses, wayward children, financial difficulties, evictions . . . How had she heard about Kabogo? How did she know that he was her husband?

Before she could turn away, Peris continued: "I didn't realize your husband was such a humble man. The general manager of a big pharmaceutical company, yet he didn't flaunt his wealth! Most other people of that caliber would have had their wives driving around in a big Mercedes and putting on airs, but you're just like the rest of us, wearing ordinary clothes and driving an ordinary car. That's impressive!"

Wanjikū was stunned. "How did you know about my husband?"

"Oh, I overheard Mama Milka asking Kaka Josiah to pray for a very close friend of hers who had lost her husband unexpectedly, and I know you two are like *chanda na pete* [a ring finger and a wedding band]. Then someone I was talking to yesterday mentioned that a senior executive

SUNSHINE ON THE CROOKED ROAD 245

at Koenig named Kabogo Mūchoki had passed away. You looked so downcast today that I couldn't help putting two and two together. It's so sad! What happened? Was it an accident or an illness? Tell me how I can pray for you. It always helps to be specific."

"Thank you, but I need to go," said Wanjikū abruptly. "Please pray for me with the information you already have. God knows the details." She walked away before Peris could say anything more and hurried to KMT, not wanting to run into anyone else. As she drove away, she shook her head at the notion that Kabogo's humility was the reason she drove an old car and marveled at Peris's ability to take random bits of information and draw a conclusion.

Nyagūthiĩ was noticeably subdued when Wanjikū told her the news as she picked her up at her school in Rirūta the previous day. Aside from the glistening in her eyes, she had a blank expression and did not utter a single word. Her relationship with her father had been strained. He'd never reciprocated her efforts when she'd tried to engage with him as a child or when she'd told him she loved him. He often just mumbled and told her to go and play elsewhere, so from an early age, she had begun to emotionally wall herself off from him. Things only grew worse after the Mombasa trip. As they drove home, she sat quietly in the car, gazing out the window at pedestrians, mkokoteni drivers, and roadside vendors.

Before leaving to get Nyagūthiĩ, Wanjikū had called Kabogo's half brother Ngotho. Of all Kabogo's relatives, he was the easiest to get along with and had always been cordial and respectful toward her. He owned a matatu business with ten vehicles and had little time for the drama and pettiness she remembered experiencing with other members of Kabogo's family after they'd returned from America, which had caused her to cease going to Kĩunangũ altogether as her relationship with Kabogo unraveled. His willingness to pass along the news of Kabogo's death to the rest of the family was a relief. She dreaded having to talk to some of Kabogo's relatives, especially his mother. Mūthee Mūchoki had passed away years earlier. Ngotho was already planning raise funds among Kabogo's friends and family to help defray funeral costs, something commonly done as a show of sympathy and support for the family of the bereaved. He would call her back after talking to the family so they could work out the details of the time and place of the burial. "Don't worry at all, Mama Nyagūthiī! We're in this together," he said encouragingly.

Afterward, she called her family and shared the news with them. Her father said they would attend the funeral and would raise funds among friends and family in Gīthakainī as their contribution toward funeral costs.

She telephoned Kabogo's company on Monday morning to let them know as well. The receptionist, with whom she had spoken on Thursday, reacted with appropriate shock and condolences and told her that she could expect to hear from someone higher up in the company once she relayed the news.

The whirl of activity shifted into high gear once it was decided that the funeral would be held that Friday at Kahunguro Presbyterian Church—where they'd had their wedding—with the burial immediately following on Mūthee Mūchoki's farm. She had no objection to this. Fortunately for her, Ngotho did most of the heavy lifting, for which she continued to be grateful.

Besides the modest obituary Wanjikū put in the newspaper, Koenig Pharma took out a large, quarter-page notice, with a picture of the handsome, sharply dressed Kabogo whose absence, they said, was a void that could never be filled. She was flabbergasted to learn that he had been the general manager of the entire company, in charge of the day-to-day operations and reporting only to the managing director. He had apparently moved back to Nairobi six months earlier to take up his position but had chosen not to tell her.

Friday came quickly. The Obonyos offered to drive her and Nyagūthiī to the funeral. Since she wasn't immediate family, Milka, who was in the same boarding school as Nyagūthiī, wasn't allowed time off. When they arrived at the funeral home, Wanjikũ found a commanding Ngotho, impeccably dressed in a black three-piece suit and wraparound sunglasses, issuing orders to the squad of younger relatives assisting him. As she approached him, his expression softened, and he took off the glasses and meekly extended his hand.

"*Pole sana* [I'm so sorry], Mama Nyagũthiĩ," he murmured sympathetically.

"Asante sana, Ngotho. These are my friends, Mr. and Mrs. Obonyo. And, of course, you know Nyagũthiĩ."

He shook hands with the Obonyos and exclaimed, "Of course, my dear Nyagũthiĩ! I haven't seen you since you were in primary school. You were still a young girl then. Oh my, you've turned into such a beautiful young lady!"

The cortege was scheduled to leave the funeral home at nine thirty. Thanks to Ngotho and his crew, they were on their way by nine twenty, headed to the church in Kĩambu. As they drove, Mama Milka encouraged Nyagũthiĩ in recounting the mischievous capers of herself and Milka at school. They seemed especially daring as the school—which the students called *Prison Barracks*—was renowned for its strict code of discipline. Baba Milka chimed in every now and then and chuckled appreciatively as he kept his eyes on the road. Wanjikũ feigned attention, with an unconvincing half smile on her lips, in an effort to hide the fact that she was brooding over how everything had changed so quickly, starting with the phone call from the hospital.

Kahunguro Presbyterian Church was full when they arrived. She could feel all the eyes turn to her and Nyagũthiĩ as they walked down the aisle to the place in the front row that had been reserved for them. There were many familiar faces in the congregation, but many unfamiliar ones as well.

A few people went up to the podium, in front of the flower-laden casket, and recounted fond memories of Kabogo, whose smiling face, blown up beyond life-size, looked reassuringly from the front of the podium, as if saying, "Relax, everyone. It's really not that bad!" Wanjikū struggled to connect the happy, self-assured man in the picture to the man with whom she'd had such a fraught relationship and whose death had evoked so few feelings of loss or sympathy in her. What she felt most was heaviness and dread at the thought that her own beaming countenance might soon be looking back at a congregation in front of a similar casket, thanks to the man in the picture, whose eyes seemed to be laughing at her. If she felt any inclination to cry, it was at the injustice of his having exposed her to HIV. He had spirited her away from her worry-free university life to one of emotional neglect, and now, as a final indignity, he threatened to take her down with him into the dark abyss of his own selfishness, which had finally swallowed him.

Koenig Pharma was well represented, with several employees and most of the senior leadership in attendance. Wanjikū listened with incredulity as Mr. Kilonzo, the managing director whom she had never seen before, described Kabogo as a humble family man and recounted happy encounters with him and his family at workplace retreats and golf outings. Nyagūthiĩ nudged her and gave her a questioning look, in response to which she shrugged in dismay and shook her head.

In the interval between the church and graveside services, people who needed to leave early came to offer their condolences, Mr. Kilonzo being one of them. There were a few people ahead of him in the receiving line, and he shifted his weight restlessly as he waited, glancing imperiously at his watch from time to time. "I'm very sorry for your loss," he mumbled when he got to the front of the line, offering her a moist, pudgy hand. As their eyes met, a brief look of confusion came over his face—as if somehow he'd ended up in the wrong line—before being hastily replaced by a phony look of compassion.

"Thank you," she replied, noting a wisp of a knowing smile appearing at the corners of his mouth as he started toward the navy-blue Mercedes waiting nearby, its rear door held open by his driver.

SUNSHINE ON THE CROOKED ROAD 249

At the graveside, there was more opportunity for those who wanted to share remembrances of the deceased in word or song. After several did—offering rambling reminiscences in Gĩkũyũ with ad hoc translations into English and Kiswahili for the city folk, or off-key bits of song—Ngotho wisely put an end to the open mic session. Many of the speakers had addressed Wanjikũ and Nyagũthiĩ directly, encouraging them to be strong and to carry on Kabogo's legacy, whatever that was. Wanjikũ nodded politely, reminding herself that they meant well, even if the Kabogo they spoke of bore little resemblance to the one she knew.

Once the casket was lowered into the grave, Mũhoro, another of Kabogo's half brothers, invited family members beginning with Wanjikũ and Nyagũthiĩ to throw the customary handful of dirt into the grave. As she tried to shake the tenacious red dirt from her hands, her eyes fell on a boy of twelve or thirteen waiting his turn to perform the ritual. What struck her was how devastated he looked—sniffing uncontrollably, his eyes bloodshot from crying—compared to how detached, even angry, she felt. He was accompanied by Njambi, one of Kabogo's sisters, and she assumed he was Njambi's son, though he didn't look much like her. For one thing, he had a light complexion—the color of a mandazi that had been taken out of the frying oil a little too early. Since Njambi was single, it was possible that the boy's skin tone and features came from a man Wanjikũ had never met.

The Obonyos had waited patiently after the burial for her to say goodbye to Kabogo's immediate family and to thank her own family and friends from Gĩthakainĩ for coming. Her relationship with most of Kabogo's family remained strained—particularly with her mother-in-law—but at such a solemn, formal occasion, there was not much opportunity for the tensions to escalate, and she was able to excuse herself quickly. Kabogo's youngest sister, Annie, whispered that she had been meaning to get in touch and asked if she was available the following week.

"Sure. I'll be around if you want to meet up," she replied. She and Annie, who was seven years her junior, got along famously. Besides Ngotho, who had done a spectacular job handling the funeral arrangements, Annie was her favorite of Kabogo's relatives, but it had been several months since they'd spoken.

As they headed away from the crowd, she looked around for Nyagūthiĩ in order to let her know it was time to leave. She saw her near the exit gate, in conversation with a couple who looked to be in their late forties or early fifties. She caught Nyagūthiĩ's attention and waved to her. Nyagūthiĩ exchanged a few more words with the couple and came over.

"Who are those people?" Wanjikū asked her.

"They're parents of a friend of mine in school. They know some of our relatives on Dad's side." Nyagūthiĩ had an odd expression on her face, which caught her mother's attention.

"Is there something wrong?"

Her daughter shook her head but didn't say anything more as they walked to where the Obonyos had parked.

Mama Milka nodded off as soon as the car began to move, and Baba Milka apologetically explained that she had been up late the previous night, talking to her sister, who lived in Germany. Even after Mama Milka woke up, they were all subdued on the ride home.

The Obonyos dropped them off at Kariokor around six thirty, so it was still light out. Wanjikū would get to have Nyagūthiĩ around for nearly two more days, dropping her off at school on Sunday afternoon. As they entered the kitchen to think about dinner, she could see that Nyagūthiĩ had something on her mind. She had intense, restless eyes like Kabogo, and when something was burning her up inside, her heavy breathing and fidgeting gave her away.

"Is everything OK, Nyagūthiĩ?" Wanjikū asked as she pulled out a large wedge of *ugali* [cornmeal] left over from two nights before and a dish of chicken stew.

Nyagūthiĩ sighed deeply. "Mom, did you see those people I was talking to at the funeral?"

"Yes."

"Their daughter, Maryann, is my dorm mate—we've been good friends since Form One. In fact, she, Milka, and a couple of others are probably the people I spend the most time with. Anyway, she's been telling me about this kid called Robert who lives next door to them and is best friends with her younger brother. I even met him once when I visited their house during the holidays. They live in Spring Valley—you know, that posh neighborhood near Sarit Centre."

"Yes, and . . ." Wanjikū tried to hide her impatience. Nyagūthiĩ sometimes had trouble getting to the point.

"Did you see that boy with Auntie Njambi at the funeral?"

"The *ka*-brown boy?"

"Yes, that one. That's Robert."

"Oh!" said Wanjikū, her voice rising in pitch and becoming slightly tremulous with anticipation. "What was he doing there?"

"Mom, I don't know how to say this. And maybe you know it already . . ."

"Nyagūthiĩ, please! Don't beat around the bush."

"OK, OK," replied Nyagūthiĩ nervously. "The day you came to pick me up from school when Dad died, Maryann told me that Robert's dad had died unexpectedly. I didn't think much about it at the time. I thought that was him at the funeral, but I wasn't sure. It was only when I ran into Maryann's parents that everything clicked."

"Where was the boy's mother? How come he was with Auntie Njambi?"

"Mom, how would I know? I didn't know anything about it until I talked to Maryann's parents after the funeral."

Wanjikū was silent, remembering the red-eyed, sniffing boy. Did he look like Kabogo? She tried to recall his features, but the only image that came to her mind was that of a sobbing light-skinned boy, hunched over with grief.

"Mom, are you OK?"

"I'm fine."

She wasn't. Despite having already given up on Kabogo years before and settling for the convenient appearance of a marriage, she still felt angry and betrayed. It wasn't that she had expected Kabogo to be faithful to her—indeed, the STD incident had led to a complete breakdown in their relationship. But another family?

"It's really unfair that you and I have been living in Kariokor all this time while Dad had another family in Spring Valley. That really hurts," said Nyagūthiī, interrupting her thoughts.

Wanjikū put her arm tenderly around her daughter's shoulders. They had always been close, but this moment would permanently redefine their relationship. For the first time, she saw her daughter not as a child but as an adult, capable of understanding the messiness and complexities of life—even though she was only sixteen.

"You know what also bothers me?"

"What?"

"Robert is twelve. I don't know when his birthday is, but I know for a fact that he's in Standard Seven, the same class as Maryann's brother. Since you have to be six to join Standard One, he has to be at least twelve. Which means that he was . . ."

Wanjikū's body froze, and her vision became blurry. She hadn't joined the dots until now. Nyagūthiī's voice trailed off as she felt her mother's body stiffen. If Robert was twelve, he would have been born around 1977. They had returned to Kenya in June 1976, which meant Kabogo had gotten into a relationship with Robert's mother almost immediately after they'd returned, much earlier than she'd thought. Had he known her before they left the country? Before the marriage?

"Mom, are you OK?"

SUNSHINE ON THE CROOKED ROAD

She nodded unconvincingly and pulled Nyagūthiĩ closer to her. "Yes, Nyagūthiĩ," she whispered, "we'll be OK."

***

Wanjikū went to the window and peered out as soon as she heard the rumble of Annie's *nduthi-nduthi* [motorcycle] in the parking lot. They had agreed to meet at noon on Monday, and Annie was punctual. She watched as the reedlike form of her sister-in-law climbed off the fiery red motorcycle and pulled the helmet from her head, tucking it under her arm as she walked toward the stairs. Smiling, she remembered Annie telling her how scandalized the family had been when she had first ridden it to Kĩunangū—the first woman in the village to ride a motorcycle. Her mother and stepmother had looked horrified, and everyone had expected Mūthee Mūchoki to let loose in outrage. Instead, he'd tottered over to where she'd stood nervously next to her new acquisition and, with a huge grin on his face, said, "Even my Wanjūgū[1] knows how to ride this one." Only after they saw the unvarnished look of boyish admiration on the old man's face did the tension in the crowd dissipate. After that day, whenever Mūthee Mūchoki heard a motorcycle approaching, he would cock his head and ask, "Is that Wanjūgū I hear?"

She had bought it from the Mūthūngū husband, Derrick, of her friend Waithĩra when the couple relocated to England. Derrick had doted so much on the bike that Waithĩra had taken to calling it *the second wife*. She was surprised when Annie asked about buying it, and Derrick was skeptical, but it took only a couple of minutes of seeing her around the bike for him to realize that she would take good care of it.

Riding around Nairobi on a nduthi-nduthi was hard enough for a man, what with having to dodge matatus, buses, and potholes. For a

---

1. Annie's Gĩkũyũ name.

woman, there were the additional challenges of catcalls from manambas when they saw braids peeping out from under her helmet, and the disapproving looks she got for wearing trousers once she dismounted. But if anyone could handle reactions of that sort, it was Annie. Life to her was an absurd joke, its humor often hidden to those who succumbed to the illusion of control over their circumstances. She met unexpected situations with a cheeky laugh or a nonchalant shrug, which Kabogo had always found maddening. Part of what had endeared her to Wanjikū was her ability to get under Kabogo's skin. He had also resented how, in Mūthee Mūchoki's eyes, she could do no wrong. Like Wanjikū's own father, the old man had been unabashedly indulgent of his lastborn child.

"Hi, Mama Nyagūthiĩ. I hope you didn't forget I was coming."

"Of course not. Come in. I was just making us some tea."

"Asante. Did Nyagūthiĩ go back to school already?"

"Yes, I took her back yesterday. Those nuns don't play around with permission slips."

"You're telling me! You know, I went to one of those mission schools. I always used to get in trouble for laughing at something the teacher or headmistress said that wasn't intended as a joke. When the attention turned to me, I'd get stressed and start giggling uncontrollably. That only made things worse, because they thought I was being disrespectful. I can't tell you the number of times I got punished for *inappropriate displays of levity*, as they called it."

Wanjikū chuckled as she dropped a tablespoonful of loose-leaf tea into the bubbling mixture of milk and water on the stove. It wasn't difficult to imagine a rail-thin Annie driving the dour-faced nuns to fury with her high-pitched *hee-hee-hee*.

"I'm sure they were happy to see me leave when I finished my time there. If Sister Agnes was still alive, I'd go back there on my nduthi-nduthi just to give her something to get worked up about."

SUNSHINE ON THE CROOKED ROAD

Wanjikũ served the tea into two large mugs, and they sat down at the dining table. After a while of sipping their tea and making light conversation, Annie's voice turned serious. "How are you coping?"

"I'm fine. I think you already know that Kabogo and I weren't very close, especially in recent years, so I'd be lying if I said I was devastated. I'm sure some things will change—particularly financially—but I'm not ready to start worrying about that yet."

"Hmm . . . and here I was thinking I would help you by bringing you more things to worry about."

"Like what?"

Annie had a solemn expression on her face.

"Did you see the *ka*-boy who was at the funeral with Njambi?"

"Who, Robert?"

"Oh, so you know him? I didn't think you knew about him."

"One of Nyagũthiĩ's school friends is his next-door neighbor. Her parents came to the funeral. That's how we found out."

"Ngatho! That must have been awkward."

"I found out only after we got home. It was worse for Nyagũthiĩ. I didn't hear anything about the boy's mother. Was she there?"

"No. She's in the hospital, and very sick from what I hear. They're saying she might not make it. I don't know the details. I've met her once, and she seemed like a nice person. Kabogo apparently even took her home a couple of times this year to visit our *maitũ*[2] . They got along quite well from what I hear."

Wanjikũ's eyes narrowed and her grip on her mug tightened. "I guess I'm the last person to find out. Even that Kilonzo guy—Kabogo's boss—knew her. You should have seen the look on his face when he saw that I wasn't the wife he had been talking about during the service. That's Kabogo for you."

---

2. Mother.

"I'm sorry. I don't like getting into other people's business. When I found out about her, I just assumed you two had separated."

Wanjikū sighed. "He was at the Mombasa office for years and came home on weekends. Apparently, he moved back to Nairobi about six months ago when he got promoted to general manager. Would you believe he never told me anything about it? He continued to come home on Friday and leave on Sunday as before. Little did I know that he would leave here and spend the week on the other side of town—that rascal!"

"Pole sana," commiserated Annie, shaking her head in disbelief. "I'm sorry Kabogo did that to you. That's very shameful."

They sat in awkward silence for a few moments before Annie cleared her throat. "So the reason I came was to tell you that when I was home for the funeral preparations, I overheard my brothers, Gītaū and Mūhoro, say that the family should push to get some of the assets Kabogo left behind, because the family had been dependent on him for financial—"

"What! Are you mad?" erupted Wanjikū. "*Ebu* say that again, so I can laugh properly. What claim do they have to his things?"

"I'm just telling you so you're not caught unawares," replied Annie calmly. "I almost choked when I heard it. I was moving around in the kitchen, and they were sitting having breakfast."

"Wait a second. Mūhoro isn't even your real brother. *Si* he's Mama Mūmbi's son?"

"If you thought the craziness in our family was exclusive to Kabogo, think again. I'm just giving you a warning so you can find a lawyer, and start filing whatever paperwork is required in case he didn't leave a will, which he probably didn't."

"OK, the soil is still fresh on the grave, and the fighting has begun. Ngatho, what madness! Is it just those two, or are there others involved? You know, your mother and I don't get along, but it would be very inappropriate to get into a fight with someone my parents' age, much less my mother-in-law."

SUNSHINE ON THE CROOKED ROAD

"I don't think Maitū or Mama Mūmbi are involved, though I can see how Gītaū, especially, could try to get them worked up, particularly by saying the money should be used to make sure Robert gets a good up-bringing. I know Ngotho doesn't have time for that kind of foolishness, so I doubt he's involved."

Wanjikū's heart sank when Annie brought Robert into it. She hadn't considered that angle. "So what is the situation with the boy? Is he living with Njambi, or what?"

"Oh, don't worry about him. He was just there for the funeral. His mother comes from old money, and despite what my brothers say, I expect his relatives will take care of him. In fact, I think that house in Spring Valley belongs to the boy's grandfather. Kabogo was still on the hook financially, including sending him to Briar Crest Preparatory School—that posh school where they pay fees in dollars, and the students take school trips to Europe."

"I've heard of it. I always wondered what kind of people sent their kids there. So that's where Kabogo's money was going while we were living here in Kariokor?"

"*Haki* [truly], I'm ashamed of my brother," said Annie ruefully. "I hope we can remain friends despite how he treated you."

"Oh, don't worry, I won't hold it against you," she said. She did wonder why no one had filled her in earlier, including Annie, but she didn't want to alienate her one source of information just as it was opening up. "Everyone is responsible for their own actions, and thank you for telling me all this. Now, I need to look for a lawyer. That's not something I know a lot about. Do you know any good ones?"

Annie's face lit up. "Actually, I might. Her name's Rebecca Mwamburi. I don't know her personally, but my friend used her when she went through a hellish divorce. Apparently, she's very professional, and her fees are reasonable. She's a Coastarian [someone from the coast] who is about this tall," she said, gesturing at waist level, "but my friend tells me that other lawyers tremble with fear when they hear her name.

My friend couldn't stop singing her praises. She said if I ever needed a lawyer or knew someone that did, she would be her number-one recommendation."

"Where is her office?"

"I don't know, but I'm sure you can find it in the phone book."

"I guess I'll start there," she said, thinking that the Obonyos might be another source of leads if this woman didn't pan out. "I don't even know if Kabogo left anything worth fighting for, but I'll still need a lawyer to help me with paperwork. I'm sure dying, like everything else, comes with its share of paperwork."

***

Rebecca Mwamburi was a memorable character, even on short acquaintance. Petite with light-brown skin and perfect white teeth, she was wearing an elegant orange skirt suit on the day Wanjikũ went to see her, enveloped by the subtle floral scent of expensive perfume.

She was very personable, and Wanjikũ was struck by the self-assured way she skipped back and forth midsentence between English and coastal Kiswahili, with its soothing singsong cadence. Most people in upscale offices conducted business exclusively in English, regarding the use of Kiswahili within their air-conditioned, high-rise office buildings as coarse and unbecoming. Ms. Mwamburi clearly had no patience for that stubborn relic of the Mũthũngũ's seven-decade sojourn in this part of the world.

The most striking thing about her, though, was the intensity of her gaze. After asking a question, she would fix Wanjikũ with her probing, impenetrable eyes, making her feel that there was something more she needed to say. Wanjikũ imagined that this could lead people to tell her a lot more than she had asked, a useful weapon during cross-examinations.

SUNSHINE ON THE CROOKED ROAD

As Wanjikū told her about her difficult marriage to Kabogo, his recent demise, and the information that Annie had shared with her, she listened with concentrated attention, making notes and occasionally asking questions. When Wanjikū finished her tale of woe, Ms. Mwamburi leaned back in her chair. "Pole sana about your marriage and your husband. Things are not supposed to go like that. Now, you said the mother of the boy is sick in the hospital. Any idea where she is hospitalized or what her condition is?"

"No."

"Your sister-in-law said she was gravely ill?"

"Yes."

"What's your relationship with your sister-in-law?"

"We're friends."

"Sawa. *Wajua* [You know], sometimes such information is only as good as the person giving it, and you always have to ask yourself why someone is telling you something. Are they trying to help you, or is the information designed to mislead you? *Waelewa* [Understand]?"

Wanjikū nodded. "I'm pretty sure Annie is reliable. I don't think she's trying to mislead me."

"OK. Do you know what assets or bank accounts your late husband owned?"

"Just his main bank account. All his checks—like for payment of bills and household necessities—came from there. I don't know if he had any other accounts."

"You said *his* main bank account—so it wasn't a joint account? Were you a signatory to that account?"

"No," she replied. She could feel Ms. Mwamburi's gaze bearing down on her as her own dropped to the polished mahogany desktop between them.

"It's not a problem. Different families have different financial arrangements. So would he give you a certain amount of money every week or every month for household expenses?"

"Yes. And for all his failings, he wasn't stingy. There was always enough money to spend, including when I needed to buy fabric for my sewing business."

"That's good to hear. Yes, I think in life, most people aren't pure devils or pure angels. Even bad people have some good qualities and vice versa. It's just that the good in bad people is usually not enough to offset the bad. What about your sewing business? How is it doing financially?"

"It brings in a little money every month, maybe enough to cover the rent for the flat and groceries, but that's about it."

"Do you have your own bank account, and do you have some money saved? Many women in situations like yours have secret accounts where they put away money in case the marriage breaks up. I've heard them called *Swiss accounts*. You know what I'm talking about?"

"Yes, I have an account, and I've saved some money."

"Enough to live on for a few months?"

"I hope so. The rent for our flat isn't very much, and my daughter is in boarding school, so daily expenses like food are not as high. You say a few months. How long are we really talking about?"

"It may take six months to a year for a letter of administration to come through," said Ms. Mwamburi.

Wanjikū was surprised. "Oh, I thought it would take two to three months."

"*Nchi gani hiyo* [In which country]?" replied the attorney with a grim smile. "Six months would be the best-case scenario. Do you have enough to make that work?"

"I guess I'll just have to make it work. It's not like I have a lot of other options. My daughter's about to finish Form Three, so I'll still have to pay her school fees to get her through Form Four. I might be able to manage that."

"OK. In the meantime, I need you to go through all your late husband's documents and see what you can find: bank statements, land

SUNSHINE ON THE CROOKED ROAD

titles, insurance policies . . . everything. There will probably be a life insurance policy and his final payout from his employer, so you need to contact his company about those. Unfortunately, if there are any documents at his other house, you might not be able to access them. If the other woman is as sick as your sister-in-law said, she might not be able to follow up on them, either.

"Since she comes from old money, I don't think they'll be interested in fighting over *tu*-small amounts of money with common people. And when I say that, I'm not demeaning your late husband—I'm just saying those wealthy families care very much about their name and don't like to look like they need money, even if they do. So if the woman is not around to take care of her son, they may take custody of him and continue paying for his private school, since the last thing they want is a scandal. In fact, even if she's still alive, they might help her with his upkeep rather than risk embarrassment. With the boy taken care of, it would be difficult for your late husband's siblings to bring a case against you as his legal wife. What basis would they have? Just because it would difficult doesn't mean they won't try. Money makes even reasonable people do strange things."

By the time Wanjikū concluded her appointment with Ms. Mwamburi, she felt confident that Annie had given her an excellent recommendation, and her fees were indeed reasonable. She promised to go through Kabogo's things in the coming days and get back to her with whatever useful information she found. She only went into Kabogo's room to clean, so it would be odd to enter it now with the intention of poking around.

Chapter 33

About a week after the funeral, Mama Milka came over to Wanjikū's house. As they sat chatting over tea and mandazi, she stopped midsentence and said, "Oh! Before I forget, I need to tell you what I discussed with the doctor that day in the hospital when I followed him out of the room."

"I thought you said it was nothing."

"Well, fortunately, that's true, but you should know. My husband's cousin died about a year ago of complications of HIV," she said, adopting a serious expression. "When his wife tried to collect the life insurance payment, they denied the claim, saying HIV was a self-inflicted injury—that's the term they use when somebody commits suicide. We were shocked! My husband tried to help her to get them to reverse the decision, calling on his many connections, but it went nowhere."

"Oh, I see."

"In the process, somebody mentioned that the whole thing could have been avoided if the doctor hadn't mentioned AIDS or HIV on the death certificate. So I thought I'd ask Dr. Kigen what he thought about that."

"*Ehe*? So what did he say?"

SUNSHINE ON THE CROOKED ROAD

"He told me that when doctors found out this was going on, many of them made a point of not mentioning HIV, AIDS, or any related conditions on the death certificate. He said, 'Sometimes you have to break the rules to do the right thing,' and that he planned to list Kabogo's cause of death as *severe meningitis* and leave it at that."

"Thank goodness! And thank you for looking out for me!"

Mama Milka's eyes lit up with indignation. "Do you know there are insurance policies that exclude anything related to pregnancy using that same clause?"

"Ati it's self-inflicted! How is that even possible?" They both laughed at that, shaking their heads in disbelief.

"Anyway, that's what I was talking to him about, so hopefully, there won't be any problems when the death certificate comes out."

"Thank you for doing that."

A somewhat uneasy silence followed as a nagging issue popped into both of their minds. The doctor had suggested Wanjikū get tested to see if she had the infection, and Mama Milka had encouraged her to do so. Initially, her response was a polite no, but when Mama Milka kept pressing—asking her if she wanted to be able to make plans for her life and think about how the results would affect Nyagūthiī—Wanjikū became defensive, eventually cutting her friend off midsentence. "What's the point of getting tested if there's nothing you can do about it! If I'm going to die, let me die without the shame. After all, it's not like I'm planning to remarry or do anything that would put anybody else at risk."

Mama Milka had averted her gaze and fallen silent, but the awkwardness of their difference of opinion on this subject continued to crop up from time to time. She changed the subject now. "Let's go together to Rirūta next weekend and see the girls. It's Visiting Day."

"Sawa, let's do that," replied Wanjikū enthusiastically. "I'm sure Nyagūthiī will be excited, even though she was here just the other day. And I haven't seen Milka since she was home for the midterm break."

Kabogo's room felt musty and forbidding when she went there to search for documents. It was almost as if his presence was still there, balefully watching as she moved about among his things. Fighting the urge to leave, she opened the window to let in the lively sounds of bustling traffic, children at play, and the scrawny, yipping mongrel from the neighboring block of flats. As she leaned over to peer into the yard, a black moth the size of her hand fluttered up suddenly from the windowsill toward her face, so that she lurched backward and let out a startled shriek.

"Wũi, Mwathani!" she exclaimed as she scurried toward the door, her heart pounding. She was terrified of flying insects, and this moth was huge. She exited the room and rushed to the kitchen cabinet where she grabbed a can of insecticide, then returned with a resolute gleam in her eye and began to spray indiscriminately. She looked for the moth through the pungent, eye-watering haze, but couldn't see it. Reasoning that it might have escaped through the open window, she stepped back out and waited. A few minutes later, she reopened the door, squirted three more bursts for good measure, then waited some more before finally returning to the room. She looked around suspiciously; it appeared that the coast was clear. She shut the window to prevent the moth—or any other insects—from coming in, then resumed her task.

She decided that rather than simply riffling through Kabogo's drawers for documents, she would use the opportunity to rid the room of all of his belongings. That turned a relatively simple undertaking into a full day's work as she loaded all his clothes into large garbage bags. She planned to place them in a conspicuous location the evening before the Kanjo truck came around to pick up trash, knowing that chokoras usually came by looking for discarded items they could either use or

SUNSHINE ON THE CROOKED ROAD 265

resell. She stumbled on a stack of lewd magazines hidden in his sock drawer and clicked her tongue in distaste. Even in death, he managed to come up with new ways to lower her already unfavorable opinion of him. Initially, she was going to throw the magazines in the trash, then thought better of it, not wanting them to fall into the hands of the street urchins. She filled a bucket halfway with water, mixed it with laundry detergent, and dropped the magazines into it to soak for a few hours, planning to disintegrate them fully before throwing them in the trash.

She found a checkbook containing the checks he usually wrote, and a life insurance policy, with her as beneficiary, valued at two million shillings, which she set apart. She found a deed for a ten-acre plot of land somewhere on Kĩambu Road, a desolate area amid coffee plantations. Unsuspecting drivers often fell prey to bandits there when they stopped after dark to fix flats caused by strategically placed planks of wood full of nails. Why anyone would buy land there was incomprehensible to her. She shrugged and tossed the deed into the pile along with some official correspondence that she wasn't sure how to interpret.

In his bottom drawer, several letters, at least half of them unopened, were stuffed in a manila envelope. Two of them were unopened aerograms from Bill and Karen Atkinson from Connecticut. She set them aside, planning to read them later. Another was an official envelope addressed to her from the Kenya Institute of Planning and Implementation. It had been opened. A frown appeared on her face as she tried to recall what this might have been about. She extracted a folded white letter:

Dear (Miss/Mrs.) Wanjikũ Kabogo,

RE: EMPLOYMENT APPLICATION

> *We are in receipt of your recent application for the position of office manager in response to our recent newspaper advertisement and are pleased to offer you an interview. Please contact our offices at . . .*

The letter was dated March 15, 1979. She didn't remember ever having seen this letter. From the date, she recalled it was from the time when she and Mama Milka had sent out a flurry of job applications after Nyagūthiĩ and Milka joined Standard One. Though Mama Milka had found a job almost immediately, Wanjikū had been crushed to receive not a single reply to the many applications she'd sent. She had half assumed, half hoped that Mama Milka had help from a social connection, and her continued encouragement to Wanjikū to keep trying had rung increasingly hollow. Now, as she looked at this letter, she felt ashamed for doubting her friend. As she flipped through the stack, she found six other official envelopes addressed to her, already ripped open. Pulling out the letters inside, she found replies to job applications she had sent. Of these, all but one were positive, inviting her for interviews. She felt the blood rush to her head, and her hands began to tremble as she tried to make sense of what had happened. Everything pointed in one direction—Kabogo!

"*Ai*, Kabogo, seriously? You would even sabotage your wife's job applications! What kind of person does that!" she said out loud, gritting her teeth in fury.

She remembered mentioning to him after Nyagūthiĩ joined primary school that she was going to look for a job. His response hadn't been noteworthy as far as she could recall. At the time, he always picked up the mail on his way home from work, before he took the post in Mombasa.

"Agh, Kabogo . . . you sick, sick man! What kind of person—"

SUNSHINE ON THE CROOKED ROAD

The phone rang, interrupting her thoughts, and she went to pick it up. It was a wrong number. As she hung up, she looked down at the envelope in her hand. She wasn't sure she could face any more of Kabogo's betrayals today. Setting it down on the countertop, she went to the fridge, took out a packet of milk, and started to make herself some tea. Going through Kabogo's things was turning out to be a lot more emotionally challenging than she had thought it would be.

**

Not until later that evening did she get to sit down and read the letters from Karen and Bill. She was surprised to see them because she'd remembered sending at least a couple of letters that went unanswered. At the time, she'd concluded their mailing address had changed and assumed she would hear from them from a new address at some point, but that didn't happen. There was a lot going in Wanjikū's life with the market stall and her dysfunctional home life, so the lapsed correspondence got eclipsed by other pressing concerns.

Both letters were dated from 1980, and reading them was like reopening a door into a part of her life she barely recognized. Karen's tone was upbeat, and the updates were routine—the weather, renovations at the library, a recent trip to Nantucket, and questions about how they were getting on in Nairobi, especially Gogie. Wanjikū smiled tenderly, her eyes misting up as she read through the letters, then put them on the countertop. She would write to Karen soon and reconnect with her old friend.

Chapter 34

March 1990

When the headaches started, Wanjikū assumed they were from all the stress of Kabogo's death and the emotional and administrative mire she'd had to wade through in the weeks that followed. The dull heaviness in her forehead rarely left her. It was present when she got up in the morning, lingered in the background all day, and sometimes even woke her from her sleep. Even without the headaches, she rarely slept through the night, tossing and turning as she listened to the patter of occasional footsteps in the building hallway or the sound of passing automobiles mixed with the slurred monologues and singing of drunkards staggering home.

She didn't tell Mama Milka about her symptoms because she knew it would bring up the issue of getting an HIV test, which she had resolved not to do. Not being able to talk to anyone about the headaches made the anxiety even more difficult to bear. Besides Mama Milka, the only other people she communicated with regularly were her parents, now telephoning them two or three times a week. She had stopped going to Hallelujah Bible Fellowship, not wanting to be harried by Mrs. Mūcene and her ilk, but hoped to return at a later time when her story faded from interest.

SUNSHINE ON THE CROOKED ROAD

By the time the headaches had been going on for three months, she began to experience numbness that came and went in her face, arms, and legs. She also began losing weight and having unexpected episodes of blurry vision, to the point where she was no longer confident she could drive safely. It was time to see a doctor, whether she wanted to or not.

She had gone downtown and was walking on Moktar Daddah Street when she saw a sign for Dr. Mwangi Gathekia outside the ground floor entrance of a three-story building without really registering it. She hadn't yet decided whom to see, or when, but sitting in the house that evening as her headache grew in intensity, she picked up a phone book in desperation, intending to make a list of doctors to check out the next day. As she put the yellow pages on her lap and flipped to the doctor section, she recognized the name *Dr. Mwangi Gathekia* in an ad at the top right-hand corner of the page. She didn't think much of omens, but seeing his name there certainly made for an easy choice. She closed the phone book and decided to go to his office the next day as a walk-in.

When she arrived at Dr. Gathekia's office on the second floor, five or six people sat quietly on plastic bucket seats in the cramped waiting room. The receptionist was relating a story on the phone about someone who got swindled out of ten million shillings in his haste to buy a prime piece of land that turned out to be in a protected forest reserve. The captive audience of waiting patients listened closely without seeming to.

After checking in, Wanjikū took one of the plastic seats and started leafing through the newspaper. The country was still reeling from the aftermath of the assassination of Robert Ouko, the erudite, highly respected government official from the Luo community whose charred remains had been discovered days after he'd gone missing from his home. Even though a month had passed, the shock and tension were still palpable, and people looked around nervously as they walked down the street, worried about riots that seemed to erupt out of nowhere. She had been at Mama Milka's when she'd heard the news. They had been talking in the kitchen, and the phone rang. It was Baba Milka, who was still at work for a late meeting. She watched her friend's expression change from relaxed to shocked as she conversed heatedly with her husband in Dholuo. Then she put down the phone and stood as if in a trance.

Wanjikũ shuddered to think what the news could have been. Something about Milka? "Mama Milka, what's going on? Mama Milka . . ."

"They killed Ouko!" she said in a strangled voice before walking into the living room, throwing herself onto the sofa, curling up in a fetal position, and bursting into sobs. Wanjikũ went and sat next to her friend and did her best to comfort her. This was the only time she had ever seen Mama Milka lose her composure. Because of the likelihood of rioting in the streets after the news broke, she planned to spend the night at Mama Milka's house. Unlike her usual visits, the house was burdened by a heavy silence, broken only by Baba Milka's polite "Good evening," when he came home.

As the three sat in awkward silence, Mama Milka spoke out in a low voice, almost as if she was talking to herself. "First, Argwings-Kodhek, then Tom Mboya, now Ouko . . . What do they have against us? We're trying to play our part in building this country, and they keep killing us! What are they so afraid of?" she said before breaking into sobs again.

Wanjikũ took in a deep breath. She felt the pain in Mama Milka's voice and recognized that while the death of Ouko was a loss to the entire country, it was especially hard on the Luo as this suave and clear-thinking leader was in many respects a modern incarnation of the brilliant Tom Mboya, gunned down in his prime in 1969 when he had so much to offer the country. Baba Milka sat in silence for about half an hour, staring at the floor, then rose up and went to his bedroom. "Good night. We'll see what happens tomorrow," he said tersely.

Mama Milka sat up from her reclining position, intending to follow. Wanjikũ rose to her feet, put her arm around Mama Milka's shoulders, and whispered, "Pole, my sister," before retreating to Milka's bedroom, which doubled as a guest room. She lay awake for several hours, churning things over in her mind. She worried about the rioting she knew would follow, planning to get up as early as possible to drive across town before things heated up. Not until about two o'clock in the morning did she finally sleep, but even then, it was fitful, full of anxious thoughts and frightening scenarios.

Now, at the doctor's office, it was only when the nurse called her name a third time that she was shaken out of her reverie. The people in the waiting room had been replaced by a whole new set of strangers. She put the newspaper down and followed the nurse.

Dr. Gathekia was a paunchy man, his belly hanging over his belt, and the lower buttons of his shirt strained to contain it. When he greeted her, his hand was like a fleshy pillow into which her hand sank. His prominent, flared nostrils made Wanjikū think of a hippopotamus lounging underwater, its nostrils sticking up above the surface, and she suppressed a smile. "So, Mrs. Kabogo, how may I help you today?" he asked in a deep baritone.

As she told him her symptoms, he listened closely from behind his desk, scribbling on a bright yellow pad.

"So you say the headaches began about four months ago? Is that correct?"

"Yes, approximately four months ago."

"And the numbness appears in different places, and it comes and goes?"

"That's correct."

He asked her several more questions, a look of deep concentration on his face, then asked her to step up on the examination couch. He picked up a bright-red stethoscope that looked like a child's toy—nothing like the elegant one Dr. Kigen draped over his neck—and she wondered if she shouldn't have done a little more research before choosing a doctor. He picked up a rubber hammer and knocked on her knees and elbows, asked her to clench her fists, smile, grimace, and a host of other things that she couldn't imagine told him much of anything.

Once he'd completed his exam, he motioned for her to take a seat in front of his desk and went behind it to scribble some more on his legal pad. Finally, he said, "You'll need to have some blood tests. I'd also like you to get a special picture of your brain called a CT scan. I don't know if you've heard of it."

She hadn't.

"It's a test that recently became available in this country, which shows us much more than you can see on an X-ray. They have a machine at Kenyatta, but because it's a government hospital, you may have to wait for a long time to have it done there. If you have the finances to do it at a private hospital like MP Shah, Aga Khan, or Nairobi Hospital, that would be the better."

"How much does it cost?"

"It can vary, but it's around two thousand shillings."

Wanjikū let out a low whistle. "Wow, that *is* expensive!"

"Yes, but preferable to waiting for months to get it done at Kenyatta."

She nodded, acknowledging the painful reality.

"OK. I'll give you order forms for the CT scan and the blood tests, then plan on seeing you back when they've been completed."

"Er, do you have any thoughts about what this might be?"

"At this point, there are so many possibilities that it would be unwise to speculate. Let's see what the tests show. Anything else I need to know?"

"No, that's it. Thank you."

As she got on a matatu and headed home, she stewed about not telling Dr. Gathekia about Kabogo's illness, which she knew might be relevant to her symptoms. She could barely bring herself to acknowledge the fact of it to herself, much less tell anyone else. Even when he had asked about her marital status and she had said she was a widow, she didn't volunteer any additional information. "Oh, I'm very sorry to hear that!" he'd said

SUNSHINE ON THE CROOKED ROAD

and moved on. She recognized that she continued to stubbornly resist putting herself in any situation that would require getting tested for the dreaded virus.

★★★

She returned to the doctor's office a week and a half later and thirty-five hundred shillings poorer, having completed the brain scan and battery of blood tests. The phlebotomist at MP Shah hospital had taken so many tubes of blood that she worried she might black out when she got up to leave, but she didn't even feel woozy.

Dr. Gathekia scrutinized the reports, mumbling softly to himself, then leaned back in his chair. "Your tests are all normal, including the CT scan!" he declared triumphantly, beaming. "That's very good news."

She eyed him skeptically and cleared her throat. "So what's wrong with me?"

"Nothing physical!" He exclaimed before tenting his fingers and looking thoughtful. "I believe your symptoms are psychosomatic. Are you familiar with that word?"

She was. "Yes. You're saying it's all in my head?"

"Not exactly. The symptoms are real. It's just that your brain is . . . er . . . playing tricks on you. We sometimes call it *Hapa na Hapa* [Here and Here] Syndrome, because the symptoms often manifest in different, unrelated parts of the body in a pattern that doesn't fit any medical syndrome."

Had she really spent all that money just for him to tell her that it was all in her head? Wanjikũ tried hard to hide her frustration, recognizing that she had withheld important information from him and that he had probably done the best he could with what she had told him. It was only nine in the morning when she left the office. Exasperated, she found herself walking toward Ronald Ngala Street to do something she would have considered unthinkable even just an hour earlier.

The sign outside the door for The Free Clinic was much less off-putting than the clinic's official name: *Venereal Disease Free Clinic*. It had taken the clinic's administrators several months to figure out why nobody was coming through the doors. Once they changed the sign, the clinic was soon filled to capacity. Still, everyone knew what services were offered without having to have it spelled out, and it was rare for someone to walk in seeking help for a peptic ulcer, foot pain, or hypertension.

Six years earlier, she had come here when she'd developed the STD, covering her head with a shawl to avoid being recognized if she happened to run into someone she knew in the vicinity. Patients were assigned four-digit numbers at check-in for anonymity and were referred to by this number in all their interactions with the staff. The ladies of the night who constituted a sizeable portion of the clientele had even started calling each other by their numbers outside the clinic and insisted on keeping the same number on repeat visits, even though they were supposed to be randomized daily. After initially resisting, the clinic staff eventually gave in and withdrew the numbers of the frequent visitors from the daily roster.

She was shuttled from nurse to doctor to phlebotomist in less than twenty-five minutes, then told to return in two days for the results. In less than an hour, she was back home. It was only then that she began to feel anxious about what she had done, but she was tired: tired of the headaches, tired of running from the virus, tired of hiding from Mrs. Mūcene, tired of being pressured by Mama Milka to get tested, tired of being haunted by Kabogo's poor choices . . . tired of everything.

Chapter 35

Mama Milka worked at a brokerage firm on Mama Ngĩna Street. The company had elegant offices on the third floor of a high-rise office building where people had to show their ID at the security desk on the ground floor to enter. She enjoyed her job and the people she worked with. In the almost ten years since she'd been there, she had risen to the rank of assistant manager of marketing, with a small but comfy office of her own.

She'd been worried about Wanjikū since the day months earlier that she'd received the urgent phone call to go to Kenyatta Hospital because her friend needed help. After that, it had been one thing after another. Of late, Wanjikū had become withdrawn and uncommunicative. When they did talk, she seemed preoccupied. She understandably had a lot on her mind, but Mama Milka couldn't get her to open up about it, just as she couldn't get her to take an HIV test. That issue was especially worrisome. She'd lost weight, her skin looked dry and unhealthy, and she mentioned that her hair had started coming out in clumps when she combed it. For all that, when Mama Milka urged her to see a doctor, Wanjikū would say dismissively, "I'm fine! There's nothing wrong with me!"

Wanjikũ could be stubborn, and Mama Milka had learned that sometimes the best thing was to let her find her own way, but it was hard to watch her friend be swallowed up by something beyond her control that she refused to acknowledge. Nyagũthiĩ was seventeen, still a year away from being a legal adult, and several years away from being ready to manage her own affairs. Mama Milka knew from Wanjikũ about the dynamics of Kabogo's family and was aware, with the possible exception of Ngotho and Annie, there wouldn't be anyone willing to take care of her, except if they saw it as an avenue to inherit whatever Kabogo had left behind. Ngotho had the wherewithal to step in, but it wasn't clear that he had the interest, or that his wife, Mũkami, would warm to the idea. Annie was a free spirit, riding around on a *piki piki* [motorbike], hardly the person to provide stability for a teenager. Besides, she was the youngest of Kabogo's siblings, and therefore the one with the least say in any such discussions. Wanjikũ's parents were too old to be much help, and despite their close friendship, Mama Milka knew little of Wanjikũ's brothers. That they rarely came up made them unlikely candidates. Plus, in situations like this, the husband's family took precedence because the wife was considered to have joined his family and left her own.

Mama Milka would be happy to help and thought that Baba Milka would be too, but she knew that as a Luo, she would be completely disqualified. She felt sure that the one thing that could unify Kabogo's fractured family was the notion that Nyagũthiĩ might end up in the custody of her mother's Luo friend. Tribalism was an irrational demon, and she had no interest in tangling with it in one of those bizarre dramas that played out for years in the courts and the media.

The only thing Mama Milka could do in this situation was pray, and pray she did. She prayed over and over again for God to help her friend, though unlike Mrs. Mũcene, she stopped short of giving the Almighty a clear blueprint for what to do. As the person who was probably most fully aware of what was going on in Wanjikũ's life, she also prayed that the person who would be most affected by it—Nyagũthiĩ—could continue to remain blissfully unaware.

She had tried calling Wanjikũ the previous night, but no one picked up the phone, which was unusual. Her friend rarely left her flat after sunset. She planned to try her again at lunch. If there was no response, she would drive to Wanjikũ's flat immediately after work to make sure she was OK.

Flora, the new receptionist, called around twelve-fifteen and told her she had a visitor.

"Who is it?"

"I didn't catch her name, but she said she was a friend."

Mama Milka gritted her teeth. Flora was useless. Mama Milka debated whether to make her get more information, but instead hung up and went and see who it was. As she walked past reception to the waiting area, she was startled to see Wanjikũ, her face swollen with crying, her tears dripping onto the polished floor.

"Mama Milka!" she bawled, walking straight into her arms, sobbing loudly. "Oh, Mama Milka!"

Mama Milka's heart sank, and she tried to steel herself for the worst as she embraced her friend. "Pole, Mama Nyagũthiĩ. It's going to be OK," she soothed, feeling Wanjikũ's body convulse with sobs against her.

"All this time!" she kept saying. "All this time!" She pushed away and held out some folded slips of paper. Mama Milka took them. Hands trembling, she opened the first one:

Date: March 28, 1990

Name: Wanjikũ Kabogo

Date of Birth: September 25, 1950

HIV ELISA: Negative

She opened the second one, then the third. In each case, the information was the same.

"I did it three times to make sure," croaked Wanjikū, sniffing and wiping her tears with the palms of her hand, which only served to smear the moisture over her face. "Twice at the Kanjo clinic and once at MP Shah. Mama Milka, I was so sure I was going to die!"

"Oh, my goodness!" erupted Mama Milka, her own tears of joy now rolling down her face. "Praise Jesus!"

They stood together laughing and crying in the visitors' area, which was fortunately empty, embracing, letting go, then embracing again.

"Wah, that man has tormented you! Even from the grave, he has not stopped harassing you. Now, you can finally be free of him."

"I hope so," replied Wanjikū uncertainly, choking off a sob. "I really hope so."

***

Dr. Gathekia had been right about the Hapa na Hapa Syndrome. Even by the time she got home from Mama Milka's office, where she had gone immediately after receiving the results of her third blood test, the headache, numbness, and blurry vision had started to improve. And the heaviness that greeted her when she woke and followed her all day until she collapsed at night had been replaced by a sense of lightness. On the matatu ride home, she even found herself smiling at the unfunny jokes the manamba was making in an effort to impress a strikingly attractive young woman seated across the aisle, who rolled her eyes in feigned contempt even as she seemed to relish being the focus of the man's attention.

For the first time in months, she was excited to be alive. Only two weeks before, she had seriously considered stepping in front of an approaching bus at the busy Kencom bus stop so that everyone would think she had died in an accident instead of from the dreaded disease. The only thing that stopped her was the thought of leaving Nyagūthiĩ with no one to care for her. Her mind had been roaming in a dark and hopeless place. Now, she was free to begin living again, eating, putting on weight, planning for the future . . . all the things she had previously taken for granted.

Rebecca Mwamburi surprised her a few days later when she called and told her that the letter of administration had come through, and she now officially had access to all of Kabogo's assets. Since they hadn't heard anything from his family in the interim, it was unlikely that there would be a challenge. There hadn't been any updates regarding either the boy or his mother. She entered the bank with low expectations, worried, in fact, that at the end of the day, she would end up saddled with Kabogo's debts. So her jaw dropped when she discovered that the total balance in his three accounts was a little over seventeen million shillings, not including the insurance payout of two million shillings that was still pending. Kabogo's final payout from Koenig of two hundred thousand shillings had already been credited to his bank account.

"Seventeen million!" she exclaimed to herself when she was back in the flat. "Kwani, how did he amass all that money?" She could imagine his chagrin if he'd known that the assets he had worked so hard to accumulate were being handed over to her. Wherever he was, he was probably gnashing his teeth and wishing he'd left a will or divorced her while he had the chance. Things seemed to be working out in ways she hadn't anticipated.

Chapter 36

1^{*991*} Nyagũthiĩ was passionate about politics, and Wanjikũ sometimes found herself watching in bafflement as her teenage daughter yelled at the TV while watching the evening news, heckling the images on the screen as if they could hear her. She'd always taken an interest in politics, often going through the newspaper even when she was in Standard One and Standard Two, asking her mother for the meaning of terms alien to her seven-year-old lexicon such as *sedition, embezzlement,* and *detention.* Wanjikũ sometimes wondered how much her daughter understood of what she was reading and tried to distract her with other activities, but even when Nyagũthiĩ could be induced to put down the paper to go out for a soda at Bhatia's duka, she would pick it right back up again when she came back to the flat.

By her early teens, she'd started watching the news on TV, and her voluble engagement made it clear that she had strong opinions about what was happening in a way that sitting quietly curled up with the *Daily Nation* had not. It was almost the same as Baba Milka shouting at the TV as he watched a football match between his favorite team, Gor Mahia, and their nemesis, AFC Leopards. Even when she wasn't in the room, Wanjikũ could always tell when the president made an

SUNSHINE ON THE CROOKED ROAD 281

appearance from Nyagūthiī's angry questions and sarcastic comments. It wouldn't do for someone passing outside their flat to overhear her, so she would poke her head into the living room to ask her to tone it down.

"Shh! Moi can't hear you, but if you keep shouting like that, someone else will. I don't want to end up in Nyati House [Special Branch headquarters] just because you can't keep those crazy ideas inside your head where they belong." But not even the threat of the dreaded Special Branch, which had eyes and ears everywhere, could silence Nyagūthiī during one of her rants.

Wanjikū relished having Nyagūthiī home now that she'd completed high school in November 1990. For the four years her daughter had been at boarding school, she'd had to be content with having her home only during school holidays or midterm breaks. The house was a lot livelier now, and Nyagūthiī had changed in many ways from the shy, awkward teenager Wanjikū had dropped off at boarding school. She was more confident, more self-possessed, and maybe a bit too emotionally invested in issues over which she had no control, such as political cronyism, sluggish economic growth, and mismanagement of government ministries. Her range of knowledge was impressive, and they would often sit for hours, sipping tea and talking about anything and everything. The nuns at her boarding school had cured her penchant for disorder. Before she went away, it had been difficult to chart a path among the piles of clothes and books on the floor of her bedroom. Now, everything was put away neatly. She even made her bed before coming to breakfast.

Given the certainty with which her daughter tackled runaway corruption, the sagging GDP, and injustice at home and abroad, Wanjikū was troubled by Nyagūthiī's inability to focus on major decisions in her own life, such as what to study at university. Milka, on the other hand, having declared with quiet confidence in primary school her intention of becoming a doctor, was on track to study medicine. Not only was

Nyagūthiī noncommittal about what she wanted to study, but she had started to voice doubts about attending university at all—the accepted path for high school students who had the required grades.

"Life is difficult, Nyagūthiī, and without a degree, you may find it a lot harder," Wanjikū admonished, trying to hide the full extent of her dismay.

"I know, Mom. But what about all those jobless graduates tarmacking after having wasted four years at university? And they still have loans to pay off."

Wanjikū had long harbored regrets about having dropped out of college to marry Kabogo and move to America. She also regretted only toying with the idea of enrolling in a degree program in Connecticut rather than pulling the trigger, an option that Nyagūthiī's birth had put on hold. Until finding the letters to her from prospective employers in Kabogo's things, she'd assumed her inability to find a job had been because she lacked a college degree. Now, she wasn't so sure. But jobs were getting ever scarcer, so that having a degree was a greater advantage now than ever. "They might be tarmacking now, but they'll eventually find jobs," she said. "And with things as competitive as they've become, they might just end up replacing people who don't have degrees, or end up being promoted faster than them. The best time to get a degree is when you're young, before life gets complicated with work and family."

Nyagūthiī rolled her eyes.

Since her daughter had finished high school, Wanjikū thought that her daily bouts with the television had made her more cynical. When Nyagūthiī came into the kitchen fuming about a breaking scandal involving agricultural supplies worth millions of shillings that had mysteriously disappeared, her scorn of the empty promises from high-level government officials to leave no stone unturned in their quest to apprehend the culprits prompted Wanjikū to say, "Maybe you shouldn't watch so much TV."

SUNSHINE ON THE CROOKED ROAD

"It's important to be informed about what's going on around you."

"I'm not saying you shouldn't be informed, but I think there's such a thing as knowing too much."

"Seriously?" asked Nyagūthiĩ, shaking her head.

"Haiya, I am serious! Tell me, in that case you just told me about, what is Nyagūthiĩ Kabogo going to do about it besides getting angry and yelling at the TV, or at me? How does she intend to solve that problem?"

"That's so defeatist, Mom! It's because of people like you not caring that everything in this country is getting worse."

"I only asked what you were going to do to fix the problem. Because if you're not able to do anything about that stolen fertilizer, and the only thing the information does is cause your blood pressure to go up, then maybe you're better off not knowing."

"Agh, Mom! What you're saying doesn't even make sense! Knowledge is power. I can still vote! I can still add my voice to that of others. But only if I know what's going on."

"But does knowledge really give you power?"

She could see Nyagūthiĩ's eyes flashing angrily—Kabogo's eyes. When her daughter got mad, she looked so much like Kabogo that it made Wanjikũ uneasy, and she backed off.

"OK, no more arguing. I just want to make sure you're also paying attention to the things that involve you directly, like what you'll do after the exam results are released."

"The results aren't even out yet, so even if I wanted to do something, I couldn't. If I get accepted to university, we'll see. Since I don't know—since I don't have the *knowledge*—" she said with special emphasis, "I don't have the *power* to act."

Wanjikũ smiled her surrender and headed to the bedroom to do some ironing. An hour later, she heard her daughter call to her urgently from the living room, "Mom, come quick and see! Your kids!" Confused, she put down the iron and hurried to the living room.

"Look, the kids from the orphanage!" Nyagũthiĩ exclaimed, pointing at the TV.

It was the choir from Upendo Children's Village, all dressed up in beautiful purple kitenges adorned with sky-blue, yellow, and red floral patterns. They were performing at an event in Nyayo National Stadium, singing and dancing in perfect unison in front of the president, vice president, and several other dignitaries. When they finished, the applause was deafening.

"Haiya! What are they doing there?" Wanjikũ asked incredulously. "Mama Jonah didn't tell me they would be performing for the president."

"Mom, your kitenges are going to be famous. Soon, everybody will be talking about them. You could make a lot of money!"

"I'm not interested in making a lot of money, Nyagũthiĩ. I make the kitenges because I enjoy it."

"Oh, sorry, I forgot about the seventeen million shillings," replied Nyagũthiĩ cheekily. "Of course you're not interested in money!"

"You!" scolded Wanjikũ. "Why are you so obsessed with that money? I should never have told you about it. Is that why you're thinking about not going to university?"

"No. You already told me you weren't going to let the money disrupt our lives, and sure enough, a year later, we're still living in Kariokor, and you only drive the good car when KMT is in the shop, which it is more often than not."

"KMT is my friend. I'll continue driving it until Owino tells me it's no longer safe."

"When was it ever safe?" Nyagũthiĩ said with a laugh.

The news coverage shifted to the commentator talking about the event. Wanjikũ glowed with pleasure when he describing the children's outfits as *maridadi kwelikweli* [exceptionally gorgeous], which got the first positive response she could remember from Nyagũthiĩ to anything said on TV.

SUNSHINE ON THE CROOKED ROAD

Of course, she followed up with a comment about the government leaders destroying the local textile industry by letting in a flood of imported secondhand clothes called *mitumba*. "Did you see them cheering! Look at those hypocrites! I can't wait to see how excited they'll be when the mitumba choir comes to perform!"

Wanjikū returned to the bedroom, heady with excitement. It had been weeks since she had visited Upendo Children's Village. She would go there tomorrow to say hello to Mrs. Makokha and tell her how thrilled she was to have seen the kids on TV.

***

She reached the orphanage about nine thirty the next morning. Francis, the security guard, smiled when he saw her. Usually a man of few words, he seemed eager to discuss the previous night's TV appearance. Despite her assurance that she had seen it, he proceeded to give her a blow-by-blow analysis of the event, to which she listened politely.

"*Hata Mheshimiwa Osotsi, yule ndugu ya mama yetu alikuwa amefurahi sana* [Even Honorable Osotsi, the brother of our lady, seemed very pleased]," he said in closing.

"*Mama mgani* [Which lady]?"

"*Huyu wetu* [This one of ours]," Francis replied, pointing toward Mrs. Makokha's office.

From the look on Wanjikū's face, he could see she had no idea what he was talking about. She practiced what she preached when it came to not keeping up with news she couldn't do anything about, and couldn't name ten Kenyan politicians to save her life—but the name Osotsi sounded familiar.

Francis, meanwhile, explained that he came from the same village as Mrs. Makokha and as a boy had done odd jobs on Mrs. Makokha's parents' farm to help with his family's household expenses. She had sent for him when the orphanage opened and hired him as a security guard.

"*Hao watu nawajua sana. Hata huko kwao reserve nimeenda mara nyingi* [I know those people very well. I've been to their home in the village numerous times]," he declared proudly. He wanted to tell her more, but she made her excuses and walked up the path to Mrs. Makokha's office.

Osotsi . . . She racked her brain trying to remember where she'd heard that name. It wasn't from the news. She knocked on the door and entered in response to the shouted, "Come in!" from inside.

"Hello, Mama Jonah!"

"Oh, hello, my dear! Karibu sana!"

"I saw the kids on TV last night. They looked amazing!"

"Yes, we thank God for the opportunity," replied Mrs. Makokha, beaming with pleasure. "It is all His doing. And those beautiful kitenges you made for the children—without them, the performance would not have been so spectacular! Thank you."

"You're welcome. I'm honored."

Mrs. Makokha sent for tea, and they settled down to casual banter. It wasn't until well into the conversation that the penny finally dropped for Wanjikū, and her eyes suddenly opened wide.

"Wait! I've been trying to remember why the name Osotsi sounded so familiar when Francis mentioned just now that he is your brother."

"Yes. He is my older brother. Why?"

"I think he had something to do with Kanjo giving me my permit after they shut down my stall. The man I went to see at City Hall mentioned that name, but I had no idea at the time who it was. It didn't click until just now."

Mrs. Makokha gave a sheepish grin, as if she'd been caught red-handed. "I don't often go outside the normal channels, but those City Council people were being very unfair. I called my brother to ask him if he knew anyone who might be able to help, and it turned out that he knew the supervisor of the department responsible for issuing permits.

SUNSHINE ON THE CROOKED ROAD   287

In fact, that man owed him a favor for helping his son get a job in the Ministry of Water—a bright young university graduate who had been unable to find a job for over a year."

"I had no idea! Thank you! I don't think I would have received that permit otherwise."

"Mama Nyagūthiĩ, I'm the one who should be thanking you for all those beautiful kitenges you've made for my children over the years. You've never charged me a single *ndururu* [five-cent coin] for labor, and the first time you even purchased the fabric with your own money. You've been very kind to us, and I'm happy to have had the opportunity to repay your kindness."

"Why didn't you tell me at the time that you had asked your brother to intervene?"

"For what purpose? The main thing was to get your permit so you could stay in business, not for me to go around blowing a *karumbeta* [trumpet] about helping you."

"Well, thank you for helping me. I would have thanked you earlier, but I had no idea you were involved."

"Maybe now that your kitenges were on TV and caught everyone's attention—including the Big Man—you might get some new customers. Maybe you should consider reopening the shop at the market so people know where to find you."

Wanjikū shook her head. "I already have as much work as I want, and I'm happy working from home. Bigger isn't always better—at least not for me."

"Well, never forget how much we appreciate your beautiful handiwork. I'll continue telling everyone I can about your kitenges. That's one karumbeta I'm happy to blow."

"Thank you, Mama Jonah. You are a true friend," said Wanjikū as she finished her tea and got up to leave.

★★★

After Wanjikū had recovered from Kabogo's death and its turbulent aftermath, she felt the need to share important information with Nyagūthiī, recognizing how close her daughter had come to being alone in the world. Whether the conversations were appropriate for a girl her age, she couldn't afford to leave them unspoken and hope for the best. She did decide to wait until Nyagūthiī completed high school, so they wouldn't distract from her studies. Once exams were completed in November and they had enjoyed the holiday celebrations in December—including a trip to her parents' home in Gīthakainī for Christmas—the conversations began.

The trip to Lang'ata Cemetery was undoubtedly the strangest. When her mother told her to get in the car so they could go for a ride, Nyagūthiī didn't hesitate. Sometimes Wanjikū asked her along when she wanted company to go shopping or to visit a relative. KMT was at Owino's, so they took the Peugeot. The somber look on her mother's face as they pulled up on the side of the road next to the cemetery alarmed Nyagūthiī. Her heart was thumping and her palms sweaty as she followed her to the cemetery fence. What potent family secret was on the verge of being divulged?

After what seemed like a long time, her mother cleared her throat and said, "Nyagūthiī . . ."

"Yes, Mom."

She pointed into the cemetery. "I want to be buried here when my time comes."

Nyagūthiī swallowed hard. "Mom, why are you . . . ?"

"Don't worry, I'm not dying. But in Gīkūyū culture, if I died today, I would be buried with my husband's family, and I don't want to be buried there. Even though your father and I were still married at the time he died, we were not together. I don't want to be with him in the next life."

Nyagūthiī drew in a sharp breath, unsure of what to say.

"When somebody dies, people want to follow tradition, so there will be a lot of pressure if you try to do something different. But many people on your dad's side of the family didn't think much of our marriage and said nothing when he started raising a child with someone else. From the look of things at the funeral, I was the last person to find out about his other family. Your father's family is part of your inheritance, but it's not part of mine."

"I have an inheritance?"

"Inheritance is about more than just money." She hesitated. "However, your father did have money and property when he died. Since I was his legal next of kin, it all came to me, though I doubt he would have left it to me if he had known he was going to die. Eventually, it will go to you."

"What about Robert?"

"From what I hear, his mother comes from a wealthy family with far more money than your father would ever have acquired. The lawyer I worked with thought it was unlikely they would want to have anything to do with this, especially since your father and the boy's mother weren't officially married. She thought it was possible that the mother might want to claim part of the inheritance, but we never heard anything—"

"She died."

"Oh. How did you know that?"

"My friend, Maryann, from school told me—the ones who lived next to them, whose parents I was talking to at Dad's funeral. Her funeral was about two months after Dad's."

"Wũi, that's sad. Poor boy! Maybe one day if things improve, you and he can make a connection. You are related, after all."

Nyagũthiĩ shrugged. "Maybe, who knows? So how much money did Dad leave?"

Wanjikũ looked around to make sure no one was nearby, then lowered her voice and told her.

"Seventeen what?" she exclaimed.

"Shh! You heard what I said."

"Ngatho! That's a lot of money."

Her mother looked around nervously. "Let's go now. We've been here long enough."

As they got back into the car and onto the road, Nyagūthiĩ was full of questions. Wanjikũ had been worried that a morbid conversation about death and inheritance would weigh down her daughter, but the amount of money involved seemed to have the opposite effect.

"So are we going to move to Lavington or Kileleshwa?" she asked.

"We're not going anywhere. Not right now, anyway."

"Wũi. Seriously, Mom? So we're going to be millionaires in Kariokor?"

She was starting to wonder whether telling her about the money had been a good idea. "Don't worry about the money. Up until now, you didn't know anything about it, and your life was fine. Even if I chose to buy a house, it will probably not be in one of those expensive places."

"Racecourse, maybe?"

"Maybe Racecourse. Or maybe we'll drive out and see that plot in Kĩambu that your father left. Who knows! It might make sense to build there, though I'm not sure I'd want to live that far out of town. Still, you never know how things go with land. I'm sure even places like Lavington and Kileleshwa were uninhabited bushland at one time."

Silence followed as they drove toward Ngong Road where Wanjikũ wanted to go to the supermarket. As they waited at the light to turn into the supermarket parking lot, Nyagūthiĩ turned to her mother.

"Do you regret marrying Dad?"

Wanjikũ didn't respond. For a moment, Nyagūthiĩ thought she hadn't heard. She was about to repeat the question when her mother sighed deeply. "Your father and I had a very difficult marriage, but if it wasn't for him, I wouldn't have you. So if you took me back to the day I agreed to marry him with everything I know now about how things would go—including that I would have you as my daughter—I would do it again."

"Oh, Mom. That's so sweet!"

The car behind them honked, and Wanjikū stepped on the gas to catch up to the cars ahead. "As far as regrets go," Wanjikū continued as they turned into the lot, "I wish I'd completed my studies when I had the chance. I could have done it later, but I didn't. I should have. Education matters, and so does having that university degree."

"If it does, Mom, then maybe you should consider going back to complete your studies. What's stopping you? There's no need to go through life with regrets," Nyagūthiī retorted, bringing a perplexed expression to her mother's face.

"What would I do with a degree at my age? I'm not looking for a job."

"Is getting a job the only reason to get a degree?"

Wanjikū was silent for a few moments as she maneuvered the car into a parking spot and brought it to a standstill. When she turned to Nyagūthiī, there was a crooked smile on her face. "You know what, Nyagūthiī? I've never thought of it that way. That's a very interesting idea! There's nothing stopping me from going back to school and completing my education, is there?"

★★★

The thought of going back to university consumed Wanjikū in the days that followed, and the more she considered it, the more it compelling it seemed. She had the time and the finances to go back to college, and there was no young child in the house to take care of. It was time to put to rest that feeling of having left something undone that had hounded her all those years.

She drove to the university a few days later and went to the registrar's office. A young man in his late twenties in an immaculate white shirt and red tie was sitting at the desk. They made eye contact, and he nodded and smiled as she approached.

"Hello, madam, how may I help you today?"

"I need information about enrolling in a bachelor's program."

"Sure, happy to help. I'll get you an information packet that you can review with the prospective student. Is he or she in a public or private secondary school? There are differences in applying, because for most—"

"I'm the prospective student."

A confused look came over his face. "You?"

"Yes."

"Um . . . er, that's a situation I'm unfamiliar with. Would you mind giving me a few minutes to check with my supervisor?"

"Sure."

He rose from his desk and was gone for about five minutes. When he returned, he was accompanied by a woman in her midthirties wearing a lavender skirt suit with stylish rimless eyeglasses.

"Hello, madam. I'm Mrs. Kinoti, the assistant supervisor. John here was telling me you had inquiries about enrolling in the bachelor's program at the university."

Wanjikũ nodded and recounted what she had said. Mrs. Kinoti listened patiently, an inscrutable expression on her face. When she was done, the two exchanged glances, and Mrs. Kinoti took in a deep breath.

"Unfortunately, our admissions process caters only for students coming from secondary schools, mainly from the public school system. There are pathways for other candidates such as students from private schools, but I don't believe we've ever admitted someone who wasn't coming straight out of secondary school. Only about fifty percent of high school applicants get admitted, so it wouldn't make sense to widen the pool of applicants when we're unable to adequately service the

SUNSHINE ON THE CROOKED ROAD

current one. So, um . . . I'm not really sure I'd be able to help you. You could try one of the private universities, though."

Wanjikū thanked her, trying hard to hide her disappointment.

"I was interested in this university because I started here as a student but had to leave when I got married and moved to America."

"You were here? When?" asked Mrs. Kinoti, perking up with interest.

"In 1970. Before they changed its name to the University of Nairobi."

Mrs. Kinoti and John exchanged astonished glances. It was clear that they now had more than a passing interest in the unusual request.

"I joined in 1975, so that was even before my time. Wow, this is interesting. I don't think I've heard of a situation where someone left and came back twenty years later, wanting to continue." She was smiling.

John, seeing his boss lighten up, took it as permission for him to do so as well. With a mild chuckle, he said, "Maybe we should try to reinstate her the way we do with students who take a semester or a year off. I don't think the policy has an upper limit regarding how long a student can be away before they're ineligible for consideration. And it wouldn't count as a new admission, so it wouldn't have to go through the admissions board."

"That's an excellent idea, John. Let's look into it. Please take down her details—name, date of birth, degree program . . . the usual information, and let's see what we come up with. Er, Mrs. . . ."

"Kabogo. My maiden name for your records is Waihenya, though."

"Yes, of course. And would you happen to have any documentation from when you were here—an admissions letter, a student ID, transcript . . . anything? We're going to look in our records, but it wouldn't hurt if you brought us anything in your possession since documents from that far back may be difficult to locate."

"I don't usually throw away documents, so I probably have them somewhere. I'll go and look."

"Perfect! Come back with whatever you can find, and we'll see what we can do. No promises, though. What were you studying, by the way, Mrs. Kabogo?"

"A bachelor of arts in literature."

Mrs. Kinoti nodded. "Well, I hope we're able to get you back into your program. Please note, however, that you wouldn't be eligible for any of the government scholarships that the regular incoming students receive."

"I wasn't expecting anything of the sort."

"Well, this is exciting," said Mrs. Kinoti, clasping her hands together to signal it was time to wind up. "I do have one question, though, if you don't mind my asking."

"Sure."

"What made you come back after all those years?"

Wanjikū smiled. "I was telling my daughter about the importance of getting an education and mentioned that I regretted not completing my university studies. She asked me why I couldn't just go back and finish if it was bothering me so much. I thought about it and realized I had no valid excuse, so here I am."

"Interesting! These young people can teach us something if we're willing to listen to them. Very well. Come back and see us when you find the documents. Even if you don't find anything, please come back because we'll also look through our old records."

Nyagūthiī was ecstatic when she learned that evening of the visit to the university. "You're going to go back to university for real? Wow!"

"I'll go back if they let me in, and they sounded quite positive about it. Maybe if you get accepted here, you and I could be roommates in the student hostel," Wanjikū replied with a mischievous twinkle in her eye.

★★★

SUNSHINE ON THE CROOKED ROAD

She found her university admissions letter and old student ID and returned to the registrar's office the following week. John and Mrs. Kinoti had been eagerly awaiting her return and had located her old records as well. Mrs. Kinoti had reviewed her request with her supervisor, who had in turn reviewed it with the deputy vice chancellor for academic affairs. All were in agreement that there was no impediment to readmitting her as a student, the only caveats being that she would begin in January 1992—the following academic year—and that she would not receive any credit for the courses completed in 1970 because the curriculum had changed significantly since that time. Also, technically speaking, her degree program had been at the University of East Africa, the precursor of the current institution, which no longer existed.

None of this was unreasonable, and she beamed with pleasure as they announced the good news. Her story had done the rounds in the department, and a handful of the other staff, curious to see the subject of this unusual story for themselves, wandered into the hallway outside Mrs. Kinoti's office and said hello as she and Wanjikũ made small talk after concluding the business of the day. Mrs. Kinoti seemed reluctant to end the upbeat conversation.

Among the people that came by was a slender woman with broad shoulders, narrow hips, and an exquisitely graceful walk. She was wearing a kitenge that swayed with the feline cadence of her steps as she strode toward them. Wanjikũ's breath caught as she recognized the outfit, and she felt her palms tingle with excitement. She remembered taking the measurements and worrying that the selected design would be flattering to everyone else in the bridal party who had larger hips, not this woman. She had thought long and hard about it, then made several tweaks to the woman's kitenge, and the end result had been fantastic. When she'd delivered the outfits to the bridal party to try at the home of the bride-to-be, the group gasped in awe as the woman emerged from the bedroom and walked into the living room to show off her outfit.

"That kitenge suits you very well!" Wanjikũ remarked now.

"Oh, thank you! I was a bridesmaid at my friend's wedding last year, and she chose to do kitenges. We went to a lady in Kariokor for measurements, and she did a fantastic job. She wasn't very expensive, either. I get compliments about this outfit all the time."

The woman hadn't recognized her, and Wanjikũ probably wouldn't have recognized her, either, were not for the kitenge. She smiled and hesitated for a split second, then decided not to reveal her identity, feeling it would ruin the purity of the moment.

"I wanted to tell you how inspired I was to hear that you had decided to come back and get your degree," continued the woman. "Mrs. Kinoti brought up your case at our staff meeting, and we're all very excited for you. All the best in your studies!"

"Thank you," replied Wanjikũ, beaming with pleasure. "I'm so glad I came here today!"

Chapter 37

Wanjikũ was surprised to get a Christmas card in March. She could tell right away it was a Christmas card from the snowflakes on the envelope and the December 16 postmark that included the phrase *Post Early Christmas* with stamps that featured a rosy-cheeked Santa on his sleigh. It was cryptically addressed *To A Friend* in a hand that gave Wanjikũ a feeling of mounting excitement as she carried it outside the post office, where it was uncomfortably hot and dusty. When she got home, she did not waste any time in opening it. Under a generic holiday greeting, it read:

Dear Friend,

Perhaps I have the wrong address, but it's the only one I have, so I'd rather try and fail than not try at all. Most kids send their wishes to the North Pole—this seemed like the best way to get mine granted.

I had a special friend once and assumed it would be for always, but life happened, and we fell out of touch. All I want this Christmas is to see her again and recapture that magic we once had.

Karen Atkinson

P.S.: My friend's name is Wanjikũ Kabogo. I don't know if she or her family are still at this address. If not, I'd sincerely appreciate any help in tracing her, as I don't know anyone in Kenya and wouldn't know how else to go about it.

As Wanjikũ read the card over a second time, she studied the address. It didn't look like the same one she had written to after she'd discovered the two letters in Kabogo's drawer.

Nyagũthiĩ paused at the door to the kitchen, seeing her mother scrutinizing the card, whispering to herself. "Is everything OK?"

Her mother nodded.

"What's that?"

"A Christmas card."

"A Christmas card? From whom? The government? They're the only ones who would send a Christmas card in March."

Wanjikũ handed the card to Nyagũthiĩ. "She was my best friend when we lived in America. After we came back to Kenya and life got busy, we lost touch. I wrote to her a couple of times and didn't hear back, then moved on. After your father died last year, I was going through his things and found two unopened letters from her and her husband that your father never gave to me. After reading the letters, I wrote to them but didn't get a reply. I assumed maybe the address from those

SUNSHINE ON THE CROOKED ROAD

letters was not current, though it's possible the letter never left Nairobi, seeing how often the post office loses mail. But this address is not the same as the one on the aerograms, so it looks like they probably moved; the other address was something like Hollister Avenue, not McDaniel Drive. And from the way she's writing here, she never received the letter I sent recently."

"Well, now that you have her new address, you need to write again, and you should do it *chap-chap* [quickly]."

Wanjikū didn't need to be prompted twice, though she did struggle with whether to start with *Dear Karen* or *Dearest Karen*. The former seemed more suitable for someone she hadn't been in touch with in over a decade, but the latter reflected how she felt. After choosing to go with how she felt, she realized she couldn't then add *and Bill*, so she decided to send him her warm regards in the body of the letter. She was soon scribbling furiously, her handwriting getting tinier and tinier as the space remaining on the aerogram grew smaller.

Nyagūthiī flipped through the newspaper as her mother wrote, checking surreptitiously on her mother's progress from time to time. She was curious about this person she'd only heard of mentioned in passing over the years, who seemed to have been a significant part of her mother's life. Her mother finished her letter, read it through, making a few corrections, then pensively folded the aerogram and sealed it shut.

"Mom, tell me about this friend of yours. I've heard you mention her name a few times, and I think you've pointed her out in pictures. Why did Dad keep the letters from you? Did she say something in the letters that upset him?"

"He didn't even open them."

"That makes no sense!"

"I gave up trying to make sense of your father's actions a long time ago."

"Ngatho! It's strange that he would hide letters from you without knowing what was in them. But why was he the one picking up the mail?"

"The post office was on his way home at the time, so it became part of his routine. Even after he changed jobs, he continued to go to the post office, and I didn't think anything of it. All that changed after he moved to Mombasa."

"Oh, I see. So tell me more about Mrs. Atkinson."

"Please call her *Auntie Karen*—that's what she would want you to call her. *Mrs. Atkinson* sounds very strange and formal."

"OK. Tell me more about Auntie Karen. How did you become friends?"

Wanjikũ began to tell Nyagũthiĩ some episodes from her life in Connecticut—the sewing machine, the obstetrics office with no appointments, meeting Karen at the library for the first time, and the day of Nyagũthiĩ's birth.

"You know, she was the only person who came and saw me in the hospital after you were born. She brought us back home from the hospital and cooked and took care of us while your father was away at a conference."

"He wasn't there?"

Wanjikũ grimaced and shook her head. "Ati. He had been working on a poster that he wanted to present. Karen's husband, who was the head of his department, almost stayed home when he found out I was in the hospital, unlike your father. It all worked out, though. She took very good care of us. You know," she said, remembering, "she even brought a camera and took pictures of you on the day you were born! I don't think I've seen them among the other photos. I must have put them aside somewhere . . ."

"You never told me you had pictures from the day I was born!"

SUNSHINE ON THE CROOKED ROAD

"I know I brought them with us, so they're somewhere in this house. Probably in one of those boxes in the storage space next to your bedroom."

"Can we go look for them?" asked Nyagūthiĩ eagerly.

"Of course! Let me make a cup of tea first." She got up and put water in the kettle to boil, then suddenly began to cackle with laughter.

"What are laughing about?" Nyagūthiĩ asked.

"Wũi, this is too funny! I just remembered the time when Karen took me to a concert in Boston. The music was so loud, it was horrible! I tried to cover my ears, but it made no difference. But you should have seen Karen! She was throwing her arms in the air and shaking her body like someone with *kifafa* [seizures]. And her hair—Wũi!—it was flying all over the place. Oh, my goodness, she was . . ." Wanjikũ was laughing so hard, she couldn't complete her sentence. Tears were rolling down her cheeks, and Nyagūthiĩ found herself giggling with enjoyment at watching her mother succumb to a rare fit of merriment.

"That's funny! I can't imagine you jamming at a rock concert." Nyagūthiĩ laughed.

"Me, I wasn't dancing. If it wasn't for watching Karen, I probably would have had a terrible time. *Ai*, Karen! The serious look on her face as she danced! As it was, I probably had a better time than she did—just watching her—though my ears were buzzing for days. They band was called The Frozen Penguins or something like that. Something to do with birds. They were her favorite band, and she had begged me to go with her. It was *cold* that weekend in Boston, even though it was only September. She had tried to get me to go to one of their concerts before, but I think I was expecting you at the time. Anyway, I left you with the babysitter, and we drove up to Boston that afternoon and didn't get back until after midnight. I must have been really been fond of Karen to leave you with a babysitter to go to a rock concert! You know what? We might even have the record she bought and inscribed for me after the concert."

Nyagūthiĩ looked like a light had just come on. "You mean The Sunburnt Woodpeckers?"

"Yes, I think that's it! I can't tell you how many times I had to listen to that record with Karen. Most of it was terrible, but there was one very nice song that even I liked."

"I think I know the one you mean. I always wondered how that one good song ended up on such a terrible record."

Wanjikū's face brightened. "Let's listen to it, if it's still there."

"I'll go put it on while you make your tea. Then we can look for my baby pictures."

***

Always my friend, you'll be to the end

Through the happy times and sad,

The smiles and tears we've had

Thanks for being there,

Showing me you care

SUNSHINE ON THE CROOKED ROAD

Always my friend, yeah, yeah, yeah

Always my friend.

The tune was as simple and catchy as the lyrics, and the raspy voice of the singer accompanied only by an acoustic guitar was heavenly. It was nothing like the psychotic rants and ear-splitting cacophony of drums and electric guitars that marked the band's usual style. She'd responded to it in the early seventies and, if anything, found it more poignant and endearing now. She wanted to listen to it over and over again. Nyagũthiĩ kept her patience through the first three hearings, but after the fourth, she got up abruptly and said, "OK. Now let's go look for pictures."

Wanjikũ had half intended to use the quest—and Nyagũthiĩ's restless energy—to sort through the old boxes that had sat neglected for two decades. However, her daughter was singularly focused on finding her baby pictures. As a result, the hallway floor, where they had dragged out the boxes, ended up strewn with clutter. They didn't find the baby pictures until the bottom of the fifth one. They were in an envelope inside a folded brown paper bag, among an untidy collection of old bills, magazines, coupons, scraps of paper, and shopping lists that had probably been swept off the kitchen countertop after everything else had been packed. How the baby pictures, which Wanjikũ remembered having put in a safe place, ended up among this assortment of detritus was a mystery. Wanjikũ didn't want to hover as Nyagũthiĩ studied the photos one by one, so she browsed through the rest: a shopping list replete with now-unfamiliar brand names, a scrap of paper on which she'd scrawled the name *Debra*, along with a phone number. She couldn't for the life of her remember ever having known a Debra. It felt like peering into the private world of a complete stranger.

"Isn't this her?" Nyagūthiĩ asked, breaking into her musings. She looked up at the picture her daughter was holding. In the Polaroid, she was sitting on a hospital bed, delicately clutching a little bundle. Leaning in next to her, with an arm around her shoulders, their faces pressed together, was a grinning woman with billowy chestnut hair. While she herself looked understandably dazed and exhausted, her companion looked radiant and full of life.

Wanjikū beamed. "Yes, that's her! That was taken a few hours after you were born."

"Haiya, she has green eyes! I hadn't noticed that on the other pictures. I've never seen someone with green eyes."

"Yes. She was the first person I'd ever met with green eyes, and the day we met, I couldn't stop staring."

"Who took the picture if Dad was away?"

"It must have been the nurse or one of the hospital staff."

Nyagūthiĩ looked pleased at this evidence that she was the absolute focus of her mother's attention from the start—and she had been an exceptionally cute baby. Wanjikū couldn't help the adoring look in her eyes as she shifted her gaze from the pictures to her daughter and back again.

"Mom, what would you say if I decided to go to America for university?" She'd been reluctant to ask, but this seemed like a good time.

"What? Are you afraid to go to the University of Nairobi and end up in the same class as your mother?" Wanjikū mocked.

"Mom! I'm trying to be serious."

"Sorry, I couldn't resist that. Of course, if you got accepted there and had a scholarship, then yes, why not? Though I would miss you. Did you have somewhere in mind?"

"Not really. I sent out a few applications in January but haven't heard anything. I'm not even sure that's what I want to do. Remember the exam I asked you to pay for last year, during August holidays—the one in Westlands?"

"Sort of."

"Well, that's the exam required if you want to go to university in America. Some of my friends were taking it, so I decided, why not? But I want to see what happens with the university selection here. I don't really want to leave you alone."

"Like I said, I'd miss you, but that shouldn't influence your decision. Besides, I'm not alone—I'll still have friends like Mama Milka and Mama Jonah to keep me company. Also, I'll be busy with school and making kitenges, so don't worry about me. What about Milka? Is she planning to go?"

"No," replied Nyagũthiĩ. "Not unless she ends up not being accepted into medical school here, which is unlikely, considering she's probably among the top twenty students in the country."

"I'm still surprised to hear that you've been considering going abroad for university. You've never mentioned it before that I'm aware of."

"It's just an option I'm considering. I don't even know if I'll get accepted or get a scholarship. Though, of course, if you want to use some of that seventeen million . . ."

"Weh! Why is that money eating you? Leave it alone! Focus on getting an education that you can use to get a job, instead of obsessing over how you're going to spend the money that happened to end up in my account. Easy come, easy go, you know." Even as said it, she knew that there had been nothing easy about ending up with that windfall. It represented years of being neglected, lied to, taken for granted . . . In that sense, she could almost see it as a divinely orchestrated reparation for time served, a sudden karmic reversal. Part of her reluctance to spend the money was because, in a way, it felt like blood money, even if the blood was her own. Having lived through all those years of low-grade hell, she still had a nagging, even superstitious feeling that their good fortune was only a temporary reprieve. Wanjikũ had withheld most of the grim details of her difficult marriage from Nyagũthiĩ, so the gap between her own apprehensions about the money and her daughter's delight in it was not so surprising.

★★★

A few weeks later, Wanjikū was in bed and getting ready to turn out the light when she heard the phone ring in the living room. She looked at the bedside clock: It was past eleven. Mama Milka often called in the evenings but rarely after nine, and her customers almost invariably called during the day. Now that Nyagūthiī was home, she got some calls from her friends and admirers, but usually not this late. Wanjikū quickly got up, put on her robe, and shuffled out to the living room in her slippers. Nyagūthiī, who had been watching TV, stood above the phone, debating whether to pick up.

"Are you expecting a call?" Wanjikū asked. When she shook her head, Wanjikū shrugged and picked up the receiver. "Hello?" she said.

She heard a few seconds of staticky silence, then a voice.

"Hello? Wanjikū?"

"Yes?"

"Hi! It's Karen. Karen Atkinson, from Hartford!"

"Karen! It's so good to hear from you! How are you?" She put her hand over the mouthpiece and said to Nyagūthiī, who was standing by curiously, "It's my friend from America!" She remembered now having put her phone number at the end of the aerogram she'd sent.

Karen sounded like she was talking from inside a cavern, a droning hiss in the background muffling her words. On top of that was a delay that made talking over each other almost inevitable, so that at first their exchange was awkward. After a few minutes, though, they settled into a rhythm of asking a question, then waiting patiently until they were sure the other's answer was complete. Not the optimal way to conduct a conversation, with its usual spontaneous give-and-take, but it worked well enough.

She was saddened to learn that Bill had passed away two years earlier from a condition called ALS that she'd never heard of before. She had already written to Karen about Kabogo's meningitis and saw no need to fill her in on the gruesome details with Nyagũthiĩ standing by. And, of course, Karen wanted to know all about Gogie and seemed floored to hear that her adorable three-year-old was now preparing to go to university.

"Here, why don't you talk to her? She can speak for herself," her mother said and thrust the receiver toward her.

Nyagũthiĩ cringed, but as it turned out, she needn't have worried. Karen's torrent of words describing all the adorable things she had done as a baby—sometimes hard to understand between the phone line noise and Karen's accent—barely required her to speak, though she did promise to send Karen a picture of herself "all grown up."

When Wanjikũ reclaimed the call, she told Karen that Nyagũthiĩ was considering attending university in America. After the call was done, mother and daughter sat up talking. Nyagũthiĩ wanted to admonish her mother for throwing her in the deep end by putting her on the phone with someone she had never met, but after seeing her mother's exhilaration from the call and hearing what she herself had apparently meant to Karen, she held her peace.

"If you end up going to school in America, we'll have to pay her a visit! She was so excited to learn that you might be considering going to university there."

Nyagũthiĩ smiled absentmindedly, trying to decide whether she liked the nickname *Gogie*.

Chapter 38

August 1991

"Mom, I think he was smiling at you," said Nyagũthiĩ on the short walk back from Bhatia's. The *he* in question was Otondi.

"No," Wanjikũ countered dismissively. "Otondi doesn't smile. Maybe he was burping or grimacing—definitely not smiling. I've known him for over ten years now, and smiling is not something he does." They had gone to the duka to pick up a package containing a few items that the Bhatia wanted to send to his son, Anuj, in Boston: loose-leaf tea, chai masala, cardamom, ginger, and Roiko seasoning. Bhatia had been excited when Wanjikũ mentioned her upcoming trip to Connecticut. Nyagũthiĩ would be starting university at the same school her father had attended more than a decade earlier. After congratulating her on her daughter's achievement, he had hesitantly asked if she might have room in her luggage for a small package for Anuj, a favor exchanged among friends that helped avoid exorbitant mailing costs and bypassed sticky fingers in the postal system. She happily obliged, knowing what a treat it would be for him to have things from his father's duka that had been tenderly packaged by his mother.

Bhatia's hair—what was left of it—was all white, and he walked with a stoop. On more than one occasion, he had remarked to Wanjikũ that he didn't know how much longer he could continue running the shop. But he worried about what would happen to Otondi, whom he referred to as *kijana yangu* [my young man], even though Otondi was probably in his forties and himself graying at the temples. Otondi still wandered off now and then to join the street people at the Globe Cinema Roundabout where he had lived as a boy, but the trips were infrequent, and it was improbable that he would go back to living there permanently. It was hard to tell whether he could even foresee the day when the old man would no longer be there to take care of him. Wanjikū didn't have any clever ideas to solve Bhatia's conundrum, but she pointed out that Otondi's mother doubtless also had worried about what would become of him after her death. Thanks to Bhatia, things had worked out well for him. That he was big and prodigiously strong and well known in the part of town north of Tom Mboya Street was some protection in itself.

Nyagūthiĩ had received a partial scholarship to the university and was hoping to study political science. Her initial ambivalence about going to college had evaporated after her mother signed up at the University of Nairobi. Reassured that her mother would be OK if she went abroad, she had no hesitation in accepting the offer to attend the University of Connecticut, a decision that was reinforced by the sense that, in a way, this was getting back to her roots, and by the reemergence of Karen in their lives. For Wanjikū, the sting of Nyagūthiĩ going so far away was soothed by knowing that her friend—who had held Nyagūthiĩ in her arms on the day she was born—would be close at hand if her daughter needed any help. Karen was beyond thrilled when they told her of Nyagūthiĩ's plans and that they would both arrive in August, with Wanjikū staying for a whole month.

★★★

This was the first time either Wanjikũ or Nyagũthiĩ had been on an international flight since their return to Kenya in 1976, so it was effectively Nyagũthiĩ's first trip of this kind. No one would know it from the ease with which she negotiated the ticket desks and airport terminals in London and New York, the same stops Wanjikũ had taken on her way to Connecticut two decades earlier. It meant that Wanjikũ could relax and leave everything to her daughter. She did notice, however, that Nyagũthiĩ seemed nervous as they waited for their bags to appear on the carousel at Bradley International.

"What is it, Nyagũthiĩ?"

"Nothing."

"You look apprehensive. Are you worried about meeting Auntie Karen?"

"Of course not!" she replied, too emphatically.

When they'd cleared customs and emerged through the sliding doors to the crowded arrivals area, Wanjikũ scanned the crowd. Then she saw Karen, vigorously waving her arms over her head, and she quickened her pace. When they reached her, Wanjikũ let go of her bags and threw her arms around her friend. Nyagũthiĩ waited awkwardly as her mother and Karen held each other in a long embrace. They stepped back and studied each other with big, wet smiles, then Karen turned to Nyagũthiĩ.

"Is that you, Gogie? Oh, my goodness! What a beautiful young lady! Come here and give your Auntie Karen a hug!"

Nyagũthiĩ smiled sheepishly as Karen hugged her and showered her with endearments. Any doubts she'd had about whether Auntie Karen would like her evaporated. Turning back to Wanjikũ, she said, "Welcome back to Hartford! You have no idea how good it is to see you."

As they made their way to the parking garage, Karen talked with Nyagũthiĩ while Wanjikũ followed a few steps behind, measuring her friend with her eyes to see if the kitenge she'd made her was likely

SUNSHINE ON THE CROOKED ROAD 311

to fit. The height was about right. She hadn't been concerned about what might happen if Karen had gained weight, since the garment was designed to be loose-fitting, but she hadn't been expected her friend to have lost weight. She looked much more slender than she'd remembered—even fragile. Sometimes kitenges could hang on thin people in a way that made them look scrawny. Oh, well. At least the fabric's sage-green background would go well with Karen's beautiful green eyes, and she hoped the minimalist white and gold patterns and the subtle gold embroidery around the neckline would suit her low-key style. She had struggled to come up with a headpiece that would be suitable for slippery Mzungu hair and finally came up with one that could be worn in a number of ways. But now as she walked behind Karen, she wondered why her friend was wearing a headscarf on a hot summer day. She was puzzled as to how much hair it was possible to conceal under that relatively small hair covering.

***

As they drove through Hartford, nothing looked familiar to Wanjikū. They reached Karen's home, which was a couple of miles away from where she and Bill lived before, and set their suitcases to the side of the staircase. Wanjikū hadn't let Karen carry any of the bigger bags from the car. In the process, their eyes met briefly, and something unmistakable passed between them—a hint of a conversation they both knew they needed to have.

"You guys make yourselves comfortable in the living room," she told them. "Lunch—or whatever you want to call this at three in the afternoon—will be ready soon."

"Are you sure I can't help?"

"Positive. It'll just be a couple minutes."

Neither of them wanted to sit after such a long time sitting, so Nyagūthiĩ inspected the knickknacks, books, and wall hangings while Wanjikū looked at the more recent pictures of Karen and Bill on the mantelpiece. Bill looked much older than she remembered, balding and slightly overweight, but still with the same warm, sincere smile that made it impossible not to like him. The mustache he'd had back in the seventies was gone. Wanjikū was studying a picture of Karen grinning impishly at the camera, her hair cascading onto her shoulders from under the brim of a straw hat, when Karen walked up behind her.

"That was in Wisconsin—our last trip together, only we didn't know that at the time," she said. "Bill had been complaining of cramping in his right leg that seemed to come and go. We didn't make much of it since he was able to get around fine. We even did some hiking. Three months later, the cramps had gotten worse, and both legs twitched. It took a few months for them to figure out what was wrong. We bounced around from one specialist to another, including a neurologist at Yale, and by the time they finally diagnosed it, he was in a wheelchair. Things snowballed after that, and he was gone within a year."

"Oh, Karen, that sounds awful," said Wanjikū, wishing she'd been there to help and provide emotional support.

"Bill was everything I had," continued Karen, her voice shaky. "After he died, I was lost. I couldn't even get out of bed in the morning. It's been two long years. Things are better now, but I still have mornings when I turn to his side of the bed, expecting to see him there. Well, I guess I'm not the only one. It sounds like you've been through more than your share of ordeals. We'll have plenty of time to talk, cry, laugh . . . all that good stuff. But right now, it's time to eat. I thought of trying to make the mushy white corn thingy I used to eat at your place—the one you showed me how to cook? I can't even remember what you called it."

"You mean ugali?"

SUNSHINE ON THE CROOKED ROAD

"That's it! The one where you put corn flour in boiling water and try to shape it with a wooden spoon as it shoots fireballs of molten flour onto your forearms. Ouch!"

Wanjikū laughed. "Yes, that sounds like ugali."

"I tried to make it once after you left, and it was *nasty*—full of lumps of uncooked flour—so I had to throw it out. Bill had a good laugh about that. So I figured I'd stick to spaghetti and meatballs today."

Nyagūthiĩ had thoroughly warmed to Karen. She liked her books and decorations, her sincerity and humor . . . and she felt sure she'd like her spaghetti and meatballs as well. After lunch, they took a tour of the campus, including the school of engineering where both Bill and Kabogo's old department was, then walked to their old neighborhood of Greenwood Park.

"You see that apartment over *there* . . . where I'm pointing?" asked Wanjikū. "Right there! That's where we used to live!"

As they turned and walked back toward campus, a lone figure on a side street half a block away stopped, stared in their direction, and hurried toward them. "Aha! I thought there was something familiar about the appearance of this fine lady here!"

Wanjikū's eyes widened as she took the outstretched hand of the well-dressed, bespectacled woman addressing them. "Lihua!"

"You remember me! How are you, Wanjikū? Karen told me the other day that you were coming. And might this be the little baby I remember from all those years ago?"

"Yes, this is Nyagūthiĩ," replied Wanjikū, grinning.

"Fantastic! It's so nice to see you both!"

"Gogie, Professor Tsai is one of your mother's friends from when your family lived here," said Karen.

"Professor!" Wanjikū exclaimed, turning to Karen.

"Thanks in large part to Bill," said Lihua.

"And since she won't tell you herself, Lihua is now head of the biochemical engineering department. Bill said she would be the best boss the department ever had."

"Stop it, Karen!" said Lihua, blushing. "No one could equal Bill. I have to get to a class, but will you pencil in dinner at our place for sometime next week? We have a lot of memories to rekindle."

"Of course. But tell me, how is your husband . . . ?" Wanjikũ couldn't remember his name.

"Chen is doing great. Still in mechanical engineering, enjoying his research. Oh, wait . . ." She rummaged in her handbag and held up a photograph of two young men in jeans and T-shirts grinning mischievously at the camera, their arms around each other's shoulders. "Either of these fellas look familiar?"

"Oh, I bet that's . . . forgive me, I don't remember your son's name."

"Yes, that's Wei, and his friend, Emeka. Remember Ugochi and her son? Those rascals have remained close friends all these years and are now together at Cambridge, doing their master's degrees."

"How wonderful! And how is Ugochi? Do you keep in touch?"

"In touch? That woman couldn't run away from me if she tried! We speak nearly every week, and every year, we either visit them in Houston or they come here. They moved to Texas from California a few years ago."

"I hope you'll tell me more about them when we get together."

"Absolutely! Well, I won't keep you folks any longer. Give me a call, Karen, and let me know what night works best for dinner."

Chapter 39

After lying restlessly in bed for a couple of hours, Wanjikū decided to get up and went downstairs to make herself a cup of tea. Karen had oriented her to her kitchen and shown her how to use the microwave, which was new to her. As she sat at the dining table, she heard the soft patter of feet coming down the stairs and saw Karen at the doorway.

"You're up early," remarked Karen.

"I'm a bit jet-lagged. And I usually find it hard to sleep, anyway, once the sun is up and I hear the birds outside."

"Were you able to sleep through the night?"

"Until about four in the morning, which is about eleven o'clock in Nairobi. How about you?"

"Not really. I was too excited knowing you and Gogie were here," said Karen, making herself a cup of black coffee. "Hey, you know what? Let's go sit on the back porch. My outside thermometer says sixty-five degrees, so it should be pleasant."

They went out and sat on the porch swing, watching birds hop from branch to branch and the butterflies flutter among the flowers. Karen had been fascinated to hear about Wanjikū's plans to return to the university and wanted to know more.

"What made you decide to go back after all those years?"

"You know, I always felt I should go back, but there was always something holding me back—being newly married in a foreign land, the potential challenges of getting a student visa, a new baby, then settling back in Kenya . . . Some reasons were good, but some were just excuses, and deep down, I knew it. Anyway, after Kabogo died, I realized how much he had taken away from me. I had the option of continuing to blame him for things that had happened in my life or trying to change the situation."

"That's an admirable decision."

"I have Nyagŭthiĩ to thank because she's the one who challenged me either to do something about it or stop whining. I'd never thought of getting a degree for anything other than finding a job, which was probably why it seemed like a strange idea at first. But I love reading, I love books, and I really enjoyed what I'd been learning before we moved here."

"Your love of books is no secret. We met at a library, remember?"

Wanjikŭ smiled, then her brow creased. "You mentioned yesterday that you're still at the library but not currently working. I don't think I understood what that was about."

"I took a leave of absence."

"Oh?"

Karen pointed to her headscarf. "I bet you've been wondering why you haven't seen me without this, even in the heat of August."

"I did notice it . . ." replied Wanjikŭ.

Karen turned to face her, an intense look in her eyes. "I was treated for breast cancer five years ago. They caught it early, and I had surgery. I was doing well, and all the scans and mammograms looked good, but in early December, they noticed a few spots on my left lung and liver. A biopsy showed the cancer was back."

"Oh no!"

SUNSHINE ON THE CROOKED ROAD

"Yes. Not the kind of news you want to hear. You can imagine what the holidays were like last year, with Bill gone and being diagnosed with stage four breast cancer."

"Wow, stage four?"

"Yes, it's already spread. The doctor says that with chemo, I have a twenty-five percent chance of living five years. Not great odds, but better than zero. Hearing that made it really clear what matters to me. One of those things is you, so I decided to write you one more time. Bill and I had given up on staying in touch with you and Kabogo after a couple of our letters went unanswered, but I wanted to give it one more try."

She took Wanjikū's hand.

"I know you're not a touchy-feely person—" her voice trailed off, and she squeezed Wanjikū's hand. She took a deep breath and composed herself, then whispered, "Just wanted to say 'Thank you' for coming. It means everything to me to see you and Gogie again!" She wiped her eyes, and the two sat in silence for a few minutes. Movement in the kitchen told them that Nyagūthiĩ was awake.

"We're out here in the back, Gogie!" Karen shouted. Then softly to Wanjikū: "Let's not tell her just yet. She's just getting to know me, and I don't want this to be the first thing she thinks of when she remembers me."

The sliding door opened, and Nyagūthiĩ popped her head out. "Are you two telling secrets?" she asked, smiling.

"Wouldn't you like to know!" said Karen. "Did you sleep OK?"

"I did, thank you."

"Get yourself a cup of tea, coffee, juice, or whatever, and come join us. We've got a lot of catching up to do."

★★★

The following day, Nyagũthiĩ began her orientation at the school, and Wanjikũ and Karen had time alone to sit and share stories of their lives during their time apart. Even knowing Kabogo as she did, Karen was stunned to hear about the callousness of his behavior. With that out of the way, Wanjikũ found she enjoyed dramatizing stories of her life in Nairobi for her friend—the carjacking, the riots, the ups and downs of her sewing business and her stall at Kariokor Market, Kaka Josiah's church, the AIDS scare, Nyagũthiĩ's childhood experiences, the visit to the university registrar's office . . . She told her about her many friends and acquaintances like Joyce, Mama Milka, Mama Jonah, Otondi, Bhatia and his connection to Ravi, Njogu, the fruit seller . . . It made her realize how eventful her life in Nairobi had been.

Karen hung on her every word and looked at her not only with affection but with admiration, as though she were the courageous heroine of an adventure novel. "My goodness, what an absolutely amazing life you've had!" she exclaimed.

For Wanjikũ, it was liberating to simultaneously take stock of everything that had happened and talk about it freely without having to hold anything back. Much of it, in hindsight, even seemed funny, such as KMT's antics during the carjacking.

"How did you keep your sanity?"

"What choice did I have? Nyagũthiĩ was depending on me. I will say, though, that when I thought I might have AIDS, I came very close to throwing in the towel."

Karen put her arm around her friend's shoulders as they swayed back and forth on the porch swing. "I know what you mean. Before you guys showed up, I was just going through the motions with the chemo, the nausea, the doctor visits, the hair falling out, the meaningless survival statistics. What did any of it matter? Now that you and Gogie are here, I feel alive! I know my prognosis hasn't changed, but I finally feel hope, because there's something to look forward to. Stage four cancer is no picnic, but loneliness is worse, the feeling that no one in the world really

SUNSHINE ON THE CROOKED ROAD

cared what I was going through, that if I died, no one would remember me."

"I'm sure there are people here who care about you and would remember you. Lihua, friends from work . . ."

"Of course, but you know what I mean. People who would remember me the way I remember Bill."

Wanjikū nodded thoughtfully as they rocked slowly back and forth on the swing, then said, "Even though I've had some misfortunes, I've always been blessed with wonderful friends. I'm so happy to see you again."

"And I'm glad for that day more than twenty years ago when you walked into the Dickinson Library! Who would have thought that we would end up with a friendship for always, just like in that Woodpeckers' song we used to listen to?"

"Funny you should mention it. I listened to it a few months ago with Nyagūthiĩ and told her all about that concert you took me to. Remember you always insisted they should have put a comma between *always* and *my friend* in the title? That's what you wrote on the cover when you gave it to me, and signed it with the letter *K*. Nyagūthiĩ always thought the *K* was for *Kabogo*."

"Oh, Lord!" Karen erupted with mirth. "I can't picture Kabogo listening to The Sunburnt Woodpeckers!"

"Oh!" exclaimed Wanjikū, suddenly remembering the kitenge she had brought. "You know what? I brought you a Kenyan dress I made. I don't know how well it will fit, but it's designed to be loose-fitting, so hopefully, it will be OK."

"Well, what are we waiting for? I want to try it on!" said Karen enthusiastically, getting to her feet. "Maybe I can wear it when we go to Lihua's for dinner. I don't get many chances to dress up and go out these days."

Seeing the sparkle in Karen's green eyes, Wanjikū knew she had chosen the right color for the fabric.

***

They were supposed to leave the house at six fifteen in order to get to Lihua's house for dinner at six thirty. Wanjikū and Nyagūthiĩ were waiting in the living room for Karen to come down from her bedroom, and Nyagūthiĩ had begun shifting in her seat, sighing and looking at her watch. "Mom, we're going to be late," she whispered urgently to her mother.

"Hush," said Wanjikū, unperturbed.

"*Si,* you go and knock on her door. It's almost six fifteen."

"You need to be patient, Nyagūthiĩ. Is this how you're going to behave after I've gone back to Kenya?"

Nyagūthiĩ harrumphed and glowered at her mother. There was some shuffling from above, and then Karen started down the stairs. "Sorry, guys, I lost track of the time."

Nyagūthiĩ's jaw dropped as Karen appeared wearing an elegant kitenge, matching headpiece, and jade earrings that complemented them perfectly. The whole ensemble brought out Karen's lovely green eyes, and her face was radiant with joy.

"Oh my! Auntie Karen, you look so beautiful!" Nyagūthiĩ gasped.

"Don't act so surprised, Gogie! This is mostly thanks to your mother's handiwork."

Wanjikū beamed with a mixture of satisfaction and good humor as she looked from Karen to Nyagūthiĩ and back again.

"Well, we'd better get going. We're already running late, which is my fault, I know," said Karen.

As they walked out of the house with Nyagūthiĩ in front, Karen turned to Wanjikū, her eyes glistening and her face radiant. She winked, silently mouthing, "Thank you!" before the two joined hands and stepped out into the warm evening air.

About the author

Ndirangu Githaiga was born in Kenya and immigrated to the United States. He is a physician, world traveler and recreational marathon runner, based in Virginia, with a passion for storytelling and the written word. His other published novels include *The People of Ostrich Mountain* (2020), *Ten Thousand Rocks* (2021) and *Place of Cool Waters* (2022).

To learn more, visit www.ndirangugithaiga.com

Acknowledgements

One of the things I cherished most while working on this novel was the research, which involved poring over old documents and news articles, watching vintage newsclips and talking to people older than me, who supplemented my childhood memories of Nairobi in the 1970s and '80s. My heartfelt appreciation goes to those who shared their recollections and helped paint a fuller picture for me: Maitū, Mama Emily, Mama Sheila, Rosemary Sinayobye, Tony Kamau and Charles Karungu—thank you for those wonderful, informative conversations.

I enjoyed learning about different cultures represented by characters in this book. Thank you Xian Qiao, Anirudh Aron, Bob Okoroajuzie and Esther Kisaakye for taking time to share valuable insights about cultures other than mine.

Thanks to Nyambura Githaiga and Joy Vermaak—my beta readers—who painstakingly went through my early drafts and provided valuable feedback.

Thanks to bookstagrammer, Wamzzy, for continued support and constructive criticism that helped me improve my craft.

Thanks to Nairobi book mavens, Sammy Muita and Lexa Lubanga, whose passion for Kenyan literature reinvigorates me whenever I start to lose sight of my purpose for writing.

Thanks to my wife and three daughters who have remained at my side during the ups and downs of my writing journey, graciously enduring my bouts of self-absorbed whining and grandiose perseveration.

And thanks to Jesū, who fills my cup daily with the wine of his grace.

Printed in Dunstable, United Kingdom